MESMERIZED

NEVAEH RYN

Mesmerized by Nevaeh Ryn
Published by Makin Groceries Media
24200 SW Freeway, Suite 402, #353
Rosenberg, TX 77471
www.nevaehryn.com

© 2025 Nevaeh Ryn
© 2025 Mesmerized Cover Art Kathryn E. Ferdinand

Mesmerized
By Nevaeh Ryn

ISBN: 979-8-88630-019-2(ebook)
ISBN: 979-8-88630-614-9(paperback)
ISBN: 979-8-88630-021-5(hardback)
Library of Congress Control Number: 2024913994

Kamika Suzanna LeBlanc's heart broke when her grandmother passed away at age 78. With a funeral looming over them, she and her mother travel from Miami to Gaville, the small Louisiana town her mother grew up in.

As Kamika grieves and reflects on her complex relationship with her grandmother, she meets up with her ex and first romantic partner, Larissa Harris, and discovers that she has changed in… unforeseeable ways.

As if grieving her grandmother's death wasn't already a challenge, her situation becomes more complicated when she meets Delaney, Larissa's charming older cousin, and a mysterious man known as Beau. Soon, Kamika's world gets turned upside down when she unearths the secrets Gaville and her family have been harboring.

To my beautiful mother, I want you to know that you aren't only a great, unpaid editor, but one of my biggest inspirations. Thank you for helping me every step of the way and encouraging me to chase my dream.

My darling Fluffy and beautiful siblings of mine, the same can be said for y'all. Albeit to a lesser degree.

Natasha, thank you so much for your help and all the effort you've put into ensuring Mesmerized won't be a dud.

Finally, Linnea, you're my favorite Swede, and your advice was invaluable to fine-tuning my cover.

First off, thank you to Warrioress Publishing for giving me a chance. Secondly, shout-out to *Bad Dragon; David* was a great source of inspiration. Finally, I have a love-hate relationship with the Twilight Saga, but its influence on supernatural romances can't be denied. I, like many other post-Twilight paranormal romance authors, was inspired by the series and make references to it throughout *Mesmerized.*

Table of Contents

Mesmerized

By

Nevaeh Ryn

PROLOGUE

Kamika

Life sucks.

I don't mean that in an 'I want to kill myself' kind of way but as a fact. Living is awful. From when our fish ancestors developed the ability to walk to now, pain has defined the human experience. I first understood that when my father was taken from me at the tender age of three. At that age, you don't understand death, or what it means when someone dies. You're just told that Daddy didn't come home last night, and you'll never see him again and wonder why.

After his passing, my mother and I turned to my grandmother to console us, since we couldn't do it for each other. My mother was too brokenhearted to provide comfort, and I was too young. Seeing her beloved daughter and granddaughter in such immense pain, my grandma couldn't bear to turn her back on us. And because of that kindness, for the longest time, I believed she could do no wrong.

But then, puberty hit. My body changed, and I started feeling and noticing new things. Before long, I realized I liked boys *and* girls.

My mother accepted my sexuality as soon as I told her, but my grandmother was a different story. She was old school, believing the only valid relationships were between a man and a woman. In her mind, bisexuals equaled promiscuous cheaters who either slept with the opposite gender for attention or because they were secretly gay. So, she discovered I was one of those filthy degenerates, I went from the granddaughter she loved to a depraved, damaged weirdo. Looking back, I was wrong in thinking that a Black, Christian woman born in 1940s Louisiana would—*could*—feel differently. Still, it devastated me to learn that the little town I spent many summers in was no longer a sanctuary.

But what was it that Nas said? Oh yeah, 'life's a bitch and then you die.'

Truer words have never been spoken. You suffer and endure tragedy after tragedy, while brief moments of happiness give you enough motivation to keep going.

Everyone else near and dear to me had no qualms about my sexual orientation. From an early age, I made it a point to surround myself with a diverse group of people who showered those they cared about with love. Yet, losing the bond I had with my grandmother still tore me to shreds. Four years before she died, I mourned her. It felt weird, grieving for a living person, but that was the only way I coped with her rejection.

And now, four years after all that bullshit went down, her greying body was resting in a casket. After my mama informed me that her mother had passed away, I felt a pang of sadness that went away as quickly as it came. Then...nothing.

I comforted my mother while she cried, and journeyed with her to Gaville, Louisiana from Miami, Florida for the funeral. However, as bad as it sounds, I didn't care that my grandma was dead. I'd mourned her already, and there was no point in doing it again. If that makes me a bad person, then so be it.

May 22nd

Kamila

I fought the urge to yawn as the preacher droned on about God's timing, how my grandmother was in a better place because she walked with the Lord now, blah blah blah. All the usual nonsense spewed after someone dies. I'd heard the same phrases too many goddamn times for them to resonate with me. My mother's quiet sobs kept me from mentally checking out. As her daughter, being her rock was my job while she grieved the loss of her mother. It was a job my sister, Zara, decided wasn't worth undertaking.

I squeezed Mama's hand, the pop-up canopy shielding us from the pouring rain. The weather was perfect for a funeral, mimicking the attitude of the attendees; gloomy and all-around sucky.

"For I am convinced that neither death, nor life, nor angels, nor rulers, nor things present, nor things to come, nor powers, nor height, nor depth, nor anything else in all creation, will be able to separate us from the love of God in Christ Jesus our Lord," my Grandma's favorite pastor droned, quoting *Romans 8:38-39* now that he finally ran out of platitudes about Miz Susie, as the town knew her.

He stood in front of my grandmother's casket. The box was propped up on the bier that'd give her over to the earth.

After hours of enduring the sight of a dead woman's face, I'd get a respite when the pastor administered the last rites, and her overly priced body box lowered into the ground. I swallowed. She'd never see the light of the sun again. Aware of what was coming, my mother's sobs increased. Her grief echoed through the graveyard.

"Go forth upon your journey, Christian soul, in the name of God the Father who created you; in the name of Jesus Christ who suffered for you; in the name of the Holy Spirit who sets us free; May you rest in peace in the love of God. Amen."

Subconsciously, I recited the words with him, a relic of the summers spent with Grandma. She adored the bible and prayer, ensuring that my mother and I memorized the most important verses.

With her body again blessed, it was time for the casket's descent into the ground. As a funerary staff member operated the lever on the bier, emotion blossomed within me. We'd grown apart years ago, but knowing she was now bound to a single location for the rest of eternity filled me with melancholy. My mother untangled her hand from mine to observe the casket descend. The pastor used the opportunity to sing 'Too Close to the Mirror' by Eddie Ruth Bradford, a hymn that used to be sung in church regularly, and one Grandma loved. I wondered if that was another request of hers, or if the holy man simply wanted to sing.

Gradually, more people trickled to watch the descent, but my feet remained rooted in place; something in me couldn't bear to watch. Grandma was dead, never to return to the living. I knew this, but seeing the wooden box lowered into the ground just felt too final. With Mama gone, I was sandwiched between two empty chairs. One was meant for Zara, but she'd chosen to stay in Miami with her father. The bastard had pumped her head full of lies, creating a rift bad enough for her to skip the funeral of her mother's mother.

Thunder boomed as the spools turned, loosening the straps, and allowing the casket to descend into the grave. Unbidden, a scowl spread across my face. The weather was being a dramatic bitch, amping up everyone's dejection, with all the damn thunder and rain. The pouring sky muddied the ground, annoying me further. We were dressed in our Sunday best, only to end up stained with dirt.

A hand landed on my shoulder, and I jumped. I fought the urge to shake off the touch. The giver of it wanted to offer comfort, no matter if I didn't know them well, or if they'd sided with Grandma all those years ago. Regardless of their intentions, I didn't enjoy strangers and hypocrites touching me so freely, but death loosened boundaries.

"Are you okay?" a soft, familiar voice questioned.

I stiffened. Slowly, I turned, my heart rate picking up.

The hand belonged to Larissa Harris, whom my grandmother disapproved of with all of her being. Grandma's disdain for Larissa had been as strong as my love for her.

"I'm…" I struggled to find the words to adequately describe my feelings, too caught up in checking out the girl who stole my heart.

She was just as gorgeous as she was when we first met. Freckles dotted her golden skin. Long, curly chestnut hair draped her back and shoulders, and her captivating doe eyes were a lovely chocolate color. When we were teenagers, mischief always filled them. Now, four years since I last saw her, they held care and wisdom. The green sleeveless turtleneck she wore made them pop. My grandmother requested that everyone wear something colorful, as she wanted her life to be celebrated amid the mourning. Despite their less than amicable relationship, Larissa had honored the request. She was still a thoughtful girl, even for those who didn't deserve it.

The immediate fallout of my grandmother discovering our relationship resulted in us losing touch. I'd shunned Gaville from my travel list afterward, and Larissa was MIA from social media. I'd had no way to check up on her. But seeing her before me, hearing her affectionate drawl, told me she was well.

That made me happy. We'd ended things on an awful note, largely against our wills, but she'd forever hold a special place in my heart.

My grandmother had her funeral all planned out; it surprised me that Larissa received an invitation. But that surprise didn't compare to my jumble of emotions. When she arrived with some of her family members at the church service, she and I only exchanged solemn nods. No words were spoken then; now, her simple question was the first thing she'd said to me in years.

"I know, silly question," she murmured as I stared stupidly at her. She retracted her hand and offered me a sad smile. "I just wanted to check on you."

"I'm...I'm holding up," I finally answered with a swallow, struggling to mimic her unreadable expression. "My mother is taking it harder than me."

Her pretty eyes regarded me with tenderness, catapulting me back to our whirlwind teenage romance. "You're probably sick of hearing this, but I'm here for you both if you need me."

"You're the first to say it," I revealed with a humorless laugh.

Since arriving in the town three days ago, I'd heard from many, "I'm sorry for your loss," and "She's in a better place now," and a bunch of other bullshit. Before the events of four summers ago, I'd been close with a lot of them. I knew people in Gaville and they knew me. Now, in the darkest hour of my life, they couldn't even offer me their time.

"I'm sorry, Kami," Larissa muttered.

My insides fluttered at her use of my nickname.

"What happened between the two of you was…rough, but I'm willing to listen to whatever you have to say about her."

"Right now, that's nothing. Everything has already been said, but I'll keep your offer in mind."

"Of course. Here, let me give you my new phone number," she said, already digging her phone out of her little black clutch.

As soon as she offered it to me, I took it, the thundering of my heart competing with the actual thunderstorm. Girlish fantasies about the two of us danced in my mind, ones I believed long ago cast aside. But seeing Larissa, being the subject of her concern, made buried feelings resurface.

Staying in my grandmother's fifteen hundred square foot home wouldn't be pleasant. The many people swarming around the living quarters emphasized its small size. At one time, it was cozy. Now, it was a suffocating box I longed to escape. The very couch where people chatted was the place of her death. Replacing the tainted furniture was on the to-do list, but wasn't our highest priority. Grandma hadn't been dead long enough for bodily fluids to seep out, and her bladder and bowels were thankfully empty. Still, the couch cover had been washed, and the leather sofa must've been wiped with disinfectant wipes a dozen times. The temporary solution ensured it was clean, but nothing made me comfortable sitting on it. The scent of stale cigarette smoke was etched into the air, mixing with the odor of cleaning products to create a noxious blend.

The ceremony had pushed memories I'd rather forget to the forefront of my mind, worsening when we arrived back at Grandma's blue house for the repast. She'd refused to accept who I was, denying me the chance to spend the final years of her life with a woman I once held dear.

"Are you sure we can't get a motel?" I asked my mother for the umpteenth time, as an old man whose name I didn't remember offered a sorrowful nod when he returned to the kitchen for seconds of fried chicken, baked macaroni, potato salad, and green beans.

"No. It'd be too expensive to stay at a motel for the entire summer," my mother said through her sad smile, her bloodshot eyes revealing that it wasn't genuine. "You don't have to stay with me, sweetie. If you want to fly back to Miami, I promise I'll be fine."

Guilt swamped me, and I shook my head. "No, I want to stay with you. I'll drop it."

After all, I was the one who volunteered to travel with her, so I shouldn't complain about our living arrangements. I needed to be a big girl and put my reservations aside to be the rock that she needed.

Mama squeezed my shoulder with a black-gloved hand "I know this isn't easy, baby."

Death never is.

"I—"

An annoyingly high-pitched voice cut me off before I managed another word. I almost rolled my eyes.

"Amia," Giselle Samson greeted, her Southern drawl thick and squeaky. I was convinced her voice was fake; Minnie Mouse had a deeper timbre. "How you doing, sugar?"

Before Grandma caught a minor case of death, she'd been a faithful, bi-weekly client of Giselle's hair salon. I had no issue with the petite woman, if I excluded what a huge fucking gossip she was. I suppose that's why she and Grandma got along so well. They were two peas in a pod, and their loose lips put my entire relationship with Larissa on blast, turning me into a spectacle and a pariah.

"I'm getting by," Mama replied, lowering her eyes. "It's hard, but I'm getting by."

At her repetition, I believed she wanted to convince herself. An ache settling in my heart, I grasped her hand within mine. The gesture caught Giselle's attention, and she turned her 'concern' onto me.

"Kamika, sweetie, look at you. You're all grown up!" she exclaimed with a phony laugh. "You're so pretty. As a lil' girl, you were a sight, but you really grew into your own. How old are you now, sugar?"

I gritted my teeth, my irritation worsening the longer she spoke. A fucking funeral was far from the time to comment on looks. Even on a good day, unprompted remarks on someone's appearance were fucked up. During a day of sorrow, it was exponentially worse.

My mother, sensing my crossness, squeezed my hand. The pressure was not only to offer comfort but a warning to play nice. On her behalf, I forced a smile to grace my lips and nodded.

"I'm twenty now."

"So Zara must be about fifteen?" she asked. I nodded, the gesture prompting her to look around the room. "Where is she?"

"In Miami," I said, refusing to elaborate, even with confusion painted across her expression.

She of all people didn't need to know how broken my family was. A dead daddy, a homophobic grandma—also dead now—and a sister misguided by a toxic sperm donor made for a fucked-up family portrait.

"You know, Colton still asks about you three," Giselle exposed.

My lips curled in disgust at the mention of her brother. I couldn't stand that scummy fuckbag. When Mama gave him a chance, he fucked over her, then harassed me about her for years afterward. Dodging him had been an annual summer activity.

Giselle pointed him out, and seeing as he wore a bright yellow vest—indicative of his career as a waste collector—I wondered how I'd missed him. "He couldn't attend the funeral, but he managed to take a break to offer y'all his condolences."

"And...he was invited?" I questioned, struggling to hide my distaste.

Crashing a wake wouldn't be something I'd put above him, a theory fueled by my knowledge of Grandma's dislike for him.

Mama smacked my hip, making me wince. She glared, and somehow, Giselle missed the entirety of the exchange. Nor did she pick up the annoyance in my tone, which wasn't shocking. She'd never been the most astute.

"Of course. Miz Susie didn't want anyone excluded."

His presence made me further question my grandmother's guest list. She was more dedicated than I thought to the kind elderly woman image she'd crafted. Outwardly, she was a sweetheart to almost everyone. But after years of hearing her belittle half the town, I understood her persona was just an act.

Mama looked at me. "Why don't we say hi to Colton?"

I shook my head. I was doing a shitty job at being her rock, but this day was taking a lot out of me, making me even snappier than normal.

"You can go, Ma, but...but I just need a moment alone."

To sell my lie, I lowered my head and allowed my locs to shield my face from view, sniffling louder than necessary. My allergies flared up thanks to the shitty weather, so the sniffle was genuine, due to congested sinuses as opposed to overwhelming grief.

Seeing through my act, Mama sidled a glare at me. She had an uncanny ability to detect her daughters' bullshit.

Giselle, however, was still stuck on stupid. "Of course, baby! We'll swing by another time to check up on y'all."

Another sniffle, followed by a nod. "Okay, thank you."

With that, Giselle guided my mother to her group of people, which unfortunately included that fucker. I'd rescue her in a few minutes. For now, I relished my solitude. Being alone in a crowd, overlooked by everyone, could be a crushing feeling. But today, it was a small mercy.

However, it didn't last very long. The front door swung open, and in walked Larissa. I perked up at the sight of her. A blond man trailed behind her, several inches taller than her 5'8 frame and holding her hand in a death grip. Based on the gentle smile she aimed his way, she didn't mind one bit.

I deflated and couldn't help my frown. Letting go of my feelings for Larissa was long overdue, but the part of my heart forever reserved for her was a side effect of her being my first love. The way things ended didn't help matters. Being forced apart denied us closure.

She shifted her gaze to me as she neared, and I pasted a smile on my face.

"Hey," I gritted, eyeing her companion. "Who's your friend?"

His grey ish eyes narrowed. "Kamika, I presume?"

"Yes, Susanne's granddaughter," Larissa confirmed before I could. He opened his mouth, but she spoke first. "Kami, this is my husband, Jack."

The wind left me, the word like a punch to the gut. "H-husband?"

Satisfaction glinted in Jack's eyes. "You know, a male spouse?"

Embarrassment flooded me. "I know what a husband is," I snapped, my cheeks warming. "I just didn't know *she* had one."

"Children, too," Jack added with glee. "Our eldest is two and a half."

Which meant she got pregnant about a year after we broke up. While I was still mourning our relationship, she was building a family.

"Jack, why don't you get us drinks?" Larissa suggested. "Please?"

The warning underneath her saccharine tone wiped away his smirk, but he nodded and walked off, the throngs of people slowing his escape. I could barely look at Larissa. It'd been years since we dated; of course, she would've moved on by now. Discovering she was not only married but fell pregnant so soon after we separated crushed me.

"So...a wife and mother," I pushed out.

I tried to sound unbothered, but even I heard my peevishness.

"Yeah," she said with a small laugh before swallowing. "I'm sorry about Jack. He's—"

I held up my hand, halting her explanation. I wasn't owed one.

"There's no need to apologize."

Sure, Jack was a little insensitive and tactless, but he *technically* didn't do anything wrong. I'd be a lying bitch if I said his words didn't worsen my mood.

Larissa smiled, the same one I once fawned over, and one I still found stunning. However, as a supreme masochist, I couldn't leave well enough alone.

"Out of curiosity, how long have y'all been together?"

"Kam—"

"He just said you have a two-year-old. Pregnancies take forty weeks, so you would've gotten with him at least three years ago—"

She placed her hand on my shoulder and stopped my rambling. "Kamika, there was no overlap, if that's what worries you."

It wasn't, but my reaction mistaken as a fear of being cheated on was better than the actual reason. I was stuck in the past, still sweet on a girl who long ago forgot about me.

"Ah, good," I murmured, sagging my shoulders in faux relief. "Umm, sorry."

"As you told me, there's no need to apologize. I met Jack a year after we broke up, and things moved pretty fast."

Her expression brightened as she spoke of her husband. Though it made my heart ache, I liked witnessing her happiness.

"Anyway, do you know Delaney?"

My brows furrowed. "Delaney...?"

Gaville didn't see many newcomers, so chances were, I'd probably met her. Yet, as I tried to conjure an image of her face, my memory blanked.

"My cousin?"

"That isn't exactly helpful."

Damn near half of the town was comprised of the Harris family. All the members resided on their property in various residences. Their land was nicknamed Magnolia Mist, due to the number of magnolia trees on the property, the misty fog that blanketed the area. Humidity, rainfall, and the water of the bayou evaporating into the air was the reason for the fog, something the logical side of me was well aware of. Yet, the eerie atmosphere it created gave me the creeps, and often, I felt eyes watching me through the mist, even when I was alone.

She chuckled. "I know, but Delaney and I were super close." My blank stare remained at her explanation, and she rolled her eyes. "Okay, she's my cousin, two years older than me, and moved to New Orleans for college."

I nodded, my confused frown still present. "Why are you telling me this?"

"Because she's moving back. Our Memorial Day party will double as a welcome back celebration, and I wanted to invite you."

That caught my attention. Unless you fancied sipping beer in a decrepit bar full of old people, Gaville's nightlife was sorely lacking. Alternatively, you could venture to Burnin'

Boots Juke Joint, a historical sight that hosted local music acts. I doubted either could hold a candle to anything offered in Miami.

"So, it's in four days?" I questioned.

I'd been looking forward to Memorial Day for weeks. My bestie, Olivia, had been hyping up her boyfriend's boat party. He was renting a yacht for the occasion and promised that we'd be partying until the sun rose, or the cops came. Whatever happened first. Most of my friends would be in attendance, including a girl I'd been eyeing the entire year. I'd planned to finally make my move, but my grandmother had to go and die, throwing a wrench in my plans.

Larissa nodded. "She's coming down in three days, and the party is the next night on our property."

I cringed at the memory of the grassy clearing reserved for the Harris's kickbacks. Somehow, someway, I always ended up slipping on a well-hidden patch of mud.

"Uh…Will there be liquor?"

No way I'd trudge through damp dirt sober.

She laughed, drawing the attention of the other attendees. "Yes, you damn alcoholic."

A grin made its way onto my face. "I like a good time. Sue me."

"You can have a good time without drinking," she admonished.

"A buzz makes it a hell of a lot easier, though," I countered.

"Makes what easier?" Jack questioned as he reappeared, two cups in hand.

He handed one to Larissa and kept the other for himself. My smile quickly fled.

"Oh, thank you, honey," Larissa said as she accepted the drink. "I was just inviting Kamika to the party."

"For 'Laney?" he asked, slinging an arm around her shoulder and tugging her closer.

She leaned into his touch.

"Yes," she confirmed with a nod, then looked at me. "So?"

"Yeah," I said. I refused to let outdated emotions stop me from having a good time. If I had to take a dozen shots to turn up, I would. "I'm never one to turn down free booze."

Larissa laughed. "Alcoholic."

"Not too much on her, babe. She has a right to drink as much as she wants right now, seeing her grandmother is dead," Jack hummed. Larissa and I stiffened. "I'm surprised you're sober right now."

Those words were the straw that broke the camel's back. More specifically, how they were said. It wasn't a poor attempt to lighten the mood, but a dig that threw salt in an open wound.

My eyes narrowed. "What the hell is your problem?"

He put his hands up in surrender. "I'm giving you props."

"Jack," Larissa hissed, delivering a slap to his pec. "Have some class."

"I'm being classy," he argued, though his previous actions falsified his words.

"No, you're being a shady asshole," I sneered.

Larissa's eyes widened.

"I don't appreciate your jabs in my house."

"It isn't your—"

"It was her grandmother's house," Larissa inserted. "By right, it is hers."

Though he shut his mouth, that was no longer enough for me. I wanted answers so I repeated my question. "Answer my fucking question. What the hell is your problem?"

Larissa's expression darkened. "Kam—"

"It's okay, Larissa," Jack soothed, rubbing circles on her shoulders. "This is a difficult time. She has a right to lash out."

"Jack, enough. It's over."

I didn't know what 'it' she meant; personally, I wasn't through with him.

"No, *it* isn't. I want to know why he's such an ass," I snapped, my eyes watering. I blinked rapidly, refusing to shed a tear. The emotional toll of the day was finally catching up at the worst possible moment. "No one is holding you hostage. If you don't want to be here, leave. In fact, I highly encourage it."

Homing in on my teary eyes, Larissa shifted. "Kami—"

"I'm fine," I reassured, a sniffle contradicting my words.

Her face softened, and she placed a hand on my shoulder. As before, her touch relaxed me, but it didn't linger. With a small snarl, Jack swiped her hand off.

My jaw dropped and Larissa sputtered.

Okay, I was through.

"I think I hear my mama calling me," I lied, all my tension returning. "When I get back, be gone."

As much as I'd been relishing Larissa's company, I prayed she and her husband left soon. Awful vibes wafted from the man she'd legally bound herself to.

"Jack, apologize," Larissa urged, displeasure dripping from every word.

Instead of complying with his wife's wishes, he huffed and pursed his lips. "Why?"

Fucking motherfucker.

At her husband's refusal, she turned her gaze to me. "Kamika, I'm so—"

Uninterested in her apology, I turned on my heels. I wanted to flee from prying eyes, but instead of scurrying away like a scared child, I forced my head to remain high. I heard Larissa still scolding him, but it brought me little satisfaction. The urge to cry intensified and I swiped my eyes. No one would blame me for crying, considering the circumstances, but shame filled me. My ex's weird ass husband being a dick was my undoing.

While passing the dining table where Mama stood, her hand shot out and grabbed my wrist, forcing me to halt. All four seats were taken. Instead of having some courtesy and giving one up, they forced the grieving woman to stand.

"Baby, what's wrong?" she asked. The people sitting near her, including fucking Colton, turned their attention to me. "What happened?"

Larissa had terrible taste in men.

"The day is getting to me," I said.

It wasn't a lie. I'd been dreading this day since I received news of my grandmother's death.

"Go sit down, sweetie, I'll find you something to drink—"

I gently tugged away my wrist. "You don't need to get me anything. I'm just going to the bathroom to splash my face."

The dining table was less than a yard away from the tiny kitchen, but I refused to disturb her peace for something so silly.

"Are you sure?"

"Positive, Mama."

With a parting kiss on my mother's cheek, I made my way to the house's sole bathroom, a single thought on my mind.

I couldn't wait for this fucking day to end.

May 23rd

Kamika

When the repast ended, Mama and I were too tired to do almost anything but get ready for bed. While she showered, I stacked the dishes, which was the extent of my tidying up. That left us with the entire house to clean the next day, something I cussed my past self out for when I woke up. Exhaustion and grief—which I was desperately trying to ignore—made me want to hibernate, but I had to drag myself out of bed and straighten up. Even after two cups of coffee, I ran on fumes, counting the hours until my head could touch my pillow again.

"We have enough leftovers for dinner," Mama said, drying off the damp dish I handed her, because we hadn't had the foresight to buy paper plates.

Ten minutes had passed since we began, and we weren't even a quarter through. Soaking them had slipped my mind last night, so food stuck to the Corelle, forcing me to scrub every plate and bowl.

I nodded, another yawn slipping out. "Sounds good, Ma."

Her weary eyes examined me. "You okay, Kami?"

No. I felt like shit, and memories I wanted to forget filled my mind. Memories of my grandmother baking me sweet treats, teaching me bits of Louisiana Creole, and modeling for me when I wanted to practice photography, back when she still loved me. Memories of Larissa and I sneaking kisses at our part-time job, sending flirty texts, and creeping around with one another. We checked off so many firsts together, and we were forced apart before we could check off more.

"Baby?" Mama prompted when I didn't answer her.

"I'm fine," I finally replied, forcing a smile. "It's just been a long week."

She nodded in understanding, a sad smile gracing her full lips. "I know, baby, but we'll get through this. Momma is home with the Lord now."

It was a struggle for me not to cringe, as I highly doubted a homophobe would see the Pearly Gates. Bible studies Grandma forced me to attend made me familiar with the scripture, and Matthew 7:1 was ingrained in my brain.

Judge not, that ye be not judged.

Judging was a habit my grandmother indulged in freely, and though she bordered on a religious fanatic, she had many failings. Smoking, drinking, gossiping, deceiving others, a short temper, and the list went on. Hypocrisy was a prominent flaw of hers, one that ruined our relationship. I once loved her despite her imperfections, and yet, she couldn't find it in herself to love me due to my orientation.

"What's on your mind, baby?" Mama asked after another prolonged silence.

Normally, conversation and music were plentiful when we cleaned, but we'd forgone the latter, and the former was sparse.

I shrugged. "Nothing."

"Does it have to do with Larissa?" she questioned, ignoring my untruthful answer because she knew me so well.

At the mention of my ex, I tensed. "What makes you say that?"

Mama snorted, a sound so familiar, so *normal*, that I couldn't help but smile. "Cut the shit. You haven't been acting right since that girl came here with her husband."

At some point, Larissa must've made her way to Mama to express sympathy, her blond bastard of a husband in tow. Hopefully, he wasn't a prick to her as he had been with me.

"That's not tru—"

"You calling me a liar now, chile?" she interrupted.

I huffed out a breath, then shook my head. "No ma'am. Just...seeing her brought back a lot of memories, Mama. Now I can't stop thinking of her, and it's just a lot."

The truth spilled from me before I could stop it. As soon as the words were out of my mouth, the tension in my shoulders eased. When I was a child, Mama insisted, *'She wasn't one of my lil' friends.'* That sentiment was ironic, seeing how close we were now. She was easily one of my best friends, and sharing my thoughts with her provided me with instant relief.

Mama ceased drying a dish, looking at me with a mixture of sympathy and concern. "That's nothing to feel bad about, Kami. She was a big part of your life, and a lot is going on right now."

"Yeah," I agreed, a lump in my throat. "But Larissa moved on. She has a whole family, and mind you, she got with her husband a year after we broke up, when it took me two to get over her."

"It took you two years to start dating again," Mama corrected, resuming her task. "That girl still has a piece of your heart, which is fine. She was your first, and you have a big heart. You'll heal in time, and don't you dare feel lesser for your feelings. God gave us spirits of love, so don't feel bad for cherishing someone important to you."

Her words brought a small amount of comfort, and I managed a weak but genuine smile. "Thanks, Mama."

"You know I'm always here for you, Kami," she said, returning my smile. "And you're stronger than you think, baby, even if things are looking bleak now. This too shall pass."

When we fell silent once again, I found myself reflecting. Seeing Larissa and her husband had opened a wound, and while Mama's words didn't heal it, it certainly soothed it. They were a much-needed source of comfort and sparked a flicker of hope.

"Let's finish the dishes, then take a break," Mama suggested after a few minutes.

"Sounds like a plan."

We finished up in comfortable silence, my mind pleasantly quiet as we completed the task. The pessimist in me promised that my relief was temporary, but I'd cherish it even if it only lasted five seconds.

When I handed her the last dish to dry, I shut off the water and grabbed two freshly cleaned glasses. Setting them on the table, I went to the fridge and retrieved the sweet tea someone had brought yesterday. Whoever it was knew what they were doing, as it was the perfect combination of sugar, tea, and lemon.

"No ice?" Mama asked as she sat at the table.

"It's already cold," I replied, sitting across from her and setting the pitcher between us.

She rolled her eyes. "Ice would make it last longer, girl."

I shrugged and took a sip, a satisfied hum leaving me at the taste. "Who brought this? It's real good."

"Wasn't paying attention," she admitted, taking a big gulp of the tea, then nodding in approval. "Wish I was. I'd ask them to bring some more."

In theory, it wasn't hard to make good sweet tea. In actuality, it required the perfect formula that was easy to fuck up.

"So, what were you and Larissa talking about?" Mama asked before another bout of silence could descend.

I pursed my lips, wishing she'd just let the conversation die instead of bringing *her* up.

"Don't give me that look, Kamika, I was just asking," she chided.

With a sigh, I forced my expression to one of neutrality. After another swig of tea, I spoke. "Larissa and her family are throwing a party for Delaney."

She cocked a brow. "And that is...who exactly?"

"One of their cousins that's moving back from New Orleans."

Returning to Gaville was certainly a choice. When you had family that gave a damn about you, it was a nice destination for a chill vacation. But living in such a sleepy town year-round wasn't for me.

"You planning on going?" Mama asked, her tone casual but her eyes probing.

I shrugged. "Maybe. I don't know."

"You should," she said, giving me pause. "It'll be something to do. Get you out of this house."

She was right. But going meant facing Larissa and her husband. If I knew anyone else, it would've been a long ass time since I'd seen them.

"Just give it some thought, baby," Mama continued as if sensing my hesitancy. She reached across the table and squeezed my hand, her skin chilled from the cold glass. "That's all I'm asking."

After a pause, I found myself relenting. "Okay…I'll consider it."

Attending the party still made me uneasy, and I already predicted that staying in bed would be more appealing than dragging my ass to Magnolia Mist. But perhaps, it wouldn't hurt to show my face, if only for an hour. If nothing else, it'd make Mama happy.

After hours of cleaning and a decent dinner, I was free to return to my room. I took a quick shower, threw on clean clothes, and then curled up in bed with my phone. My feet were thankful for the respite, and I kept my mind empty by scrolling through stupid videos my friends sent and reacting with emojis. Simple interactions that required no emotional strain.

After two or so dozen videos, a text came through. From Larissa, of all people.

FREE HER: Hey. I'm so, so sorry about yesterday. Jack's behavior was inexcusable, and I tore into his ass when we got home. FYI, you're still invited to the party. I'll keep Jack on a shorter leash, promise 🤍

Despite myself, a small smile tugged at my lips. The name I saved her number under echoed my sentiments about her husband. They didn't mesh well together; she was too sweet for him. But, knowing she wouldn't shun me for his behavior provided relief.

> Me: lol thanks.

> Me: And yeah, I'll come. Don't wanna miss out on a good time.

I considered adding a heart emoji of my own, but at the last second, decided against it.

> FREE HER: Awesome 👍

She'd upgraded from text talk, which I always complained to her about, to proper grammar and emojis. A change I could get behind.

> Me: 👍

My text sent, I went back to watching videos, ending the day feeling better than when it started.

May 25th

Delaney

As a teenager, Delaney Harris vowed to escape the humdrum life that Gaville offered its residents. Despite the secrets it harbored, it was far from an exciting place to live. Both the pack she hailed from and the humans who'd settled around them were stuck in their ways, creating an oppressive environment worsened by the slow pace of things. She achieved her goal when she graduated high school and got accepted into New Orleans' Tulane University, one of the best colleges in Louisiana. College life had been a beast she was eager to tackle, and living in

America's supernatural capital meant things were never dull.

Yet six years later, she was back in Gaville, an older and wiser woman than when she'd left.

Her life in New Orleans had given Delaney the excitement she craved, but with it came a slew of drama that left her soul weary. Break-ups, backstabbing bitches, a tiring job, and co-existing with a slew of other creatures had grown exhausting. Not to mention, the college workload. She'd gone from one extreme to the next, from having too little to do to having too much on her plate. It resulted in her graduating two years later than she'd planned, making her crave the simplicity of pack life.

Finally, after weeks of planning, she was back home.

The Uber ride from New Orleans to Baton Rouge cost her over a hundred dollars, but she hated driving, so she'd considered the price worth it. She'd sold most of her things, getting rid of everything that wasn't special or essential. When it was all done, the life she'd made for herself fit into three duffle bags, making moving via a standard vehicle a breeze. After a night at a motel to regroup, she hailed another Uber around 7 AM, this one heading to Gaville. An hour and a half after her pick up, she grinned as she read the sign welcoming newcomers into the small town. She retrieved her phone, firing off a text to Larissa that she'd arrived in town.

"You stay all the way in the boonies, huh, girl?" Gerald, her Uber driver, said with a hearty laugh. His Cajun accent was thicker than his potbelly, and over the ride, he shared his entire life story. In return, she shared that she was returning to her hometown. "Rarely come up here."

Something about the old man smelled off, but she couldn't pinpoint what. Perhaps, the lingering scent of cigarettes and fast food was to blame, not Gerald himself. For a human, the car would be hard to handle if you weren't accustomed to it. For her kind, the pungent combination was eye-watering. When she first opened the door, it took everything in her not to gag.

"You've been to Gaville before?" she asked, looking out the opened window to cleanse her nostrils, reminiscing as she took in the familiar buildings.

After years away, little had changed.

"Drove through a few times with my ole lady. Her folks stay in Shreveport," he shared, one snippet of information she'd had yet to learn.

He began to prattle on about something else. Delaney nodded along, pretending to listen. In reality, her mind was elsewhere, excitement stealing her ability to focus. She was growing anxious, eager to let her wolf come out and play. Little compared to the freedom of running around her home turf, pushing her muscles past their limit as the wind tickled her fur. Memories of racing her cousins and engaging in family hunts filled her with nostalgia. As fun as New Orleans had been, any time she wished to shift into Canidae form, she had to leave the city to achieve the endless greenery she craved. The parks dotted around the city, the green spaces located around Lake Pontchartrain, and the trees decorating fancy neighborhoods were all too risky for her to shift. Unlike in tiny, rural Gaville, a wolf roaming around New Orleans was far more likely to garner attention.

Finally, Gerald pulled up to the entrance of her family's property. A chain-link fence encased the many acres, keeping out unwanted visitors and clearly defining their territory. Trees shielded the property's core from view, and the long gravel path winding through the land lay just behind the gate. He stopped right at the edge, peering around the seat with furrowed brows.

"This the right place, girl?" he asked, shock and concern mingling. "Looks like a bunch of trees to me."

Well, no shit.

Taught to respect her elders, and knowing he meant no harm, she held back the retort. Instead, she just smiled and nodded.

"Yes sir, you got the right place," she said, unbuckling her seatbelt.

He let out a low whistle. "Your family got land, huh?"

An understatement. The area was in the ballpark of twenty acres, large enough for all two hundred members of her pack.

"Lots of it," she confirmed, reaching into her crossbody bag for her wallet.

Her job had only paid cash, so she'd gotten into the habit of using physical currency for everything. Though the distance from Baton Rouge to Gaville wasn't much larger than the distance from Louisiana's capital to New Orleans, the ride cost her a hundred bucks extra, not including the tip. She supposed the area wasn't as developed, making the trip more of a hassle, and the late hour she'd left New Orleans minimized the amount of traffic present on her trip to Baton Rouge. During her journey to Gaville, patches of traffic extended the travel time, jacking up the price. Not that money was an issue for her. Bounty hunting earned her a pretty penny, and the portion of her inheritance she had access to was nothing to scoff at. The fare for her ride was already paid for, but she'd always tipped in cash. Pulling out a few twenties, she handed them to a surprised Gerald.

"Keep the change," she said, closing the door once she exited the vehicle.

He was very chatty, nearly to the point of being annoying. But he was friendly and good company, earning a large tip.

When she popped open the trunk, she heard the gate creak open and turned to see her cousin emerge. Or rather, her cousin-in-law, Jack Reese-Harris. As he approached, he offered Delaney a smile. It slipped when he saw Gerald sitting in the driver's seat, still ogling the money. His grey -blue eyes darkened, his lips flattening into a thin line. The poor bastard wasn't fond of humans; being shot in your wolf form and watching your brother die would do that. The incident ultimately led to him meeting Larissa and becoming a mated man. It was a concession of sorts, but love wouldn't erase the mental scars of something so traumatic.

"Let me get those," he said, grabbing two of her duffle bags before she replied.

Less work for her, so she wouldn't complain.

She hauled the final one over her shoulder. Slamming the trunk closed, she stepped back and waved, earning a honk of the horn as Gerald pulled off. The loud noise made her flinch, the pitch irritating her ears.

"C'mon, Larissa's waiting for you," Jack grumbled, throwing a sour look her way.

She returned his glare with one of her own. "What crawled up your ass and died?"

Despite the insult, he held the gate open for her, allowing her to step foot onto the property first. Breathing deeply, Delaney relished the crisp, refreshing scent, so missed of late. Even after years in another city, it still smelled like home. Jack closed the gate behind them, flanking her as they walked down the path that led up to the residence he and Larissa shared with his mother-in-law and her aunt, Galena. As one of three healers and the wife of their former beta, she was invaluable to the pack, holding a high position that extended to her immediate kin. Delaney's body was buzzing with excitement to see her beloved aunt again, who took her in after the passing of her parents.

That excitement was replaced with annoyance when Jack opened his mouth again. She swore the man was only ever happy in Larissa's presence. "Why'd you bring so much stuff?" he complained, adjusting the bag that she damn well knew was a breeze to carry.

If they'd been human, she could see where he was coming from, but shifters possessed a higher weight threshold.

"It's three bags. How the fuck is that a lot?" she replied, wishing her cousin or aunt had been the one to greet her. She had no issues with Jack, beyond the fact that he didn't like most living beings. "Why'd you come instead of Larissa?"

Surprise flickered across his face. "She didn't tell you?"

"Tell me what?"

"Okay, obviously she didn't," he muttered under his breath, as if that'd stop her from hearing him. "She might be expecting again. She was about to take the test when you texted."

Ah.

That explained his irritability. On a good day, he had attachment issues. Anxiety over if his mate was carrying a new family member would worsen them tenfold.

Delaney let out a low whistle, playfully punching his shoulder. "Three under three years. You've been putting in some work. Keep going and y'all could start a pack of your own."

Jack's lips twitched into a smile, the show of positive emotion doing wonders for his looks. With his usual scowl, the man appeared utterly unapproachable. With it gone, one could actually notice his handsomeness.

"Larissa loves it here too much for us to ever branch out," he said. "Plus, running our own pack would be a lot of fucking work."

"Good thing I was joking," Delaney fired back, before returning to the topic of her cousin's potential pregnancy. "You hoping it comes back positive?"

"I'm hoping for whatever she's hoping for," he answered, a sweet yet cliché reply. "We have more than enough help available, especially with you back now."

She recoiled. She liked babies, truly, she just didn't want to be responsible for any. One of the many joys of being an older, childless relative was making fond memories with the little ones, whilst leaving all the shitty parts of kids to the parents.

"I'm not a nanny," she protested, ignoring the side eye. "And I'm only staying with y'all until my cabin is finished, so I won't be available for long."

Jack shared the common wolf belief that the whole pack should help raise the pups. When it came to protecting from threats and providing resources, Delaney agreed. Anything more hands-on than that was a no-go for her.

"Babysitting wouldn't kill you."

"What if it vomits on me and it gets in a cut? Then I could develop an infection and die."

A frustrated huff left him. "Stop being dramatic; that isn't even possible. And we don't even know if she's pregnant yet, so this discussion is pointless."

A sentiment she could agree with.

The house finally came into view. Jack got a pep in his step, walking faster. If he was in wolf form, she'd bet money that his tail would be wagging a mile an hour. Upon opening the door, she was hit with the artificial scent of lemon and pine. Aunt Galena was a clean freak, leading to her home always having an overpowering scent of chemicals. Delaney's nose was sensitive, even by wolf standards, allowing her to pick up the more noxious notes others would miss. Wrinkling her nose, she followed Jack through the halls of the mansion, one of the largest homes in the pack and second only to the alpha's residence. It was essentially a luxurious cabin, the sort of vacation home rich people would blow several bags on. Though she had some complaints about the smell, she adored the wooden interior, the pictures of family and friends lining the hallways, and the cozy environment the furniture and decoration created.

A high-pitched squeal made her wince, though her lips twitched into a smile at a baby's laugh. Jack quickened his steps, practically running to reach the living room, the source of the ruckus. When they breezed through the archway and he saw Larissa and their kids, he unceremoniously dumped Delaney's bags on the floor. Their youngest, Cyrus, was cradled in her arms, the six-month-old giggling as his big sister, Shay, toddled around, still in pajamas. Two coffee mugs were on the table, with a pink divided plate next to them, crumbs and chunks of fruit lying abandoned on the plastic dish.

"Hey, beautiful," Jack greeted, settling next to his wife and wrapping an arm around her shoulder.

The tender kiss they shared was a touching sight that sent a pang through Delaney's heart. She'd never been much of a traditionalist, but one thing she'd always longed for was a mate. In her life, she'd had two potential mates. One in high school, a girl from another pack who just wanted things to stay platonic. The second had been more serious, a witch from one of New Orleans' Voodoo Covens. Their relationship had been hot and cold, but Delaney had been sure Toria was the one. What relationships didn't have trouble, after all? Ultimately, that wasn't the case, and she wasted three years of her life being strung along.

Looking at her cousin, she felt envious, wishing finding her true love could've been as easy as it was for Larissa. It was an innate want; mates were sacred among shifters. The people who could've fulfilled that desire turned out to be duds. If fate granted her another potential mate, she prayed the third time would be the charm, or she'd lose her shit.

Shay instantly became Delaney's favorite when she slapped Jack's leg, making him yelp and them separate. Giving him the stink eye, she weaseled her way in between the two.

"My mommy," she declared, nuzzling into her mother's side.

"My wife," Jack countered, tugging the little girl into his lap.

Shay screamed as if she was wounded, making Delaney's ears ring, but not robbing her of amusement at the scene before her. Based on Cyrus's giggles, he found his big sister's antics funny, too.

Shay recoiled as if burnt when Jack kissed the top of her head, crying out, "Cooties!"

Delaney couldn't help but laugh, while Jack groaned. "Cooties aren't real."

"How she'd even learn about them?" Delaney asked, dropping her duffle bag and leaning against the archway, not venturing to move closer.

Because, as amusing as the scene was, she felt like a giant third wheel. Once she greeted her cousin, she'd be on her way, leaving Jack and Larissa to their little hellion.

Larissa looked at her and waved, biting back a smile of her own. "The Alpha's youngest, Dex. He made it his mission to educate the other kids about them during his parents' anniversary dinner last week."

Delaney snickered. The communal dining hall was used on special occasions, and the youth had their own seating area. Older kids watched over the younger, the goal to teach them responsibility and give the adults a damn break. However, it could also lead to a world of mischief, as it so often had when Delaney and Larissa were children.

"Shay, that's enough," Larissa said in exasperation when the little girl shrieked again, shaking her head. "She's not normally so bratty, I swear."

Delaney shrugged. Truth be told, she didn't give a shit how the child acted on the regular. The kid didn't come from her loins, so it wasn't her issue. But, instead of saying that, she went with the more diplomatic, "It's all right."

"I concur," Jack inserted, trying to hold a wiggling Shay as he stared at his wife. "She's been testy with me since I surprised you with a date."

"You cut into her play time," Larissa replied, before focusing on her daughter, her demeanor becoming stern. "Missy, show your father some respect. Now apologize to him, or you'll get time out and no dessert tonight."

That got the little girl under control. Whereas Delaney got her ass whooped a lot as a child, the thought of no sweets was enough for Shay to do a complete 180. Though her lips were pursed into a pout, she looked at her father and did exactly as her mother asked.

"Sorry, Daddy," she muttered, finally escaping his arms. "Hugging mommy okay."

"Thank you for your permission, oh great one," Jack responded, his sarcastic reply undercut by the goofy grin on his face.

Shay was too young to grasp sarcasm, because she just nodded, then ran to the toybox and began playing again.

"Come sit down," Larissa said, patting the empty spot on the sofa. Cyrus whined in protest at the movement. "We have a lot to catch up on."

"Girl, be for real. We call each other every week," Delaney replied. "What the test come back as?"

Luckily her cousin wasn't one to pull rank, because the defiance could've gotten her into shit with a more traditional wolf. Delaney was two years older, but just the daughter of two gammas. Larissa, meanwhile, was the daughter of a healer and a beta. She was also learning her mother's trade, while for the time being, Delaney would be a freeloader.

"Negative," Larissa answered, then nodded to the baby in her arms. "Which I'm happy about. I want to get these two out of diapers before we have a third."

Delaney nodded, falling silent. She didn't have much to say about the topic, and frankly, she was anxious to stretch her legs after being cramped in a car for so long.

"I'm gonna say 'hi' to Aunt Galena, then go for a run," she said, pushing off the frame.

"Momma isn't home right now," Larissa revealed, then looked at Jack. "Would you mind watching the kids for a bit so I could go with her?"

He shook his head, scooping Cyrus from her. "Nah, babe. Go catch up with your cousin."

"Best husband in the world," she chirped, kissing his cheek before standing.

She was still in her bed clothes, but instead of changing, she just fell into pace with Delaney.

"You're lucky Shay didn't see," Delaney teased when they entered the hallway.

Larissa shook her head. "Don't even get me started. That girl thinks the male species is diseased now. Thanks to Dex's PSA, she doesn't even want to touch her little brother and is convinced her daddy will contaminate me."

"Apparently, she doesn't think Dex is diseased," Delaney pointed out. "If she took his words so much to heart."

"Sure doesn't," Larissa confirmed as they reached the foyer. "She still follows him around and hangs onto his every word. All the kids do."

Even when young, the wolf shifters' hierarchical structure was evident. It was something Delaney had once rebelled against, but it looked like her baby cousin was more of a conformist.

How sad.

"Besides, is she wrong?" Delaney teased as they removed their shoes, her excitement growing. "You got two kids from Jack contaminating you."

"Oh my gosh, shut up!" Larissa ordered, her skin becoming flushed. "You're so fucking nasty."

A giggle tumbling from her undercut the insult. The happy chime heightened Delaney's amusement. Larissa grabbed her hand and tugged her down the central hallway toward the massive oak doors. Her anticipation getting the better of her, Delaney pulled away and started running.

"Race you to our spot!" she called, her head start giving her the lead.

"Cheater!" Larissa said, leaping forward.

They raced across the manicured parts of the property to go into the thicket of their woods. In the midst of running, Delaney unbuttoned her flannel shirt, revealing the high-neck tank top underneath. She too popped the button of her jeans, determined to shift into wolf form the moment the race ended. Greetings flitted in and out of her ears when they passed pack members, to which she responded with a wave. It wasn't long until nature replaced the wooden buildings, and flying creatures replaced the people. When they reached the biggest magnolia tree on the property, the race came to an end. It was close but Delaney edged out the win by an inch. Her tactics might be unorthodox, but the results were impossible to argue with.

Out of breath from the run, neither of them spoke as they undressed and folded their clothes, stacking them in neat piles underneath the tree. Delaney was nude within seconds, having zero shame in letting it all hang out. She knew she looked good, and moreover, modesty was a hindrance among her kind.

So, imagine her slight annoyance when she noticed her cousin still wore her pajamas.

"Why are you still dressed?" Delaney asked, pushing away the thought of how weird the question would sound out of context.

Larissa indicated her body. "Stretch marks, baby weight, and less than firm boobs thanks to breastfeeding."

Just one more reason not to push out a pack of pups; it'd wreck your self-esteem and permanently alter your body.

"I didn't even notice," Delaney said honestly.

"It's the same thing Jack says."

"He wouldn't lie to you, Rissa, and unless you want to walk back in torn clothes—"

"Shut up," Larissa grumbled, quickly stripping out of her clothes. Once naked, she nodded toward the wide expanse of land, bordered by oak, acacia, and magnolia trees. "Ready?" she echoed.

"You were the one holding us up," Delaney mumbled under her breath, shrieking when her cousin threw a small rock at her, which she easily dodged. "Yes, woman, damn!"

Snickering, Larissa broke into a run, leaped into the air, and shifted midway through. She landed on her front paws. Prancing around, she lifted her yellow gaze to Delaney.

Needing no further encouragement, Delaney sprinted off, the fragrant green grass cool and soft beneath her feet, the air redolent with the scent of blooming flowers. She soared up, the breeze cutting over her naked skin and then swirling through her fur. She landed next to her cousin, shutting off her mind as she let instinct take over.

They stared at each other. It had been so long since they'd been together in their most primal forms. Delaney dipped her head to Larissa, in a show of deference to their rank. Larissa nudged her nose against Delaney's snout, then dashed forward.

She raced to catch up with her cousin, pleasure shooting through her.

She was finally home.

Kamika

Three days after the funeral, I started dreaming about my grandmother. The dreams were always short, glimpses of the past that made my heart ache. When the memory ended, I'd fade into oblivion and awake with melancholy nostalgia. Remembering Grandma made me want to waste the day away in bed, scrolling on my phone until my thumb was numb.

Alas, things had to be done, so that wasn't possible.

Mama and I didn't take long to settle into a routine. Get up, have breakfast, clean up, lunch, more labor, and then dinner. Grandma had kept her home orderly, but we had to sort through her many belongings. Her bedroom was cluttered, in a cozy sort of way, and the knick-knacks and pictures were signs of a well-lived life. Nothing exemplified that more than the bookcase in her room, dedicated to her journals.

I suppose love for the written word was genetic, as both Mama and Zara adored writing. That trait skipped over me, as photography was my first love.

The start and end dates were on the spines of the diaries. The first dated back to 1960, when she was just 13 years old. However, it wasn't until 1979, when she got pregnant with Mama, that Grandma started consistently journaling. Per Mama's dictate, going through the dozens of journals would be our final task, and only after she met with the lawyer. Contacting him had been a challenge, so what Grandma wanted done with her possessions still wasn't known.

If she wanted her innermost thoughts to remain a secret, we'd seal them in a box and never read them.

Even with her copious belongings, Mama had Grandma's bedroom organized within two hours. The same couldn't be said for the attic, filled with boxes and bins. It needed to be cleaned out, and spending hours in a dark attic with who knows what hiding amongst the mess was something neither Mama nor I wanted to do. So, we unanimously decided to bring everything into the living room.

Good idea in theory. Troublesome in practice.

No matter how much we sorted through and lugged down the steep wooden staircase, too much shit remained. It seemed like there was no end in sight, until finally, only seven containers were present. Granted, they were the largest of the bunch, but not impossible to move. Mama had stayed up late to clean the kitchen and start sorting through the boxes, so I repaid her by getting up early to remove the final batch of clutter from the attic. My latest dream of Grandma had been surreal, and shook me up. It made the attic even spookier, but I wasn't going to let baseless paranoia stop me from doing shit.

When I lugged the fourth container down, I heard footsteps downstairs.

"Kami, baby?" Mama called up the staircase. "You need help?"

The fact that she wasn't making her way up the stairs confirmed her exhaustion. We agreed to get the heavy ones out together, and if she was running on a full battery, she'd be barging up the steps and scolding me for starting without her.

"No, Ma, I got it," I yelled back.

My reply was a simple, "Okay," followed by her footsteps fading away. Likely to the kitchen to start breakfast, coffee, and toast. Simple fuel that prevented us from starting our day on an empty stomach. My stomach grumbled at the thought of food. Labor before sustenance was unusual, and my body was protesting. However, there wasn't much left in the attic, and I assumed removing the final boxes would be a breeze.

If only.

I was making good time, but it was anything but easy. I couldn't understand how my grandmother had dealt with thirty-plus-pound containers. She was active for her age, but still an elderly smoker. If *I* struggled, I could only imagine the hell she went through whenever she had to retrieve one from the attic.

"Fuck!" I exclaimed as the cardboard box I carried came apart at the seams, leaving me with a pile of belongings at the top of staircase.

Thankfully, nothing but the stupid goddamn box broke, but that still presented me with a mess to clean. Kicking the shit aside, I decided it could wait until I finished moving everything else. I took my time moving the other boxes and bins down the stairs. Finally, when an ache was settling into my back, the last of the containers had been brought down. A joyous moment, undercut by the sheer shit now scattered everywhere. The mess created a maze that was hella annoying to navigate through, the tiny living room barely able to contain everything.

The smell of bacon infiltrated my nose, my mouth watering. Swallowing, I made my way to the kitchen, finding my mother at the stove, music playing on her phone. I glanced at the clock on the microwave. 10:45 AM. We were getting a late start to the day, which explained why I was so goddamn hungry. Normally, our bellies were full by 10 AM.

"Whatcha cooking, Mama?" I asked, unable to stop my laughter when she jumped.

She turned around with a scowl, snatching her phone off the counter and pausing her music. "Shit's not funny, girl. You scared me!"

"Sorry, sorry," I replied, raising my hands in a gesture of surrender. I walked closer, peering into the pan. Sure enough, strips of salty pork sizzled in its own fat. "There was bacon?"

"Found an unopened pack in the bottom drawer." She shooed me, returning to her station. "Figured we'd use it before it went bad."

Grandma certainly wouldn't be needing it.

"Coffee is already brewed if you want a mug, and I'll do our toast while the eggs are frying."

My stomach growled again, the hearty breakfast sounding heavenly. Typically, big breakfasts were reserved for special occasions, but I certainly wasn't complaining about the influx of food.

"I'll have my coffee with my food," I said, grabbing a roll of plastic garbage bags from the counter.

"What's that for, baby?"

"A box broke in the attic."

Her mouth formed into an 'O', and she nodded. When she resumed her music, I took it as my sign to leave until breakfast was done. To no one's surprise, I found the mess exactly where I left it. Plopping down, I yanked a bag from the roll and opened it. The pile was mostly papers, with a miscellaneous object here and there. If I were a more patient person, I might've scanned through the documents. Instead, I gathered the loose sheets into stacks, then shoved them in the bag. They could be sorted and examined downstairs.

One bag could've fit everything, but I didn't want a repeat of the box breaking. So, I used three bags to contain everything. Since I wasn't inspecting anything, it took me less than five minutes. The final objects caught my attention, making me halt and actually look closely. Among the remaining papers was a picture dating back to the 40s. It was my great-grandmother, a floral silk scarf wrapped around her head and large earrings dangling from her ears. She looked radiant, every bit the beauty

Grandma had told me she was. It flattered me that she'd always maintained I looked just like her mama, although she'd wrapped the compliment up by commenting on how much darker I was than her. Flipping the image around, I saw '*Mommy—1945*' scribbled in my grandmother's handwriting. It was taken two years before she'd been born, and when her older siblings had been five and three, respectively.

I admired the image for a few more seconds, before carefully placing it in the bag. As soon as the plastic encased it, the hair on the back of my neck stood up. A chill ran down my spine, and despite being alone, I felt eyes on me. I looked around, wondering if some rodent had found its way into the attic.

Nope.

I was all by myself.

"Oh, hell no," I muttered, raising to my feet.

Any care I took handling the stuff disappeared. I threw everything into the last bag, cussing when something clattered to the floor. Picking it up, I found a jewelry box. Cracking it open, I saw the same necklace Great-Grandma had been wearing. Goosebumps erupted on my arms as the temperature plummeted, adding to my growing unease.

"What the fuck?" I whispered, closing the box and tossing it into the bag, ready to get out of the damned attic.

I fought the instinctual urge to run for my life, my mental reminder that the horror-movie like creepiness was just my imagination becoming a silent chant. It smelled like mold and old people, with a hint of Grandma's favorite perfume. Which made sense, seeing as it was her house. However, my imagination took the odor as another omen, leading me to carry all three bags down at once. I grasped the two lighter bags in one hand, stumbling down the staircase. Perhaps I was being paranoid, but this was some scary movie shit, and I wasn't going to loiter any longer.

The relief I felt when my foot touched the last step was ridiculous, though in my hurry, I failed to notice my mother. I bumped into her, the bags I held dropping to the floor. Thankfully, they didn't tear, and she didn't drop the coffee mugs.

"Something wrong, baby?" she asked, looking at me with furrowed brows.

I'm almost entirely positive this house is haunted.

I wouldn't voice my suspicion, though. Mama wasn't a skeptic, per se, nor was she religious to a fault. However, her Christian upbringing installed in her a belief that souls either went up or down. Ghosts, in her mind, simply didn't exist. So, I just shrugged.

"Thought I saw a mouse."

"A mouse?" she repeated, her voice raising in alarm. "There's mice in this house?"

"No, no," I quickly reassured, rolling my shoulders to stretch out the ache that'd settled. "I thought I saw one, but it was just...uh...paper. My mind was playing tricks on me."

She eyed me slowly, as if she knew I was lying out my ass. I squirmed under her gaze, but whatever she saw, she didn't find it suspicious enough to question me any further.

"Alright. I was coming to tell you the food's ready. Go eat before it gets cold."

"Yes, Ma'am," I said, accepting the mug she handed me and trailing behind her to the dinette table.

As I sat down across from my mother, I tried to push my lingering unease away. Unlike Mama, I was a believer. Grandma had filled my head with stories about her visits to New Orleans, rampant with ghosts and witches. Maturing destroyed my belief in the latter, but, I'd bet money the former were real. They may not be able to hurt the living—the British and French still existed—but I didn't relish the thought of a dead person spying on me. In fact, I fucking hated it. Some believers were wholly into all things paranormal, whereas I tried to stay far away from that shit. Even horror movies about ghosts and ghouls were a challenge to watch sometimes, because they made me jump at every little noise and closely inspect every shadow.

So, experiencing a scene that was right out of a mediocre horror movie didn't sit right with me, and made me all the more eager for Labor Day to arrive. Come September 2nd, I'd be back in Miami, and able to forget about my Grandma's little house of horrors.

"Penny for your thoughts?" Mama asked as I bit into my last piece of bacon.

Oh, right, I hadn't said anything. Typically, our meals were filled with idle chatter.

"The attic just creeps me out," I confessed, seeing no reason to withhold that information.

After all, I wasn't saying why it creeped me out. Her mind could jump to conclusions behind my wariness.

She nodded, finishing off her plate and washing it down with a sip of coffee. "I feel you, baby. I kept expecting a mouse, spider, or a damn snake to be waiting for us in one of those boxes."

I shuddered just thinking about that. My scream would've been heard around town. "No way I would've stayed in this house if that happened."

"Baby, I would've been out the door with you," she said with a laugh, the sound encouraging my own giggles.

Our laughter filled the kitchen, pushing away the quiet tension. Yet, I sensed her question lingering in the air. She could read me like a book and likely knew that I was bullshitting.

"So, the attic is cleared out?" she asked after a heartbeat of silence, pushing away her empty cup.

I finished off my coffee, then nodded. "Yeah. Nothing but dust and cobwebs up there now. We can start sorting through all that stuff today."

That wasn't a task I looked forward to. When Mama first said we'd be staying until Labor Day, I thought it was overkill. Grandma had always prided herself on having her business in order. Yet, the sheer amount of shit she hoarded meant staying for weeks was necessary to thoroughly sort through everything, and there was no telling when her lawyer would finally set up a face-to-face meeting.

"You still going to Larissa's party?"

I shrugged. Larissa had made it known I was still welcome, and Mama had made it clear she thought I should go. Yet, following Jack's outburst, attending a Harris kickback no longer held its appeal.

"I still think you should," she continued, standing from her seat and collecting the cups. "I'd hate for you to be stuck here all summer without shit to do."

"Stuck implies I'm here against my will," I replied, getting to my feet to help her clean up. "I knew what I was signing up for when I agreed."

"I know, baby. But I was thinking, now that the attic is cleared, I can sort through the stuff by myself."

I shook my head. "No, that'd be too much work for one person."

"It'd be time consuming," she agreed, setting the dishes in the sink. "But not physically demanding. I'd just have to sit my ass in one place for a few hours every day."

That was still very labor intensive, in a different way than emptying out the attic had been. In theory, sorting and categorizing wasn't much work. In practice, that shit could waste precious hours of your life and be utterly mind numbing.

"I don't mind helping you," I insisted, feeling like shit that she thought I wouldn't be up for the challenge.

Yeah, I might've complained about many things, but that didn't mean I'd abandoned the duty I'd volunteered for.

She squeezed my shoulder, offering me a small smile. "I know, Kami. But I want you to go out. If I need help, I promise I'll let you know."

Accepting help had always been a problem for my mother. Why I thought that habit wouldn't make itself known during this trip, I didn't know. And while I appreciated Mama's concern, helping her sort through a bunch of shit seemed more comforting than navigating through social landmines at a party I was hesitant to attend.

Yet, at her insistence, I found it hard to refuse. As a toddler, Mama told me I was a complete Daddy's girl. When Grandma and I were still cool, she was my favorite person in the whole wide world. But since entering adulthood, my bond with my mother became stronger than ever, and I understood how many difficulties she'd been through. She always managed to emerge stronger than before. However, I knew losing her mother had her in more pain than she was letting on, and I didn't want to add to her stress because she was worrying about me, thinking I was shutting down.

Like I had when I was forced to break up with Larissa, and Grandma declared that I was dead to her.

Just the memory was hurtful, and since then, Mama had become a worrywart over my wellbeing. But, I guess seeing your child damn near catatonic for a month and a half would do that to a parent. The trauma my grandmother inflicted strained Mama's relationship with her mama, leaving Grandma isolated from family during her final years.

After a very pregnant pause, I sighed, deciding to relent. "Okay, I'll go to the party. But, I'm going to help you, too."

Mama looked at me as she scrubbed a dish, her eyes softening. "Alright, baby. I can accept that compromise."

Anxiety assaulted me at the thought of facing Larissa and Jack—*especially Jack*—again. But I didn't voice how the prospect had me on edge. I just returned her smile, praying that tomorrow would be a break as Mama seemed to think, and not another challenge I had to face.

CHAPTER FIVE

Beauden

"If you put your shoes on my goddamn dashboard one more motherfucking time, I'm throwing your ass into flames," Beauden Hugo Valois snarled, tired of warning Cruz to keep his feet planted on the floor.

Beau's black 1968 Cobra Jet Mustang was his baby, only second to his cat, Snowball. He adored the black feline so much that he had some witch bitch cast a spell on her to make her immortal. Their life forces were now entwined. As long as Beau lived, so would Snowball. Being a vampire, his life would only end if he made some dumbass mistake. He liked to think of himself as above error, but bringing Cruz along on a trip to the boonies proved that notion false. The fucker knew how to have a good time, but he grated on Beau's nerves like no one else.

Cruz waved him off with a chuckle, his goddamn boots still on his spotless dash. "Oh, relax, my friend. 'Tis just a car."

Beau recoiled as if he was hit, the comment insulting him. "The fuck it is. I've had this ride since the '70s, and I'm not letting you fuck it up."

Cruz's response was more grating laughter, but he knew not to test Beau. With an unnecessary sigh, he removed his feet. "There."

How their friendship had lasted a century, Beau hadn't a clue. But one day during the summer of 1923, Cruz Sánchez waltzed into a bar. Beau was frequenting the establishment; it had made for good hunting grounds. That night, they had their eyes on the same target, a pretty little thing from rich stock, looking to slum it with the poors and the coloreds. They made a game of hunting her, and they'd been tight ever since.

When Cruz got too tiring to deal with, Beau took a trip down memory lane to recall all the good times they had. It was an excellent way to avoid killing him, because, fuck, he'd miss the asshole if he bit it. So, instead of risking an accident and snapping his neck—as he'd done so many times before—he just ignored his dearest friend.

Or tried to, as Cruz liked attention too much to shut the fuck up.

"Now that I've been a good boy and did as you ordered, will you get your ass off your shoulders, Beauden?" Cruz asked, his vaguely Caribbean accent thickening with the infusion of sass. Beau grunted in response. Cruz sighed. "Still not happy, friend?"

"I'm fucking thrilled, pardner," Beau grumbled, turning the radio up and wishing they'd arrive at their destination already.

Michael Jackson's 'Off the Wall' was the latest cassette to enter his car's player. The titular song of the album started to blast through the speaker. Beau bobbed his head to the beat, the music a great distraction. They'd been on the road since 9 AM with no stop. It was a little past noon, and they were just entering the neighboring town, Fleur. The endpoint? Gaville, Louisiana, a little town on the Mississippi, surrounded by swamps and forest, and three hours away from Beau's beloved New Orleans, not including traffic. He was born and raised there, and couldn't imagine living anywhere else, but his job took him all over the country.

The moment the song ended, Cruz lowered the volume. Seeing as they had advanced hearing, the action was unnecessary, only pissing him off more.

"I'm hungry," Cruz announced. "Can we stop for food?"

"You got money for food?" he replied, knowing damn well he wasn't talking about a restaurant.

Some human cuisine made for a good palette cleanser, but it provided little nutritional value unless blood was an ingredient.

Like a petulant toddler, Cruz huffed and crossed his arms. "Unless we're eating the staff, I'm not talking about a restaurant."

Beau's frustration was starting to boil over. He, too, was hungry and tired of dealing with a man-child that expected his every whim to be indulged. Cruz was his best friend, but he didn't have the patience to constantly put up with his bullshit.

"GPS says we're almost to Gaville," Beau said, trying to rein in his temper. "Hold tight for a minute."

Ideally, until nightfall. Hunting during the day was always risky. They were old enough that the sun didn't hurt them, but more people were milling about. More people, more witnesses, and sunlight allowed for increased visibility.

Cruz was well aware of this; he hadn't gotten so old by being a jackass. Yet, he lived to challenge Beau, and that time was no different.

"I bet we could pick up a target within the hour. Be back on the road within two."

"That's two hours wasted, when we can be in and out of this bitch, and back home in New Orleans by tomorrow."

That was an exaggeration. The coven that hired him provided him with an obituary of some old bitch that had a renegade witch for a mother. Said mother took some papers she wasn't supposed to, and now they wanted them back. Finding the home address had been a breeze, and with the lady dead, whatever protection spells cast would only last so long.

Unless, of course, they were cast by someone powerful. If that was the case, his plan of heading to the house, ransacking the place, then torching it to conceal evidence wouldn't cut it. And that plan was banking on the papers being within the home. For all he knew, they could be buried in the swamp, presenting a headache.

Just thinking of all the potential complications had a pang of regret going through him. Bounty hunting had long stopped being exciting to him, but lately, each job felt more taxing. A career switch had been on his mind, but he didn't know what the fuck he'd do, and the money he made was too appealing to walk away from. It was why he accepted the coven's mission, even though Beau fucking hated dealing with witches. Dead or alive, those bitches were tiring, and if they hadn't offered such a pretty penny, he would've laughed in their faces.

Alas, Lavina dangled a big paycheck in front of his face.

He'd push through and get the job done. It was what he was known for, pulling through for his employers no matter the difficulty. Sure, he'd been getting lazier as of late, but he would squander his payday, and he sure as hell wouldn't let ghosts best him.

Cruz tsked. "We cannot head straight to the home in daylight, Beau. If we have to wait until darkness anyway, why not do something fun with our time? Fleur is a college town, you know."

Beau sidled a glare, annoyed that the attempt to sway him was working. Co-eds were a favorite of theirs.

"And it's a Sunday. Plenty of them will be off," Cruz announced in a singsong, sensing Beau's change of heart.

"We're leaving when the sun sets," Beau said, parking on the side of the road.

Grabbing his phone, he canceled the GPS, rolling his eyes at Cruz's snicker. He wasn't giving into the prick but making a logical decision. His line of work was hard, and thinking was always easier on a full stomach.

They, in fact, did not leave when the sun set. Instead, Beau found himself in a strip mall nightclub, in a booth tucked away in a dimly lit corner, nursing whiskey on the rocks. Human alcohol had little effect on him; he'd need to down a full bottle of Everclear to even feel a buzz. But sipping liquor prevented them from standing out, seeing as just about everyone had a cup or flask in their hand. He and Cruz were surrounded by drunk twenty-somethings who should probably be studying for a test, not getting lit.

But, hey, humans with a good head on their shoulders made for fucking annoying targets.

Fleur boasted a population of around 15,450, over six times more people than Gaville. The primary reason for that difference was the large community college, decent enough to attract over three thousand students. Amongst those students were many all-American girls. Blonde haired, blue-eyed beauties experiencing their first taste of freedom. Good Christian girls eager to rebel, free to explore things that would've never flown in their conservative households. That included fucking around with guys who weren't handpicked by Mama, and who wouldn't shrink back at their father's threats. The kind of guys that'd make their religious mothers balk, and their strict daddies fume.

The kind of guys that they were raised to believe were beneath them.

Girls like that made for the perfect prey, especially with liquor flowing through their systems. Plus, they were far more entertaining than the homeless guy Beau wanted to snatch up. The cops might ignore a dead hobo, but part of the fun was getting away with the crime.

"What about her?" Cruz asked, pointing to a petite redhead dancing on a table.

Nope. Her friends were filming her antics. Too many witnesses, who'd be quick to identify them. In the modern world, escaping the law wasn't impossible, but it wasn't as easy as it had once been, before technology consumed everyone's lives.

"Too popular," Beau answered, scanning the crowd to select another victim. He spotted a curvy redbone, licking his lips as he admired her curves. He pointed his chin at her. "Wanna take her down?"

A peek at Cruz revealed he was just as interested, his hazel eyes growing darker the longer he stared. "I'd hate to kill that one."

"We don't gotta kill her to sample her."

Cruz hummed in agreement. But, before either man could stand, another one entered the equation. A tall, lean, brown-skinned man with a fade greeted her with a kiss. Beau groaned, disappointment swamping him.

Cruz didn't tear his eyes away. Instead, he began admiring the guy. "We could take them both. Double the fun."

"Hell no," Beau immediately replied, picking up on his friend's meaning.

Cruz swung both ways, and while Beau respected his choice, if a woman wasn't directly involved, he wasn't interested. Fucking a chick with another man was the most he'd ever do with the same sex.

Cruz threw his head back and laughed, shaking his head and taking a swig of his rum and Coke. "I'm just jesting, Beauden. We'll file that one away, just in case."

Beau rolled his eyes. Cruz was the only asshole he allowed to use his full name. When his surrogate father died, he dropped it almost entirely. His jaw tightened at the memory of the man's gory demise, disdain flaring up. The woman who took away his humanity had been the same one to take away his father-figure. She'd been a French Creole broad, looking down on Blacks and Yankees alike. But that hadn't stopped her from pitching pussy to both groups.

He took a swig of his whiskey, needing to wash away the bitter taste in his mouth.

"I want a brunette bitch tonight," he declared.

Preferably, one with curly hair and soulless grey eyes.

"Thinking of her again?" his friend questioned, familiar enough with that statement to decipher his intention.

When Alosia Sinclair haunted his mind too much, he cleansed her from his system by fucking and killing one of her doppelgangers. It allowed him to relive her death, the euphoria he felt when he'd finally managed to best her, and get payback for all the shit she'd done.

Beau shrugged. Cruz, thankfully, didn't press the issue. That was the one topic he knew not to push.

He downed his drink, then stood up, clapping his hands together. "If it's a brunette you want, then that's what you shall have."

With that, he disappeared into the crowd. Cruz had never met Alosia, but Beau had described her enough for him to get an idea of how she looked. Less than ten minutes later, he was returning to the table, a woman in tow. His selection ticked off many boxes that Alosia had.

Tanned brunette with curly hair? Check.

Tall and plump? Check.

Pouty lips, button nose, big, pale eyes? Check, check, check.

Her eyes were blue, not grey, but other than that, she was perfect. So much so, that his lip nearly curled in disgust. Beau had to give it to the man. Finding a woman that could pass as Alosia's sister wasn't easy, but he'd managed to do it in a crowded club within minutes.

The woman's gaze swept over Beau appreciatively, her breath hitching ever so slightly. Her tongue darted out, moistening her red lips. She peered at Cruz, looking at him with just as much lust. "This is Hugo?"

Beau smirked at the shock in her voice. He'd admit, Hugo wasn't the most attractive sounding name, but he felt more comfortable using his middle name when hunting. Cruz, on the other hand, usually pulled some alias out of his ass.

"Sure is, sweetheart. He's gorgeous, isn't he?"

"Agreed," she breathed, holding out his hand. "Bella."

He accepted her hand, but instead of shaking it, he kissed it. Her giggle told him that he had the desired effect.

"A beautiful name for a beautiful lady." He let his eyes drag over her, feigning the optics of attraction, an easy job. He'd admit, she was pretty, just as Alosia had been. "You got a man waiting for you at home?"

"No," she said, crossing her arms over her chest. "I kicked his ass to the curb, so you don't got to worry about that."

Her tone hinted that she was still salty about whatever went down, not that he gave a fuck. If anything, it was a good thing. Pigs always investigated boyfriends and exes first.

"So, you two got anything planned tonight?" Bella asked, looking at him through her lashes, trying to play coy, a ploy he could see through easily.

"That depends on you, love," Cruz replied, his voice smooth as honey.

His accent was noticeably thicker. He played it up when they hunted, knowing how it turned women across the country into goo. Outside of the South, Beau's twang garnered its share of attention, but deep in Louisiana, it didn't stand out much.

Bella bit her lip, her cheeks turning pink. "I...I don't typically do this, but I live nearby. If you two...want to come over for some drinks."

Her excuse was one they'd heard a million times before, but a sign that they had her exactly where they wanted her.

Beau raised an eyebrow, a smirk tugging at his lips. "Is that an invitation, sweetheart?"

"If you're interested," she purred, her blue eyes dark with desire.

Big mistake on her part, but a win for them.

Cruz looked between them as Beau rose to his feet, his lips stretched into a grin. "Shall we get out of here, then?"

When Bella nodded, no further words were needed. Little was said as they followed her out of the bar. The route they took lacked security cameras. It was as if fate was sanctioning her eventual death, quelling any guilt he might've felt. When a victim was too risky, Beau let them be, taking it as a sign they were meant to live. That wasn't the case with Bella, leaving his conscience clear. The evening breeze brushed against their skin, cooling them down as they walked to her apartment. Bella's complex was just blocks away from the bar, a little rundown, but not the worst he had seen. She led them inside her place, her demeanor jumping between confidence and nervousness. It only fueled his anticipation.

Beau would make sure to enjoy the night. Come morning, he and Cruz would be in Gaville, stomach full and balls empty. Bella, however, would be dead, one victim among many.

May 26th

Kamika

When Memorial Day rolled around, Mama's advice was still lingering in my mind, convincing me to drag my ass to Larissa's party. At that point, boredom was setting in, and I missed Miami more than ever. Before we even boarded the flight out of the city, I'd become homesick. When we landed at Louis Armstrong International Airport, that sensation intensified. The more people offered vain words of comfort, the more unbearable the feeling became.

Baton Rouge Metropolitan Airport was closer to Gaville, but there was no nonstop route from Miami to Baton Rouge, so flying into the city would've cost more time and money. The humble town of Gaville was about an hour northwest of Louisiana's capital and had a humble population of 2,311 people. I could only do a handful of things to distract myself, which didn't bode well for someone who became bored easily. One of the many things I loved about Miami was that there was always something new to do, and the city's nightlife was anything but lacking. Gaville was the exact opposite.

Perhaps that's why I listened to Mama and took Larissa up on her invitation. Sure, her husband wasn't my biggest fan, and I'd lost contact with almost every friend in the town, but attending the small kickback gave me something to do.

Well, it was supposed to be small. Instead, dozens of people crowded the property's clearing. It wouldn't surprise me if every teenager and twenty-something in Gaville were in attendance. It reminded me of the barbeques and get-togethers Larissa used to invite me to, teeming with every member of her large family, and whoever they held dear. Then, the raging parties thrown gave me life and often ended with Larissa and me sneaking off with a bottle of alcohol to find a secluded corner to enjoy each other's company. Now, I wanted to hide at the number of people. Most of them insisted on talking about my grandmother the moment they saw me. The soberer of the bunch offered condolences, while the drunker ones asked if we'd reconciled by the time she died. Either way, it dampened the party atmosphere I longed for.

Instead of mingling with peers that I hadn't seen in ages, I traversed the property's gravel trail alone, sipping on a cheap hurricane cocktail. The path led me to the more secluded area that once frightened me. Light never penetrated here and my imagination ran wild. My vow to enjoy myself looked like it would be broken, as I felt nothing but annoyance.

I made my way to a small iron bench, rusted from being exposed to the elements. Taking another sip of my cocktail, I set the cup aside, then retrieved my phone from my bra. Big tits made for convenient storage. Surrounded by flora, my signal wasn't the strongest, but I still managed to access Instagram with no problem. Mindlessly scrolling would be better than stewing in anger. First, I checked my DMs, a smile gracing my face seeing how many drunken wishes for my return were present. Some were accompanied by videos and pictures taken just for me. Knowing I was in my friends' hearts, even when they were absolutely hammered, lifted my mood. However, the envy and dejection I felt refused to fuck off, and they only worsened when I moved on to checking my friends' stories, highlighting just how much fun they were having on the boat.

I closed the app out, but because I was a sucker for pain, I moved on to my text messages. They were notably drier, but I made sure to respond to the few I had. Seeing Zara's name made my annoyance return. The simple *'Hey,'* I sent last night sat unread. Sighing, I powered off my phone, staring blankly ahead. Southern Magnolias filled the Harris land. The trees were still in bloom, infusing the air with a nostalgic sweetness and dotting the grass with white flowers. I inhaled, humming in delight as the floral aroma entered my nostrils. If I'd brought my camera, I'd snap a couple of images. My phone's camera was fucked, preventing it from being a viable option.

Loud rap music traveled from the center of the party, echoing throughout the property. 'Swing' by Savage was the latest to be played, a throwback song my mother used to love. I bobbed my head to the beat and contemplated migrating closer to the music to dance. I quickly dashed the idea. The thought of hearing more about my grandmother was greatly unappealing.

I'd have had a better time if I didn't let the comments affect me, but I couldn't control my mood souring whenever someone mentioned her. I lacked that level of emotional regulation, and the insensitivity many regarded me with didn't help matters. The town was small; everyone knew about the rift between me and my grandmother. During the funeral and repast, people had enough tact to ignore that fact. But in a party setting where liquor flowed freely, sensitivity disappeared.

Jamie Brown took the cake when the jackass had the nerve to ask me if I was happy my grandmother died. An awkward silence settled over everyone within earshot, and after replying with, "Fuck you," I made my escape to a remoter part of the property. I didn't want to deal with stupid fuckheads, and dancing under the moonlight sounded like a strangely therapeutic vibe.

Pagans used to do that shit frequently, so it had to have some benefit.

"Kamika," Larissa called, catching my attention.

My head swirled in her direction. A tall, gorgeous woman who made me doubletake trailed behind her. With caramel skin, cat-like brown eyes, perfectly full lips, and enviable waist-length locs, something about the stranger reminded me of Zoë Kravitz, a long-term celebrity crush of mine. Her features were sharper than Larissa's, her skin a touch darker, and her hair thicker, but the women shared a resemblance.

"H-hey," I said with a wave, maintaining my composure by a thin thread as Larissa and the woman neared, red Solo cups in their hands. "Who's this?"

A smile accompanied my question. The stranger fixed her gaze on me, and my stomach somersaulted. She inhaled sharply, her body stilling.

"Kamika, this is Delaney, my cousin," Larissa announced with excitement, practically bouncing on her heels.

Well, that explained why she was so fine. The Harris family had some good ass genes.

I stood and held my hand out to Delaney, hoping my palms weren't sweaty. "Nice meeting you."

She accepted my outstretched hand; I squeaked at her tight grip. I tried to retract my hand, but her hold remained firm as she stared at me with uncomfortable intensity.

I swallowed, deciding to greet her again. "Uhm, hi?"

Nothing. Frustration welled within me. I attempted to yank my hand away; her grasp tightened to the point of pain.

"Fuck!" I exclaimed, my hand feeling like it was being crushed.

Why the hell was she so strong? More importantly, why wasn't she letting me go?

The thought of throwing my drink in her face crossed my mind, but I wasn't in the mood for a fight. Moreover, I'd likely get dragged from one corner of the property to the other. I could hold my own well enough, but I knew my limits.

"Delaney," Larissa hissed, smacking her cousin on the head as she continued her mission to break one of my bones. "Let her go, dumbass."

At her cousin's sharp words, Delaney's arm jerked back as if she touched fire. I rubbed the cool plastic of my cup against my sore hand, unable to control my glare. Pacifism was momentarily forgotten; my hand hurt too much for that shit.

"Are you out of your goddamn mind?" I snapped, regretting dragging my ass here.

A sound scarily close to a growl escaped Delaney. She slapped her hand over her mouth and dropped her drink. My mouth slackened; my pain forgotten, unease sweeping through me as I examined the crazy bitch before me.

Was Larissa on a goal to surround herself with weirdos?

I glanced at her for an explanation, but she watched her cousin with wide eyes and a tight jaw. Guess she was just as lost as me.

Delaney turned to her cousin. "Is she…does she—?" she mumbled.

Her unfinished questions confused me.

Larissa seemed to understand. She shook her head, her expression turning from bewildered to sympathetic. Something seemed to click in her mind, something that I was still missing.

Delaney's shoulders sagged. "I'm sorry."

"What the fuck is going on?" I asked, wanting to make sense of the exchange that just took place.

All Larissa mustered was, "Umm," while Delaney continued gawking.

In a moment of liquid courage, I placed a hand on Delaney's arm to feel her temperature. Maybe the swampy Louisiana heat was overwhelming her, triggering some type of episode. "Are you ok—?"

"I'm fine," she snapped, shaking off my touch. She stepped back, her hands twitching.

My brows furrowed at her odd reaction.

She finally looked at Larissa. "I'm…Imma be around."

With that, she hurried off toward the epicenter of the party, leaving me confused as hell and further questioning my ex's choice of company. Family or not, the sheer size and population of the compound allowed for avoidance. Most importantly, why the hell would she introduce me to someone off their rocker?

"Larissa," I began, watching Delaney retreat. "What the hell was that?"

Another, "Umm," escaped her.

I pinned her with a glare.

She heaved a sigh. "It's...a little complicated."

Perhaps something was wrong with Delaney that only her family was privy to, or she couldn't hold her liquor well. Whatever it was, her reaction was far from normal.

"Do I stink or something?" I joked, hoping humor might coax out the truth.

She laughed. "No, exactly the opposite."

The corners of my lips twitched at her words, and I tried to ignore the way my heart fluttered at her compliment. Still, I couldn't help but cherish the privacy in this secluded corner.

No past. Grandma.

No present. Jack.

Just us.

"So, what's her issue?" I lowered my voice, using the tone that always got me my way with her.

She ignored my question, and asked, "How much did you know about Susanne, Kami?"

I frowned, so fucking lost. It burst my bubble, and if she wanted a subject change, I would have preferred any other topic but that one.

"What the hell does my grandma have to do with your cousin acting weird?"

Larissa scowled. "Delaney has her reasons."

"Not from my viewpoint."

"Answer me. What did Susanne tell you about the LeBlanc family?"

I huffed out a breath but decided to humor her. Because, well, it was her, and I'd spoken about my grandmother to enough people already. What difference would it make if I added another person to that count?

"Her mama and her siblings are from New Orleans, and her daddy is from Gaville. Both of her parents died before I was born, and my aunt and uncle went back to New Orleans as soon as they could, so I've only met them a handful of times. Happy?"

She wasn't; she continued her delve into my family's history. It was something we'd never spoken of when we were together because neither of us was interested. Gaining an interest in the topic now, of all times, nearly destroyed the last of my frayed nerves.

"Did she, like, ever say why her mama came to Gaville?"

"Jesus, Larissa, I don't know. She barely talked about them!" I snapped, fed up with the irrelevant interrogation. "And what does that have to do with anything? And if you say, 'umm,' so help me God…"

Even before her passing, my grandmother was a sore subject, so Larissa randomly bringing her up irked me to no end. Before I received a proper answer, Jack stalked out of the darkness. I clicked my tongue. He was the last person that I wanted to deal with.

"What the hell is wrong with 'Laney?" he asked, not even acknowledging me.

I was too caught up in figuring out the same thing to care about an asshole ignoring me.

"Kamika, Jamie has been asking about you," Larissa said with a smile.

Both me and her husband gave her confused looks. Not only didn't I want to see that bitch, but it irked me that Larissa couldn't stay on the subject. This behavior was so unlike her, that it only increased my reluctant curiosity.

"She was by the bonfire last I saw her," she continued.

But then, we hadn't been close in years. I didn't truly know her anymore, and that was devastating.

"Nice way to avoid the question," I sniffed and poured my cocktail onto the ground, inches away from Jack's feet. "But I think I'll be going. Nice seeing y'all."

Not.

I stomped away before she responded. I knew when I wasn't wanted somewhere, and the entire goddamn party was a bust, anyway. The other partygoers couldn't shut up about a dead woman I had fallen out with. The guest of honor had an odd aura about her, and the woman who invited me was pushing me to someone else. Anyone else from what it seemed. First Delaney and then Jamie. I should've just stayed home.

With incomparable and shocking speed, Larissa appeared in my path, scaring the hell out of me and forcing me to stop.

Jack, thankfully, was nowhere in sight.

"What?" I snapped, ready to curl up in bed, while ignoring the random thought that Grandma's spirit might haunt the house I was staying at.

"I'm sorry," Larissa breathed. "When I said it was complicated, I really meant it."

"I fail to understand how my goddamn grandmother relates to those complications or Delaney's behavior."

"Refer to my previous comment."

I ground my teeth together, struggling to keep a level head. However, my annoyance and tipsiness made that a challenge. So, I opted to remove myself from the situation.

"Larissa, I'm leaving—"

"No!" she nearly yelled, earning a confused look form me. She took a breath. "I'm sorry, but I think Delaney wants to apologize to you. Alcohol always makes her act...strange."

I barked a laugh and spun in a circle, not seeing the attractive weirdo anywhere. Larissa was fucking with me; I was sure of it at her silence. I narrowed my eyes. "Okay. Where is she?"

"The house," she blurted. "She texted me. Just...give her a chance. Let me walk you there."

I wasn't drunk enough to deal with this bullshit.

"I know the way, Larissa. Is this a ploy to kidnap me or some shit?"

My words were sarcasm, but her insistence on seeing a woman who nearly crushed my hand concerned me.

"I promise you'll retain your freedom," she reassured with a smile. "You and Delaney got off on the wrong foot, but you can both use a friend right now."

Her words triggered a realization.

My eyebrows shot up.

Under normal circumstances, I would be ecstatic that she was trying to set me up with Delaney. However, tonight wasn't normal, partially because of the very cousin Larissa was pushing me towards. And with life continuing to fuck me over, I just wanted to leave.

I could admit Delaney was attractive, and as a vain bitch, that made her very appealing. And sure, maybe alcohol was the reason for her odd behavior, and I needed to have a proper conversation to judge her. But, fuck, I couldn't deal with extra bullshit this summer, and something told me reinvolving myself with the Harrises would lead to that. I wanted entertainment, not drama. On the other hand, Delaney was far from the worst person I'd encountered since returning to Gaville, and for all I knew, she could have intense social anxiety. That didn't explain away Larissa's questions, but it certainly painted her cousin in a more positive light.

Fuck.

I couldn't actually be considering this.

"I'm not going to the house tonight, Larissa. I'm leaving," I declared, settled on a plan, one against my better judgment.

She deflated and opened her mouth to speak.

I held up my hand. "If your cousin is truly sorry, maybe we can meet when she sobers up...*maybe.*"

I was, indeed, considering it.

It wasn't a foolproof plan, but based on how Larissa lit up, she was satisfied with it and chose to ignore my lingering hesitancy.

"Yeah, yeah, I'll text you!" she promised with newfound enthusiasm.

I knew it was dumb, but my impulsivity was craving some summer entertainment, and a distraction from the misery in my life might be what I needed to endure Gaville without ending up in therapy.

Delaney

Delaney was familiar with lust. The pursuit of pussy had driven her to do stupid things, things she never would've done if the ache between her legs and promise of a good time hadn't urged her on. That pesky feeling blossomed as she stared at Kamika's retreating form. She breezed past her without noticing Delaney pacing behind a tree, fully unaware of the admiration she garnered. Her tank top and jeans shorts clung beautifully to her curvy figure. The bright yellow of her top complimented her rich brown skin, and her shorts revealed thick, toned thighs that she wanted wrapped around her. It wasn't mere lust that created such erotic images in her mind, but an instinctual want that she'd only felt twice before.

The crunching of grass caught Delaney's attention. She turned to see Larissa stomping up to her, shoving past partygoers and glaring at her. When she reached Delaney, she slapped her arm. "Have you lost your damn mind, girl?"

A growl slipped past Delaney's lips at the aggressive tone, and she stepped back. Big emotions always led to her temper rising, and she didn't want a good night to end in bullshit. Moreover, hierarchy gave Larissa the right to do whatever she pleased.

"She's pretty," Delaney said, instead of answering her cousin. "How'd you know her?"

Larissa scoffed, the friendliness she showed to Kamika morphing into irritation. "You didn't only do that shit because she's pretty. You want her."

"I wouldn't mind fuckin—"

"Don't finish that sentence," Larissa warned, with an intimate protectiveness Delaney didn't quite like. "I know you're not dumb enough to do that bullshit for a quick fuck, and even if you were, Kamika deserves better. You *want* want her."

Delaney looked around. Not too many party-goers were nearby, and they were on pack land, giving them the right to say whatever the hell they wanted. Yet, there were many attendees not related to them and in the dark about the truth of their world. Revealing too much would lead to trouble she wouldn't feel like dealing with.

With a sigh, Delaney finally spoke. "Does she really not know…about us?"

"She doesn't," Larissa repeated. "But she can learn about us if I'm catching the right vibes."

"She isn't one of us," Delaney stated, trying to ignore the hope that sparked within her at Larissa's words. "I'm not…I can't…I won't."

She wouldn't allow fate to fuck her over twice. One whiff of Kamika let Delaney know what kind of blood flowed through her veins, tantalizingly sweet, even for a non-blood sucker. The powers that be may have found it funny to give her two witches as potential mates, but she wouldn't be dumb enough to make the same mistakes. She sure as well wouldn't fuck around with one that didn't know of her heritage.

"Refer to my previous statement," Larissa said, shifting feet, then huffing out a breath. "If you really want to play yourself because of that cunt, then I'll tell Kamika not to come over—"

"No," Delaney interrupted, the thought of not seeing her again tightening her chest.

Damn instincts. No steps had been taken to solidify the mate bond, but every fiber of her being screamed to seek Kamika out.

"Then let's establish some ground rules," Larissa began, looking at Delaney intently. "One, you'll get a damn grip, and not nearly crush her hand."

Delaney scoffed. "That was a fucking accident."

"Doesn't matter. It still could've ended badly. Now, two, you'll treat this seriously."

"What if she only wants casual?"

Delaney didn't cherish the thought, but she wasn't delusional to think Kamika would see her as a 'forever' partner.

Larissa shrugged. "Minds change."

"But—"

"Finally," Larissa interrupted. "No sex until she knows the truth."

Fucking hell. Out of all the conditions, that one would be the hardest. Delaney rushed into sex in all her relationships, enjoying the sensation and intimacy that came along with it. It was the closest she'd ever be to another being, and after she left *thou who shan't be named*, it became an excellent way to forget about a bitch who'd never truly cared about her. Moreover, shifters had higher libidos than humans, and her fingers weren't always enough to satisfy her.

Did she understand the importance of waiting? Yes, she did. Did she relish the thought? Fuck no.

"Sex may hurry things along," Delaney protested, her lips pursing.

"And it kicks off the damn solidification process, which Kamika has to choose."

"And if she doesn't?"

"Then you move on, Delaney. There are other fish in the sea, and you seem to have no shortage of potential mates."

That much was true. In her 24 years, she'd had a grand total of three, more than others in her pack.

"Do we have a deal?" Larissa asked, holding out her palm.

Tsking, Delaney nodded, and accepted her hand, sealing her cousin's terms with a handshake.

Kamika

Nothing in the world compared to a Louisiana summer night. The scorching heat of the day turned into a pleasant warm breeze, creating the perfect lounging temperature. My locs were piled into a bun, and the gentle wind blew against the back of my neck. The air was thick with the scent of magnolias and night jasmine, perfuming the darkness with a sweet aroma. Concealed by Gaville's bountiful plant life, the creatures of the night created a natural symphony.

I preferred it that way. I adored the town's flora, but the fauna consisted of too many insects, amphibians, and reptiles for my comfort. Trekking past them on my way home scared off most of them, but my least favorite of the bunch—insects—chose to keep close. Mosquitoes hunting for a midnight snack refused to leave me be. The fuckers always flocked to me and gorged themselves to death on my precious blood.

Greedy assholes.

"Goddammit!" I swore, swiping another pest off me, just as another dropped to the ground after consuming too much blood.

My tank top and jean shorts were good party attire but exposed a lot of skin for insects to devour. I hadn't taken the bugs into account when I'd chosen my outfit for Larissa's kickback. Temperature and vanity had been my primary focus.

I regretted not asking Mama to borrow the car. Gaville wasn't big, and as a teenager, I'd walked everywhere, so I didn't see harm in doing it now. However, I should've taken advantage of my ability to drive, something I lacked back then. A layer of sweat wouldn't coat me, nor would bugs be feasting on me.

But, dummy that I was, I chose to walk across town. It was twenty minutes from my grandmother's house to Magnolia Mist, but that was more than enough time to leave me itchy and grimy.

The town center consisted of rows of colorful Creole-style architecture, a more rundown version of New Orleans' famed French Quarter. Most of these buildings dated back to the 19th century, with a few modern buildings sprinkled into the mix. Main Street marked the halfway point of my journey. I couldn't wait to take a hot, steamy shower and wash away the side effects of a Southern summer.

Yet, my steps slowed as I hurried down the currently abandoned street. Loud blues boomed from a car's speaker—Muddy Water's 'Mannish Boy' if my ears weren't mistaken—and bright headlights shone ahead. A classic black Mustang sat on the side of the road; its trunk popped open.

I'd seen enough horror movies and true crime shows to be wary.

A news report from earlier in the day flickered through my head, a brief segment covering a missing college student from the next town over. Maybe, I should call Mama for a ride. Sure, waking her up might piss her off, and, yeah, she might scoff at my reasoning, but my dismembered body parts wouldn't end up floating in the Mississippi River.

Laughter burst from me at my absurd thoughts, the part of my brain not affected by cheap rum recognizing the very unlikely scenario.

"Hello?" a male voice called, the trunk slamming shut and revealing the outline of a large man. "Who's there?"

Shit.

"Umm, just passing by," I announced as he neared, my eyes widening to saucers as he strolled into the light.

Holy shit. Setting sight on him rapidly increased the temperature.

The tall man holding the car kit could easily pass for a model. Streetlights reflected off his smooth, dark skin—he was glowing. The tight black T-shirt and grey sweatpants he wore revealed his muscular physique. His waves would benefit from a touch-up, but it didn't take away from his attractiveness, and his beard was perfectly maintained with no patchiness.

He had to just be passing through. First Delaney and now him. Gaville didn't have this many fine people the last time I visited.

He leaned against the Mustang's hood and evaluated me with just as much scrutiny. Based on his smile, he liked what he saw.

For a moment, neither of us spoke. Once again, his gaze traveled up and down my form. I shifted. He licked his lips. I contemplated dashing away. I shouldn't have started this. Fine or not, this random man might be dangerous.

But maybe his lips were chapped, and I was overreacting?

No! No self-doubting. That's how horror movie characters die.

A powerful gust of wind cooled my flushed body. His eyebrows shot up, a soft "oh" leaving him and breaking our long stretch of silence.

"So, uh, I'll be going now," I said awkwardly, waving goodbye and preparing to go on my merry way.

"Wait!" he called.

I contemplated just ignoring him, but I'd seen too many news stories about the fate of women who ignored strange men, so I stopped in my tracks.

"You from here?"

"Just visiting relatives."

Technically, it wasn't a lie. I just didn't mention that the relative was dead. And now, he was aware that I had people who'd notice if I disappeared.

He nodded, his eyes flickering to my exposed chest. "You know any car shops?"

I cocked a brow. "You know it's past midnight, right?"

He copied me. "You know 24-hour shops exist?"

"You're seriously overestimating Gaville's vibrancy."

His gaze again strayed from my eyes. Following his line of sight, I noticed a big ass mosquito chilling on my chest. Screeching, I smacked it away, cursing the vampiric pest when I saw speckles of blood.

"Fucking bugs," I hissed, shuddering.

My skin crawled. It felt like thousands of little creatures now roamed my body.

He chuckled. The deep sound made me shiver for a completely different reason. "It's just a little bite."

"You like being bitten?"

As soon as the words left my mouth, I wanted to take them back.

A smirk spread across the stranger's face. "You want the actual answer?"

"You know what I mean!" I groaned, trying to ignore just how nice his smile was, and how pleasing I found his drawl. "You know what? Forget it. Why don't you call a tow truck?"

The only towing service was in Fleur. It'd take a minute to get to Gaville, but it was better than nothing.

He dug into his pockets and held up his smartphone. "Phone's dead."

Perhaps, he was the ill-fated horror movie character. He had all the right makings to be the victim of a deranged slasher or vengeful ghost.

"You got money to pay for one?" I questioned, digging out my phone.

"You think I'd take a trip broke?"

I shrugged. "Some people are stupid." Shit, he might think I was insulting him. "N-not that you are," I clarified, my stammering making the situation more awkward than necessary. "And I didn't know you were taking a trip. Like, I don't know you."

Jesus, shut up and just call the truck.

"Beau," he said, as I dialed the number to the repair shop.

My head tilting to the side, I regarded him again. "Your name?"

He nodded. "Is Beau. And you are?"

"Kamika," I answered, waiting for someone to pick up the phone.

"Kamika. A real pretty name for a real pretty girl," he hummed.

My name leaving his mouth sounded oh so right. But with his voice, I'm positive it would be a challenge for him to say anything that sounded bad.

"Dammit," I muttered when it immediately went to voicemail.

It was supposed to be open 24/7. Redialing got the same results. Giving up on getting a response, I ended the call and put my phone back in my shorts pocket.

"So, they aren't answering, but there's a motel not too far away from here. You should've passed it on your way here."

"So...how Imma get there?"

"Walking or Ubering?"

"And leave my ride?"

Fair point, though Gaville didn't see much crime; his car would be safe.

I remained silent, and he tsked. "You know what, we'll just sleep in the car."

"We?" I repeated.

"Me and my pardner, Cruz," he said, nodding his head toward the vehicle.

I finally took note of the figure in the passenger seat, a handsome, ambiguous man with tapered curls. He was staring holes into my head, and I quickly turned my attention back to Beau. My eyes darted between him and the car. It was a miracle his tall ass could drive the vintage Mustang, and I seriously doubted that he'd get a comfortable night's sleep.

"Your poor back," I murmured under my breath.

"My poor back?" he repeated with amusement, his grin returning.

Shit, he heard that.

"It'll be fine. I've done this shit before."

"Your homie will be okay with that?"

He shrugged. "Don't give a damn if he is. He's free to walk his ass to a motel if he got a problem."

All I could get out was an, "umm," my tipsy, tired brain failing to compute a proper reply.

"But you know what?" he said, finally straightening. I shook my head and waited for him to continue. "Since you worried about me, why don't you give me your number in case we need some help?"

Damn, that was smooth as hell.

My jaw slackened, and I slapped my hand over my mouth fearing a bug might fly in. At that moment, I thanked God for my skin tone. If I was lighter, I'd be the color of a tomato.

"Umm, I thought you were just passing through," I breathed, dropping my hand and hoping like hell I didn't look as flustered as I felt.

His look led me to believe he was aware of my rattled state and delighted in it.

"Clearly, I'm staying longer than I thought," he said and nodded at his car. "My ride broke."

It was a miracle it hadn't done so sooner, because nice as it was, car problems were inevitable with a decades-old vehicle.

"So?" I shot back, my logic cautious to give my number to him. "You'll be leaving as soon as you get it fixed."

So many horror stories started in this manner. However, many rom-coms did, too. The romantic in me couldn't help but think what a cute story this would be to tell in the future. Or, at the very least, one that was fun as hell to tell my friends when I returned to Miami.

"I can extend my visit," he said with a shrug.

Suspicious.

"For a girl you just met?"

"I've done more extreme shit for less."
Impulsive.

Impulsivity could be a dangerous trait, but it could also lead to a hell of a good time. Only one way to find out. Worst-case scenario with giving Beau my number, I'd end up brutally murdered. Best-case scenario, I'd end up getting some bomb dick. Honestly, that's a risk I was willing to take. And if luck shined down on me, I wouldn't need to involve myself with the Harrises for entertainment.

When I got home, I tried my best to silently open the front door. My mother was aware that I'd gone out. Adulting gave me a significant amount of freedom. However, she was never happy when I disturbed her slumber. It was an agreement between the two of us. I could stay out as long as I wanted if it didn't interfere with her sleeping.

Unlike me, she wasn't a night owl. She went to bed at a reasonable hour and was always awake by 8 AM. It was well past her 10 PM bedtime, so I knew I had to be quiet.

Or I thought I did. Because instead of being curled up in bed, my mother sat on the couch with a blanket around her, documents strewn all over the coffee table. A repeat of today's earlier broadcast on the flatscreen TV served as background noise. She wasn't watching it, too immersed in the papers, her brow creased.

"Ma?" I called when she didn't greet me. "I'm back."

She offered a small wave but kept her head down. "Hey, baby."

I studied her. She was ready for bed but showed no indications of tiredness. Instead, she looked perplexed. The more she read, the more confounded her expression became.

"You okay?" I questioned.

Translate: Why the hell was she up so late?

"I'm fine, sweetie. Go to bed."

Well, this was unusual. Maybe, directness was better.

"Uh, what are you doing up?"

She finally looked at me, cocked her brow, and raised a paper, before returning to browsing over it.

Point taken.

Clearly, she didn't want to be bothered. Without saying anything else, I went to gather things for a shower.

Perhaps this was Mama's way of dealing with grief. She was staying in the house she grew up in, sleeping in the bed her mother once occupied, in a room filled with knick-knacks the woman collected throughout her life. It would be understandable if sleep was avoiding Mama, causing her to seek out a distraction.

Yet, her behavior was odd as hell, and her reaction hinted that something more complicated was amiss. Regardless, I couldn't help but wonder why the fuck everyone around me was acting so weird.

When I checked my phone over coffee the next morning, Beau's simple text greeted me.

Flat tire: Got home safe?

A small smile tugged at my lips, and I quickly fired off a response.

Me: Yeah. Thanks for asking :)

May 30th

Kamika

Days after the party, I hadn't accepted any of Larissa's invites to come over. It was all she was texting me about, some more subtle than others. I was quickly growing tired of repeating the same answer. So tired that seeing her name pop up in my notifications filled me with annoyance, giving me the strength to mute her texts. An ache went through me when I did so, but the sweet silence was worth it.

Well, it wasn't exactly silent, since I'd been texting friends back in Miami and Beau. However, that was a welcomed conversation, and what I was doing as Mama started preparing dinner.

Me: Got your car fixed yet?

It'd been my daily question to him, with the answer always some variation of 'no.'

Flat tire: Still in the shop. Take you on a spin when it's out.

I rolled my eyes, but I couldn't stop the smile that spread across my face.

"Kami, can you...what got you smiling like that?" Mama asked, sounding amused without knowing the details.

Proper rest did my mother good, soothing whatever the hell was wrong with her when I returned from the party. She still looked a tad frazzled, but that was to be expected when sorting out your dead mother's business. Each time I tried to help Mama, she shooed me off, insisting I get out and catch up with old friends.

Ha.

"I met someone on the way home from the kickback," I answered without looking away from my phone. "His name is Beau."

"I'm going to ask you about him over dinner, but right now, I need you to go get me some garlic bread, parmesan, and pepper flakes."

I barely heard her, too caught up in texting to process the request.

"Kamika, girl!" she called, making me jump as my attention returned to her.

Sheepishly, I set my phone aside. "I'm sorry. Can you repeat that?"

She rolled her eyes. "Go out and get garlic bread, parmesan, and pepper flakes. And get some ginger ale, too."

My shoulders slumped. I didn't feel like going anywhere and interacting with people. Outside of a select few people, I couldn't be bothered. But, instead of voicing any protests, I nodded and stood.

"All right. Anything else?"

"Just get whatever you think we need," she directed, then returned to the tomato gravy. "I'll Cash App you half back."

"Only half?" I teased.

"You're eating half, aren't you?" she replied, not bothering to look at me. "So, stop complaining and get to going."

I suppose I couldn't argue with that logic.

"Yes, ma'am," I said, before exiting the kitchen to carry out the task I'd been assigned.

I headed for my room, grabbing my purse, keys, and shoes. As I stepped into my slides, I sent Beau another text before setting my phone to silent. I found it too distracting to drive with my notifications up loud. If it was important, the sender would call me.

Me: Gotta run, talk later.

Flat tire: Aight. Be safe.

I smiled at his simple response, then slipped my phone into my bag. With all my needed belongings gathered, I ventured out of the house, counting down the minutes until I could return.

The drive to the store was uneventful, the familiar streets of Gaville passing by in a blur. I'd thrown my playlist on shuffle the moment I entered the car, but I wasn't listening to the music. Some new businesses had opened, and there was also a new apartment complex, likely to accommodate the 200 or so newcomers. Beyond those additions, little had changed. My mind kept a mental map of the area, and I reminisced as I passed familiar sights. Memories of sneaking out to the playground with Larissa, eating at the diner with Grandma after church, and going to the movies with Mama filled me with nostalgia.

Between the ages of three and five, I resided with Mama in the small town. We embraced its slow-paced lifestyle that helped us mourn my father completely. Soon after we returned to Miami, Mama found work and met a guy, resulting in Zara's birth, and I began school. I'd look forward to spending my summers in Gaville. Mama would accompany me on the trip down to Louisiana, spend a week in her mother's company, and then return to Miami until it was time to retrieve me. At the time, Zara was too attached to Mama to go an entire summer without seeing her, so my little sister would only stay in Gaville as long as Mama did. The routine was the highlight of my year, even before I began exploring the town without Grandma by my side.

Never did I imagine that the comfort the town provided me would disappear. However, the moment my grandmother cast me out and ruined my relationship with Larissa, Gaville stopped being a second home to me. Now, I felt like an outsider.

My mood was thoroughly dampened by the time I arrived at the store. The presence of others, be it my mother's quiet strength, getting to know Beau over the phone, or texting my circle back in Miami, allowed me to ignore the bothersome thoughts. But once I was alone, I couldn't shut my brain off.

I wrestled with memories as I parked near the convenience store entrance and turned off the engine. Most big retailers had chosen to invest in Fleur. Gaville, however, ran on convenience stores and locally owned businesses, and the residents liked it that way. Luckily for me, *Jayson's Food Mart* was the closest to Grandma's house, and if my memory served me right, it had everything I needed to get, saving me from driving all over town. While I collected my things and exited the vehicle, I mentally recited the items I had to fetch.

Garlic bread, parmesan, pepper flakes, ginger ale. Garlic bread, parmesan, pepper flakes, ginger ale. Garlic bread, parmesan, pepper flakes...

The ingredients became a mantra within my head, quieting down my gloomy thoughts. Any time they tried to return, my internal voice chanted louder. As I grabbed a cart, I nodded at the middle-aged worker sweeping by the door, mimicking their polite smile. I wanted to return to the comfort of home—er, well, my temporary accommodations—as soon as possible. With the basket secured, I began to speed-walk, heading to the frozen section to grab the garlic bread. *Jayson's Food Mart* wasn't the biggest store in town, but it had dinner staples and basic food items, with signs everywhere that allowed customers to easily navigate the space. When I took hold of the garlic bread, I crossed it off my list, my mantra dropping the item.

Garlic bread, down. Parmesan, pepper flakes, and ginger ale are left.

The parmesan and pepper flakes were in the same aisle, allowing me to check those two off simultaneously. The only thing left was the soda, then I'd be free to return home, and waste time texting Beau. Anticipation filled me. The butterflies he sparked were a pleasant feeling, somehow giving me the illusion that everything was right with the world. When I talked to him, I wasn't a dead woman's granddaughter visiting a town as an outcast, but just a girl getting to know a guy.

After successfully securing the last case of ginger ale, I proceeded toward the small checkout counter. There was only one person ahead of me, and the teenage boy manning the register was moving efficiently. It didn't take long for me to have enough room to place my four items down, and within five minutes, it was my turn. With nothing else to do but wait, I quickly noticed the guy's intense staring. I might've been flattered if he were older or if I were younger. But he looked no older than seventeen, leaving me thoroughly uncomfortable.

"Is something wrong?" I asked as he scanned the pepper flakes.

He blinked, social awareness returning to him. "No, ma'am, I'm sorry," he replied, a sheepish expression on his face. "But, uh, you don't remember me?"

It was my turn to blink in surprise. I studied him, trying to recall which family he was from, and if he'd shown up to Grandma's funeral. Though he was vaguely familiar, my mind came up blank for a name.

"I'm sorry, but I don't," I admitted, fishing out my wallet to pay as the case of soda was checked out. "Should I?"

"Probably, since you babysat me every summer for three years straight, *Kamika,*" he said casually, having composed himself from his little blunder.

It took me a second for his words to process, but when they did, my memory was jogged. My lips morphed into an 'O' shape as realization dawned, a name finally coming to me. Jayce Caissy, the eldest boy of Mr. Jay and his wife, aka the folks who owned the store. From ages thirteen to sixteen, I watched his brothers, Avery and Reese. His parents deemed Jayce old enough to look after himself, but too young to look after his siblings. Hence them hiring little ol' me. If I did my math right, he was about sixteen now, the same age I'd been when I'd last babysat for his family, before everything had gone to hell.

"I hardly recognized you," I replied, memories of when he was a little boy popping into my head.

From when he was born, Jayce was smaller than most children his age. I distinctly remember sitting in church as a preschooler, listening to Grandma's group theorize about his true age and why his parents kept his prematurity secret. It was ingrained into my brain, as that was when I became aware of my grandmother's love of gossip. Now, he was nearing the six-foot mark. He'd been an adorable kid and was shaping up to be a handsome guy. My mind flickered to Zara, and the guy she had a crush on throughout middle school. Jayce resembled him, and had she and I been closer, I might try to play wing woman.

But we weren't, so thoughts of how cute they'd be together were quickly dismissed.

"And I didn't babysit you," I said as he handed me my bags. "I watched your brothers."

He scoffed playfully, coming around the counter to set the case of ginger ale in the cart. It was a simple task that I could've done easily, but I wasn't one to refuse free help.

"Be so for real. You watched me as much as you did my brothers," he stated, returning to the register and clicking some buttons. "Your purchase will be $15.92."

I selected the option to pay by card and inserted it into the payment terminal. Seconds later, it was confirmed I wasn't destitute, a chime reminding me to remove the card when the payment was approved.

"Have a good day," I said as I put my card back, offering him one last smile.

He returned my grin and waved, his rich brown eyes sparkling. "Bye, Kami. Don't forget me again."

I laughed and waved back, my mood considerably higher than it had been when I entered the store. As I placed my groceries in the backseat, it dawned on me that he hadn't mentioned my grandmother once, a pleasant change of pace. Even at a party, I couldn't escape the ugly reminder of her death.

It didn't take long for me to load the items into the car. Just as I slammed the door shut, someone calling my name made me pause.

"Kamika, right?"

At the sound of the raspy voice, I peeked over my shoulder. My eyes widened when I saw Delaney. Her locs were in a ponytail, and her outfit consisted of jean shorts and a white tank top. She was dressed simply but still looked stunning. But no matter how pretty her exterior was, wariness invaded me thanks to our previous encounter.

I spun around and faced her with a scowl. "You have an excellent memory. Nice seeing you."

Not.

A knowing gleam lit her eyes, and she smiled. "Chill. I just wanna talk."

Well, I didn't. First impressions were everything, and she'd fucked hers up royally.

"I have to go. My mother's waiting for the stuff I picked up."

Her smile faded, and she winced. "Hey, listen. I'm sorry, okay?"

Well, that caught me off-guard. I eyed her. "Apologies in a sweet voice win you no points."

Her smirk made a triumphant return, and she puffed her chest out. "You think my voice is sweet?"

As sugary as cane syrup.

"I misspoke," I said with a sniff.

"I call bull, but okay," Delaney said with a laugh, easing the tension a little more and entrancing me in her gaze. She held out her hand. "I'm sorry for how I acted. Truly. Can we start over?"

For a moment, I stared at her hand as if it were a gun. Then, I realized I was being overdramatic. Our first meeting was ass, but that didn't mean being cordial wasn't an option.

Besides, I received enough judgment in Gaville. I wouldn't garner more by being unnecessarily rude. So, reluctantly, I grasped Delaney's hand and shook. "You have one more time to act like you just stepped out of a circle in hell, and I'd cuss your ass out if you come near me again. Am I clear?"

Delaney nodded and reclaimed her hand. "Perfectly."

We stared at each other. Something inside me unfurled, but I wasn't sure what. I didn't want to *recognize* what. I didn't want to travel the same road as I had with Larissa. The reaction it caused haunted me. Not only did my grandmother call me a hoe after catching us in a compromising position, but the slurs she threw out would forever haunt my mind. The whispers, the rumors, and the stares irrevocably changed me.

At that moment, I decided *I'd* only explore whatever was developing with Beau. Delaney would be off-limits under all circumstances. She was too close to Larissa to be a viable option, and even if my grandmother was gone, most of the people who threw fuel onto the flames of our fallout were still around. Everyone in Gaville knowing everyone meant getting into a relationship with another Harris girl would again make me a topic of unwanted conversation.

"I really have to get going. My mother sent me to the store and she's waiting for me."

"Cool." Delaney rocked on her heels, not in a rush to move. "Come over, Kami. I want to make up my behavior. Please?" she continued when I remained silent. "Larissa will be there, too."

I wrinkled my nose, easily finding an excuse to rebuke her. "That means suffering Jack's company."

The words slipped out before I could stop them, adding to the awkwardness lingering in the air. She was close to Larissa, so chances were high she was close to her husband.

Delaney laughed, a sound that sent tingles down my spine and eased my nerves. "He's a little intense, but he loves Larissa and isn't that bad when you get to know him. I promise."

Her words reminded me of how quickly Larissa moved on with Jack, dampening my mood again.

"Just think about it," Delaney pressed.

Damn, she was persistent. It was flattering that she wanted to be in my company so badly, and I wouldn't deny that I was curious about her. Both drove me to give in and nod.

"I will," I promised in a subdued voice.

That was enough for her.

"Bet." Delaney offered a last smile, then turned, and rushed into the grocery store without looking back.

"Mama, I'm back!" I called as I breezed through the door, carrying our groceries.

Delaney was still plaguing my mind, how normal she seemed today a stark contrast to her odd behavior at the party. I was already thinking about going back on my pledge to avoid her. She was a beautiful woman, and I'd be gone by the end of the summer. Causal wasn't easy for me, but it wasn't unheard of for me to just fuck around with someone. Why couldn't I grant her access to that very exclusive club? A summer fling would provide a cheerier story to tell my friends back in Miami, and *two* would be hot gossip we could all laugh over.

Then again, if anyone caught wind of it, my remaining time in Gaville would be awful. Most folks in town were older and old school, looking down on queers and girls deemed fast. A queer woman acting fast would be seen as the devil reincarnated, and I wasn't sure I'd be able to endure such criticism a second time. The first had nearly destroyed me, and though I was older and more cynical, I was only human. I should just entertain Beau and forget about Delaney.

But, fuck, she was hard to forget.

Shit, why was I acting like this was life or death?

Come Labor Day, I'd be back in Miami, never to step foot in Gaville again. There was nothing here for me anymore.

"You okay?" Mama asked when I breezed into the kitchen.

Nope. Too busy stressing myself the fuck out, overthinking.

My expression must've betrayed my inner turmoil. I tried to mask my emotions with a smile. Explaining everything going through my head was a discussion I didn't have the energy to engage in.

"Peachy," I replied, her huff letting me know she didn't believe a word I said.

Luckily, she didn't push the issue, content to let me deal with my shit myself.

"Don't think I forgot, girl. I want to know who you were texting," Mama said as I set the groceries on the counter.

I paused. She might not have forgotten, but I certainly had.

"Tell me more about Beau," she continued.

I crouched down and got a cookie sheet for the garlic bread. The oven was already preheated, so once I protected the metal with some cooking foil, I plopped the breadsticks down and slid them into the hot machine. Only then did I look at my mother, whose brow was cocked.

"He's 26, from New Orleans, and staying in town for a little while with his friend," I finally replied, returning to the table and plopping down. "Oh, and he has a black cat named Snowball."

He'd sent me a few pictures of his furry friend, earning many texts of me fawning over her cuteness. My dream pet was a hyacinth macaw, the largest of all parrots and a gentle giant that could live for decades. However, that didn't stop me from acknowledging the adorableness of more common pets.

Mama frowned, focusing on nothing else but his age. "Ain't he a little old for you?"

"It's only six years," I argued, immediately feeling the urge to defend him.

She'd have an aneurysm if she knew I was talking to a 30-year-old last year. It was one of the few times I didn't tell her about someone I was interested in. Seeing her reaction to Beau's age, I decided that was the right choice.

"Those six years can make a big difference, girl," Mama huffed, grabbing the parmesan and pepper flakes and adding them to the sauce. "But if you like it, I love it. Is he in school?"

"He graduated."

"His major?"

I searched my mind and came up blank. "He didn't say."

She tsked. "What does he do?"

"He's a flexible freelancer," I said, using air quotes. "His words, not mine."

Her "hmm," reeked of disapproval, but she made no further comments. Instead, she ended her little questionnaire with, "Is he cute?"

"You think I'd talk to someone ugly?"

"Remember James?"

That shut me up. He was my rebound from Larissa, and I'd gravitated toward him because he was fun, not because he was a looker. He was fit, yes, but his face was painfully average.

"Exactly," Mama said with a laugh. "So, answer the question, Kami."

"James was a low point, and yes, Beau is cute. He's fine as hell."

"You got a picture?" she asked, looking back at me over her shoulder.

"He doesn't have any social media," I said, my lips pursing.

In a quest to learn more about him, I sent what I knew to my sleuth friend back in Miami. Even she yielded no results. He was totally under the radar.

"He's a freelancer, with no social media? And what kind of freelancer, girl? What the hell does a 'flexible freelancer' even mean?"

As much as I hated to admit it, her first point was valid. No matter what type of freelancer he was, certainly, Annika would've found his business accounts, even if he had no personal ones.

But, instead of voicing my doubts, I said, "He does a bunch of odd jobs around his city, and maybe he uses a freelancer website."

"Or maybe he's unemployed," Mama replied, banging the spoon against the edge of the pot to remove the excess gravy, then fishing the garlic bread out of the oven.

Admittedly, him being unemployed was better than my second leading theory; he was a drug dealer. The first was that he was a contractor without a license, and got customers through word of mouth to avoid getting into hot water. Still a criminal, but a decidedly better one.

"But like I said, if you're happy talking to him, don't let me rain on your parade," she continued, glancing at me over her shoulder. "Now get some plates, dinner is ready."

I grabbed a few plates from the cabinet and set them on the table, trying to push aside the doubts that Mama had planted in my mind. It proved to be challenging, and as we sat down to eat, I couldn't help but wonder if I was making a mistake by pursuing this summer fling with Beau. Was I being too impulsive, too caught up in the idea of a distraction? Was grief clouding my judgment?

On the flip side, why shouldn't I allow myself to have some fun and enjoy the moment? Life was short, and Beau was better than the alternative, being alone and stewing in depression.

Delaney

Restlessness was consuming Delaney, pulsating through every fiber of her being. It'd only been a few days since she last saw Kamika, but time seemed to have slowed to an unbearable crawl. Each time Larissa's phone vibrated in her presence, she prayed it was Kamika texting that she was coming over. She'd fumbled by not getting her number herself, a mistake she was kicking herself for.

Or perhaps, it was a blessing in disguise, as the number of texts she would've sent by now would make her come across as a creeper. She had a nasty habit of going all in too early.

Her ex had always described Delaney as a stage five clinger. Clingy, jealous, controlling, and borderline obsessive. It was a title she'd vehemently denied. It was natural for her kind to become consumed in their mates, even if the bond wasn't solidified. Toria would flip-flop between relishing in the attention and screaming at her for being too smothering. The latter often ended in an argument, or fucking like rabbits for hours.

Looking back, she should've left that bitch long before she caught her in bed with someone else. Their relationship had been toxic, and not even the red strings of fate were enough to keep them together.

Despite what her ex claimed, Delany didn't normally cling to her partners. She was perfectly rational with other girls, even managing days of silence. Some might even call her a player or a fuck girl, two other titles she denied. Kamika crossed her mind again. If she'd give her a chance, Delaney would try to do better, finding a happy medium between co-dependent and a tad neglectful. Though their start was rocky, she'd do better than she had previously.

Because, certainly, she'd learned something from the other two girls that fate had guided her towards.

Delaney shoveled more popcorn into her mouth, topped with butter and grated parmesan. Larissa hated the combination, so she and Jack shared a bowl, their only flavor being butter and salt. She wondered how Kamika liked her popcorn, then tried not to wonder, forcing herself to focus on the TV. The kids were in their rooms, taking a nap as the adults binged *House of the Dragon.* She and Larissa had been big fans of *Game of Thrones and* vowed to watch the spin-off together when they finally reunited. Two seasons in, and that had finally happened.

"Aemond is so fine," Larissa breathed, earning the side eye from both Delaney and Jack.

Thankfully, the credits rolled before Jack pitched the remote at the television.

Delaney snorted. "He's a goddamn red flag."

"What's so fine about him? He's average at best," Jack grumbled, his lips pursed into a childish pout.

Delaney had to admit, the sight was amusing. If her hands weren't so greasy, she might've snapped a picture to laugh at later.

"See, you just don't understand the female gaze," Larissa said, her gaze locked onto the screen as another episode started. When her little crush didn't quickly pop up, she spared a glance at Delaney. "Look me in the eye and tell me he's not attractive, cuz."

"I'm gay; I'm outta this discussion," Delaney replied.

She'd take the fact she found Aemond Targaryen handsome to her grave. Men weren't her thing, let alone murderous white boys.

Larissa clicked her tongue. "Gay or not, you have fucking eyes."

"Unlike Aemond, who only has one," Jack muttered, still sulking.

Delaney couldn't stop the laugh that burst from her, and though Larissa balked, she saw the amusement glinting in her cousin's eyes.

"How can you be attracted to a damn pirate?" he continued, though the sight of his wife's smile made him lighten up.

"Ableism," Delaney quipped, just to fuck with him.

"No," Jack quickly denied. "Pirates wore eyepatches, like Aemond. If that's Larissa's thing, I'll get a Jack Sparrow costume to spice things up."

Delaney snickered. "Tryna get to that booty, huh?"

Jack turned red and shrugged, chuckling as he refocused on the television. At this point, Delaney didn't have a clue what the fuck was happening on the show. Larissa guffawed, grabbing a pillow and hitting her on the arm with it, causing some popcorn to spill onto the floor.

"Nasty ass," Larissa said, still chortling.

"You started it!" Delaney cried, inching away to avoid being attacked by another cushion.

"Just watch the show, you two," Jack ordered, going back to his usual self now that he was composed.

Just as Delaney started to pick up the plot of the episode and fill in the blanks, Larissa's phone vibrated. Her gaze snapped to the coffee table, staring at the device as the screen lit up. To her disappointment, it wasn't Kamika calling, but a scammer. It was her turn to pout.

Larissa eyed her, putting a hand on her shoulder. "She'll call eventually, trust."

"And how do you know that?"

Since the party, she wondered how close her cousin was to Kamika. She couldn't recall Larissa ever mentioning someone of that name.

"If she said she'll show up, she will," she explained, sounding confident that she was right. "Just trust me 'Laney."

Delaney hoped her cousin was telling the truth. She knew the girl was mourning her grandmother, so it was possible grief was stopping her from reaching out. And though her rational mind knew she needed to give her time, her instincts wanted her close. She'd even considered stealing Larissa's phone to get

Kamika's number. Larissa wouldn't give out her digits unless Kamika consented. Respectable, but it put Delaney in a bind.

The phone rang again. This time, it was Larissa's mother. A whine left Delaney's throat, earning her the side eye as her cousin answered the phone.

Fucking hell, but she needed to get a grip.

However, Delaney's stupid instincts were flared, registering that Kamika could be 'the one'. They stopped her from even considering friendship before pursuing her romantically. Never mind that friendship provided a solid base for a relationship, or that Kamika hadn't even graced Delaney with her presence. Their run-in at the store didn't count, as that'd been a happy coincidence that Kamika hadn't seemed too pleased with.

"Hey, Mama," Larissa greeted, smiling at Jack when he paused the show.

The call volume wasn't high, but the benefit of shifter hearing was the ability to eavesdrop with zero effort. Or drawback, if you weren't the nosy type. Delaney was indeed nosy, and the new conversation was a welcome distraction.

"Hey, sweetheart, are you busy?" Aunt Galena responded, sounding winded.

Larissa's brows snapped together, and though her mother couldn't see her, she shook her head. "No, Mama, I'm just watching TV with Jack and Delaney. What's up?"

"Can Jack watch the kids for some hours? We need you at the hospital," she said, prompting Larissa to stand.

Both women looked at him. Jack nodded.

"Yeah, Mama, I'll be down ASAP," she replied, her voice fading as she trekked to the stairs.

Aunt Galena was working a rare shift at the hospital, stationed between Fleur and Gaville. Most of the time, she stuck to the pack lands, but one of her long-term patients was due to give birth. As a PCP with OBGYN training, she was prepared for anything pregnancy might throw at a woman. Larissa was following in her mother's footsteps, aspiring to be a nurse practitioner and a nurse midwife. With a Bachelor of Science in Nursing, she had secured a part-time on-call position at the hospital and assisted her mother's department.

"Welp, looks like our marathon is over," Jack said, reaching into his pocket and retrieving his phone. Delaney glanced over, watching as he viewed his children's rooms. "Kids still asleep, so that's a relief."

Delaney hummed in response. Moments later, Larissa returned in scrubs, her phone pocketed.

"Okay, one of the nurses called out sick, so I'm going to cover for her," she explained, coming around the couch to hug Delaney, and kiss Jack. He huffed when she pulled away, and she rolled her eyes. "Boy, shush. I'll be back later."

With that, she breezed away. Larissa's dual-credit classes in high school enabled her to earn her core credits before graduating, allowing her to complete her BSN in just two years and become a registered nurse. A twinge of jealousy passed through Delaney. Because she spent her first two years of high school slacking off, she had to spend her last two catching up to achieve a decent GPA, which made dual-credit courses impossible.

But, shit, the consequences of your actions and all that.

In the end, she graduated with a major in Art History, a minor in Civil Engineering with a focus on Water Resources, as well as Certificates in Electrical Engineering and Environmental Management and Resilience. Her major was her passion, while everything else was intended to help keep the pack's community running smoothly. Besides the alpha and the beta, there was a council to oversee everything. The council members managed the small but significant details. Aunt Galena served on the board, representing the healers. Delaney would be working in the civil section to maintain their electrical and water systems. If she could work her way up, she may one day sit on the council of one of the largest packs in America.

After seconds of silence, Jack's phone chimed. Delaney perked up, before remembering Jack wasn't Kamika's friend…right?

She opened her mouth to ask, but he answered her unspoken question. "Just a nanny cam alert. It detected movement."

Delaney slumped, then nodded. "Oh."

He took a moment to study her. "Who did you expect it to be?"

"You know who."

Jack snorted. "I'm not close with Kamika, 'Laney. Only met her twice, and I could've done without it both times."

The reply raised her hackles, a growl slipping out. Kamika was nice at the party, and she even humored her in the parking lot.

"What's that supposed to mean?"

"It means I don't want to see my wife's ex, who's clearly still hung up on her."

At his reveal, everything seemed to come to a screeching halt. Delaney wondered if he was lying, or if his answer was pure speculation. She listened closely for any physical indications that he didn't speak the truth, but nothing. His heartrate did spike ever so slightly, but that could be attributed to the anger written on his face. Shifters were protective of their mates, and ex-lovers were deemed threats. At one time, it wasn't uncommon for exes to be killed. Nowadays, that practice varied from pack to pack, with several factors determining the likelihood of a formal fling surviving their ex's mate. Humans, generally, were left alive.

"You're lying," she declared, the painful pang of jealousy that'd gone through her disappearing.

"They were literally each other's first—"

"Not that part," she hissed, his words adding salt to the wound.

That part made sense. Kamika still being hung up on Larissa didn't. Delaney had seen the way she'd appraised her at the party, and at *Jayson's Food Mart*. She'd sensed the hitch in her breath, the accelerated heart rate, the way her pupils dilated, the beginnings of arousal. Someone pining for another wouldn't have such a reaction—she knew that from experience.

"I saw how they interacted, how—"

"I'm going for a run," Delaney announced, glaring down at Jack. "But even if she still has feelings, Larissa loves you, so get over yourself."

She left the room in a huff, consumed by envy and a confusing sense of betrayal. Mentally, she chanted her advice to Jack. Larissa had been with him for years, and she adored that man. Her love affair with Kamika was over, but that didn't stop it from burning Delaney up inside. She didn't care that Kamika had a dating history—most people did. Yet, a primal part of her brain rued that she wouldn't be her first, that another shifter had gotten their paws on her before she did. Relationships with another human were easier to dismiss than a relationship with a fellow wolf. The former meant nothing, the latter was a very real threat.

Worse, they'd been each other's *first*.

A growl slipped from her. She undressed in the hallway, needing to be in her wolf form as soon as possible. She was so happy Larissa was gone, otherwise, any logic she was holding onto would've flown out of the door.

The moment she was outside, Delaney felt a familiar pull. Her body tingled, the sensation spreading through her fingers and toes.

"Goddamn," she whispered through gritted teeth as her bones began to crack and reshape.

The process was quick, but no less painful. The entire transformation took thirty seconds, and within moments, her baser instincts started to take over. Her pesky human emotions faded away, giving her a reprieve from the jealousy that'd threatened to consume her.

She headed straight for the tree line, wanting to be engulfed by nature. Forest separated the heart of Magnolia Mist from the swampland surrounding Gaville. Wildlife often found their way into the thicket, and Delaney enjoyed a good hunt. It's what made her a great bounty hunter; tracking down her targets never lost its thrill. It didn't take long for her to find prey, a white-tailed buck that should make for a good chase.

She crouched low, hiding among the bushes and bunchgrass. The creature remained unaware, munching away like it wasn't about to become a meal. She crept closer, taking care not to make any noise. Any time the deer swiveled its head, she went still. Finally, when she felt that she was in lunging distance, she took her chances and leaped forward. Had it stayed still, the hunt would've ended there. Unfortunately, it finally realized it was being stalked and took off. She let out a frustrated growl, before giving chase, refusing to be bested.

Had she been in a better mood, she might've let the creature go on living. But at that moment, she needed some way to relieve her stress. Blood coating her snout should do the trick.

She lost track of how long she chased the thing. The sun started to dip below the horizon, vivid colors streaking the sky. But she paid it no mind, determined to chase the deer until it collapsed into an exhausted heap.

However, it just wasn't her day to hunt. As the deer's legs finally buckled, another scent caught her attention, this one far more unwelcome. It was faint and might've gone unnoticed if it wasn't so windy. Yet, it didn't, and she immediately identified the scent as belonging to a vampire.

And not just any vampire.

Beauden Hugo Valois, aka the fucker who'd stabbed her in the back.

Just as my Mama pulled out of the driveway, my phone buzzed. The car's Bluetooth system notified me of yet another text from Larissa, interrupting 'I'll Be Around' by Timbaland and CeeLo Green. Mama chuckled when she saw the contact name, and I needed only a second of deliberation before I opened it up.

> FREE HER: Hey. You busy today?

Note to self: Change Larissa's contact name. It wouldn't be hard to do, but I'd save the task for my future self when I was in a place with more stable WIFI than a moving vehicle.

Me: Unfortunately):

FREE HER: That sucks lol

FREE HER: Wanna come over this week?

I sighed, gnawing on my bottom lip as I stared at the request. She was absolutely relentless.

Me: idk.

Me: I'll see this weekend.

It wasn't hanging out with Larissa that I was opposed to. It was dealing with her husband and cousin. The former was undeniably worse, but the latter filled me with...well, I wasn't sure. Delaney was gorgeous and seemed so normal at *Jayson's Food Mart*. Maybe that was the cause of the intense butterflies each time I thought about her. But even that wasn't enough for me to venture to Magnolia Mist. If anything, it only made me want to stay further away.

> FREE HER: Okay. Hope to see you

My stupid, naïve heart fluttered at the text. It was a challenge to ignore the giddiness that swept through me. Larissa didn't want me anymore; she was married and trying to play matchmaker. The most we could ever be were friends, and that'd only be possible if I finally got it through my head that she and I were a past item.

Logically, I knew that, but the feelings that were revived at my grandma's funeral refused to be reburied.

> Me: Yeah, I'll text you

> FREE HER: Can't wait

I waited a few seconds to see if she'd say anything else. When no other texts came through, I powered off my phone, placed it in the cupholder, and looked out the window, admiring the town's scenery.

"Any chance 'Free Her' is Larissa?" Mama guessed, lowering the music and glancing at me for a split second.

I nodded, looking at her through the corner of my eye. "Yep. Jack is an ass."

"He could be a sweetheart to her," she replied, her expression neutral.

"Wouldn't make him less of an ass," I grumbled, huffing like a petulant child at the notion that my mother was defending him.

Mama tsked. "But it would mean she wouldn't need freeing."

I rued that she was right. From what I saw at the repast, their relationship was fine. Great, even. Jack was just a prick to everyone else.

"I'll change the name when we get home," I said, watching as we pulled into the plaza that our destination was located in.

I'd hoped for a miracle to be bestowed on us, and we'd be back home before June ended. Preferably, by June 11th, my mother's birthday. Yet, I'd quickly realized that dream wouldn't be fulfilled. It was only ten days away, and a dent had barely been made in Grandma's belongings. Not to mention, my grandmother's lawyer had given Mama a call, asking to meet with her next week. It fucking took him long enough. Maybe I was impatient, but I saw no reason why the meeting hadn't been scheduled earlier.

Today, my mother had taken a break from sorting through the piles of documents littering the living room to visit Giselle's hair shop. Turns out, she'd made the iced tea for the repast. The glass pitcher was long empty, cleaned, and ready to be returned to its owner. For whatever reason, Mama had asked me to tag along. And, though I couldn't stand the Samsons, I agreed. She'd seldom left the house since the funeral, and perhaps she needed someone to lean on as she ventured into town.

Snagging an empty spot by the salon was surprisingly easy. The place was simply called *'Gaville's Beauty Avenue'* and offered an array of things. Box braids, cornrows, twists, dreadlock maintenance and installation, silk presses, Brazilian blowouts, wash-and-goes, and more. The cheap prices advertised on the window shocked me. Back in Miami, even unlicensed stylists who operated out of their homes charged an arm and a leg.

When we entered the quaint building, the bell above the door rang, alerting everyone to our presence. Giselle's station was near the door, and she was in the midst of sweeping up hair. At the chime, she looked in our direction. Surprise flickered across her face before she covered it up with a grin and approached us.

"Hey, ladies! Y'all came earlier than expected," she said in that artificially cheery voice.

Mama held up the pitcher. "We just came by to bring this back to you."

"Y'all came all this way just for that?" she replied, accepting the pitcher and setting it on the receptionist counter. "You could've texted me to come pick it up, instead of giving me a heads up that you two would swing by."

"I didn't want to be a bother," Mama said, forever a sweetheart.

Giselle waved her hand. "Awww, girl, that's so sweet. Thank y'all."

Did she expect us to just keep her shit?

"It's no problem," Mama said, ignoring the condescension or just not picking up on it.

The former was more likely.

The visit could've ended there, but unfortunately, Giselle didn't seem keen to let us go so soon, launching into a new topic after a heartbeat of silence.

"So, how are y'all holding up?"

Ugh.

Not this question again.

"Bad," I answered before Mama could, delighting in the way Giselle's smile faltered.

Truth be told, despite the ache in our hearts, we were both handling it decently. Yet, that stupid ass question deserved a pissy reply.

"It's tough," Mama elaborated, far more diplomatic than me. "But we're holding up. It's all we can do."

Giselle nodded. "Amen to that."

The smirk she gave me was unnecessary. If she had any sense, she'd understand my frustration, but then again brainless assholes ran in her family. Why would I expect any logic from her, the town gossip?

Mama exchanged a glance with me. My heart went out to her at how uncomfortable she looked. At one time, Mama and Giselle were good friends, but that was before Colton's raggedy ass and roaming dick infiltrated Mama's life. My mama was a good woman who hadn't deserved his treatment, but Giselle still sided with her little brother. Misplaced family loyalty triumphed over sisterhood.

"Well, uh—"

"Amia, chile," Giselle interrupted Mama with a wave of her hand and a gleam in her eye. "You shouldn't be cooped up in that raggedy old house going through Susie's ancient shit."

My grandmother and I had our problems, but Giselle was awful. "You went to that raggedy house more than once," I hissed. "You were Grandma's good friend."

"If I don't see to it, then no one else will," Mama added with a hint of irritation creeping into her voice. "And her house wasn't raggedy, nor does the age of her belongings make them less valuable."

I couldn't help but grin at Mama's reply. Typically, she held her tongue. The fact that she responded to Giselle's insult directly–even if Mama was still too polite for my liking–spoke volumes on how much Giselle had bothered her.

"Dear me, y'all are so sensitive." Giselle fanned her hand in front of her face. "Give a body anxiety. I didn't mean nothing. Even Susie referred to her house as raggedy."

Doubtful. Granny was proud of that place, but the more we engaged, the longer we'd stay.

"Enough of that," Giselle said briskly. "I'm trying to invite you two to my book club." She tittered and lowered her voice. "We call ourselves the Smut Sluts. We love us some sexy men and good loving. The more explicit the better."

"I'm not sure," Mama hedged, her temper cooling as quickly as it had flared. "I have so much to do. I might not have time—"

"Nonsense! Each member gets to include a book in our monthly poll. We only have ten members—twelve with you two—so we need at least seven votes for the book to be chosen."

"Or you can add an eleventh member and have someone to break a tie," Mama suggested.

"Thirteenth," Giselle corrected. "You two are in, remember? And, no, that's too much trouble. My way is better."

Mama nodded. "Of course, you're right, Giselle."

Not.

Often, Mama took the route of pacifism to avoid bullshit. I blamed Grandma, as her strong personality required a level-head to deal with, and logical pacifism could easily come across as meekness.

I pasted a smile on my face. "I can only join if you promise inclusion. I'd want some wuh luh wuh romances."

I knew someone like Giselle was unlikely to be familiar with the meaning of WLW, and the playful pronunciation would be completely lost on her. But I wouldn't pass up the opportunity to fuck with the annoying little woman.

Giselle frowned. "Sorry, sugar. I don't have a clue what that is." She beamed at Mama. "Young people."

"It's It means women loving women. Aka female/female," I said, getting her back for her earlier smirk with one of my own. She stiffened and I did a little happy dance inside. "You know? Lesbian?"

In truth, I had no issues with reading straight romances. My issue was how pushy Giselle was, and her blatant disregard for our wishes. If a functional braincell was present, she might notice that my mama and I weren't interested.

"You're welcome to add whatever book you'd like to the poll," she said coldly, storming behind the receptionist's counter, bending down, and coming up with a tattered book. She stomped back to us and held it out to Mama. "This is our current read."

Mama took the book and turned it over to read the blurb. "What's it about?"

I couldn't stand around and listen to Giselle's annoying voice another moment. "I'll wait for you outside, Mama." Manners urged me to address Giselle. That, and not wanting guff from Mama. "See you soon, Giselle."

Before either of them responded, I turned and walked outside, breathing in air not polluted by Giselle's fakery. Being surrounded by nature and stationed on the Mississippi River, Gaville's air always had a crisp note. It soothed me, allowing me to calm down. I was always a bit of a hothead, something I blamed my grandmother for. The old woman had a temper like no one else.

I'd gotten a firsthand taste of that many times, none more hurtful than the final time I saw her.

Could I have been more polite to Giselle? Most definitely.

Did she deserve my politeness? Hell, no. She was a bitch to her brother's bastard.

My mood deteriorated again. When I realized my quest to get away from Giselle resulted in me forgetting the car keys, I almost screamed. I didn't want to go back inside and be swept into a dull conversation filled with shade, so I opted to lean against the hood of the vehicle and scroll on my phone.

Whatever.

Prolonged exposure to fresh air might do me some good, and Mama shouldn't be too long.

Beau hadn't texted me since last night, Zara had yet to reply to my greeting, and my circle in Miami had slowed down with their texts. It ground my gears. I decided that playing a mobile game would be the best way to waste time. Word searches were a favorite of mine, something my friends joked was a 'granny' hobby. I called it mental enrichment, but to each their own.

Getting caught up in searching for random words thoroughly distracted me, just as I wanted. But the downside to my distraction was not being aware of my surroundings. I only noticed someone had gotten too close when a hand clamped down on my shoulder, making me jump. I whirled around to confront the bold motherfucker, just to come face-to-face with Colton Samson. Being able to suppress my scowl should've earned me an Oscar. I despised him with every fiber of my being. He was tall, handsome, and made bank as a sanitation worker. It turned him into an arrogant bastard, so far up his own ass, that he thought nothing of cheating on my beautiful mama.

When he grinned, I forced a smile, my hands balling into fists. Mama wanted me to play nice to the townsfolk, so I'd be a good daughter and not start shit.

"Kamika, girl, look at you! All grown up," he said, his eyes sweeping my figure.

Fucking ew.

His creepy leer reminded me of the time he'd hit on my grandma, making her slap the fuck out of him. If he was so daring with me, I'd honor Grandma's memory by doing the same thing.

"Yep. I'll be 21 in November," I replied, returning to looking at my phone, hoping he got a clue.

He didn't.

"You know, I remember when you were a little girl, always clinging to your mama or grandma," he prattled on, adjusting his bag of whatever the fuck was in his hands.

Based on the smells wafting from the plastic, it was a meal plate from the seafood joint down the street, simply called *La Mer*. It smelled fucking amazing, and my growling stomach irritated me more. Clenching my jaw, I tried to ignore my unwanted shadow.

"Speaking of, I would've gone to Miz Susie's service, but duty called," he said with a chuckle.

What was funny, I hadn't a fucking clue. I wished duty had called his ass away from the repast but he'd managed to darken our door anyway. He was only bringing my grandmother's services up to be a shady motherfucker.

"Sorry about your loss, and all that," he continued, his insensitive words hurting my heart. "I didn't have a chance to talk to you that day. I want to correct that now." He snickered again. "I know how tight you and your grandma was before she found out you wished you'd been born with a dick."

My jaw clenched, and my grip on the phone tightened. Even for him, speaking of my grandmother's passing so callously was low. But one glance at him as he rambled on, it was clear he had no remorse for being a fuckhead.

Figures.

Even when he had a baby on my mother and shattered her heart, he displayed no remorse whatsoever. Narcissists weren't known for their character growth, so why would this be any different?

"I don't need your shitty condolences," I snapped, my voice laced with anger as my patience ran out. "And I certainly don't need you looming over me."

Colton's smirk faltered, but he regained his composure within seconds. "Just tryna catch up with you, girl. Seeing your mama reminded me how much I missed her. Speaking of, how is she?"

A scoff escaped me. "As if you give a damn."

He mumbled something about disrespect, but I couldn't give a fuck about what he had to say.

"She won't take my calls," he complained, his whining giving me a headache.

"And she never will," I huffed, pocketed my phone and stomped to the salon's door. If I'd stayed in his presence a moment longer, I would've caught a case. The memories of his betraying my mother haunted me, something I'd never forgive him for.

Cross me, fine, but don't play with my mama.

Just as I opened the door, Mama emerged. Her presence was both a blessing and a curse. A blessing, because it meant we'd be heading home soon. A curse, because Colton descended on her the moment he laid eyes on her sundress-clad figure. Without hesitation, I planted myself in between them, refusing to allow him to get too close.

"You ready to go, Ma?" I asked, not sparing him a glance.

She nodded; a brow cocked as she peered around me. "Yeah, baby. I thought you'd be in the car already."

"I forgot the keys."

Colton wasn't content with being ignored. He cleared his throat, drawing her attention.

"Amia, honey, you looking damn good."

Her smile was notably more forced than it was with Giselle. "Thank you, Colton. How've you been?"

"Can't complain," he said, holding up the takeout bag with a yellow smiley face. "Here to bring Giselle some lunch. She's in her 40s, and that girl still doesn't know how to eat properly."

If he noticed how phony my Mama's giggle was, he didn't comment. Instead, he continued prattling. "Anyway, like I said the day you dropped your mama in the ground, I'm so sorry for your loss. I have a very strong shoulder, chest, stomach, thigh–" He laughed and finished his statement, "to cry on."

One way my mother kept her cool was by zoning out. Her blank stare let me know she was employing that tactic at the moment, disassociating to tune out Colton's crappy flirting. When I was a little girl, she advised me to do the same when someone was getting under my skin, though I never managed to perfect it as she had.

"It was a hard pill to swallow, but it's getting easier," Mama replied when he finally shut up, inching closer to the car. "Kamika and I gotta go. I hope you and Giselle enjoy the meal."

Mentally, I applauded my mother for keeping the conversation so brief. However, in actuality, I just settled for a smirk. When we were both secured in the car, I finally relaxed.

"I hate him," I declared as I buckled my seat belt.

Mama shook her head, starting up the car. "Hate is a strong word, Kamika. He may be a dirty dog, but what happened between us was years ago. He could've changed."

We must've been talking to two different motherfuckers, because the one I'd just spoken to had shown zero growth.

"Or he could be exactly the same, or even worse," I countered.

My mother, ever the diplomat, always tried to see the best in people. An admirable trait, but one wasted on someone like Colton.

"Whatever he may be, don't give him power over you by holding a grudge. Don't expend any energy on him. You're better than that."

Personally, I disagreed, but I wouldn't shit on my mother's words of wisdom by saying that. So, I just nodded in response, though something told me she sensed my true feelings. Mama was just eerily intuitive like that.

June 3rd

Kamika

Flat Tire: Ride out the shop. Where you wanna be picked up from?

My eyebrows rose as I saw the text, a smile tugging at my lips as I reread it. He'd remembered his promise.

Me: Bold. Meet me at La Mer, and I might give you the honor of bringing me home.

Heavy on might. Despite the connection I felt with him, he was still a stranger. Giving him my address when we hadn't properly hung out was a dummy move. Sharing a meal wouldn't disqualify him as a threat, but it would allow me to get a better feel for him than was possible over the phone. Body language, facial expressions, and tone of voice exposed more than words on a screen ever could.

Definitely wasn't a date.

Nope.

Just a way to smoke him out.

Flat Tire: You wanna go to the beach or something?

My brows furrowed at the question until I remembered the restaurant's name translated into the sea. A chuckle escaped me as I replied.

Me: You're stupid

Me: It's a seafood restaurant

His knowledge of French deepened my attraction to him, and made a question pop into my head.

Me: How do you know French?

Flat Tire: My Daddy taught me a little. His Grandparents from Bordeaux.

Me: You ever been 👀

Flat Tire: Nah, haven't traveled outside North America. What time you want to meet up?

As I typed my response, I made a note to ask him about the destinations he'd been over our meal.

Me: 3pm?

Flat Tire: Aight. It's a date

Flat Tire: My treat.

...Okay, maybe it *was* a date, and though I tried to convince myself that I was indifferent to the title, the giddy giggles that spewed from me said otherwise.

Despite the fancy-sounding name, *La Mer* was a humble bistro. It wasn't a small place, but there were visible signs of wear and tear and layers of grime on the outside that might make some people second-guess stopping by. Yet, health inspection hadn't shut their asses down, and the food was good enough for me to ignore what some might call red flags. It wasn't dirty to me, but well-loved by the people of Gaville.

Me: I'm here

I knew he wouldn't—or at least, shouldn't— reply while driving, so I settled on one of the benches outside. I smoothed down my cowl neck sundress, the blue floral pattern complementing my skin tone nicely.

And, more importantly, the low neckline showed off my tits.

Less than five minutes after I sat down, '*I've Got a Woman,*' by Ray Charles was blasting from a vintage black Mustang, one I instantly identified as belonging to Beau. The song choice made my eyebrows raise, but I wasn't complaining. Grandma had been a big fan of

Brother Ray, and I had several of his songs on my playlist.

"Ray Charles fan?" I asked when he exited his parked vehicle, standing from the bench as he approached.

"One of my favorites," he confirmed, bypassing my handshake.

An undignified squeak left me as he pulled me into his strong arms. He found my surprise amusing, his throaty chuckle sending a wave of heat through me. His closeness allowed me to sample his cologne, an ambery fragrance with spicy and floral undernotes.

He smelled good enough to eat.

"What cologne is that?" I asked when we pulled apart, trying to conceal how turned on a simple hug made me.

He offered me a cheeky grin. "You like how I smell or something?"

"Why else would I ask?" I replied, accepting his arm when he held it out to me.

A gentleman. I liked that.

He answered my question as he held the door open for me, both gestures scoring him extra brownie points. "*Dior Homme Parfum.*"

My eyebrows shot up. "*Dior*, huh?"

He must be a helluva freelancer.

He just shrugged, wrapping an arm around my waist as we stood in the short line to the hostess stand. I pretended his height and muscles didn't impress me. Not wanting to gush too much and give away how fine I found him, I studied my surroundings, enjoying the pirogue hovering above the entrance to the main dining area. Little had changed since I'd last been there. Fish nets crisscrossed the ceiling. Fake shrimp, crawfish, and fish dotted the slatted wood walls. A taxidermized gator hung on the wall across from the hostess stand. Beneath it was a huge lobster tank crowded with meals waiting to happen.

"Table for two."

Beau's confident voice broke into my contemplation. He ignored the flirty smile of the hostess and pressed his hand against my lower back as he guided me to our table. Perhaps I was lonelier than I thought, because the contact nearly made me swoon.

"Your waitress will be right with you," the chick purred, winking at Beau, which I didn't appreciate at all.

I might have no claim on him, but the girl could show some damn respect. I didn't recognize her, so I concluded she must be a college student from Fleur, who snagged a job wherever she could find one.

"Are you okay?" he asked, looking less than amused. "Is something in your eye?"

The girl glowered, and I fought to suppress a smile. Huffing, she stormed away.

"Some women have no damn couth," he murmured, holding out my chair.

I didn't want my tongue to get ahead of my brain, so I forwent a reply. So far, our date was going well, but it was still early. "So, uh, tell me about yourself."

He leaned in and claimed one of my hands, then brought it to his lips. "What do you want to know, Mika?"

I cocked an eyebrow. Mika was different. Anyone who'd ever shortened Kamika referred to me as Kami. "Whatever you want to tell me. Where are you from? Where are you going? Shit like that."

"I'm from here, and where would you like me to go?"

Giggling, I rolled my eyes. "Careful, that's a little corny."

He winced. "I haven't been hit with that charge in all my years of existence."

"You're not even thirty. All the years of your existence," I repeated, deepening my voice to poorly imitate him. "Makes you sound like an old man."

He squeezed the hand he hadn't released. "You get the point, Mika."

"I do," I responded, his deep voice calling to me. Trying to control whatever was flaring between us, I allowed the rest of his words to sink in. "What do you mean you're from here?

Gaville's a small place. I would've run into you one of the times I've visited."

"I'm from the 504, baby," he said, drawing the word out to show off his New Orleans drawl. "Not Gaville."

"So, why'd you say you're from here?"

I couldn't suppress the suspicion in my tone; trusting pee-pee owners wasn't something I made a habit of doing. Already, I'd given Beau more leeway than I did most men. A handsome face and charming personality did wonders, though deep down, I knew that was a dangerous combination that could lead to a world of fuckery.

"New Orleans is in Louisiana, ain't it?"

"Right. I knew you were too beautiful to be from Gaville," I replied, the cliché flirtation slipping out before I could stop it. My mind scrambled for a topic change, settling on the first one that popped into my brain. "What's New Orleans like?"

His roguish smile told me he knew he was a sexy motherfucker, but he did me a favor and answered my question.

"Never a dull day there," he answered, fondness creeping into his tone as he leaned back in his seat, relinquishing his grip on my hand. "There's no place like it, and I've been all over the continent. You ever wanna come visit me down there, I'll be happy to give you a tour, sweet."

"Sweet?" I echoed, charmed in spite of myself. I put on a faux-southern accent, attempting to mimic Scarlett O'Hara. "Your old-fashioned manners and words are beguiling, sir."

To my own ears, I didn't do half-bad. Beau's amused chuckles made me second-guess myself.

"So you think I'm a Casanova or some shit?"

My face heated, and I shook my head. "I didn't say that."

"You said I was beguiling. Same shit."

"Casanova is only famous for being a hoe with connections," I declared, putting an end to his teasing. "Plus, he was a scam artist and a perverted dickhead. He abused little girls and had a baby with his own daughter."

I realized too late that my choice of conversation was not everyone's cup of tea, but thankfully, he didn't seem to think me odd for it.

His eyebrows shot up. "That's some nasty ass shit."

"Right?"

"I take it you're a student of history?"

"Mostly Louisiana history, with some exceptions," I replied. Despite being from Miami, it was the Pelican State that'd captured my heart. "Particularly Gaville's. My grandmother was an important member of the community and knew a lot about the area. She passed on her love of history to me."

"*Was* an important part?" he repeated. "What happened?"

I didn't want my grief to seep into my date. Grandma would understand. She may even applaud me, believing I was finally on the right track by going on a date with a man, and not trying to mess it up. Still, at Beau's expectant look, I found myself answering.

"She passed away recently. It's why me and my mama came here. For the funeral, and to sort out her business."

He studied my face. "What was your grandmother's name?"

"Susanne."

He squinted.

I cleared my throat, quickly coming up with a subject change. "Anyway, what type of freelancer are you? Besides a flexible one who does odd jobs around New Orleans."

I was positive you needed a contractor license to do a host of shit, so if he was selling his services without one, that could lead to a hefty fine.

"I do a lot of contract work, fixing shit," he said, all but confirming my theory that he was an unlawful handy man.

But, hey, that was a hell of a lot better than being a drug dealer.

"Hi, my name is Ally, and I'll be your server today," the cheery voice interrupted my response. She sat a loaf of French bread and a crockery of soft butter between us, along with small plates and knives. "If you know what you'd like for drinks and appetizers, I'll be happy to take your orders."

Unlike the bitchy hostess, she was vaguely familiar. Maybe I'd encountered her during one of the many church services Granny dragged me to, filled with other kids and teens not allowed to sleep-in on Sundays. I couldn't place how I knew her, and she didn't seem to recognize me, so I didn't say anything.

"We didn't get menus," Beau said, just as I spotted them sticking out from a small wooden crate on our table. It was pushed against the wall and sat between the salt, pepper, Tabasco, and ketchup.

I nodded to the menus.

"Give us a few minutes," he instructed, not unkindly. Even if he'd been a rude motherfucker, I don't think it would've fazed Ally. Like the hostess, she seemed totally enamored of Beau.

The thought doused some of my attraction. My stepfather was a cheating asshole. Colton was, too. What always seemed like harmless attention from women turned out to be ego strokes and commitment issues.

I snatched the menu Beau held out to me. Not commenting on my rudeness, he opened his menu while I did the same and looked over the selections.

"I'll have the peach and melon slushy," I said, not bothering to look at the appetizers before setting my menu back into the mini crate.

"I was thinking about the crawfish beignets, fried green tomatoes and remoulade sauce, calamari, and oysters on a half shell for our appetizers."

"While I like a man with a big appetite, that's too much, especially if we're ordering an entrée. And," I added, shaking my head. "I don't eat raw oysters."

"They're good for the libido."

"They're also good for cemeteries. They kill you."

He laughed. "It isn't a particular concern of mine."

"Good for you, Mr. Invincible. I don't believe in tempting fate."

"You won't be, Mika. Just trust me."

"Ha. Famous last words." I removed my napkin from around the utensils and sat it in my lap, then reached for the bread.

"I'm serious, sweet. Live a little. If the worst happens, I'll move heaven and hell to find a remedy and revive you."

He was a certified sweet talker, and I was a simping bitch for allowing his corny pick-up lines to thaw me.

"You're so full of shit," I said around laughter, not paying attention as I grabbed the knife and accidentally cut my finger.

Droplets of blood dripped onto the little plate and the tablecloth. Beau gripped the edge of the table, which I found funny.

"Hey, big, strong dude, it is just a little cut." I wiggled my injured finger, and his eyes darkened. "You're squeamish?"

"Not...not..." He swallowed. "Not really," he finally pushed out.

"Well, you're something." I wrapped the towel around the injured digit, pushed my chair back, and got to my feet. "I'll be back once I see to this in the bathroom."

I strutted away, barely feeling the pain of a minor injury that had Beau all in a tizzy.

Beauden

He couldn't help himself. The moment Kamika was out of view, Beau picked up the plate with her blood on it. He did a cursory glance around the dining room, ensuring no one was watching him as he lapped up the red ichor. It was a reckless move, but humans were often too consumed with themselves to pay attention to anyone else. Everyone had phones, and they were an excellent distraction, letting his strange behavior slip under the radar. Flavors exploded on his tongue, the sweetness nearly euphoric. He bit back a moan, setting the dish down again, his saliva replacing Kamika's blood.

Not only was she a pretty little thing, but she tasted fucking delicious. Neither was shocking. New Orleans' Voodoo Covens produced beautiful women, and witches' blood was always blissful on the palette.

Already, the outing was proving productive. His sampling confirmed Kamika was of witch stock, and Susanne was the name of the dead bitch who'd brought him to the town. Fate had been on his side, putting her granddaughter in his path. Whether she knew of her heritage or about the supernatural world was of no concern. Beau would bet a lot of fucking money that some of the business Kamika and her mama had to sort out were the very documents he was in search of.

Beau smirked at the emoji, then set his phone on the table. Kamika had yet to return from the bathroom, and some of her blood still stained the knife. Taking his chances, he trailed his finger along the blade, collecting the droplets before they could fully dry on the cutlery. He sighed as he licked his fingers clean. Witches' blood could be deadly, but Kamika presumably had no powers. If that was the case, the toxins that'd turn her plasma into poison weren't present, leaving him free to indulge.

"What the fuck?" a man said, making Beau whip his head up.

Immediately, he wrinkled his nose, the smell of dirt and dog clinging to the blond giving away his species. So caught up in Kamika's life essence, he hadn't realized a werewolf had entered the establishment.

"May I help you?" Beau said coolly, eyeing Mr. Blondie with distaste.

He didn't bother to hide his scowl. The intruder was exactly the kind of prick to think he's the shit; blond-haired, blue-eyed, and conventionally attractive.

"Don't play dumb, asshole," Blondie growled, glowering down at him. "I saw what your bloodsucking ass did."

Beau didn't like being talked down to, and he despised how the dog was standing over him, high-and-mighty on a damn high horse.

Beau's chair scraped against the tile as he stood. Satisfaction roared through him at his height advantage, not that the mutt realized he was at a disadvantage. He was a young and dumb pup, likely eager to prove himself to his pack, intimidating the big, bad vampire passing through his territory.

"Move before I *make* you, *pardner*," Beau ordered, shoving the bastard so he was forced to inch back. He wouldn't be able to go all out in front of so many humans, but even when his strength was scaled back, Beau was efficient at whooping ass.

Jack snarled and returned the shove. The whispers that reached his ears gave both men pause, and before things could escalate, Kamika's sweet scent infiltrated his nostrils. He breathed deeply, turning to see her marching to the table. His tongue darted out, moistening his lips as he admired her. That blue dress hugged her perfect curves and showed off perky titties he wanted to feel. Her dreadlocks flowed down her back, revealing her thin chain necklace and hoop earrings. She looked damn good, even with her glossy lips tugged down into a frown.

Miz Susanne had fantastic genes.

"What's going on here?" she demanded, taking her position at Beau's side.

When Blondie's gaze flickered to her, Beau wrapped an arm around her waist, silently warning him she was off limits.

Outrage crept into the fucker's expression. "You're here with *him*?"

They knew each other. Ironic, how she seemed to attract supernatural company without even being aware of it.

"What's it to you, Jack?"

Jack, huh? A generic name for a stereotypical mutt.

"You don't think it's dangerous to date random, strange men?"

"Motherfucker, don't start with me," Kamika snapped, her aggression shocking Beau and the mutt. It was almost comical how a little human girl rendered them both speechless. "Beau isn't random and strange, and you have no goddamn right to tell me who to spend time with. I swear,

I don't know how Larissa got with your raggedy ass."

Jack's lip lifted into a snarl. "And I don't know how you downgraded from her to him. If nothing else, I thought you had taste."

Well, ain't this interesting.

The two seemed to share a lover, Jack's current mate and Kamika's ex. Everything Beau knew about werewolves dictated that Jack should be trying to get Kamika out of the picture, cutting down the competition, and all that. And yet, he was trying to protect her.

Clearly, Beau was missing something.

"Besides, what about Delaney?"

And there it was. Another dog was trying to stake a claim on her. Based on the name, he'd wager the mutt blondie spoke of was the same pup he met back in New Orleans. A helluva twist which could complicate his plan, but not make it impossible. He wouldn't be so good at what he did if such a minor issue got in his way.

Kamika scoffed. "Oh, you're helping Larissa play matchmaker now?"

"That's my wife," Jack replied with a haughty sniff.

"Then be a good mutt and go back to your mistress," Beau taunted, raising his eyebrows when Jack growled, silently daring the motherfucker to try something.

It was only when their waitress returned that it sank in what a scene they might be causing. The biracial blonde looked confused, glancing between Jack and Beau.

"Uhm, are you with their party?" she asked, sparing a smile for Kamika.

Beau liked that. The hostess bitch tried to pretend she didn't exist.

"No, he's not," Kamika said, returning to her seat. "He stopped by to say hi, but he was just leaving."

Beau remained standing, refusing to be the one to back down. He may not have started this bullshit, but he'd finish it if needed.

"Yep," Jack agreed through gritted teeth, seeming to realize this was a battle he couldn't win.

When he stepped away from the table, Beau sat down again, leaning back as he eyed the pup.

"Came to pick up food, but the hostess let me come say hi to my…old friends," he continued, wincing when the words left his mouth.

With one last glare at Beau, Jack left, leaving them in peace.

Delaney

"Bad news," Jack announced as he stormed into the kitchen, carrying the takeout that Larissa had sent him to get over an hour ago.

When he didn't see his wife, he stopped and looked around. Delaney cocked a brow at his frown. "I'm listening," she said, pausing the mobile game she'd been playing to give her cousin her undivided attention.

"Where's Larissa?" he asked.

She scanned Jack for injuries, relieved to find him unharmed. Besides his disgruntled demeanor, something about him was off. Her stomach growled, and she decided it could wait until after dinner. If he wasn't running to the alpha with his discovery, it couldn't be that serious.

Then again, she hadn't told anyone about Beau, and that was pretty serious.

"Delaney," he hissed, slamming his fist on the counter. "Where's Larissa?"

"Changing my grandson's diaper," Aunt Galena answered as she entered the room, wiping her hands with a napkin as she eyed the bag of food hungrily. "Thank God you're back. I'm starving."

She reached for the bag, and her son-in-law gave it up without a fight.

"I'm still waiting," Delaney said, wondering what had his hackles raised.

She could sense his agitation and unease. She ordered Larissa to come back ASAP, because it seemed as if he was seconds away from losing his shit. As her aunt warmed and plated the food, she willed herself to ignore the delicious scent wafting up her nostrils. Her hunger made ignoring the food a challenge, but she managed.

The scent she picked up on made her stiffen.

It was faint, fainter than it had been the other day during her hunt, but it was definitely Beau. He fucking adored that *Dior* cologne, and nothing could cover up the scent of decay that seemed to cling to vampires.

Shit.

That was bad.

Beau was staying. Which meant he likely had a job in the area. Hopefully, he was riding solo, and that annoying bisexual hadn't tagged along.

"You alright, baby?" Aunt Galena asked as she handed Delaney her plate.

She forced a smile and nodded, accepting the steaming pile of food. "Just hungry."

"Ditto, cuz," Larissa said, breezing into the room, Cyrus on her hip and Shay toddling behind her.

Typically, when Jack was around his wife, he calmed down. No such luck this time. Her presence did prompt him to talk, confirming what she suspected.

"A vampire's in the area, and he's targeting Kamika."

"What?" Larissa and Delaney echoed.

Delaney shot from her seat, dread and anger slamming into her. The protective fury in Larissa's voice was of no concern. Only Beau's boldness mattered. First the fucker stabbed her in the back, and now he targeted her future mate. She was going to make that fucker pay.

"Where are you going?" Aunt Galena demanded as Delaney stalked to the archway, intending to hunt his ass down. "Sit down and eat, girl. Don't go doing stupid shit."

"We have his scent and his last known location," Delaney snapped, unable to do nothing as a threat ran free. "Let's nip the problem in the bud before—"

"Kamika isn't a member of the pack or a permanent resident of the town," her aunt replied as she stood.

Delaney's jaw dropped at the callous response.

"So we shouldn't do anything?" Larissa said, sounding as shocked as Delaney felt.

"We don't know if she's in danger, or who this vampire is affiliated with. Striking first could get us into a world of trouble."

Delaney couldn't suppress her growl. As a member of the council, her aunt's decree held weight and echoed the pack's longstanding policy: no going on the offensive when it came to outsiders. Jack cast her a brief, pitiful glance before giving his attention back to his children. They were too young to grasp the tension.

"This is bullshit! She may not fit your criteria for protection, but she is *mine*," Delaney hissed, glowering down at her aunt. "I won't let anything happen to her because of a stupid fucking rule—"

The slap that cut her off wasn't unexpected, but it only inflamed her further. She clenched her jaw as her head snapped to the side, rubbing her sore cheek as she looked back at her aunt. She remained composed, her face neutral.

"I'm aware she's your potential mate, so I won't fault you for feeling so strongly about the matter. But watch your tone," Aunt Galena warned, returning to her seat. "I'll inform the Alpha of the situation tomorrow. You have my permission to protect your mate, Delaney, but do not engage with the bloodsucker unless absolutely necessary."

It wasn't exactly what she wanted to hear, but it was better than leaving Kamika out to hang. So, she nodded and returned to her seat when her aunt gestured to her plate of food. Her appetite had dwindled, but she'd shown enough of her ass for the evening. While she chowed down, she'd formulate a plan to keep her mate safe.

As for Beau, she'd only get in trouble for fucking that motherfucker up if she got caught, and she'd become very adept at sneaking.

June 4th

Though keeping vital information from her pack might seem like a betrayal, there was a reason Delaney never told them of how she made money in New Orleans. Bounty hunting had a complicated reputation in the supernatural community. In more urban areas, it was an important profession that allowed factions to outsource their dirtier work and track down those who wronged them. In rural areas, it wasn't quite so cut-and-dry. The Harris Pack, for example, saw it as meddling in others' business, which could lead to a world of trouble. Their assessment, though grossly simplified, wasn't entirely wrong. Delaney had made more than a few enemies due to the job, Beau being one of them. When she first sensed him, she kept her mouth shut to avoid her family's ire and prayed he was just passing through.

That wasn't the case, and now, Kamika could be caught in the crosshairs.

Delaney thought of the dead girls found between Gaville and Fleur, who were dominating the local news cycle. Just the thought of Kamika joining them made her heart hurt. She refused to let that happen, and her determination to protect her mate led her to watch Kamika's house from afar. Some might call her a stalker, hiding amongst the flora, her attention solely on the blue shotgun home. She'd say she was just being a good mate and doing her duty to her pack by protecting their territory.

Besides, she'd gotten permission from her aunt, and the Alpha himself, so naysayers could go fuck themselves.

Delaney had decided to stay in wolf form. Her instincts were sharper, and her body was stronger. Someone stumbling upon a large canine might cause a stir, but Gaville had an array of wildlife. And, more importantly, she didn't intend to be sighted. Under the cover of darkness, avoiding detection was a breeze. When she grew too restless, she circled the home and peered through the windows, looking for any signs that something was amiss. She found none, Kamika and her mother safely lodged inside.

Perhaps Toria hadn't been entirely wrong when she said Delaney was possessive and paranoid. Why else would she be camping outside the house of a girl who could barely stand her, a girl that she hardly knew? On the other hand, the protective feelings towards potential mates were incomprehensible to non-shifters, and Delaney's own...quirks made her more prone to questionable behavior. Only when the solidification process began could another species grasp the devotion they felt.

At least, that was what she heard from others. Sex was a vital part of the solidification process, and yet, Toria often seemed indifferent to her. Maybe her ex was just a coldblooded bitch, incapable of love. It was better than the alternative, being fated to those who could never understand the fidelity she felt.

A branch snapping caught her attention. Looking around, she saw no one, but when she listened, she heard footsteps. Her lip pulling back into a snarl, she lowered herself, preparing to launch her body at any threat. As the steps drew nearer, it wasn't Beau's scent that assaulted her, but Larissa's. She relaxed, cocking her head to the side. Sure enough, Larissa emerged from the tree line, in human form and holding up a change of clothes.

"Shift," she ordered, tossing her the garments.

If she could, she would've rolled her eyes at the bossiness. Instead, when her cousin turned her back, Delaney obliged with the command. Once she was back into her two-legged form, she quickly tugged on the outfit her cousin had brought her.

"I'm decent," Delaney announced, frowning at Larissa when she turned to face her. "Why'd you come here?"

"You've been gone since sundown, and it's almost 1 AM. You need to get some rest."

Delaney scoffed and shook her head. "Vampires are notoriously fond of the darkness, cuz. The leeches are too weak for the sun."

Not Beau. He was well over a century, allowing sunlight to have little impact on him. That made him an even bigger threat.

"Well, in case you forgot, the vamp sniffing around Kamika was out in broad daylight, so depriving yourself of sleep won't do much good."

Delaney glared, crossing her arms over her chest. "That isn't comforting."

"But it's the truth," Larissa shot back, before her expression softened. "Look, I get how you feel. I don't want anything to happen to Kamika, and I'd go out of my mind if I thought Jack was in danger. I did when Mama and I first found him. I never cried that much over a stranger before."

Years later, Delaney could still hear the pain in her cousin's voice and see the way her face twisted as she remembered the first time she met her husband. Delaney herself could still recall the day Larissa called her, sobbing, barely able to get words out as she recounted discovering her potential mate. The bullet had come dangerously close to taking Jack's life, and Delaney had held Toria a little tighter that night.

She knew her cousin could relate, and thanks to Jack, knew that Larissa and Kamika had been an item. Both facts should enlighten her as to why Delaney was pulling an all-nighter. Sacrificing sleep to avoid Beau possibly attacking Kamika was worth it.

Unfortunately, Larissa didn't seem to agree with her.

When she tugged on the sleeve of Delaney's jacket, she stepped out of arm's reach. "If you understand how I feel—"

"Just because I understand doesn't mean I'll allow you to neglect yourself. Mama made me pull my shit together, and you need someone who won't let you turn into a malnourished stalker."

A burst of laughter left Delaney. Her amusement died when the underlying insult sank in. "I'm not fucking stalking her. I'm—"

"Keeping her safe," Larissa finished, the pointed look making Delaney flush and look away. "And I hate to tell you this, but hiding in bushes and watching someone's house is a classic stalker move."

Delaney's cheeks burned with embarrassment. Despite her intentions, she couldn't deny the truth of Larissa's words. But, fuck, she knew Beau. He could be a cruel bastard, and when he wanted something, little could stop him. He wasn't renowned for his niceness, but for his ruthless efficiency.

"Those college girls...what if Kamika ends up like them?"

"The reports show the attacks were likely done by a human," Larissa said, her attempt to soothe falling flat. "No bite marks were found."

Ridding victimsof bitemarks wasn't as tricky as Larissa seemed to think. Delaney considered sharing her history with Beau but quickly dismissed the notion. If it got back to the council, she could be blamed for bringing trouble to their doorstep and face repercussions. She could take being relegated to the tasks no one wanted to do, or even a beating, but endangering the pack could get her exiled. She'd be forced to leave Gaville and cut communication with everyone she held dear, and that she wouldn't be able to take.

"Were you this blasé about her safety when you two were together?" Delaney grumbled, the words slipping out before she could stop them.

Larissa froze, her eyes going wide. She looked at her cousin warily, taking a defensive position.

"I'm not going to fucking attack you," Delaney snapped, insulted that her cousin would think that lowly of her. "Just forget I said anything."

"No," Larissa said, clearing her throat and composing herself. "No. If you plan to pursue Kamika seriously, this is something we need to talk about."

"What is there to talk about? You two dated at some point before Jack, and now you're close friends."

And, if Jack's words were accurate, Kamika was still hung up on Larissa. Delaney prayed he was letting his jealousy cloud his judgment and reading into something that wasn't there.

"Close friends is an overstatement. We haven't spoken in years and only reconnected at her grandmother's funeral. I just think she needs a friend right now, and there's nothing more to it."

Right. Susanne was her grandmother. Before she left for school, Delaney had seldom interacted with the half-witch bitch, finding her too fucking judgy. She hadn't been powerful enough to be so high-and-mighty, but no one in the pack ever checked her for the bullshit she handed them. She'd been the only one who could maintain the protection spell her mother had placed over the town, before she decided to limit the boundaries to just her house over some petty shit. However, it seemed her daughter and granddaughter were ignorant of their heritage and the supernatural world, and that made Delaney dislike Susanne a little more.

"How'd you find out?" Larissa asked, recapturing Delaney's attention.

"Jack."

Larissa huffed. "Of course."

Based on the look on her face, she was going to tear into her husband when they returned to pack lands.

"Kamika and I did care for one another," her cousin continued after a moment of silence, holding Delaney's stare. "She was one of two people I dated before Jack, and the only woman I've ever been with. It was one of the best summers of my life, and I was devastated when we broke up, but that's all in the past. When I met Jack, I knew he was the one. No one else mattered. I won't pretend that I don't still care for her, but everything I feel is platonic."

Her words brought Delaney some relief, but it was how Kamika felt that truly concerned her. Because, God forbid, what if Jack was right? That'd make pursuing her all the harder.

"Is...did Jack break you two up?" Delaney asked slowly.

From Larissa's recount, she couldn't imagine any other reason why they'd come to an end.

A sad smile spread across her face, and she shook her head. "No. Uh, let's just say not everyone approved of us."

She wondered if Susanne was one of them. Everything she knew about the old woman led Delaney to believe she'd been one of the loudest critics.

"How about this? Stop creeping around their place, come home, and I'll get Kamika to come over. She can't be hanging around the vampire if she's with us, and he wouldn't be dumb enough to cross pack boundaries."

True. Beau was many things, but he knew how to pick his battles. Trespassing in the core of the Harris's territory would be a surefire way to get fucked up.

Delaney took a minute to mull over Larissa's proposal, then nodded. "Alright. But if she hasn't come over by next week—"

"Then we'll figure something else out," Larissa interrupted, her exasperation clear. "Now, can we please go home? I left my mate and our warm bed to come fetch your creepy ass."

Delaney chuckled softly, her tension easing at the playfulness seeping into her cousin's tone. "Fine, fine. Let's head back," she conceded, brushing a wayward loc from her face.

Larissa's arm looped through hers, guiding her away from the colorful home. Still, Delaney couldn't help but throw a glance over her shoulder, needing to ensure the area was clear. Afterall, she'd be a pretty shitty mate if she couldn't protect one human girl.

June 7th

Kamika

This wasn't my grandmother's house. Everything was identical, and yet, in my heart, I knew it wasn't the home I'd spent so much of my time in. It carried an eerie feeling, and I felt as if I was being watched. It made my skin crawl. I wanted to leave. I didn't know where my mama was. I'd searched the entire place, and she was nowhere to be found. Swallowing, I made my way to the front door, deciding a walk would clear my mind.

My plan was perfect, except for the fact that the handle wouldn't budge.

I double-checked that I'd unlocked the door. When I confirmed I wasn't going insane, I tried again.

Same results.

My panic grew. I pinched myself, wondering if this was a strange dream. It did little good. A throaty chuckle sounded behind me, filled with amusement. It was so familiar, and as a little girl, I would act so silly just to hear the sound. Now, though, it only filled me with dread.

The dead couldn't laugh, and they certainly shouldn't be in my presence.

"That don't work here, little girl," Grandma said, sounding even closer. "It'll take more than a pinch to wake up before I want you to."

The door still wouldn't open, but when her words processed, I calmed a bit. This was all a dream, albeit a strange one. I would be lying if I said I didn't miss her, specifically the version that was present before I entered my teens. My subconscious must've conjured her up in the most unsettling way possible. The situation bordered on nightmarish, and the intense alarm I felt was ultrarealistic. But it wasn't real, giving me the strength to respond.

"And when will that be?"

"You've always been an impatient one, Kamika," she chided, shaking her head. "That's why I caught you and that dyk—"

"Don't," I warned, wondering why my brain decided to torment me.

Maybe it was trying to remind me what an awful person my grandmother was, to get rid of the grief that lingered.

"That's right, she stopped being gay," Grandma said, reaffirming my theory. "Got herself a nice white man, huh?"

I suppose she would've known about their relationship years before I did. Gaville was small, and my grandmother had been a nosy woman, keeping tabs on any and everyone.

I tried to will myself to wake up, to exit this lucid dream, but nope. My subconscious was holding me hostage with a homophobic dead woman.

The small smile on Grandma's face slipped. "That's how you think of me, now, girl?"

Great, she could hear my thoughts, because why not torture myself further? Dream journals weren't something I made a habit of keeping, but when I woke up, I'd jot this one down. A few of my friends back in Miami were majoring in psychology. Hopefully, they could dissect this.

"Nothing to dissect, girl. I didn't come down here to be a nuisance—"

"Down here implies you went to heaven," I replied flatly, seeing no point in a show of respect in my dreams.

Her eyes narrowed. "Watch it, girl. I'm still your grandmother."

"Something you forgot when you all but disowned me for falling in love."

"The Bible says—"

"What does it matter what an old book written by dead fucking men says?" I snapped, moving away from the door to get in her face. "I idolized you, and had always tried to be respectful to you, to show my love. And for what? For you to turn your back on me as soon as I fell in love with someone you didn't approve of? Who, by the way, was a sweetheart with a promising future. But you didn't care about that, because you're a bigoted bitch. That's why you died alone, surrounded by fakes who only attended your funeral to keep up appearances."

By the end of my rant, I couldn't keep still. I started to pace, my eyes feeling misty as my body shook with anger I'd struggled to suppress, and a deep hurt. The wound she'd caused had never healed, and now that she was dead, it never would.

"You and your Mama came," she said after some seconds. I didn't still, nor did I look at her. I tried to tune out her words, but when she continued to speak, I couldn't help but listen. "And not due to obligation. Those tears your Mama shed, those tears you tried to hide, they were real, Kamika. And I know I wasn't perfect. I know I could've handled that situation better, but believe me when I say, you were better off without Larissa. And in the end, you would've lost her no matter what I did. As soon as that white boy pranced up in here—"

"Larissa isn't a cheater," I interrupted, stilling to glare at her. "If she and I were together when Jack showed up, she wouldn't have stepped out."

She laughed again, but this time, it held no humor. "Is that what you think? Oh, baby, you don't know shit about her kind. When they feel that pull, they go towards it, no matter who it may hurt. And this ain't 'homophobia' talking," she said before I could blast her ass. "It's fact. Larissa and Jack were meant to be together, and try as she might, he would've won over you in the end."

My jaw clenched, and I looked away. I've had some bad dreams, but this one ranked amongst the highest. Certainly, there were other ways my mind could've chosen to reflect.

"People are too soft on themselves, Kami," she murmured, the use of my nickname making my heart clench. "We lie to ourselves, try to deny truths we don't want to hear. Believe it or not, I'm doing this because I love you. You need to hear this, just like you need to hear what I'm about to say next—"

"I'm not interested," I interrupted, angrily swiping at my eyes. "I'm ready to wake up now, so—"

"And I'm not done. Like I said, you ain't waking up before I want you to."

Even as a figment of my imagination, she was a control freak, holding me hostage to get her way.

"And when will that be?"

She studied me for a moment, her stare so intense that my discomfort made a grand return. Typically, in my dreams, faces were hazy and out of focus. Yet, hers was crystal clear, and her eyes held a striking level of detail. So many emotions passed through them, emotions I didn't think her capable of, and emotions no person I've dreamt of had ever expressed.

That eerie feeling from earlier returned. I wanted this odd dream that I was trapped in to end.

"I suppose this is my fault," she finally sighed, tearing her gaze away. "If all had gone to plan, you'd know what I'm talking about."

"Then make it clear so I can wake up."

She tsked and shook her head, the sound grating on my nerves. "Can't do that, baby girl. You'd brush me off until you put the pieces together. Until that time comes, I'm speaking as clearly as I can."

Oh, great, a fucking riddle. My friends were going to have a field day with this one. I could already hear Morgan droning on about the importance of therapy, or Rowan lecturing me on how healing is a journey that takes time, and I have to do XY and Z to become whole again, when nothing in me was broken. I just had a little baggage—dare I say trauma—like everyone else. Show me a person who claims to have neither, and I'd show you a brazen liar.

"Ain't no riddle, girl. You'll know what I'm talking about soon enough, with the way things are going," she muttered, the last part barely audible. My brows snapped together. "But I'll say this. I'm watching over you and your mama. And that watching let me know the company you're keeping ain't the best. The Harris girls aren't ideal, but they won't hurt you. That boy, though? He's trouble."

I knew immediately that the boy she spoke of was Beau. It made my skin crawl, and while some found it comforting, a ghost spying on me was nightmare fuel.

"Ghosts aren't harmful, Kami. It's the living you have to worry about."

I looked at her, wondering if she realized the irony of her words. Because of her, I was acutely aware that those breathing could do the most damage.

"I know," I said finally, feeling so fucking drained, despite being asleep.

An energy drink would be needed when I woke up. I preferred coffee, but I suspected I'd need something with an extra kick.

Grandma smiled at me, that gentle, loving smile that used to put me at ease as a child, one I'd longed to see for so many years now. "You've always been a smart girl, Kamika, but you're still young and flawed. I need you to trust your instincts, and if anything feels off, leave that situation. Your gut will never lead you wrong, baby. Can you promise me that?"

She had a lot of nerve, asking anything of me. And yet, I found myself nodding. Because, even if the messenger was far from ideal, the advice was solid.

"Fine," I huffed, ready to be released from this state of limbo.

"Good," she said simply.

She pulled me into her arms, taking me aback so much, I nearly shoved her away. I caught myself in time and opted to remain stiff and unmoving.

"You can wake up now," she whispered, the words causing my surroundings to start to fade away. She stepped back, a bright light emitting from her. "I'll be seeing you again soon, Kamika."

I didn't have a chance to ask her what she meant, or to tell her to stay in the afterlife. She disappeared into the blinding glow, and within seconds, my subconscious shut off.

I awoke with a gasp, my eyes flying open. A layer of sweat coated me, making the sheets and my pajamas stick to my skin. I felt uncomfortably hot. Kicking off my covers, I sat on the edge of my bed and looked around. Everything was as it should be, and that oppressive feeling from my dream—no, my fucking *nightmare*—was gone.

The discomfort, however, stuck around.

I heard my mother in the kitchen, and the smell of coffee wafted to me. The clock revealed I had just twenty minutes before my alarm sounded. I was awake now, though, and doubted I could get back to sleep. But I was still frazzled and didn't feel like explaining to Mama what had gotten to me. So, instead of preparing myself for whatever the day would throw at me, I grabbed my cellphone and started to scroll through my notifications.

The check-ins from my friends were dwindling, so the number of messages I had to reply to started to lessen. The growing silence from my circle in Miami wasn't only what bothered me, but the fact that I hadn't heard from Beau since our date. Jack's interruption had dampened the vibe, but we bounced back once our server brought out food. Before and after the arrival of that blond bastard, things were good, leading me to believe it was something *I* did that turned Beau off from me. Maybe he read too much into Jack's remark about Delaney and believed I was involved with someone else.

With a sigh, I pushed thoughts of Beau away and confirmed with Olivia that I hadn't thrown myself off a bridge. Having replied to my last friend, I glanced at my remaining notifications. I groaned at seeing the emails from school.

I'd graduated from Miami Dade College just a week before Grandma died, with a Pre-Bachelor of Arts. The goal had been to hone my photography skills, hopefully leading to professional opportunities, and preparing me for life at a four-year college, per Mama's request. She supported my dreams, but wanted me to pick a practical, back-up degree. I intended to choose teaching, just like she'd been before she became a freelance editor. Unlike her, I wouldn't teach English. If my dreams of opening a photography studio failed, I could teach elementary kids arts and crafts.

Yet, my grandmother's demise put an end to celebrations. With it, I'd stopped considering further education. Neither my head nor heart was in it, and I was so thankful that school had concluded before she decided to die. Though her death had impacted me, it hadn't stopped the world from spinning, and the college's career center continued messaging me about potential job opportunities and four-year universities to apply to.

I marked all their emails as read, without opening a single one.

Few notifications remained now. Most were from the games I had installed or notifying me of someone liking one of my social media posts, or following my photography account on Instagram. They, too, were quickly dismissed. Unlike the text from Zara, which was immediately opened. I hadn't heard from her since the day before I left Miami, when I'd begged her to reconsider staying in the city. Of course, my pleas did nothing and resulted in radio silence. I suppose calling her daddy a raggedy liar had earned her ire. Which, in retrospect, I understood, even if my words were true.

Zara: Hey. U okay?

A smile spread across my face at the simple question. Whenever we argued, once her anger fled, that was the inquiry she used to break the tension. It hadn't always been appreciated, but now, it was greatly cherished.

I gnawed on my bottom lip as I sent the text, then glanced at the clock. Twelve minutes had passed, and the smell of breakfast was growing stronger. Mama would be calling me soon.

My hope crashed and burned. Though he was at fault, he never forgave Mama for leaving him. If Zara's attendance depended on his approval, she would be unfortunately absent.

Another reason to hate Mr. Roman Leston.

I didn't say that to her, though. We'd just gotten back on speaking terms, so I wouldn't destroy the uneasy peace.

Just like that, the conversation ended. I contented myself to playing the latest mobile game I downloaded, an infuriating screw game. Winning should've been simple. Collect all the screws, sorting them into the properly colored box. In practice, it was a motherfucker to win, with microtransactions the easiest path to victory. I refused to spend a dime, resulting in many headaches.

Before I could raise my blood pressure, my mama's voice rang out, two minutes before my alarm was due to sound.

"Kamika, breakfast!" she yelled.

"Okay," I called back, standing from the bed and slipping into my house shoes.

As I headed to the living space to start my day, my weird ass nightmare crept back into my mind. I willed the dream to be forgotten and prayed I wouldn't have another one anytime soon.

And yet, something told me that my prayers wouldn't be answered.

Kamika

Grandma's intrusion on my sleep prevented me from feeling rested. Midway through the day, I started to crash. Over the last couple of days, while Mama dealt with the documents, I cooked and cleaned. I didn't want her to put too much on her plate, and to be of use, I needed energy. Coffee hadn't done the trick, so I set out to *Jayson's Food Mart* to buy an energy drink. Additionally, we lacked the ingredients for Alfredo sauce, which needed to be rectified if I were to prepare my planned dinner of shrimp pasta, garlic bread, and a modest garden salad.

"Kamika," Jayce greeted as I entered the store, offering me a small smile and a wave. "How you doing, girl?"

He sounded humorously like his father, and I suppressed a giggle. Smart kid that Jayce was, he picked up on my amusement quickly, his grin growing. "Whatchu laughing at?"

"You," I said without hesitation, walking to the empty counter. "You're too young to sound so old."

The store wasn't crowded today, so I saw no harm in spending time with him. In the grand scheme of things, he wasn't that much younger than me. When I babysat for his family, I was more lenient with him than I was with his brothers, leading to many banter-filled conversations as Avery and Reese snoozed. Nostalgia drove me to do the same thing once more.

"Mature," he corrected, drawing himself up taller. "And I got to. I can't sound like a lil' boy when talking to an older lady."

Ouch.

He made me sound as if I were my Mama's age.

"I'm twenty, not middle-aged," I grouched, stepping away from the check-out station.

He held his hands up as if surrendering. "Ay, I don't mean it as an insult, Kamika. Just that I need to carry myself in a certain way to impress you."

If it wasn't for his shit-eating grin, I'd think he was flirting with me. Instead, I recognized it as teasing, and a way to cover his ass. Still, I played along.

"I'm still too grown for you, lil' boy."

He dropped his arms. "Age ain't nothing but a number."

"And jail ain't nothing but a place, huh?" I rebuked, grabbing one of the nearby abandoned shopping baskets.

He nodded in agreement, chuckling. "Exactly."

I rolled my eyes, but I couldn't stop my own laughter from bubbling up. "Boy, bye. Let me shop in peace."

"Alright. I'll be here when you need me."

The end of our conversation was perfectly timed, because as I wheeled my cart away, another customer walked into the store. I recognized the elderly woman as an attendee of the local church and one of the mourners at Grandma's funeral. I couldn't recall her name, and the look she gave me made me disinterested in asking. So, I went on my merry way and picked up what I needed. My list was small. An energy drink, half-and-half—which was also used for coffee—Italian-blend cheese, shrimp, fettuccine, and garlic bread. We weren't in short supply of seasoning, so when those five items were in my basket, I carried them back to the counter. The old woman wasn't in sight, and no other customer was in line.

"Welcome back," Jayce greeted, getting to work as soon as I set the basket on the counter. He held up the Mango Lemonade *Celsius*, nodding in approval. "Good choice."

"It's the best flavor," I said simply, the vibrating of my phone drawing my attention away.

Out of the corner of my eye, I saw him frown as I pulled out the device, but I paid him no mind. Larissa's message was my focus.

Rissy: Not giving up 'til you come over

I finally got around to changing Larissa's contact name, opting to save her under the moniker I gave her when we were dating. But not even sweet memories dulled my annoyance. After her husband nearly caused a scene, she was still insisting I come over. Maybe he hadn't told her I was on a date, but certainly, my absence from Magnolia Mist should send a clear message. Then again, Larissa was nothing if not persistent. When she set her mind to something, she didn't stop until she had it done. And right now, her mind was hyper-focused on setting me and Delaney up.

Admittedly, I was curious and ducking her was growing tiring. My pride was the only thing that stopped me from accepting, and the fact that I seemed to have greener pastures in the form of Beau. Unfortunately, he'd dropped out of sight, reigniting my spark of attraction to Delaney.

Perhaps, going over wouldn't be so bad. If things were too awkward, I'd leave. And if I saw Jack, I could ask him if he was out of his goddamn mind fucking with my date.

"Your total is $22.37," Jayce announced, breaking into my contemplation.

"Alright," I muttered.

Before I could talk myself out of it, I shot Larissa a text, asking if it'd be okay if I came over after dinner. I ignored my phone while I paid, even if my heart leapt when it vibrated again. Still, I waited until I said my goodbyes and carried my groceries to the car. Only when I was in the driver's seat did I take a moment to see what she said.

> Rissy: That works!

> Rissy: Can't wait :)

I told myself her response didn't matter, pretending that the addition of the smiley face didn't lift my mood. I tried convincing myself that I was only going out of boredom, and to confront Jack. Yet, even as I drove away from the food mart, my small grin remained, betraying my true feelings.

Thank God no one was around to call me out on it.

If there was one thing I adored about my grandmother's house, it was the hallway of built-in bookshelves. When I was around four, she transformed it into a cozy reading nook, the wooden shelves framing the doors. As a little girl, the day would conclude with me, Mama, and Grandma huddling on the couch and reading a storybook.

Years later, it looked much the same, making me reminisce about better times. Times when I thought I'd found the love of my life at the tender age of sixteen. Times before I fell out with my grandmother and death took her, when she still loved me dearly and always had my back.

"Mama, I'm about to go," I announced, strolling into the living space, where my mother was still on the couch.

The News was on again, and the anchor was droning on about another missing college student. I spared the broadcast a glance, but I focused on Mama. She took her duty of sorting out my grandmother's unfinished business very seriously. As the days dragged on, she spent more time glued to that couch, a document of some sort in her hand. After dinner, I cleaned up my mess, then went to freshen up, while she returned to the papers.

"Ma, you heard me?" I questioned when she didn't respond.

She snapped her head toward me and nodded. "Yeah, baby."

Back to reading she went, with no additional questions. No inquiring about my destination or who I was meeting. No asking when I'd return or what I'd do. None of her typical questions. My brows furrowed.

"Have fun."

"Yeah...I will. I'll be at Larissa's," I said, tugging my sneakers on and awaiting her reaction to that piece of information.

I expected my announcement to spawn some questions, a warning that we'd have a discussion later. It didn't.

Instead, she murmured, "Be careful," indicating she was only half listening.

I bit back a sigh at her atypical behavior but cut the conversation. Throwing out, "Love you," over my shoulder, I began my journey to the Harris's property. I was starting to miss my regular walks, so I forwent the car and decided to travel there on foot. The heat was countered by a pleasant breeze, and with music flowing through my headphones, I arrived there before I'd even realized it.

Me: Just got here. See you in a sec

With my arrival announced, I saw no harm in climbing the fence instead of waiting for someone to open the gate. A pathway made navigating between the many buildings a breeze, most of which Larissa hadn't let me see. The greenhouse, the gazebo, and her house were the only places I'd been allowed to venture to. When I thought she and I would be together forever, I vowed to discover what secrets the family was hiding. That hadn't happened, so some things would forever remain a mystery. Larissa's home was easy to find. When I was with her, I only saw her and her mother. Her father had died years prior, and the cousins who'd stayed in the many spare rooms never made themselves known.

But, as Jack emerged from the house, I was forced to reconcile with the fact that her husband and children had joined the fray.

Out of sight, I could forget about how fast she moved on. Gazing upon her husband, holding a tanned toddler with curly blonde hair, that was impossible. Most of the little girl's facial features resembled Jack's, but her deep brown eyes were a carbon copy of Larissa's. Without asking, I knew who she belonged to.

Internally, I groaned. I didn't feel like dealing with his bullshit or unpacking the way my gut twisted at the sight of a child, the perfect mix of both her parents. The bone I had to pick with him needed resolving, but arguing in front of a child felt tactless. So, I opted to ignore him, and with it, my supposed reason for coming over fell apart.

If Beau hadn't been in the picture, I likely would've folded sooner, even with my reservations about Delaney and dislike toward Jack.

"Hello to you, too," he muttered as he passed me, making me freeze before I ascended the steps.

"I have nothing to say to you," I replied coolly, leveling a glare at him, my resolve to pretend he didn't exist crumbling.

He paused, bouncing the toddler as he glanced at me. "Your date had awful energy. You should thank me for—"

"For jackshit," I hissed before I could stop myself. The girl gasped; Jack's eyes narrowed. I ignored them both. "Don't act concerned. It wasn't any of your business."

"I, personally, don't care what you do. But Larissa does, and Delaney—"

"Doesn't know me, so interfering on her behalf isn't justification."

"Papa, Dex," the little girl demanded, squirming in his arms.

Hearing her voice broke through my haze of anger. I took a breath to calm down. Jack's gaze softened as he glanced at his daughter, and he nodded.

"We're going, baby girl," he cooed, a soft smile gracing his face. "Daddy's just talking with Mommy's friend."

"Kamika," a husky voice greeted, instantly grabbing my attention.

I peered over my shoulder, observing Delaney and Larissa bounding down the stairs of the porch. Larissa glided to her family, while her cousin stopped feet away from me. She smiled, lighting up her face.

"I'm happy you came," she said, her raspy voice melting my insides. "Finally giving me a chance to make up for my bullshit."

Thoughts of Larissa flew from my head as I focused on her cousin, taller, toner, and more seductive, for a reason I couldn't put my finger on.

"Hi, Delaney," I murmured, cringing at my breathlessness.

My panting embarrassed me, but fuck, the woman was gorgeous. Her long legs were endless, smooth perfection that she showed off in a short, red romper. It clung to her figure, and the neckline scooped low, revealing her cleavage. I cleared my throat and refocused on her face, reminding myself that looks meant nothing. A pretty package could conceal a lot of ugliness.

"I had nothing better to do," I said once I got a hold of myself.

"Well, hopefully we can entertain you," she replied, her face falling ever so slightly, even as her smile remained pasted on.

Jack cleared his throat, recapturing my attention. All eyes turned to him. I cocked a brow, awaiting to see what bullshit he'd spew now. He took a breath and offered a sheepish smile. "I'd like to apologize for my behavior at the restaurant, and you're grandmother's wake. It was...inexcusable. For everyone's sake, I'd like to start anew."

Well, I'll be damned.

I was tempted to look up, to see if airplanes were falling out of the sky, or if the blue of the atmosphere had changed color. But nope, everything was as it should be. Seeing Larissa's nod of approval, I realized she'd said something to coax the apology out of him. It was still too soon to forget his behavior, but he'd extended the olive branch, coerced or not. If I didn't accept it, I'd look like a messy, vindictive bitch.

I swallowed my feelings and smiled. "Apology accepted."

He sighed in relief. "Truly, I am sorry. I'd like us to start over, if possible."

Mentally, I chanted the old adage, *forgive but don't forget*, and nodded. "Of course."

"Okay, that's done, let's go inside," Delaney said, grabbing my wrist and tugging me up the steps.

I squeaked, and Larissa groaned. Delaney paused, and she looked at me sheepishly. Her hand fell away.

"Uh, sorry," she muttered. "Bad habit."

"Extremely bad," Larissa chided, appearing behind us. She took a second to wave to her daughter and Jack. "Have fun at Dex's, Shay!"

"Okay, Mommy!"

The sweet reply made me smile. I wasn't around many children, so the little beasts made me anxious, but it was hard not to soften at their cuteness.

When they disappeared from sight, Larissa walked into the house. Delaney spared me a glance, then followed her. I fell into pace, looking around the house that I'd once spent so much time in. Her entire home had a rustic feel, both the walls and the floors being made of wood. Family pictures hung in the hallway that connected the living room and foyer, showcasing happy memories for any guests to see. A right turn led us to an archway and into the living room. Delaney headed for the couch, plopping down and grabbing the remote. I sat to her right, and Larissa sat to her left, sandwiching her between us. Despite the couch's absurdly large size, the three of us huddled together.

Not that I was complaining. In fact, a teensy, weensy part of me wished I were the one in the middle.

The silence echoed as Delaney tried to connect to a streaming service, her frustration becoming evident with each failed attempt.

"Your shit won't connect," she grouched.

"What do you mean?" Larissa demanded. "Jack and I just watched our show last night."

Our show. I bit the inside of my cheek to prevent a frown.

"You're literally watching me trying to connect my account," Delaney said. "And I can't. The QR code won't work. When I try to log in on my phone, it says the account doesn't exist. That's bullshit. It's your fucked-up internet."

"It's your fucked-up phone," Larissa retorted. She snatched the remote. "Girl, give me this shit and go sit down somewhere."

"I'm already sitting down," she huffed, crossing her arms and sulking like a child.

The imagery of the strong, seductive woman doing something so juvenile made me giggle. Her annoyance melted away, and she turned her stunning gaze to me, smirking.

"Something funny?"

"Your reaction," I replied.

Her smile grew, and I found my own lips twitching upwards.

Those cat-like brown eyes assessed me, even when she addressed her cousin. "Hey, Rissa. Kamika's our guest. Once you connect, let her choose the movie."

Less than a minute later, Larissa sat back down and handed me the remote.

"What do y'all want to watch?" I asked, half-heartedly flicking through some films.

"We're letting you choose, remember?" Delaney responded.

"Whatever you choose is good, Kami," Larissa added.

With a nod, I began scouring the platform. As I searched, little was said, the two giving their phones their undivided attention. A peek revealed that Delaney scrolled through social media, while the music coming from Larissa's phone hinted she was playing a mobile game.

"You can turn the music down, y'know," Delaney said, not tearing her eyes away from her device.

"Girl, it isn't that loud," Larissa replied with a huff, but ever the diplomat, she lowered the volume. "Happy now?"

"Overjoyed," Delaney quipped.

The exchange made me smile, and by the time they quieted down, I'd found my movie.

"Okay," I announced, capturing both of their attention.

They cast their phones aside and then looked up at the screen. Frowns spread across their faces, and two sets of eyes glared at me.

"No," Larissa and Delaney chorused, staring at me in disgust.

"C'mon, they're classics," I protested with a pout,

My dramatics earned an eye roll from Larissa and a snort from Delaney.

"Did you just call *Twilight* a classic?" she asked, outrage and amusement mixing.

"It was literally a cultural reset," I reminded Delaney, the slight annoyance in her tone taking me aback.

Less than twenty minutes in her presence, she'd already earned a strike against her for not liking a movie that defined my childhood. It may not have been a pinnacle of cinema, but that didn't stop the franchise from holding a soft spot in my heart.

"It's literally ass," Delaney shot back, her grin broadening as my pout grew. She patted my clothed knee and gave me a look of faux sympathy. "There, there, the truth can be a hard pill to swallow."

She squeezed my knee, garnering my undivided attention. Her hand lingered for a second before she returned it to her lap. Larissa used the opportunity to attempt to pry the remote from my hand. Delaney scooted closer to me while I tightened my grip on the device. She sent a nasty glare her cousin's way, using her body to shield me from her.

"Sorry," Larissa murmured, shrinking away.

Odd, but I wouldn't question the defense on my claim to the remote.

"I'm a guest! Don't you want to be an excellent hostess?"

"And be tortured?" Larissa questioned. "No, thanks."

"Stop being dramatic. We used to watch them all the time!"

Delaney frowned. "You did?"

Larissa shot me a look, and I smirked. Guess she didn't like being exposed as a fangirl.

"Yes, and she never complained then," I said in a smug voice.

"Yeah, yeah, whatever," Larissa grumbled.

Delaney sighed, slinging an arm over my shoulder. Since I arrived, she'd made sure to touch me in some way. Though forward, I wouldn't complain. I knew what I was getting into when I agreed to come over. Essentially, it was a date that Larissa was monitoring to make sure nothing went awry. At that thought, Beau's handsome face flickered through my mind. Maybe I was fickle and too eager for a companion, but I saw nothing wrong with playing the field, allowing me to feel little guilt at entertaining another suitor.

"Put the damn movie on. *Now!*"

The moment the movie's opening rolled, Delaney released a deep sigh.

"Hush," I ordered, my gaze glued to the screen.

"How can I?" Delaney protested. "I pride myself on never finishing this series."

I bit back a laugh. "It isn't that bad," I admonished her dramatics, turning to her cousin. "Tell her, Rissy."

Larissa leaned forward to glare at me. "I used to think so. Edward *was* hot, but I'm a grown-ass woman now. He's two thousand ten years old and jonesing for a child!"

Valid point, but I refused to admit that aloud.

"Fuck off," I huffed, glaring at the two women. "Edward was born in the late 1800s, forever frozen in time. Technically, seventeen, too. And he just...had poor social skills."

The cousins stared at each other before they broke into peals of laughter. The sound sent shivers down my spine, my body responding to the amusement of both women. It was music to my ears.

My attraction to them didn't take away my offense, however. I elbowed Delaney and reached over to slap Larissa. They laughed harder at my violence.

"I hate you both!" I yelled, but their amusement was contagious, and I joined in their delight.

At one time, I would've been too up in arms about the franchise to join in on the fun. Now, I knew it wasn't that serious, and that their disdain for the movies didn't take away my love for them.

"Do you really still like *Twilight*?" Larissa demanded when our chuckles died down.

I nodded. "Nostalgia's a bitch. Underneath everything, I'm a romantic. I believe in true love, soul mates, and all that bullshit."

"True love? Edward liked her because she was 'different.' If she were a regular human, he wouldn't have looked at her twice," Larissa pointed out.

I flipped her off, though I couldn't argue her point. The books supported Larissa's theory. She'd just completely brushed off the great romance.

"Do you believe in imprinting?" Delaney demanded.

I stared at her, because, fuck, what a weird question. Her bewildering intensity made it sound as if *she* believed it to be true. Some of my hesitation toward her returned, though not enough for me to recoil from her touch.

"The werewolves?" she questioned when I remained silent.

She sounded...*vexed*. I was missing something. But people were passionate about the series. It was either loved or hated. There was rarely an in-between. I took a moment to consider her question, pushing aside the alarm bells ringing in the back of my mind. In theory, the notion of fate taking care of everything seemed fantastic. I glanced at Larissa. A time ago, I was convinced we were made for each other, but that notion had proven to be very incorrect. Something so romantic didn't exist in real life, and the examples the series provided weren't ideal.

Finally, I nodded. "I mean, I don't think it's weird, though *some* of the imprinting has become weird as fuck now that I'm older. But a mate for life sounds cool as shit. Dating would be easy if forces beyond our control could decide for us. You'd instinctively know who's right, and who's wrong."

"Theoretical compatibility doesn't mean you're meant to be together forever," Larissa inserted, making me frown at her.

Perhaps I was reading too much into it. However, it felt personal, like a rejection of me. Most likely, it was. Year after year of spending my summers here—and with Larissa—meant she knew me well.

"Let me tell you how dumb those movies are," Delaney said before I replied. She leaned forward and turned toward me. "First," she started, ticking off a finger, "werewolves don't have telepathy. They can't hear each other's conversations."

I snapped my brows together. They weren't real, so I didn't understand the level of conviction in her words. For argument's sake, however... "Those do."

"Second," she said, slapping another finger with undue force and ignoring me, "werewolves don't need vampires to trigger transformation. Third, werewolves aren't only male—"

"Leah wasn't male," I cut in, triumphant.

"Leah was an anomaly," Delaney retorted. "Remember?"

Larissa elbowed her cousin, and the two of them shared another look beyond my understanding. Delaney's weirdness had rubbed off on her cousin, and left me confused. True, *Twilight* werewolves were unique from most other depictions of the creatures, but that was a part of their charm. And, at the end of the day, it was fiction, so creative liberties need not be taken so seriously.

Begrudgingly, I had to admit I was enjoying myself. Being around them was comforting, and bantering came naturally. That kept me glued to my seat, even with their...quirks.

"Fuck those fake ass werewolves," Larissa announced. "My issue is with the vampire and his interest in a child."

"So was he!" I fumed, before sagging. "Kinda..."

"You don't even believe that shit! That motherfucker was like a hundred-fifty," Delaney said, laughing. "Worse than a centenarian. Just an old ass motherfucker. Viagra won't even help him."

I couldn't help but cackle, even as a shudder ran through me. "I don't want to think about his dick! Just watch *Twilight* as a comedy for a better time."

"Isn't it?" Delaney questioned, snickering when I stuck my tongue out at her. Then she bopped my nose.

I blinked at her in surprise.

"You're too cute."

Her arm tightened around me. Somehow, she pulled me closer, and her earthy, citrusy scent engulfed me. A part of my mind screamed to pull away, but my body melted against hers. I felt contented, as if I was embracing a cherished person I'd known for years, and not a weird woman I'd known for less than two weeks.

Was I really so fucking touch starved?

Yes, yes, I was, because I snuggled closer and started the movie, looking forward to spending the next two hours in her arms. I'd dissect my emotions later, but for now, I'd enjoy the film and the company around me.

Delaney

Soon after the movie ended, Kamika decided it was time for her to go. It filled Delaney with disappointment, because she wasn't ready to leave her presence. So, being the sweetheart she was, and to protect her from the bloodsuckers lurking, she offered to walk Kamika home. Though she'd thawed considerably, Delaney halfway expected her to shoot her down. Instead, she'd simply said, "Okay". The word had never sounded so sweet, and Delaney was hot on her heels as they exited the wooden mansion.

"You live across town, right?" Delaney asked before she could think better of it.

As far as Kamika knew, Delaney had never been to her place. She worried the slip-up would freak Kamika out. When she side-eyed her, she feared she was cooked.

"Larissa told you?" Kamika questioned.

Delaney nodded and breathed a sigh of relief as an out was given. "And I knew your grandmother. I'm sorry for your loss, by the way."

Correction, she'd known *of* Susanne, but she couldn't recall even speaking five words to the woman during her life. However, the old lady wasn't around to call her out, so she saw no harm in the white lie.

Kamika stiffened, and she realized just how insincere her offer of condolences sounded. Delaney cleared her throat, and her mind scrambled to assemble a sentence that didn't seem quite so callous.

"I...I didn't know her very well, and know jackshit about y'all's relationship. But losing a loved one is never easy," Delaney said, having firsthand knowledge of the words she spoke.

Her father had thought she was a dreamer who lacked discipline, while her mother had thought her too unstudious and unruly. Her relationship with both had been strained, but when they passed, it felt like she'd lost a part of herself.

As the silence stretched on, Delaney made the snap decision to open up to Kamika. If she wanted things to progress with her mate, she would have to take the first steps to make up for the damage she'd done.

"When my parents died, everything felt off kilter," she revealed, her heart lurching when she heard Kamika's soft gasp. "I'm not the best at offering advice, and we're basically strangers, but if you ever need to talk, you know where to find me."

More silence. For a moment, she worried she'd reopened an old wound for nothing. But then, a reply finally came. As soon as Kamika spoke, Delaney gave her undivided attention.

"I get what you mean," she said quietly, staring ahead as they finally made it off the sprawling property. "My grandmother and I haven't been close for years, but knowing that she's gone…it's weird. I felt the same way about my father for a long time. I don't have many memories about him, but after his death, it took a while for things to feel right again."

The sadness Delaney sensed in Kamika mirrored her own. They'd finally found common ground. Unfortunately, it was morbid, and a pretty fucked up thing to share with somebody. But, hey, on the bright side, it gave them the chance to have a proper conversation.

Just the two of them, with no third party to interrupt their bonding.

"I don't remember much about my parents either," Delaney revealed, forcing the words out. "I was ten, and I think the trauma of losing them at such an early age blocked out all my memories."

Even fourteen years later, the mere thought of them sent waves of grief through her. However, Kamika needed to know her history before she forged a proper future. Delaney knew Kamika wasn't ready to hear that they were fated to be together, and she especially wouldn't want to hear about the mate bond. Or how Delaney felt as if a bolt of lightning shot from the sky and electrified her body the moment she saw Kamika. To the pack and to her, Kamika was her fate, her mate, and she'd see her as such from here on out. Hopefully, it didn't end in Kamika's rejection and Delaney's broken heart.

Kamika turned to Delaney. "I'm so sorry," she said softly, taking Delaney's hand in hers and squeezing gently. Although she released her just as quickly, Delaney felt Kamika's brief touch to the depths of her soul. "If it's too hard to discuss, I understand. Despite everything, my grandmother's death is still so painful for me, and I don't know what I'd do if I lost my mother."

Delaney nodded. Kamika seemed almost too perfect to be true. She had a valid reason to be wary of her and to keep the wall she'd erected between them up. Yet there she stood, sincere in her concern.

She started off again, so Delaney did, too. She'd never been good with emotions. It was one reason she'd fought with Toria so often. Big-girl talks were neither of their strong suits. She needed to change the direction of the evening, lighten the mood that felt so heavy.

"Vampire or werewolves?" Delaney asked.

Grinning, Kamika sidled a glance at Delaney. "I already told you I was Team Edward. Surely, you can read between the lines."

"You like Edward in the movies, but what about in other cases?"

She huffed out a laugh. "Well, they don't exactly exist in real life for me to have another reference."

Right. In Kamika's world, supernaturals didn't exist.

"Pretend they do," Delaney insisted. "Or better yet, reference other depictions of them, because there are many, and most have something in common."

What's seen in the modern era is based on folklore dating back centuries. What's now dismissed as oral tales were often real eye-witness accounts. Aka, they were steeped in some truth. Even *Twilight* didn't get everything wrong, though Delaney rued to admit it.

"I would say if Edward were a werewolf, then I'd like werewolves," Kamika announced after a moment of consideration, making Delaney groan.

What the fuck was so great about that pale, sparkling white man, anyway?

"Disqualified!" Delaney chortled, easily covering up her twinge of jealous annoyance. "You're telling me you like the dude, not the species. I am specifically asking you to take yourself out of that damn movie, and then answer me."

"Vampires?"

Delaney laughed again. "If you have to question me, then you aren't sure."

"Here's the thing. Vampires are cold and dead—"

"Undead."

Kamika ignored her and continued without missing a beat. "Werewolves are people who turn into overgrown, psychopathic canines."

Ouch.

Certainly, there were kinder ways to summarize her species.

"That's a little harsh," Delaney grouched, her lip nearly protruding into a pout.

Kamika shrugged. "I guess I don't like one more than the other."

Delaney supposed that was the best she was getting out of her, and she wouldn't push the issue further when she was finally making progress. Per the old adage, she'd quit while she was ahead.

A new question popped into her head, one she wasn't quite so passionate about. "Cats or dogs?"

Delaney, personally, didn't have a favorite, but she was curious to hear which fluffy creature had captured Kamika's heart.

"Birds," she replied after a second of deliberation.

Huh.

"Birds?" Delaney repeated, her brows furrowing. "That wasn't one of the options."

"No, but I love parrots," Kamika explained, a small smile playing at her lips. "A hyacinth macaw, to be specific, but it'd need a lot of space. Plus, they can cost $10,000."

"Goddamn!" Delaney exclaimed, the thought of spending so much money for any pet mind boggling. "Why are they so fucking expensive?"

Kamika tittered at her reaction. "They're endangered, for one, so you'll need a wildlife license in a lot of areas. They're also difficult to breed on mass, and they have high maintenance cost. And because they have so many desirable pet traits, they're in high demand, so the few available get snatched up quickly."

Delaney nodded along, storing all the information away. She was fortunate enough for $10,000 dollars to barely make a dent in any of her accounts. Once the bond was solidified, that boujee ass bird would be gifted to Kamika.

"Sounds like you've done your research."

"More than I should, considering I'll probably never own one," she replied, strengthening Delaney's resolve to one day get her that bird. "But, to answer your original question, both cats and dogs are cool with me. They're both cute, and have their ups and downs, so I don't have a favorite."

Well, there was another, less grim thing they had in common. Dogs were more practical for her kind to own, because felines were often spoked by their wolf forms. For a long time, she thought herself a dog person for that reason. However, she'd grown fond of Toria's cat, and missed the sweet ragdoll more than she did the woman.

"Same here, but the only pet I've owned was a Golden Retriever when I was a kid," Delaney said. "After Zuzu died, I kind of swore off pets."

Gloom crept back in at the thought, but she quickly shoved it away, refusing to bring the mood down when she was making such great progress. Kamika didn't seem to pick up on the dip in her mood, going on chatting merrily.

"I get what you mean. My grandma used to have this adorable King Charles Spaniel named Honcho. I only saw him during the summers, but I was crushed when she told me she had to put him down."

"The death of a pet is so devasting," Delaney agreed.

"Yep. It's why I started wanting a macaw, because they live so long. Fifty years in the wild, up to seventy-five years in captivity."

That certainly increased their appeal. It'd be bullshit if you dropped ten bands on an animal, just for it to die in a decade or less.

"Have you ever owned a bird before?" she asked, eager to get off the subject of death.

"My Mama got me a budgerigar parrot for my tenth birthday." A fond smile graced Kamika's pretty face. "I named her Tweety, because I used to love *Looney Tunes*. It was why I started wanting a pet bird. I was ecstatic when I got her. She was so chirpy, and a sweetie. I cried for weeks after she died when I was seventeen, because they only live up to ten years. Mama and Zara, my sister, were upset, too, because they took care of her during the summers."

Well, so much for a happier topic.

"I'm sorry," Delaney stated, unsure of what else could be said.

Kamika shrugged. "Don't be. It happened a while ago."

Delaney didn't know what to say, so her future mate's simple reply led to another bout of silence, one that was broken minutes later by Kamika.

"What was your major, by the way? Larissa told me you graduated recently, so…" she said, trailing off as she awaited an answer.

Delaney could've jumped for joy. Kamika was showing an interest in her, small as it was. Never did she think small talk could bring her so much happiness.

"Art history," she replied, applauding herself for how composed she sounded. "With a minor in Civil Engineering, and a couple of certificates."

"What are the certificates?"

"Electrical engineering and environmental management and resilience."

Kamika's low whistle made her puff her chest out. "Impressive. Sounds like you'll be making a lot of money one day."

Ha.

If only.

While the pack didn't struggle, payment wasn't given for the jobs done. Everyone had a role to play to keep things running smoothly, so earning money was an unlikely reward.

But, she couldn't reveal such dynamics to Kamika, so instead, she said, "Yeah. What about you?"

"I have a Pre-Bachelor of Arts. I want to open my own photography studio one day," she revealed.

Knowing that they both had creative interests brought a smile to Delaney's face. The more they talked, the more she discovered they had in common. She could only hope that Kamika was noting the same thing, and that it was earning her some brownie points.

"Pre-Bachelor...you planning to get a bachelor's degree, then?"

"I'm thinking of getting a degree in educational studies, just for a backup plan. I wouldn't mind being an elementary art teacher, if all else fails," she said, the way she deflated contradicting her words.

For the sake of keeping things simple, Delaney pretended not to notice it. "A backup plan is smart."

"Yeah."

Delaney admired Kamika's practicality, but it was obvious her heart didn't lie with teaching. If that was the case, a career dealing with snot-nosed brats would make her miserable.

No matter.

Once she claimed her, she'd be free to pursue her passion.

The pack job may not come with a salary, but the Harrises were sitting on a pretty penny. Thanks to her grandparents, Delaney would inherit a nice chunk of cash. They'd died well before she was eighteen, but the caveats in their will meant she'd only received a small portion of her inheritance. However, once she turned twenty-five next year, it'd be fully accessible to her. She'd happily fund Kamika's dreams, and if all worked out, it'd prove to be a wise investment.

Before she knew it, the blue shotgun was in sight, marking the end of their journey. Delaney would be a lying heifer if she said it didn't disappoint her. The day had been a dream, all because Kamika had been by her side for a decent portion of it.

"Today was fun," Delaney said as they approached the house, silently vowing to harass Larissa until Kamika accepted another invitation.

She would ask for Kamika's number, but she didn't want to be too pushy. So, as much as she hated having to rely on her cousin to communicate with her mate, she'd make do until their relationship had progressed.

"It was," Kamika agreed, bringing a smile to Delaney's face. "Even if you have bad taste in movies."

She chuckled, shaking her head. "That'd be you."

Kamika joined in on the laughter, the sound of her giggles the sweetest chime Delaney had ever heard. "Whatever. I'll see you soon."

With that, Kamika climbed the steps and unlocked the door, disappearing into her house without a second glance. Her parting words shocked Delaney too much to say anything else, because it meant that finally, Kamika had overcome her reservations, enough so to consider seeing her again.

If that was the results of opening up, Delaney needed to do that shit a bit more often.

She lingered for some minutes, ensuring she didn't need to double back for anything and Kamika was safely inside. The sun was starting to set, and as orange and pink streaks started to outnumber the hints of blue, Delaney decided it was time to take her ass home. With one last glance, she turned on her heels and started walking the way she came. Her smile remained, and she couldn't wait to gush to Larissa about the progress made. Despite her cousin's past with her mate, she was more than supportive of Delaney's efforts to woo Kamika.

The girlishly cheerful mood was cut short by the sight of a black vintage Mustang, a car she was all too familiar with, and whose owner she despised.

Beau loved riding with his windows down, and when he drove by her, she was able to confirm that it was indeed him. He stopped at a red light, and she considered just walking past him, ignoring his existence. It's what she should've done, but the moment she heard him calling out to her, she was unable to be the bigger person.

"Still can't drive, huh, Delaney?" he said, the smirk on his face making her long to punch him.

She rued not taking a different path. Sidewalks were more convenient in human form, but they bordered roads, which wouldn't have been a problem if Beauden wasn't one of the drivers.

"Fuck off," she barked, stopping to glare at him.

The light was notoriously slow, giving her the time to get some things off her chest. She folded her arms, disgust slamming into her when his eyes flickered to her exposed legs. During the one job they worked together, he hadn't hidden his attraction to her, and was annoyingly persistent, even after she revealed she was gay. It was one reason among many that she disliked him, although leaving her to die definitely ranked at the top.

He tsked. "C'mon, girl, don't be like that."

"Refer to my previous answer. Oh, and by the way, you have one more time to fuck with

Kamika before I rip you to shreds," she hissed, uncaring that they were in a very public location.

The primitive urge to protect and attack stole Delaney's common sense, making it hard for her to remember what she'd be risking if she did attack him.

His smile faded, his onyx eyes narrowing into slits. "She isn't claimed, so you can't dictate her choices."

Yeah, but that was something she'd remedy soon enough. For now, she'd ignore how much his factual statement stung.

"She's under my family's protection, so I very much can."

He opened his mouth to say something else, but she wasn't interested in hearing it. So, she just powerwalked away to get away from the stoplight. She veered off path, heading into the patch of trees that surrounded Gaville's downtown, and led to her family's property, if you knew where to go. Looking around, she ensured no prying eyes were around, then began to undress. Her body was buzzing with anger, and she longed to go back and maul Beau. However, that wasn't possible, so she'd settle for working off some tension by shifting into wolf form and running back home. When her paws hit the ground, her jaws dug into the material of the red romper she'd been wearing, lifting it off the forest floor. Her cheap flip-flops would have to be left behind, but she could deal with that.

The dirt was cool, the trees serving as protection from the Louisiana sun. It helped chill her too-hot body. With a low growl, she broke into a sprint. The exhilarating run provided a primal release of frustration. The flora passed by in a blur of green, brown, and white, the scent of magnolias, wood, and earth filling her nostrils and calming her nerves. Her instincts guided her through familiar undergrowth, a shortcut only a special few were privy to. She slowed when she reached the edge of her family's land. Her adrenaline faded as she shook herself free of leaves and twigs, scattering them across the ground. The scent of Beau's cologne lingered in her nostrils, a bitter reminder of his presence and their confrontation. She vowed to deal with him later, but tonight, she'd focus on the weary contentment she felt at her progress with Kamika and share the good news with Larissa.

She wouldn't let that bloodsucker dampen her happiness, just as she'd do everything in her power to ensure he stayed the hell away from *her* mate.

June 11th

Kamika

As predicted, Zara wasn't able to make it down for Mama's birthday. She did, however, call our mother while we ate breakfast, an obvious source of joy for Mama. It set a good tone for the day, even though nothing would go as planned. Mama's 45th birthday was supposed to be a big deal. Before Grandma's death, I planned to treat her to a spa day with money I'd made doing some photography gigs, then take her to that blues bar she'd been wanting to go to for weeks. Giving her gifts had always been a challenge, since she insisted love was a sufficient present. I knew that was cap, as the one year I'd gotten her nothing, she'd been upset. So, this year, I decided to give her a gift card that'd allow her to purchase anything she wanted.

Luckily, I had the foresight to pack it with me, as well as a teddy bear that wore a pretty necklace meant for her, and a pop-up card I'd selected at the last minute. The gifts were the only thing present of the original plan, much to my disappointment. Still, I was determined to make it a good day for her.

"Zara's sending me a card," she announced as I returned from my bedroom, her attention on her phone while she finished her coffee.

"That's nice," I said, carrying the gift bag containing all her goodies.

She looked up. When she saw what I carried, she cast her phone aside and gulped the rest of the brew down, a smile spreading across her face. "Baby, you shouldn't have."

"You don't even know what I got you," I countered, setting the bag on the table. "Happy birthday, Mama."

"I told you to get me nothing, so this is already too much."

My wallet would've loved if her words were true.

"Mama, I appreciate the sentiment, but we both know you're disappointed whenever I don't get you gifts."

"You calling me a liar?" she asked with mock offense as she pulled the bag to her.

"Nope," I denied, reclaiming my chair and watching as she removed the gift paper. "Your expectations just don't match your words."

She snorted, pulling the teddy bear out. When she saw the bling it wore, a soft gasp left her. Gold leaf pendants extended from the chain, each one containing a small pearl in the middle, the birthstone of June.

"Oh, Kami, this is beautiful," she breathed, holding the necklace up to the light. "How much did you pay for this?"

I groaned. "I can't tell you the price of a present."

A guy from school had a not-so-secret crush on me, and he happened to work at the jewelry store closest to my house. Because of him, I got a discount on the piece, information I'd take to my grave.

"Well, however much it was, I love it," she said, placing the necklace back on the bear and pulling out the two envelopes.

The smaller one contained the gift card, and the larger one contained the birthday card. The latter made her laugh, while the former made her grin grow. When she was done, she returned everything to the empty bag and stood. Stopping by my chair, she wrapped her arms around my shoulders. I snuggled into her, pleased to know my gifts were sufficient.

"Thank you, sweetheart."

"You're welcome, Mama."

With one last squeeze, she pulled away.

"This was a good birthday," she said, collecting our breakfast dishes.

My brows furrowed, her words puzzling me. Unless my eyes were broken, it was only 11AM. Aka, plenty of hours left until the day ended. And while I'd try to give her a fantastic birthday, the verdict couldn't be decided until the clock struck midnight.

"Why are you speaking in the past tense? The day has just begun, Mama."

"I have a lot to do, honey," she explained, bringing the dishes over to the sink. "We'll celebrate my birthday when we return to Miami. Today, we'll treat it as any other day."

I frowned. True, there *was* a lot to be done. But if we planned to stay until Labor Day, we had months left to get everything in order before it was time to depart. There was no reason to skip celebrating my mother's birthday.

Unless, of course, she didn't want to.

It was possible Mama's heart wasn't in it, grief over her mother's death zapping away any joy. Yet, her body language said otherwise, and disappointment seeped from her words.

"Taking a break today won't kill you," I replied, making my way to the sink. Mama stepped back and lifted her brow, so I immediately took over the task of washing the dishes. "And no chores for you today. Birthday, remember?"

"I won't complain about that."

Mama returned to her phone, while I scrubbed the dishes that'd accumulated since last night. It wasn't much, but the five or so minutes it took me gave me enough time to come up with a convincing argument. Birthdays were always treated as a major deal by us, and to skip such an important one felt sacrilegious.

"We at least have to go out to dinner today," I declared as I dried off my hands. "We can't do nothing, and it'll be my treat."

She didn't look up from her phone, and for a moment, I worried she didn't hear me. Then, she nodded, glancing at me. "Alright, baby. We'll leave this evening, but until then, we'll proceed as normal. This house is a mess, and—"

"I understand," I said quickly, interrupting whatever spiel she was about to go on.

The doorbell ringing brought our conversation to an end. I strolled to the front door before Mama could stand, uncaring that my attire consisted of a headscarf, oversized sleep shirt, and ill-fitting plaid pajama pants. While Grandma's lawyer had yet to go over every detail of her will, he made it clear over a telephone call that the house was ours. Within it's walls, I could wear whatever I wanted, and anyone who had a problem could fuck off. However, when a look through the peephole revealed that Giselle stood on the other side, I rethought my stance. I'd never forget when she accused my twelve-year-old self of being 'fast' for daring to wear pajamas around her grown-ass brother. Grandma's response had been to laugh, something that pissed Mama off when I shared with her what occurred.

It's funny. When Grandma and I were close, all her good qualities took precedence in my mind. Only when she pushed me away did her many transgressions start flooding my memory, and now that she was dead, I didn't know how to feel about her.

"Who's there?" Mama called, prompting me to disengage the locks.

"Giselle," I replied, pasting on a grin as I opened the door. The bright envelope and cake she carried made it clear why she was here. So, instead of saying 'Hello,' I greeted her by saying, "She's in the kitchen."

"Thank you, baby," she said, bouncing into the house with an extra pep in her step.

I wondered if she and Mama had been talking without me realizing it, because I saw no other reason for her presence. Yet, today, I'd ignore the past. Unless she was here to stir up some bullshit, I wouldn't question someone celebrating my Mama's life.

"Amia, girl, happy birthday!" Giselle exclaimed when she caught sight of my mother. "Any big plans today?"

"Kamika is taking me to dinner," she said, gaze glued to Giselle's offering. "What's all this?"

"Girl, what does it look like? A gift and a cake," she answered with a chortle, setting the cake on the dining table and holding out the envelope. "Go on, open it."

Mama and I exchanged a brief look before she obeyed. Inside the envelope was a generic card, containing another gift card for fifty dollars, and a flyer promoting a band I'd never heard of called Acrylic Bayou. A close inspection revealed they were performing at Burnin' Boots Juke Joint, from 8-10 PM.

"My eldest son's band is putting on a show tonight, and I figured y'all would need something to do, so there it is," Giselle said, a satisfied smile on her face as if she'd done us a great favor.

Well, that explained her presence.

I couldn't begrudge her being a good mother and promoting her kid's music, though I could've done without the dig.

"We'll see if we can make it," Mama said, her tone not indicating her emotions.

"Y'all really should come; it'll be a blast," Giselle replied, gearing up to leave now that her task was complete. "Oh, and the cake is chocolate and vanilla swirl. I didn't know which y'all preferred."

Okay, that was actually thoughtful.

"All cake is fine by me," I chimed in, earning polite laughter from Mama and Giselle.

"Amen, girl," Giselle said.

She began walking to the door. My mother and I both trailed behind her. "I'll let you know if we're coming after dinner," Mama stated as Giselle stepped onto the porch.

"Okay, girl. Keep me posted."

"You wanna go?" I asked when we were alone again.

Admittedly, my interest was piqued. I loved concerts, but unlike Miami, Gaville didn't have the widest selection of musical acts or a venue suited for big acts. Whoever was playing at Burnin' Boots would have to do, and going to the juke joint could allow us to properly celebrate Mama's birthday.

"Like I said, I'll tell you after dinner. And you're free to go without me, even if I don't go."

"And deal with Giselle alone? Pass."

Mama chuckled, shaking her head. "Fair enough. It could be fun, but I don't know how tired I'll be."

I nodded, unable to deny the spark of excitement I felt. A night out could be exactly what we needed, even if it wasn't a part of the plan. But, I'd learned the best experiences tended to be the spontaneous ones, and after the emotional rollercoaster of the last few weeks, we both deserved a night to let loose and enjoy ourselves.

At Mama's behest, we spent the sunlight hours cleaning, as had become routine. Today, she allowed me to help her sort through the many, many things Grandma had left, instead of shooing me as usual. Once the afternoon sun began to dip below the horizon, I put a halt to things and escorted her to her bedroom to get ready. Before I retreated to my room, I picked out her outfit, a simple but elegant black jumpsuit that complemented her figure. When she wanted to, Mama could dress nicely, but often, she chose comfort over style. Both were important, so I made sure her outfit was comfy, but still looked nice. Likewise, I wore a pair of black split hem jeans, with a red backless high-neck halter top. Comfortable and cute. The extra-long tie made it appear as if I wore a scarf, and the color popped against my skin. Hoop earrings, minimal makeup, and comfortable wedges completed my look.

I looked damn good, if I did say so myself. Pictures would be a requirement.

"Well, look at you," Mama said when I emerged from my bedroom. "You look nice, Kami."

"Same to you," I replied, grinning when I caught sight of the necklace I gifted her.

As gorgeous as it was on the bear, it was stunning on her, the perfect addition to her outfit.

"Selfie?" I questioned, though I was already striding to her.

Obediently, she posed for a couple of photos with me. When she was ready to go, she just stepped out of view of the camera, a big enough hint for me to tuck my phone into my glittery clutch. By the time we made it to the car, the sun had set, the sea of stars lighting up the night sky. If there was one thing Gaville had Miami beat in, it was natural beauty. The relative ruralness of the area minimized light pollution, showing the brilliance of our atmosphere.

"Where are we going?" Mama asked as I drove through the streets of Gaville, the late hour minimizing traffic.

"Remember *Pasta Parish*? That Creole-Italian fusion place? There."

Italian was one of her favorite cuisines, and based on how her eyes lit up, I knew I'd chosen right.

Though the streets weren't crowded, finding a decent parking space was surprisingly difficult. After precious minutes of my life had gone down the drain, I found a spot. As we walked to the restaurant, jazz music flowed from the building. The cool air of the night felt amazing against my skin, and the many flowers planted around *Pasta Parish* gave the air a lovely floral smell. Inside, the live jazz band was nearly deafening but created a nice atmosphere. It was cozy, with dim lighting, classic Italian restaurant décor, and tantalizing smells. It'd undergone a renovation since I'd last been there, giving it a more boujee vibe than I remembered. I was just happy the place still accepted walk-ins. *La Mer* had great food, and would've been a sufficient backup, but I wanted to treat my mother to somewhere a tad nicer.

"*Benevenute*," the hostess greeted, a polite smile plastered on her face. "Table for two?"

"Yes. It's her birthday," I answered, gesturing to my mother, who rolled her eyes.

She hated her birthday announced at restaurants, as she hated the spectacle some made of it. I, however, would happily allow for some moments of attention for a free dessert, or even better, a discount.

"Oh, well, happy birthday," she said, grabbing two menus and stepping from behind the station "Follow me."

Once we were seated, it wasn't long before our waiter appeared, a middle-aged man who was nice but reserved. The loud music didn't allow for much conversation, but every now and then, Mama and I yelled to each other as we waited for our food to arrive. When it did, we weren't disappointed. As we neared the end of our meal, the contentment in her smile and relaxation in her shoulders made me feel triumphant. It was exactly what I had hoped for. Unfortunately for Mama, as we waited for the check to arrive. the jazz band caught wind that it was her birthday and performed a special rendition of 'Happy Birthday' just for her. I made sure to take a video and many pictures of the moment. The check came with two slices of cake. I gobbled my piece immediately, while Mama took hers to go. As we left the restaurant, I turned to Mama, happy to see her smile still present.

"That was...surprisingly lovely," Mama admitted, making me grin. "Even the birthday song."

"He had a nice voice," I said, nudging her with me elbow. "And he was into you."

She groaned. "Girl, he was just doing his damn job."

"Not the singing! The wink, and he literally told you to call him."

My argument didn't convince her. She shrugged and said, "Performers flirt for tips all the time."

Maybe it was unfair to treat Colton as the root of all evil, but I blamed him for her lack of confidence in herself. Attention from the male species wasn't the best indication of attractiveness, as famously, penis owners would stick their cocks anywhere. Yet, she received loads of it, and it went unnoticed. What her ex-husband had started, Colton finished. When her divorce was finalized eight years ago, she and Zara had stayed in Gaville the entire summer. She'd used him as a rebound, a temporary man to bounce back from Roman.

 But, instead of getting her confidence back, he destroyed it further.

"Agree to disagree," I finally said, deciding to change the subject. "Anyway, are we checking out the band, or calling it a night?"

She fell silent as she considered my questions, before nodding. "Why not? If they sound like shit, we'll just go home."

I giggled, her words amusing me to no end. "That's the spirit."

The atmosphere of Burnin' Boots was lively, the chatter of the patrons and the vibration of the music thrumming through me as we weaved through the crowd. Mama had called Giselle in the car, and she'd promised to meet us outside. Her vow had proven false, as she was nowhere to be seen. So, we just made our way to the bar to see if she'd pop up. Ten minutes before her kid's band was set to take the stage and twenty minutes after we arrived, we finally caught sight of her. Mama waved her over, and it was only when she arrived that I realized Colton was also accompanying her. It made sense that he'd come out to support his nephew, but the mere sight of him pissed me off. I kicked myself for not accounting for his presence and urging Mama to go home instead of coming here.

"Well, look at y'all!" Giselle shouted over the music, giving me and Mama brief hugs. "Y'all look so pretty."

Colton whistled lowly when he caught sight of Mama. "Damn right. You lookin' like a million bucks, girl."

Good Lord, how in the world did he ever pull my mother? Or any woman, with corny pick-up lines and the appeal of a wet sock. I didn't join in on the faux laughter Giselle and Mama offered. He needed to know he sucked.

"Thank y'all," Mama said politely, looking between the Samson siblings. "You two look nice yourselves."

"Why, thank you," Giselle replied, tugging at the collar of her wrap dress. "Got it at the thrift shop near my salon. They got some cute stuff. And Kamika, you can find a real shirt there."

Oh, that bitch.

"Her shirt is cute, Giselle, and you know you used to wear shit like that when you were younger," Mama said, her defense of me allowing to hold my tongue, though it was a challenge.

Instead of acknowledging Mama's words, she commanded her little brother to take us to our seats while she ordered drinks. He grabbed

Mama's wrist, and she grabbed mine, giving me a look of warning as we were lead to their table. Giselle's shady ass returned minutes later, taking a seat across from Mama.

"Okay, they'll bring our drinks in a minute. I got a beer for you," she said, gesturing to her brother, before waving her hand between her and Mama. "Wine for us, and a non-alcoholic Arnold Palmer for Kamika," she finished, flicking her wrist at me.

Huh. That was uncharacteristically sweet. I wonder if she poisoned it.

"Thank you, girl. I'll pay you back when we come to your book club," Mama said, making me frown.

Were we really going to spend hours around Giselle and her judgy ass friends, discussing a lame ass book?

She waved Mama off. "Girl, I'm a Christian, so I'm always happy to extend a hand to the less fortunate. I know things ain't easy for y'all right now, so don't even worry about paying me back."

Her words could've been misconstrued as generous, if not for her smug tone. But, seeing as she was covering our portion of the tab, I could overlook that. We weren't poor. We were frugal and loved a bargain.

As soon as our drinks were brought out, the act we came to see stepped onto the stage.

"What the fuck is up, everyone?" the lead singer, a pale guy with a finger mohawk, yelled. His words earned some shouts and hoots, making him grin. "Y'all ready to have fun tonight?"

More hollers. This time, Mama and Giselle joined in.

"We're Acrylic Bayou, and first up is our song, Dancing into the Abyss."

The singer had a gothier aesthetic than his bandmates. When he started to sing, it was evident that his unique vibe bled into their music, the way he screamed the lyrics not matching the instrumentals.

"Is this their first gig?" I asked. Their nerves were easy to see, and only the lead singer seemed prepared to engage with the crowd.

"Yep," Colton answered, then looked at his sister for confirmation. "Right?"

Giselle nodded, her gaze glued to the guitarist, who wasn't half bad. "That's my baby right there," she exclaimed, pointing to a lanky boy playing the guitar.

The band was kind of fire, and I was shocked at the level of skill. However, the singer seemed overconfident in his abilities and did best when he wasn't trying to burst the eardrums of the attendees.

"Go, Dayton!" Giselle shouted during her son's first guitar solo, which was, admittedly, the best part of the song.

The beats were a fusion of classic rock and blues, Dayton and the drummer syncing wonderfully to create a pleasant sound. Yet, their talent didn't take away the fact that Mohawk was a fucking migraine to hear. Two songs in, and I was ready to call it quits. Unlike the adults, who were chatting amongst themselves, I didn't have alcohol to wash my nerves.

"I'm going to the bathroom," I declared when I finished my Arnold Palmer, needing to flee to somewhere quiet.

"Okay, baby," Mama said half-heartedly, engrossed in whatever topic they were talking about.

My pounding headache prevented me from processing the words being tossed around. If Mama wasn't enjoying herself, I'd regret coming.

The small hallway that led to two bathrooms was tucked away, dulling some of the noise. Not completely, though, as even in the tiled bathroom, Mohawk's bad singing was audible. It dampened my intention to hide in there for a song or two, feigning a stomach bug to escape the ear abuse. The condition of the bathroom didn't help either. In their, the building's age was very evident. The water heater dominated most of the room, but it was easy to ignore when you took in the full bathroom. Holes and cracks were in the walls, evidence of water damage stained the ceiling and floors, and the plastic plant had a layer of grime that made it unappealing to look at. I did my business as fast as possible, then left the decrepit little room.

In my rush to exit the bathroom, I bumped into someone. The spicy, ambery scent flooded my nose and clued me into who it was. His hands grabbed my forearms, steadying me. When I pulled back, I found myself staring into Beau's eyes, confirming what I already knew.

"Hey," I said simply, tugging out of his arms.

He tsked when I turned to walk away, grabbing my wrist. "A hey is all I get?"

His cheek annoyed me to no end. I tugged my arm away, leveling him with a glare. "It's a greeting, isn't it? And more than you deserve, after you fucking ghosted me."

I hated how bothered I sounded, but unfortunately, it reflected how I felt. Things had been going well, and one little bump in the road was all it took for him to go MIA. It was possible he wasn't that into me, yet that thought only worsened the sting. Even if he'd left town–which clearly wasn't the case–there'd been no reason he couldn't have given me a text to notify me of his departure.

"I didn't ghost you," he argued, his perfect lips pursed into a frown. "I've just been…busy."

"Okay," I said simply, turning to walk away.

I had no claim on him, so I couldn't dictate how he spent his time. Moreover, if he couldn't make time for me on his vacation, then I wouldn't waste time on him.

"Kamika, c'mon—"

"It's no big deal, Beau. You're not into me, and that's okay. You don't owe me an explanation."

My words not only rang true, they gave me an air of maturity that, in truth, I didn't possess. I was under no illusion that Beau would ever be more than a short fling, but I'd been enjoying getting to know him. I thought the attraction was mutual, and knowing it wasn't came as a blow.

He scoffed, the sound grating on my frayed nerves. "So, you not even gonna give me a chance to explain?"

"What is there to explain?" I held up my hand before he could answer. "Look, I did not come here for this. It was nice seeing you, Beau."

"I'm not just here to fuck around, Kamika," he said, his annoyance palpable. "I have some business in Fleur, but it's cheaper to stay in Gaville."

I cocked a brow. "And you're telling me this...because?"

He huffed. "So you know I'm not blowing you off for nothing, damn."

I couldn't imagine what kept him so busy that he couldn't reply to my texts, when he'd clearly read them. Taking a couple of minutes out of your day to respond wasn't a monumental task.

"And what exactly are you building, Beau, that keeps you away from your phone?"

He opened his mouth, then closed it, caught in a lie. "Some old couple wants me to fix up their place," he said after seconds passed. "Do some repairs, build a bigger shed, shit like that."

"And what's their name?" I asked.

"Ain't that confidential shit?"

Dodging the question again, I see, when I hadn't even had a chance to call out that him just 'passing through' was complete and utter bullshit. But, I was committed to seeming unbothered. Instead of failing further, I just nodded and said, "Okay". My simple reply obviously annoyed him, but before he could say a thing, a third party joined the conversation.

"So, this is what's holding you up," an accented voice purred, drawing my attention away from Beau. It took me a moment to place the familiar face as Craig, Beau's friend. "The little lady at our table will be disappointed by the change of plans, but I'm not complaining."

The fucking nerve of this asshole! How could he be upset that I moved on from his ass—*false*—while flirting with other women? Then again, it was in line with everything I knew about raggedy motherfuckers. Roman and Colton had been supremely possessive over Mama, while fucking over her.

Beau glared at his friend, pointedly ignoring my sharp look. "Shut the fuck up, Cruz," he barked.

Oh.

That was his name.

No matter, I'd heard enough. Cruz's smirk remained, his eyes flitting over my figure. It only increased my irritation.

"Aww, don't leave so soon," Cruz called as I retreated from the hallway. "I was just playing."

I didn't dignify his words with a response. Assholes flocked together, and this brief interaction told me Cruz was a supreme one.

Thankfully, neither man tried to stop me. It was a struggle to keep my face neutral as I returned to my table. Mohawk was finally singing a song within his range, although I couldn't appreciate it due to Beau. Not only did I like him, but I also didn't appreciate his attempt to play me.

"Where were you, girl?" Giselle asked as I slid into my seat.

"Bathroom was crowded," I answered, the lie coming out easily.

Movement drew my attention to Mama...who had Colton's arms wrapped around her shoulder, his chair closer than it had been when I left. When she caught me staring, she *did* pull away, and Colton *did* allow his arm to drop to his side. I would've thought it was him being him, but his annoyed expression and Mama's guilty one told me everything I needed to know.

How fucking lovely.

Beauden

Beau slapped the back of Cruz's head as soon as Kamika dropped out of sight. The exaggerated yelp pissed him off to no end, and before Beau knew it, he was gripping his friend's collar and slamming him against the wall. The door frame rattled, and if it wasn't for the music, the thud would've been audible to the humans milling about.

"What the fuck was that for, you goddamn asshole?" Beau snarled, his anger and guilt shocking him.

He hadn't been lying when he told Kamika he'd been busy, but unbeknownst to her, she was now key to their operation. Confirming that the documents were likely in the dead bitch's house had been easy. It took one glance in the window to see the piles of paper scattered around the living room. The issue was that he didn't know what was what, and the place had a protection spell around it that prevented him from breaking in. Most protection spells could be nullified with an invitation. He was unsure if Kamika inviting him inside would work, since she wasn't the one who cast the spell, but it was better than nothing.

However, Cruz had to appear and fuck shit up.

True, Beau had been an asshole to ghost her. Not only was it a stupid move when he needed to get close to her for their job, but it was plain rude. Yet, the minimal mending his words might've done was destroyed when Cruz opened his stupid ass mouth.

Cruz shrugged, making no move to struggle. "I was simply asking a question."

Beau's blood boiled. Cruz acting like their meal for the night was anything more than that gave him more work.

"If that's who you want for the night, I'm not complaining," Cruz continued, causing Beau to drop him to the floor. He grunted, then dusted himself off. "She's a pretty thing, so—"

"That's the granddaughter, you dumb fuck," Beau hissed, pacing the hallway. "And you just added to my workload, you miserable nitwitted asswipe."

Motherfucker had the grace to look regretful, but not the intelligence to shut up. "There's no need to sound so angry, Beauden. She's just—"

"Key to the goddamn mission! Those witch bitches are paying us too much for you to fuck shit up."

Cruz's smirk finally dropped, and he huffed out a breath, holding out his hands. "I'm sorry, okay? Let's just bring the blonde back to our place for tonight. Filling your belly and emptying your balls will put you in a better mood."

Before seeing Kamika, Beau had been all for the plan. Bars always provided easy prey, doubly so when one hosted a concert. But now, the thought of returning to the willowy blonde, so opposite of Kamika, filled him with distaste. He wanted to chase her down and get her to listen. Not only for the mission, but for the sake of his ego. He wasn't used to rejection, so her disinterest stung.

"Go by yourself, asshole," Beau grumbled, beginning to leave the hallway.

Cruz snorted. "Oh, c'mon. Don't tell me you're actually upset over her. If it's that big of a deal, just corner her and compel—"

"Her kind can't be compelled, you dumb fuck," Beau said through clenched teeth, whirling around to glare. "And that bullshit ain't my style. You might need compulsion to get attention—"

"No I don't," Cruz interjected, actually sounding offended.

Beau ignored him, continuing as if he hadn't spoken. "But I don't. Next time you see me with her, don't fuck things up."

His creator had used compulsion on him more than once, giving him a distaste for the practice. If he refused a request, it was her go-to, even once she turned him. She'd been a far older vampire, so it wasn't an issue to hijack his mind. Each time, she made sure he remembered everything. When the fog cleared, the memories he never wanted to exist remained when she'd had the power to make him forget everything if she'd chosen.

"Maybe I should tell you that, Beau," Cruz muttered after a moment of silence. "Because feelings tend to derail plans, and our paycheck will be too high for a little crush to ruin everything."

"Don't try to flip shit around on me, when I'm the one doing all the work," Beau sneered, making a note to beat Cruz's ass this week.

Beau had about fifty years on Cruz, so whooping his annoying ass would be a breeze.

Despite possessing advanced hearing, the ability to tune people out was crucial when dealing with Cruz. So, this time when he stormed out of the hallway, he made sure to ignore whatever the motherfucker was saying. If he was going to salvage things with Kamika, he needed to focus, which was impossible with the asshole of a friend he kept in his company.

"Motherfucker," Beau grumbled, his mood ruined.

He stalked through the throngs of people, intending to return to the motel. Burnin' Boots was a time capsule to the Old South, when juke joints were scattered across the region so Black people could turn up in peace. It was one of few original jukes still standing, dating all the way back the 1920s or '30s, if Google hadn't lied to him. Modern life came with many benefits, but Beau often missed the olden days, where life was simpler, hunting was less risky, and the world still held some mystery. The old shack had been renovated and expanded, but it kept its vintage feel, reminding Beau of those good ole days.

Even with the subpar singing, the beautiful women milling about and the memory of days gone by allowed him to enjoy the evening, until Kamika showed her pretty face. The blonde bitch throwing herself at them had lost her appeal, and Cruz's comments about her left Beau wanting to escape his friend's presence.

He found himself searching for Kamika as he navigated through the exit. Her scent, sweet and decadent, was smothered by the many other bodies present, most stinking of alcohol, sweat, and bad body sprays. It worsened his annoyance and reaffirmed his need to dip.

Otherwise, he might do something stupid that'd inadvertently fuck with his payday, and that just wouldn't do.

June 14th

Kamika

Turns out, Mama was serious about going to Giselle's book club. Unbeknownst to me, she'd been reading the book Giselle had given her every night before bed and ended up loving it. Given the name of the book club and the content they read about, the piece of information didn't sit right with me, but who was I to judge? Mama needed a hobby and a friend more than ever, and the book club would give her both. If she liked mafia throuples, then I loved them. Well, not really, but that was neither here nor there.

"Just come in and say hi," Mama insisted as I pulled up to Giselle's house, a French colonial townhome just blocks away from her beauty shop.

The plan was simple. I'd drop Mama off, make some groceries, do something else productive to kill time, then come and pick her up. I was content with doing things that way, as even if I'd read the book, I wouldn't subject myself to the torture of a discussion *or* Giselle's company. However, it seemed as if Mama thought I could use some socializing. And damn it, I couldn't just throw her to the wolves. So, I nodded, turned off the car, and followed her to the front door. Seconds after I rang the doorbell, the door swung open.

"Y'all came!" Giselle greeted with a smile, enveloping Mama in a tight hug, sparing me a wave when she released her. "C'mon, we're just about to start."

She stunk of wine and based on the way she swayed on her feet, I didn't think it would be a stretch to say she wasn't entirely sober. We followed her to her living room, her house smelling faintly of cinnamon and flowers. It was pleasant and homey, a contrast to the aura emanating from the women sitting around her coffee table. Three empty bottles of wine confirmed my theory. It wasn't even 4 PM, and yet, alcohol was flowing freely.

"Ladies, this is Amia and Kamika, they'll be joining us—"

"Oh, I'm not staying," I said quickly, offering an apologetic smile. "I just popped in to say hi. So, uh, hi."

"No, sit, sit, sit," Giselle insisted, waving her hand to punctuate her order. "I want to hear your opinion on *The Don and His Two Broads*."

I snapped my brows together, because, what the fuck kind of book title was that? Mama laughed, exaggeratedly, widening her eyes to warn me to shut the fuck up. I huffed, shook my head, and folded my arms, wondering how the fuck I'd gotten myself into this situation. There was such a thing as agency. Staying in the safety of the vehicle would've been a proper use of it, but instead, I was lured inside.

Giselle sucked her teeth and wagged her finger at me. "None of that, missy. You should be ashamed of yourself, showing such disrespect."

"Kami has a lot to do," Mama inserted, and I wondered if her smile was real. My anger sure the fuck was. "She didn't intend to stay."

"She has no choice, Amia," one of the other women said. "We are required to attend every meeting and can only miss once every six months if we have a valid reason."

"I didn't read the book," I said, unable to think of a more valid reason to skip out on the session.

Besides, y'know, not wanting to stay in the first place.

The gasp that echoed through the room would make it seem as if I confessed to a great crime. My mother, the traitor, seemed to find humor in this situation.

"Girl, you've had weeks!" Giselle admonished, before massaging her temples and sighing. "No matter. We'll fill you in."

I could only blink at her. How in the world could I participate in a discussion of a book I knew nothing about?

"Well." Mama pursed her lips, uncertain how to respond.

I didn't possess her gentility, though I knew exactly what the fuck to say. Before I had the chance to blast them and get the hell away, Liliana breezed into the room in her bare feet and with a durag on her head. When Mama and Zara stayed for a week or two, my little sister and Liliana sometimes had playdates. We ourselves were never close, but her bond with my little sister made me have a soft spot for the fourteen-year-old. Based on the smile she spared me, and the glare she sidled at everyone else—including her mama—she echoed my sentiment.

"Sleeping in, girlie?" I asked, since no one else seemed inclined to talk to her.

"Avoiding narrow minds and drunks from the vine," she retorted, pausing long enough to impart those words before continuing toward the kitchen.

"You should be praying for forgiveness and coming correctly," Giselle replied with a glare.

Liliana didn't respond, stomping to the kitchen and slamming through the door with more force than necessary.

"That child is a disgrace," another one of Giselle's prissy friends exclaimed.

Mama wrinkled her nose. "I wouldn't say that, Oletha. She's just a child."

"That girl is just like her daddy. Satan in slippers," Oletha said, lifting her brows at Giselle.

Instead of tossing the lady out for disparaging her child, she nodded. "He was Satan in a suit," she agreed. "I can't believe I fell for Liliana's lies."

I really didn't have a dog in this race, except I was curious, and I couldn't exactly defend the girl without the facts. "What did she lie about?"

"She pretended she wanted to research Gaville," Giselle said darkly. "When she really was researching genealogy, and more importantly, demonology."

"Satan, I say. Just plain devil's work," Oletha cried. "You should give her another whooping."

"Two's enough," Giselle said decisively. "And she's grounded for three months. The same number of months she pulled the damn wool over my innocent eyes."

"What is wrong with Liliana's research?" I asked, genuinely baffled. "Maybe she was working on a school project."

I realized too late that it was summer, and thus, school was out of session. Liliana had always been a smart girl, so I doubted she was in summer school. However, my lapse in logic didn't catch their attention. Instead, it was the mere notion of my idea.

"No school around here would want information on such foolishness," Oletha said heatedly. "We're a Christian town with Christian values."

I held my peace. To me, 'Christians' didn't need to go to church. Most of them were awful human beings. "Demonology aside, why would she get in trouble for the genealogy? You gave her two beatings, so it must've been for both."

"If she needs to know something about our family, she should ask me," Giselle said tightly. "If I don't tell her, that means I don't want her to know. That does *not* mean she goes behind my back and looks into the information anyway."

"Unless you have something to hide, I don't see why she can't look into her family tree," I snapped, shocked how these grown ass woman were endorsing beating a child for something so minor.

Giselle narrowed her eyes. "I didn't ask you for your opinion, Kamika. Besides, I'm humiliated that she wants to be a demon. That reflects so poorly on me and my parental skills." Her hands flew to her mouth and she sniffled. Her eyes were dry. "I can't believe that child—a girl from *my* blessed loins—did this to me. If Dallacia hadn't called me and told me what was up, I never would've known."

Dallacia was the town librarian, and someone else my grandmother had been close to.

"And she came here, at a book club meeting, to out me."

"I don't think she wants to be a demon," I said with exasperation. "She's probably researching both to try and figure out if there are demons in the family. *Or,*" I amended at the gasps and horrified looks directed at me, "Gaville is filled with all kinds of legends. She might've been trying to discover if any of it is true."

"Kami is probably right," Mama said calmly, making me stand straighter, knowing she was on my side. "Besides *Dallacia*? She's one to tell anyone's secrets."

The other two ladies who'd barely spoken nodded their heads and laughed, while Giselle sat up straighter.

"Chile, I know that's right," Oletha said imperiously. She patted her Afro. "I heard she left Mr. Jones for Warrenta Thales, then realized she needed dick and left that hoochie mama. I couldn't believe Jones took that heifer back."

"She sucks good cock," one of the women said. "That's what Billy told Oris who told Jeanatay, who told me."

I listened to these gossiping heifers— barring Mama, even though she participated— and wished I hadn't. I knew more about who was fucking who, who *wanted to be* fucking who, and who *went back* to fucking who than I cared to. I'd known most of the women since I was a child, and didn't want to imagine them getting freak nasty.

"Girl, we've gotten so off track," Oletha declared an eternity later. "Let's get back to the book and Signore Sergio Calcagni. I stopped at the chapter where Marie Elena was pitching a bitch because she found out Sergio made love to Patrizia while she was at the fashion show."

"I think Sergio has more feelings for Patrizia," Mama said, and I pressed my lips together. She raised her hands at the incredulous looks. "Just saying."

"I disagree," Giselle said. "Patrizia is twenty and Marie Elena is close in age to Sergio. Generational differences won't allow him to prefer Patrizia."

"Girl, but young pussy will," one of the nameless women said, making my eyes bulge out of my head.

"And she was freaky, chile," Giselle chortled, pouring herself another glass of wine. "Licking his ass was crazy."

Okay, that was enough.

I jumped to my feet, my face feeling as if it'd be set on fire.

"Uh, bye," I managed, offering a halfhearted wave as I barreled towards the door.

I'd wasted enough time surrounded by those hypocrites. How in the world could these women punish a child for expanding her knowledge under the guise of Christianity, while drinking like fish, telling everyone's business, and reading pure filth? Last I checked, that wasn't Godly behavior, either. And how did my sweet, gracious Mama appear to be having a good time? Mysteries that I'd never figure out. One thing was for certain, I'd be damned if I ever attended another one of these meetings.

The woods scared the shit out of me. Whenever I had the misfortune of going through an area bursting with trees, all I thought about were the dangerous animals lurking out of sight. In Louisiana, swamp creatures added more stress. It was terrifying. The tantalizing break from the summer sun didn't alleviate my fears. I could handle heat pretty well, but I absolutely hated being sweaty. Hence why I chose to trek a gravel walking trail, only a few other souls frequented. It featured many soaring trees, their canopies shielding me from the sunshine. A pleasant breeze blew, cooling me off and rustling the leaves.

It'd been a long time since I visited Riverfront Garden, Gaville's nature park with many walking trails. But, after dealing with those book club bitches, I needed to decompress, and jogs always did the trick. Like every corner of Gaville, the park made nostalgia roar through me. The community garden had expanded, and soccer goalposts were placed in a formerly empty section. But little else had changed, which pleased me. The Garden was the perfect place to get a taste of nature bursting in and around Gaville, without some of the nastier drawbacks.

Namely, mud and things that could kill you. Minus mosquitos—those fuckers were everywhere. A bug buzzed by my ear.

"Fuck off," I hissed, swatting at the pest.

It only made me run faster, aided by the crack of a branch. Logically, I knew deadly beasts shouldn't lurk, outside of the gators and snakes the signs warned visitors of. Those were bad enough, and the fantastical side of my mind worried that a stray wolf or bear would find its way to the trail and maul me to death. But such was the risk of sprinting through a forest.

Fear, I found, was a great way to run fast. And the faster I went, the more calories I burned. The sweat was a drawback, but the peace of mind it gave me wasn't. The sneakers and sweatpants I wore weren't my typical jogging attire, but they made do. I intended to jog away my frustration until Mama called me to pick her up. Instead of grocery shopping as intended, I'd just pick up something to eat for dinner, and run the errand another day.

Quite frankly, as vicious as I knew Giselle and her circle could be, the way they referred to Liliana was shocking. Even more shocking was Mama choosing to stay around them. Like mother, like daughter, I suppose, because Grandma also had a fondness for those raggedy bitches. Unlike her mother, though, Mama wasn't a judgy woman. Though she was a Christian, she was accepting and open-minded, the complete opposite of what I witnessed today.

I could only hope those heifers wouldn't corrupt my wonderful mother.

Just the thought re-sparked my anger. I pushed myself harder, even as my lungs burned. A little breathlessness was preferable to annoyance. At the end of the day, running was a way to unwind. Even as the fear of mauling or kidnapping by a lunatic looking for victims lingered in the back of my mind, the activity calmed me.

It being a great workout was just a bonus.

I hadn't intended to stop at The Garden. Else, I would've brought my camera to snap photos for memory's sake, and to show my mother what she was missing holing up with those bitches. Yes, she needed friends and a hobby, but certainly, better company could be found. She needed a breather, not another stressor. Besides, fresh air did the mind and body good. Who knew? It might've even boosted her energy to finish the task Grandma had left us quicker. And once that was done, we could return to Miami and forget about the hypocrites of Gaville.

Because, as much as I missed the town, I could do without most of the residents.

I forced myself to push them aside, as the more I thought of them, the less relaxed I became. Instead, I took some deep breaths and admired my surroundings, hoping nature's serenity would transfer to me. The Mississippi created an absurd number of streams throughout Louisiana. One such waterway was in the middle of the park, hence the Riverfront part of the name. As my will to run dwindled, I took a breather on a bridge overlooking the stream. Every now and then, the surface of the water rippled as some aquatic animal disturbed the flow. Turtles and ducks wandered along the edge. Trees provided cover from the sun, and the low-lying plants acted as food and a hiding spot. I was fortunate to capture the beautiful scenery with my phone. Even my mediocre camera couldn't ruin them, and while they might not have been of professional quality, I couldn't wait to show off the photos.

I jumped as a mosquito landed on my skin, ruining my shot. Before it had a chance to sink its antenna thingy into me, I tried to slap it off. But the asshole flew away at the last minute, and I hit my own arm.

"Ow, you bitch!" I yelled in the direction it flew, cursing Noah for sheltering those insects on the arc. "Annoying ass bugs."

On cue, another one—or possibly the same bitch back for revenge—droned by my ear. I flailed my arms like a mad woman to shoo it off, keeping a tight hold on my phone to not lose it in the waters below.

"Ya mama, bitch," I seethed, recoiling at another buggy noise.

It wasn't as close, but it was louder.

A chuckle tore me away from battling the insects. "You make a habit of arguing with bugs?"

Lord, what a voice. Deep and sultry, with a hint of a Southern drawl. Even with my lingering annoyance, I couldn't deny it was pure perfection, designed to entice, and one I'd know anywhere.

"When they piss me off, yeah," I sniffed, turning to face Beau. He stood feet away in a hoodie and sweatpants. I frowned as our last encounter entered my mind. Until now, I'd been successful in ignoring it. "Going from ghosting me to stalking, huh?"

He rolled his eyes, the corners of his lips quirking upwards. "Gaville is small, Mika. Ain't that hard to run into someone often."

I pretended his nickname didn't soften me. Allow a man to fuck over you once, they'd make a habit of it. Minor infraction or not, fling or not, ignoring me for days, then expecting everything to be hunky-dory wasn't a good sign.

"Considering you successfully avoided me for days, I doubt that," I scoffed, turning my attention back to the water.

The wooden bridge creaked as he came close. "Still holding that against me?"

"It literally just happened, so yeah."

"Will an apology get me back in your good graces?" he murmured, his hand settling next to mine on the railing.

Dammit, girl, remain strong!

But, fuck, I was fighting a losing battle. His scent, his voice, and his mere presence were messing with my brain. At Burnin' Boots, the scent of sweaty bodies and stale liquor prevented me from falling victim to his cologne, and my headache aided my annoyance, shielding me from his charms. Here, in the peace of the park, such obstacles didn't stand in his way.

"...It'll be a start."

I peered at him through the corner of my eye, spotting his grin.

"Well, then, I'm sorry, *Kamika*," he said, the emphasis he put on my name making me shudder.

A throb settled between my legs, cluing me into the core issue. I was fucking horny, making me suspectable to a fine ass man giving me attention. Unfortunately, my vibrator wasn't high on the list of things to pack for my grandmother's funeral. With my wave of grief starting to lull, my libido was charging up to full force. That could prove to be an issue. But, luckily, the solution was standing right next to me, and Delaney was another contender. They both seemed eager enough for my attention, and some depraved part of my mind imagined what a threesome with them would be like. Mistake, because the images it produced only aroused me more. I squeezed my thighs together to alleviate the bothersome ache, hoping he didn't notice how flustered I was.

"Well," I finally breathed, trying to hide my reaction. "I'll consider forgiving you."

When he spoke again, I swore his voice sounded huskier, as if he knew the effect he was having on me. "Shit, it's better than nothing, so I'll take it."

I giggled and turned to face him again. Under the hood, I spotted a beanie. My brows scooted together. It was hot as hell, and he was dressed for a tundra. "You aren't hot in all of that?"

"Nah, I run cold."

"It's 91 degrees out," I pointed out, wondering how in the world he was still standing. "With a feels-like temperature of 150,000."

And the bridge was one of the few areas that lacked shade, meaning the sun was beating down on us.

He grinned. "You worried 'bout me?"

"Someone passing out on me would seriously ruin my day," I quipped, not confirming or denying his words.

Although, it would certainly dampen my arousal, so it wouldn't be all bad.

"Well, we can't have that," he said, his hand brushing against mine.

"No," I squeaked, before clearing my throat. His grin grew, and I spun back toward the stream. Silence befell us, and as I tried to think of what else to say, a question popped into my mind. "Umm, how long have you been out here?"

I didn't recall seeing him as I jogged through the park. The bridge we stood on marked the halfway point for just about every trail, so unless he was an Olympian, I at least should've seen him approaching the structure.

Alternatively, I was scarily unaware of my surroundings, a thought I didn't relish. Awareness was a woman's best friend, and a lack of it can lead to an array of brutal deaths.

"I've been here for a minute," he said.

My brows furrowed. Before I asked how this was the first I'd seen of him, he spoke again.

"By the way, it if was 150,000 degrees out here, I don't think either of us would survive."

Changing the subject, I see.

Lucky for him, I wasn't in the mood for an interrogation.

Smiling at his wry tone, I turned and drew in a deep breath. "It's hot as piss was what I meant. And 'feels like' is bullshit. If it feels like

102 degrees or whatever the meteorologist said, then that's what the hell it is." I gave him the once-over. "Except you're dressed like it's - 102."

Added to his abundance of clothes was that lush, thick beard. I wished he'd drop the hoodie just so I could admire it in its full glory. My gaze locked on his lips, perfectly shaped and longing for a kiss. His nose was straight and sharp, and the depths of his dark eyes mesmerized me.

The heat and his nearness held me spellbound. Masturbation was definitely on the menu tonight.

"So?" he murmured.

"So what?" I managed.

"You and me." He stepped closer. Instinctively I tipped my head back. "Another date." His head descended. A flash of sunlight gleamed on diamond incisor grills. "What do you say, Mika?"

His lips brushed my sweaty skin, suddenly so sensitive I shivered each time his breath fanned across my neck.

"Girl."

Grandma's voice rose in my head as if she stood right next to me. To say it was a vibe killer was an understatement. I stumbled back, and my eyes shot to Beau's face. His fangs protruded from his mouth.

Wait...what the fuck?

Gasping, I blinked; the grill remained, but the fangs were gone. A moment of anger swept over his face, and yet another blink from me cleared that, too. Perhaps I should be worried because it seemed I was experiencing heat-induced hallucinations. A heat stroke was nothing to play with, so I needed to cut this conversation short and retreat to my air-conditioned car.

Our gazes clashed, and I felt knocked off balance, completely overwhelmed.

"Uh, I...when..." My thoughts jumbled in my head, and I searched for the train of thought I seemed to have lost.

Beau smiled. "I was hoping we could do something today," he said helpfully. "Right now."

Squeezing my eyes shut, I ordered myself to act with dignity. Not looking at him helped my equilibrium and reminded me that I had to pick my mother up and find something to feed us. I popped one eye open, then immediately closed it at the overwhelming lightheadedness swarming me. Turning, I staggered to the bridge railing and opened my eyes. "I'm busy today."

He stepped behind me and placed a hand on my shoulder. Ice layered with fire swept through me. His touch was cold, but his nearness was hot.

"This might be your only chance," he drawled. "As soon as my job is done, I'm dusting this place."

Right. He'd said he was passing through and—

Wait a fucking minute.

"If you're just passing through, how'd you know about Riverpark Gardens?" It was a cherished place for the locals, but off the beaten path for everyone else.

Jesus, maybe he really was stalking me. The thought further cooled off my libido.

"Google Maps," he replied, easing some of my suspicion. "After I saw it in Fodor's."

"There's a Gaville Guidebook?" I asked in shock. Hard to imagine as small as the place was, with not much to see or do.

"There is, in both eBook and paperback. Riverpark Gardens was recommended as a lovely little off-the-beaten-path getaway."

His mimicry of what I was just thinking gave me pause, but perhaps my trust issues with the male species clouded my judgment of him.

His phone buzzed, signaling an end to the moment. He groaned, fished it from his pocket, and groaned again. "Dammit," he grumbled, declining the call.

"Problem?" I questioned, studying the water and feeling so out of fucking sorts.

I was hot, sweaty, confused, and in need of a fucking shower. Once I went home, the first thing I'd do was freshen up.

"It is beautiful out here," I said after many seconds, receiving no answer. "Beau?"

I glanced around, expecting to meet dark eyes that put a spell on me. Instead, I found emptiness.

He was gone, disappearing without a single noise.

"Dangerous."

Grandma's voice echoed in my head again, making me wonder if I was losing my mind. This time, all alone and confused, it creeped me out 10x more. Hearing a dead woman wasn't comforting in the slightest and prompted me to pocket my phone and resume my run. I needed to pick up Mama, anyway. And if she wasn't ready, being surrounded by the Smut Sluts no longer sounded quite so awful. Hypocritical as they were, they were living and familiar, something I knew how to handle.

But Beau?

Hearing my dead grandmother?

Yeah, those two things were out of my range when it came to coping.

CHAPTER NINETEEN

June 19th

Kamika

After our encounter in the park, Beau went back to ghosting me. This time, though, I wasn't upset. Even if I could ignore his assholery, I couldn't ignore that our last interaction was uncomfortably odd. It made me hesitant to see him again, allowing me to see his radio silence as a blessing in disguise.

However, my mind being free of Beau left more room for Delaney to occupy my thoughts.

Unlike him, my last encounter with her was pleasant. Amazing, even, and with nothing planned for the day, I toyed with the thought of asking Larissa if I could visit. Mama had finally been able to schedule a meeting with Grandma's lawyer. He was located in Fleur and warned her that going over everything my grandmother left wouldn't be a quick affair. She promised to pick up dinner on the way home, so once she left, I spent an hour tidying up. When that was done, I was left with nothing to do but scroll on my phone. Going on a walk was an option, but not one I was fond of.

So, possibly against my better judgment, I gave in to the urge to text Larissa.

Me: Question...

Less than five minutes later, she responded.

Rissy: Answer.

I couldn't help but smile at the response, my fingers gliding over the screen as I typed out my inquiry.

Me: Y'all free today? I wanna come over

Me: I'm bored lol

I gnawed on my bottom lip as I waited for her to respond. Once again, she answered quickly, but my nerves made the time seem longer than it actually was.

> Rissy: Yeah, girl, you're always welcome!

A wave of relief washed over me, her text all the confirmation I needed.

> Me: Bet. Be there soon

> Rissy: Delaney's gonna be hyped lmao

My smile made a return, and I tried to ignore the stomach butterflies that flared to life. If I sought a fling, all the signs pointed to Delaney being an ideal candidate. And yet, though that was my initial goal, only seeking sex no longer held appeal.

Was Delaney hot as hell? Yes.

Had I imagined us in some...lewd positions? I pled the fifth.

But the million-dollar question was if I would pursue her. The answer to that one wasn't clear. Having done some reflecting, I'd conclude that forming a connection would be better than frivolous carnality. If she and I hit it off, that'd be great, but I wouldn't let my loins guide my decisions. Because, while sex could be a distraction, it could also be the source of many complications. Most of all, it wouldn't erase...however I felt about Grandma's death. Even time might not mend those feelings, so taking pleasure in someone I barely knew wouldn't do much. It would only put the issue off temporarily, turning me into a ticking time bomb awaiting a meltdown. So, as much as it disappointed my pussy, I'd do the big girl thing and sort out my feelings before jumping into anything.

All I could hope was that my future self would thank me for giving her time to heal and not want to beat my ass for not seizing the opportunity to smash a certified ten.

Delaney

Delaney felt as if she were floating on cloud nine. When Larissa announced that Kamika had finally reached out, asking to come over, she thought she was dreaming. It just sounded too good to be true. But she was very much awake, and stupidly giddy to see her mate. Their day together had done more mending than she realized, because after weeks of avoiding them, Kamika was now seeking out their company.

Hopefully, Larissa would soon be removed from the equation entirely.

As much as she loved her cousin, she wanted Kamika to herself again, as they'd been when she walked her home. She knew she hadn't imagined the connection between them, though she couldn't tell Kamika that without sounding like an obsessive creep.

Which, she most certainly was not.

"What's that?" Shay asked as she settled next to Delaney, examining the drawing she was working on.

"An outline," she replied, sparing the girl a brief smile.

She cocked her head to the side, her sandy blonde curls cascading down her shoulders. "Of what?"

"My future bedroom."

Construction of Delaney's cabin had begun days before she arrived, but she'd approved the final floor plan via emails and video calls. Her sketchbook was filled with ways she could decorate her space, and of what would make for the ideal furniture layout. She knew she'd forever be welcomed at Aunt Galena's home, but it'd pass down to Larissa, and she was rapidly growing her family. Sooner or later, Delaney would end up moving, and she wanted it to be on her own volition, rather than being forced out with nowhere to go. Besides, as much as she loved her family, she'd gotten used to having her own space back in New Orleans.

Shay's little brows furrowed. "You have one here."

"But not forever, sweetheart." She sighed, setting her drawing supplies onto the coffee table. Shay was feeling chatty, Jack was out running errands, and Larissa had stepped out to deal with Cyrus. Delaney would entertain the little girl until her mama came back, but it would be a task requiring her full attention.

"Why?"

"Because I'm having a home built for me."

"Why?"

"Because I want to."

"Why?"

Goddamn, was that her favorite word? Delaney tried to stamp down the annoyance she started to feel, knowing the little girl meant no harm.

"Because Delaney likes her own space, sweetie," Larissa answered as she breezed in, carrying her sleeping son. She loved to hold that little boy, and Delaney swore Cyrus spent more time being carried than in his crib. "She's a lone wolf."

She winked at Delaney.

Delaney rolled her eyes, her lips quirking upward. "Haha, very funny."

Shay remained confused, but when her mother giggled, so did she. The child's favorite person arrived, so Delaney returned to her drawing. She gave the bed a bookcase headboard, as extra storage was always convenient. She wondered if Kamika enjoyed reading, or if she would fill the space with knick-knacks.

Fuck, what if she didn't like Delaney's interior design style? She adored colorful mid-century modern looks, but that wasn't everyone's cup of tea. Kamika might prefer traditionalism, or God forbid, modern minimalism.

Okay, maybe she was being a tad unreasonable.

She shook her head, casting her sketchbook aside when she finished the bed. The two hadn't even been on a date yet, so worrying about how she'd decorate their home when they moved into together was silly.

The doorbell rang.

Delaney was on her feet immediately, dashing to the door. On the other side stood Kamika, her blue flared jeans and white tank top hugging her beautifully. She licked her lips at the peek of cleavage, before forcing herself to focus on Kamika's lovely face. Ogling her wouldn't earn Delaney brownie points.

"Hey," she said simply, stepping aside so she could enter.

"Hey," Kamika repeated, giving her a polite smile as she glided through the doorway.

The familiarity with which Kamika moved through the house reminded Delaney that she and Larissa had once been an item. As much as she tried to ignore it, it filled her with jealousy, and she couldn't help but wonder if Kamika visited for her or her cousin. The thought created a goal: obtaining her number before she left. If she rejected her, that'd answer Delaney's question.

Should either be the case, she wasn't sure what she'd do.

"Hey, girl," Larissa greeted as they came into view.

Cyrus slept in her arms, while Shay cuddled into her mother's side. When Kamika and Delaney stepped in, she perked up, zeroing in on them. The toddler offered a wave, which Kamika reciprocated.

"Hi," Shay chirped.

"Hello," Kamika replied, her smile to the child nervous.

"Don't let her intimidate you," Delaney whispered, amused at how timid her mate seemed at the sight of the child. "Children pounce on weaklings."

Thankfully, Kamika understood it was a joke, giggling at the warning. "I'll keep that in mind."

Grinning, Delaney took her hand and led her to the couch. She made sure to station herself between Larissa and the kids, in an attempt to prevent Kamika from sitting next to anyone but her. Her plan worked swimmingly. The closeness and scent of her nearly drove Delaney into a frenzy. Clearing her throat, she forced herself to behave, leaning forward and swiping the remote from the coffee table.

"Did you draw that?" Kamika asked, a peek revealing she was laser-focused on Delaney's earlier sketches.

"I did," she confirmed, picking up her sketchbook and handing it to Kamika. "Just trying to decide how I want to decorate my home. You can flip through it."

"You're moving out?" Kamika asked, and maybe it was wistful thinking, but Delaney swore she heard disappointment.

"Kind of," Larissa answered, bouncing Cyrus as he started to stir. "She's having a cabin built on the premises."

"Yeah," Delaney confirmed with a nod, watching as the tension left Kamika's shoulders.

"I'll have the same address, just in a different home."

"I forget how big y'alls property is," Kamika confessed, finally accepting the notebook. She tentatively flipped through the pages, casting glances to Delaney every few seconds. "These are very nice. You're talented."

She puffed her chest out in pride. "Thank you."

"So, what are we watching?" Larissa asked after several seconds of silence.

"Well, since we watched *Twilight* last time, the reasonable choice is *New Moon*," Kamika announced, searching for the movie as soon as Delaney handed her the remote.

Both Delaney and Larissa groaned. Kamika smirked.

"Hush, both of you," she ordered. "Besides, since y'all hate Edward, you should be happy that this movie is focused on Jacob."

Oh great, instead of vampires wearing body glitter, they'd deal with fake werewolves.

"You're the guest," Delaney grumbled, unable to stay grumpy when Kamika smiled so proudly.

"Willingly watching a *Twilight* movie?" Larissa said with a dramatic gasp. "Character development."

"Or regression," she replied, chuckling when both her cousin and mate giggled.

In the first half hour of the movie, the kids were calm. Shay watched with apt interest while Cyrus slept, his little coos and squirms hinting that he was in the midst of a dream. But then, the creepy biker made his appearance, shattering the peace.

"Corn, Mommy," Shay demanded, Bella's thrill ride with a man double her age making the child lose interest.

Larissa giggled and pinched her cheeks. Shay frowned.

Her response was to kiss her daughter's cheek. "Popcorn, sweetheart, and we don't have the kernel-less kind, so none for you."

"But, Mommy—"

"It's rude to talk during movies, sweetheart," Delaney inserted, interrupting the little girl's complaint.

Shay huffed, crossing her arms over her chest and pouting. "I'm hungry!"

"Daddy will bring dinner home," Larissa said calmly. "Your favorite, chicken nuggets—"

"No!" Shay screeched, the little brat gearing up to throw a tantrum. "I want 'corn!"

Her hysterics woke her brother up, who began to wail at the interrupted sleep. Sighing, Larissa offered Kamika and Delaney apologetic glances.

"Do you two mind pausing the movie while I deal with them?"

"Not at all," Kamika said, grabbing the remote and putting a stop to Bella and Jacob's conversation.

"Thanks," Larissa murmured, cradling Cyrus on her hip as she grabbed Shay's hand and dragged the fussy child out of the living room.

"Free birth control," Kamika sighed as the seconds turned into minutes. Guilt crossed her face immediately. "Don't tell Larissa I said that."

Delaney shook her head with a smirk. "It's all good. I don't foresee kids in my future, either."

She held her breath as she waited for Kamika's response. At twenty, it was reasonable if she didn't tolerate children now but planned to have some when she was a more established, mature woman. Delaney, however, was content with being childless until the end of her days.

"I might foster older kids when I have a solid career," Kamika said, immediately capturing Delaney's attention. "Adopt a couple if it's cool with them, but I can only handle younger children in small doses."

"Define younger," Delaney requested, noting her mate's words.

Luckily, her cabin had two spare bedrooms. One would be used as an office, with a sofa bed if she had guests, and the other as a gym. However, if Kamika wanted to fill them with kids, she'd happily oblige.

And if any of their adopted babies discovered the truth of their new family, Delaney would just gaslight them into silence.

"In the foster system, kids are considered older when they hit seven, so I guess six and below."

Her brows snapped together. "Only seven? That's a little…"

"Fucked up?" Kamika supplied, to which Delaney nodded. "Yeah, I agree. Some systems and articles define eleven and upwards as older, but still, children above the age of six have decreased odds of being fostered or adopted. Even lower when they hit double digits. It's sad."

"Yeah, that's pretty fucked," Delaney agreed, unable to help feeling sympathy for thousands of kids she'd never meet.

At the sounds of screaming children floating into the living room, she grimaced. Though Shay preferred Larissa, it was Jack who spoiled her rotten. Larissa used a firmer hand, which meant not indulging her every little whim, much to the child's chagrin.

"Do you want to play the five-second game?" Kamika asked, grabbing her phone and tapping the screen.

"The five-second game?" Delaney echoed. "What does it entail?"

"I tell you to name a group of things, and you have five seconds to do it. For instance, name five supernaturals…and *go*."

"Wait! Shit. Five?"

Kamika made the sound of a game buzzer. "Time's up."

"We don't even have a stopwatch!"

She flipped her screen, revealing a timer which had been set to five seconds. "No, but I have my phone. And if you don't want to rely on that, you can just count. One one hundred. Two one hundred. Like that."

"Or," Delaney said, her lips quirking into a smile. "I can just say one, two, three, four, five, like a normal goddamn person."

"It'll go too fast for an actual second to pass," Kamika protested, then shrugged again, her phone still clutched in her hand. "But whatever. Don't complain when you don't have enough time."

"Let me try it," Delaney said, appreciating Kamika's willingness to compromise, overlooking the petty remark. "Name ten countries in Africa."

"Oh, shit. Uh…uh…South Africa, Morocco, Zimbabwe, uh, uh, uh—"

"Time's up!"

Kamika groaned. "Let me try it while I'm not under such stress."

"Be my guest, Kami, but you can't name the three you just gave me."

"Hard ass," Kamika complained, capitulating immediately and setting her timer to stress herself out again. "Kenya, Botswana, Nigeria, Egypt, that island with meerkats, Democratic Republic of Congo, Liberia, Sudan, Lesotho, East Sudan—"

"Disqualified," Delaney announced. "What's the name of the island? And it's South Sudan."

"I was close!" Kamika protested. "C'mon, give me half a point. At least I knew there are two Sudans."

"Nope. I'm a competitor. If I give you half a point, that might come back to haunt me, and I lose the game. My turn," Delaney said brightly, ignoring Kamika's glare.

"Name five verbs that describe movement."

"Oh, I see how it'll be," Delaney said, amused that Kamika was taking a page out of her book. "You won't make this easy for me."

"Tick-tock, tick-tock, tick-tock," Kamika said, waving her phone.

"You didn't say the timer started."

She tapped her smartphone's screen pointedly. "It starts now!"

"Sex, running, swimming, walking, and... uh, riding!"

The timer went off, and they burst out laughing.

"Okay, freak-a-leek. Very telling that the first and last one are something nasty," Kamika chirped, her teasing tone going straight to Delaney's heart.

"What the fuck else could I say?" she protested, no real heat in her tone. "Besides, you're the pervert for thinking that riding means something sexual."

"Be so for real. You started off with sex, so obviously, your mind was in the gutter. And, by the way, you could've said dancing, jumping, hitting, pulling, rolling—"

"Okay, damn, I get the point, girl," Delaney interrupted, another giggle leaving her, the girlish sound not one she made often. An idea struck her, one that had her grinning like a Cheshire cat. "Anyway, my turn."

Kamika hummed, focusing on her screen as she geared to reset the timer. "Alright, go ahead."

"Give me your number in five seconds or less," Delaney said in a sing-song, making Kamika sputter. As amusing as she found it, she was quick to add, "Only if you want to."

If she wasn't quite ready, that meant Delaney would have to put in a little more work to get in her good graces.

"Nah, I don't mind," Kamika reassured, looking at her phone before handing it over. "It just took me aback."

Delaney was pleasantly surprised to see Kamika had pulled up the option to add a new contact. Without hesitation, she entered her info, then sent herself a simple text greeting. When her own phone buzzed, she quickly picked it up, replied, and saved Kamika's number under her name.

"Oh, and by the way," Kamika said when her phone was back in her possession. "You can call me Kami if you want. A lot of people do. Or Mika, but only one dude who I don't want to talk about calls me that." She wrinkled her nose at the mention of the mystery man.

Delaney frowned, not needing to be told the 'dude' Kamika spoke of was a romantic prospect. Perhaps a situationship, or maybe an ex. Whoever it was, she immediately disliked him for messing with what was hers.

"Noted," Delaney said, doing a remarkable job at hiding her emotions. "And you can call me 'Laney, although most people just add the extra syllable. Personally, I don't give a shit."

"Noted," Kamika mimicked, her smile returning.

The conversation came to an abrupt end when Larissa returned, her children noticeably absent.

"Okay, Cyrus is sleeping in his crib, and Shay is in her time-out corner until Jack returns," she announced, sitting back down on the couch. "He can deal with his daughter, then."

"Uh, can't she just walk away?" Kamika inquired, making Delaney snicker.

"Nope. It has a child gate, and her only seat is a pillow, so she can't climb out," Larissa explained.

"Well, it's better than a spanking, so she got off light," Delaney added, shuddering to think about how her parents would've handled such brattiness.

The belt entered the equation for lesser offenses than Shay's tantrum.

"Spankings are only reserved when she puts her life or someone else's in danger," Larissa said, rubbing her temples.

"Like when she tried to smother Cyrus," Delaney volunteered.

Larissa groaned and Kamika's eyes widened.

"She did what?" her mate exclaimed, jaw agape.

"It's a long story," Larissa grumbled, letting her hands fall to her side. "Gosh, I hope I never have to do that again. It was so hard."

Delaney put a hand on her cousin's shoulder. "Hitting anything is easy if you're angry enough."

Larissa shrugged off her touch with a glare, while Kamika guffawed and muttered, "Oh my gosh."

"Girl—"

"I'm putting the movie back on," Kamika announced, interrupting Larissa's reprimand.

Delaney couldn't help but to stick her tongue out at her little cousin, who just rolled her eyes and focused on the TV screen. As Bella's stunts grew more reckless, Delaney's hand crept closer to Kamika's. When their fingers made contact, she spared her mate a glance, finding her face impassive. Emboldened, she grasped her hand in hers. Kamika's brows furrowed, but she didn't pull away. Euphoria shot through Delaney when she squeezed her hand. For the rest of the movie, they held hands, a simple, innocent gesture that meant the world to Delaney. Because, as minor as it was, it signified that she was on the right track.

If things kept going well, it wouldn't be long until she could call Kamika hers, a day she couldn't wait for.

CHAPTER TWENTY

June 20th

Kamika

Ever since I was a child, I have had a resistance to heat. Hot summer days did make me sweaty and tired, but compared to many others, I held up pretty well. However, being bred in Miami and having spent considerable time in Southern Louisiana, such a trait isn't remarkable. I was used to high temperatures, so it reasoned that I had a high tolerance to them.

What was most unreasonable was my inability to get burned.

Touching hot pans, boiling water splashed on me, coming into contact with flames, none of it left a lasting mark. To say it was painless would make me a liar, but it wasn't excruciating. A little aloe applied to the wounded area, and I was as good as new. Yet, the road to discovering this was quite stressful, namely for my mother. One of my first memories was when I was around three years old, months before my fourth birthday. I'd wandered into the kitchen unsupervised, causing all hell to break loose. It was as clear as day, especially now, as I watched the events unfold from the corner of the kitchen.

There my little self was, entering the kitchen as Mama and Grandma watched a TV show. I could never remember which program, as it was a very unimportant part of the story.

"I can't believe this shit," I heard Mama murmur as I embarked on my little adventure.

"Why you got me watching this shit?" Grandma grumbled, though she remained seated. "I gotta go finish cooking."

"The water for the spaghetti isn't even boiling yet."

"That was our mistake, y'know?" Grandma said, materializing in front of me and making me screech. "Leaving a bad ass little girl unwatched."

The version of my grandmother in front of me appeared years older than the woman on the couch, still blissfully unaware of the commotion I was about to cause. Immediately, I concluded this was another weird, ghost induced dream, except this time, my brain had tried to ease me into it.

"I was a kid that didn't know better, and it's not like I got hurt," I replied, feeling the need to defend the actions of my past self.

"No, but you did stress me and your Mama the hell out, and cause a big ass mess," Grandma countered, shaking her head as my toddler self grasped the handle of the pot and yanked.

The water cascaded over my head, the pot falling onto my little toes. That, I remember, was the reason I screamed so loudly.

"Kamika, baby?" came my mother's frantic call.

I was rooted in place, screaming my little head off. Not because I had been soaked in hot water, but my foot had been hurting like a bitch. However, all things considered, I came away pretty unscathed.   The severe burns from that hot liquid might have permanently altered my life if I'd been a different child. Fortunately, I came away from the incident with an injured toe and sore ass. Grandma had been the one to administer the spanking. Like Larissa, she had a policy that harming myself or others warranted a whooping. Perhaps the mention of that brought on the dream.

"What the hell, Mama?" my mother screeched, pulling me into her arms before Grandma could deliver another blow, cradling

me protectively and leveling her mama with a nasty glare.

Grandma administered the spankings before Mama could interfere. Evidently, it irked her.

"And your mother was pissed about that, let me tell you," dream Grandma said, shaking her head. "Tore into my ass for putting hands on you when we got you to settle down."

"It's fucked up to hit an injured child."

She snorted. "Girl, it was three firm pats to the behind, not a damn beating with a bat. You needed to know what you did was wrong."

"Pretty sure a pot falling onto my toe and boiling damn water getting all over me was enough of a learning experience."

"You needed to be punished for causing me and your mama such stress."

It was my turn to snort. "Ever the protector, huh?"

She rolled her eyes, and I refocused on the conversation. They'd settled their mini-argument, deciding my injuries, or lack thereof, should be the focus.

"W-we need to take her to the hospital," Mama stammered, the tears streaming down her face wracking me with guilt.

This was just six months after my father passed, and she'd still been mourning. Now, we laughed at the memory, but she'd also shared with me the terror she felt at that time, the worry that she'd have to bury her firstborn. Boiling water can cause third-degree burns, which could be deadly. Of course, that hadn't been the case with me; my skin had been just fine.

Grandma—the dream one, not the memory version—was as silent as I was. Unlike me, though, she had a small smile on her face, making my brows furrow. I knew she'd freely offer her thoughts, so I stayed quiet, still observing the chaos I'd caused.

"We can just wrap her toe here—"

"I'm not talking about her toe, Mama," my mother yelled, struggling to calm me down.

"Amia, she's fine," memory Grandma snapped as my mother carried me to the front door. "The water didn't do shit to that child."

"It's boiling water, and what if the pot broke her foot, and—"

"If she had burns, it would be obvious by now, girl," my grandmother interrupted Mama's panicked words. "Boiling water can melt skin, Amia, and Kamika's ain't even wrinkled. I'll clean up the mess. You tend to your daughter. If you find a burn, we take her to the hospital; otherwise, drop it."

"That was when I knew you were different," Grandma said as the scene faded, the home transforming into the eerie living room I'd been trapped in last time. "It was such a relief,

knowing you wouldn't be completely helpless in this world we live in."

Considering I didn't want to be a firefighter or work with burning materials, heat resistance wasn't the most useful thing. However, in the case of a fire or any unfortunate accident, it could prove to be a lifesaver.

"It could be more useful than you know, Kamika." She sighed, shaking her head. "If only I could've explained everything to you and Amia. You wouldn't be doing so much dumb shit currently."

I bristled, giving her my undivided attention now that the trip down memory lane had ended. "And what dumb shit might that be?" I asked coolly, cursing my mind for subjecting me to this old woman once again.

Did I miss her and the bond we once had? Yes. But I thought I'd mourned her while she'd still been alive and threw me away.

Did I want to deal with her interrupting my sleep to criticize me? Hell, no.

"The company you keep isn't indicative of smart decisions, but I suppose you'll have to learn that the hard way."

Oh, this again. Even in my dreams, she found a way to disparage me. Maybe my subconscious was reaffirming my idea not to pursue anyone and just chose a fucked up way to do it.

"Just keep this in mind, Kami. Being alone ain't so bad. It could allow you to focus on yourself, your own strength, and reflect. You don't need…questionable people around you 'til you get back to Miami. Learn to enjoy your own company."

"What's so questionable about Delaney?" I asked, already having the answer to what was wrong with Beau.

I liked him, yes, but even a fool could see that he was a shady motherfucker. But whether that only extended to being a horrendous flirt and leading on multiple women at a time, or something more sinister, well, I couldn't say.

"That girl ain't everything she appears to be," Grandma warned, her ominous words only frustrating me. "When you first met her, you sensed something was off. That's your gut trying to warn you."

"We've been alone a few times now," I snapped, feeling the need to defend her. "If she wanted to hurt me, she could've done so already. Liquor can just make people act…funny."

She studied me, her unblinking stare unnerving. Still, I held her gaze. She was like a shark. If she sensed any weakness, she'd pounce.

"Not the most pleasant animal to be compared to," she whispered under her breath, before finally—thankfully—blinking. "There are more ways to harm someone than just physically,

Kamika. And by the time you realize what I mean, it may be too late. You'd be ensnared in her trap, unable to escape."

"So stop speaking in riddles and spell it out for me," I yelled, my voice echoing through the faux-living room.

A flicker of something akin to regret crossed her face, but it disappeared as quickly as it appeared. "I wish I had, when I was still breathing. But everyone has rules we must follow, baby. Even the dead."

My eyes widened, but before I could question her, she disappeared. Last time, the light that took her was blinding. This time, a huff of smoke engulfed her and swept her back to the underworld. When I was alone, the dream began to unravel. The living room melted away, leaving behind a smoky void of purple and gold. Grandma's signature scent of roses and white sage lingered in the air.

My mind raced a thousand miles an hour. Sleep was supposed to be a time of rest, but just like the last time, Grandma's intrusion left me restless. Only when everything went black was my mind allowed to shut off, granting the peace my grandmother and subconscious had denied me.

When I woke up, the scent of Grandma's perfume was still strong, to where I had to pinch myself to ensure I was actually awake. The sting let me know I was. I scrubbed a hand down my face, my grandmother's voice more potent than any blaring alarm clock ever could be. It was fucking terrifying, and had me wondering where the nearest Catholic church was for some holy water.

With a heavy sigh, I rubbed the sleep from my eyes and grabbed my phone. Just like last time, I had twenty minutes before my alarm sounded. And just like last time, a message from Zara greeted me.

Huh.

What a coincidence.

Zara: You alive?

My lips quirked into a smile at the question.

Me: Yeah lmao

Me: You?

Zara: Yeah, lol

Me: Happy to hear that

She didn't reply, and I doubt she'd text again this week. Radio silence from her had become commonplace since she moved in with her father. I didn't know what lies he fed her, but since she hadn't cut me or Mama off completely, I figured they weren't irreversible. Regardless, Roman Leston was owed an ass whooping for the damage he did. I, unfortunately, was too weak to administer justice. But when the day came that karma bit him in the ass, I'd throw a fucking party to celebrate his downfall.

June 21st

Delaney

In Delaney's opinion, Eve got the short end of the stick. Both she and Adam ate the fruit. Since Adam was the older being, he should've been held to a higher standard. But God disagreed. Adam couldn't think for himself, so his punishment was to become a farmer. Eve listened to a fucking reptile, causing all of womanhood to endure pain during periods, and for childbirth to become one of the most dangerous endeavors of a woman's life. Delaney was far from a Christian, and yet, whenever her cycle rolled around, she cursed that bitch for listening to a talking snake. Certainly, she had to sense something was off. Then again, the 'forbidden fruit' could've been a smokescreen for an explicit act not sanctioned by the Big Man upstairs, involving mouths and genitalia.

Eve's punishment was so severe that her curse didn't only extend to human women. Wolf shifters were unfortunate enough to suffer from periods, too. A small silver lining was that werewolves experienced a canine heat cycle rather than a human menstrual cycle. That meant periods only inflicted their wrath on female shifters 2-4 times a year, though, like healthy human females, it lasted anywhere from 3-10 days. Bleeding was the easy part, as the estrus cycle lasted for a week or two. It left victims achy, unbearably hot, overly sensitive to everything, and so fucking emotional.

The worst part, though?

The insatiable horniness that never seemed to go away.

Delaney understood why, as this was when a shifter was most fertile, and craving sex increased the chances of procreation. Put simply, this was the ideal time for her kind to breed.

Her understanding of it didn't lessen her disdain for the process. She never planned to carry kids, and her attraction to 99.9% of men was non-existent. She'd asked Aunt Galena about fellow shifters who specialized in gynecology to rid herself of that affliction. A hysterectomy was appealing to Delaney, simply because she wouldn't have to deal with her fucking heat. However, she didn't want to risk kickstarting menopause so damn early in life. Thus, she had little option but to lie in bed and suffer, stuffing her face with junk food, and fucking herself with fingers and toys until her wrists got sore. But no matter how many orgasms wracked her body, it wasn't enough.

If Eve had no haters, Delaney was dead and buried, likely burning in hell for questioning the existence of any biblical figure in the first place.

A knock sounded, intruding on her thoughts.

"Go away!" she shouted, her frustration mounting as the power of her rabbit vibrator began to slow.

For the last six years, she'd always found partners during her heats. When her and Toria became an exclusive item, the bitchy witch would be at her disposal until the worst was over. If, of course, they weren't arguing. Then she'd laugh at Delaney's suffering, before popping in headphones and playing some stupid fucking game on her Switch. Toria had been well aware that a potential mate eased the side effects of estrus like no one else. That was likely why Kamika hadn't left Delaney's mind since the cycle began early that morning.

Kamika had shown herself to be kinder than Toria ever was, and that—in conjunction with being fucking stunning—made her more attractive than anyone Delaney had ever met.

She only hoped that Kamika possessed a high sex drive. If she did, she'd be absolutely perfect. If not, endurance could always be built.

The knock sounded again, just as the vibrator died. Growling, she hurled the stupid toy at the door, her failed attempt at orgasm leaving her in a pissy mood. "I said go away, for fuck's sake!"

"Are you decent?" Larissa asked from the other side of the door, sounding remarkably calm, despite Delaney's moodiness.

She realized Larissa wasn't going anywhere until she was granted entry. As children, they would make a game of annoying one another. Knocking relentlessly on Larissa's door had been Delaney's favorite method, so she supposed this was her karma.

Huffing, she slid under the covers of her bed and hiked her oversized shirt down, hiding her nude body. "Yeah."

The door opened, and Larissa entered carrying a tray of food, a gift bag dangling from her wrist. Her nose wrinkled in disgust, likely picking up on the scent of Delaney's heat and the odor of a sweaty body. But a heat was a trying experience, and wolves didn't turn their backs on packmates, so she soldiered on. That didn't mean she was without comment, though.

"Showers can help, you know," Larissa said as she set the tray on the bed.

"Shut up," Delaney grumbled, her mouth watering at the food before her, a cheesy pastrami sandwich on French bread with broccoli cheddar soup and chips. "I've taken two already."

Larissa's eyes widened. "For real?"

"Refer to my previous answer," Delaney said, picking up the sandwich and taking a big bite out of it.

She nearly moaned at the taste, the meat, cheese, and bread making her taste buds dance in delight. She'd raided the pantry earlier, collecting candy and chips, but this meal would be her first real form of sustenance all day.

"Good?" Larissa asked, setting the gift bag on Delaney's dresser.

Pacified for the time being, Delaney nodded, too focused on her meal to speak.

"Did you know a sex shop opened in Fleur about a year and a half ago?" her cousin asked, smirking at Delaney. "Jack and I went, and not long after, I popped up pregnant with Cyrus."

Delaney chose to ignore the second part of her sentence. "Why the fuck would I know that, when I haven't even been back a month, and you never told me?"

Larissa tsked. "So grouchy, when I have a gift for you."

"You're one to talk. You would become a demon three times a year."

During their teenage years, Larissa's cycle had been pure misery for everyone in the house.

"In my defense, PCOS worsens heat cycles," Larissa said, her grin growing. "And it mellowed out once I got mated to Jack, although they come four-ish times a year. A trade-off, I guess. Tamer cycles but more frequently."

"Stop fucking bragging."

Delaney's cycles came two or three times a year, always irregular, and always intense. However, it was different when the mate bond was solidified. Instead of a max of four times a year, it was common for the estrus cycles of mated females to come up to six times a year and not be quite so crippling. The commonly accepted theory was that when cycles were frequent but weaker, as Larissa had put it, sex was more likely, resulting in more pups. As someone whose mate wouldn't possess balls filled with sperm, things might be different for Delaney, though she'd accept the trade-off that her cousin had been lucky enough to receive.

Larissa rolled her eyes. "It's girl talk, not bragging."

"Go 'girl talk' to someone else," Delaney replied, moving onto the soup as soon as she took the last bite of her sandwich.

The soup was just as good, rich, creamy, and spicy. The delicious food allowed her to ignore her aching cunt and stiff limbs, giving Delaney a semblance of sanity.

"So, back to what I was saying, my gift to you," Larissa began, pausing to pull out two boxes, setting them next to the empty bag. "Are those."

Delaney set the half-empty bowl back on the tray and wiped her hand over her mouth, her brows furrowing, before her jaw fucking dropped. The first box wasn't too offensive, a simple strawberry caramel perfume. It confused Delaney, as the scent profile of her favorite body spray consisted of bergamot, sandalwood, and honey, something Larissa was aware of. However, solving that mystery could wait, as the knotted 'monster' cock dildo had her completely flabbergasted.

"What the fuck is that?" Delaney said, her jaw still unhinged.

Thanks to freaky humans, toys resembling the dicks of male werewolves were now widely available. Some were more accurate than others, but judging by the preview on the box, Larissa had selected one complete with a giant knot.

"That is the body spray Kamika has worn since high school," Larissa replied, her answer explaining its presence and piquing Delaney's interest. "And that is a sex toy, meant to give the user pleasure, and made for people who like to shove things in their—"

She'd definitely make use of the body spray, but her sex toys worked just fine—when they didn't die on her.

"I know what the fuck a sex toy is," Delaney snapped. "I meant, why the fuck did you get me that?"

"Well, you don't have a real one at your disposal, so I thought it would help."

While female shifters had cycles that were a cross between human and canine, the males had…equipment that was a cross between the two creatures. Back when Delaney was convinced that she was confused, she'd slept with two shifters. One from the Harris pack, and another from a visiting pack. Neither had done it for her, but it had allowed her to study their junk in detail. She'd noted their pointed cockheads, and how the base of their dicks were rounded, hinting at the knot that'd emerge when they came. That fucking knot had forced her to deal with both men for half an hour after the encounter. The awkwardness was amusing now, but at the time, it'd been torture.

"I'm not using that," Delaney declared when she got hold of herself, finishing off her cooling soup with a few loud slurps.

She set the chips aside, done with the processed fried potatoes for now. But she was quick to crack open the root beer, taking a deep sip to wash down the meal.

"I spent a lot of money on that, and it'll help, trust," Larissa said, holding up her hand and giving a three-finger salute. "Scout's honor."

Delaney rolled her eyes, but didn't say anything. When they were little, Aunt Galena had signed both her and Larissa up for the Girl Scouts. They had long since grown out of the organization, but the salute was the quickest way for them to convince the other of their honesty.

"You can take my tray away," Delaney mumbled, chugging her soda and tossing it into the empty bowl. "Or not. I'll bring it down after my shower."

Larissa gasped dramatically. "You're leaving your lair?"

"Shut up," Delaney ordered as Larissa collected the tray. "Fucking pervert."

She followed her cousin out, rolling her eyes at the loud chortle. They went in opposite directions, Larissa to the staircase and Delaney to the bathroom, but the former's laughter rang out through the hallway. Hot showers were one of life's simple luxuries, but Delaney's body was too warm to subject herself to that. Yet, freezing cold showers were not something she took willingly, so the water that rained over her was lukewarm at best.

She was well overdue for a retwist and hadn't washed her locs in two weeks. Her scalp was beginning to itch, which would drive her crazier when her heat returned from its break. So, she tackled her hair first, lathering her dreads in her favorite shampoo that smelled of grapefruit and oranges. She used a scented hair mist and moisturized her hair daily, a ritual that allowed her dreads to prosper for the past eight years. The hair moisturizer she favored was thick and oily. Her hair loved it, but the tradeoff was the amount of buildup it sometimes caused. It took two washes to get the damned shampoo to lather. She massaged her scalp when little white bubbles appeared, sighing at the pleasant sensation.

Standing directly under the stream, she kept her eyes half-open as the product ran down the drain, her thoughts returning to Kamika. With it, the heat that'd been kept at bay started to make its return. Swearing, she decided to skip conditioner, vowing to use a deep conditioner and a hot oil treatment when her body stopped torturing her. Some dreadheads avoided the product, but Delaney swore by it. She wondered what Kamika's hair care consisted of. She'd need to learn before they moved in together, to ensure she had all the proper products.

As soon as the thought crossed her mind, she scowled. The two hadn't even gone on a date yet. Thinking so far into the future would only make her rush things and result in a massive blunder. But, fuck, she was a tiny bit irrational when it came to her mate, and the relentless arousal pulsing through her only made things worse. That arousal forced her to cut her shower short. Delaney lathered up her washcloth and gave her body a thorough scrubbing, her movements rough and jerky. Impatient, she fidgeted as the body wash went down the drain. She wanted to return to the safety of her bedroom, locked away from the world as she rode her heat out.

Delaney toweled her hair first, squeezing softly to let all the moisture escape. She wrapped that towel around her head and retrieved a second one for her body. Brushing her teeth took less than a minute, not ATA recommended, but better than nothing. Her moisturizing spray was the only hint of hydration her skin saw. As soon as she set the bottle down, she decided enough was enough and hurried back to her room.

Once the door clicked shut, she dropped her towel and headed to her dresser. She ignored her usual body spray, opting for the one Larissa had gotten her. She sprayed it all over herself, wanting to smell like her mate. While missing Kamika's nutty shea butter scent, it would suffice. Setting the bottle back down, her eyes landed on the dildo. A huff of laughter escaped when she noticed the unopened lube bottle next to the box.

"Unbelievable," she whispered, shaking her head.

Despite her fierce opposition, curiosity flared to life. She picked up the box. Like any good packaging, the back of the box hyped up the product within, designed to hit every vaginal and anal pleasure point with 'life like' and 'unbelievably addictive' sensations were. She clenched her thighs together, her mounting lust shaming her.

"I can't be considering this," she said to herself, opening the box to get a closer look.

The dildo, bestowed the name *David* by its creator, was wrapped in a layer of plastic. It came off easily enough, allowing her an unbridled view of the toy. It was indeed accurate to a male werewolf's junk, possessing a soft, pointed tip, and a cumbersome knot at the black base. The sleek, maroon silicone of the shaft seemed to gleam in the dim light in her room. Hesitantly, she traced the curves and contours with her index finger, the smooth surface cool against her heated skin.

Her nipples beaded.

She looked at the box again, promising pleasure beyond one's wildest dreams. Delaney swallowed hard. The rational part of her brain screamed in protested, telling her to get a goddamn grip. However, she only had two toys in her possession, a rabbit and a wand vibrator, both dead from overuse, and tame compared to the beast before her. Despite her shame, the primal urge to be filled and stretched was overpowering.

Biology didn't care that she was a gay woman who didn't want kids; it only registered that she was a fertile woman of ideal breeding age.

"Fuck it," she breathed, gathering the lube, dildo, and body spray and hurrying to the bed.

Items one and two were set on the nightstand as she drenched her bed in the artificial odor. She longed for Kamika's presence, but that wasn't possible, forcing her to settle for a weak imitation. Step one complete, her fingers trembled as she grabbed the unscented lube and *David* from the nightstand. She pursed her lips when she realized she hadn't opened up the lubricant.

"Goddamn it," she muttered, quickly remedying her mistake.

When David was slathered up and glistened, Delaney lay back against her pillows, inhaling deeply, biting her lip as she imagined Kamika there with her. Her aching want became unbearable. Every nerve was alight with need, increasing her restlessness, her longing for release. Spreading her legs, she positioned the dildo at her entrance, but didn't impale herself just yet. Pride made her hesitate, and in the back of her mind, she was concerned *David* wouldn't fit comfortably, if at all. Her free hand drifting to her clit, peeking from its hood and begging to be touched. Her breath hitched as her fingers massaged the bud, the sensations making her all the wetter.

Maybe, on a different day, she would've drawn out this…uh…self-love session a little longer and savored the build-up. Today, though, Delaney needed release and was tired of waiting. Slowly, she pushed the toy inside of her, gasping as the tip breached her core. Everyone in the house knew what dealing with a heat entailed, and yet, she bit her lip to stifle a moan. Her hips bucked as she pressed the dildo deeper, her slick and the lube dulling the stinging stretch.

"Fuck," she moaned when the knot lay just outside her entrance, the last challenge before *David* was snug within her depths.

One hand teased her clit, while the other guided *David's* movements. Her clit throbbed, and her body trembled with the effort to hold back. She squeezed her eyes shut, her imagination getting the better of her as that damned body spray invaded her nostrils again.

Why the hell had she sprayed so much? Was she trying to torture herself further?

Apparently, so, because she turned her head to get a better whiff, increasing her arousal. Her imagination took over, and she envisioned Kamika there, watching, *teasing,* satisfied that Delaney was so desperate for her. Typically, she was the dominant one, but her heat made her annoyingly submissive. Toria had delighted in it, but Delaney wondered if Kamika would enjoy taking control, or just play the role of a doting partner, tending to her every need with eagerness.

No matter which it was, Delaney would be satisfied, as long as Kamika was by her side.

She whimpered, her fingers moving faster, her hips rolling against the thick dildo. Her breaths were coming in short, ragged gasps, her muscles tightening as she teetered on the edge of euphoria.

"Oh my gosh…" she panted, overcoming the final obstacle as she pushed the dildo deeper.

As big as the shaft was, the knot stretched her pussy nearly beyond her limits. The sensation was uncomfortable, in the best way possible. Every thrust teased her G-spot, the tip poking the hidden pleasure point that lay deep inside. When she'd conquered the knot, all it took were very jerky rubs to her clit to come undone.

"Shit!" she cried, her vow of quietness forgotten as her body convulsed with pleasure. Her orgasm hit her hard, the muscles of her cunt clamping down on the toy as she desperately ground against it, drawing out the ecstasy she felt.

Only when she floated from her high did she stop. Her body trembled from aftershocks, and her breaths came in shallow gasps. With a whine, she pulled the dildo out, her face heating as she realized what she'd just done, how creepy it was to masturbate to the thought of someone she wasn't yet dating.

If anyone ever found out, she'd deny it to high heaven, before flinging herself from the nearest cliff due to her embarrassment.

Worst of all, her heat wasn't over, not by a long shot. She foresaw *David* getting a lot more use. As much as it pained her to admit, Larissa had been right. The thought increased her shame in her post-nut clarity, and reaffirmed her feelings.

She really fucking hated Eve.

June 22nd

Kamika

As much as I hated to admit it, and despite how difficult it was for me to adhere to it, my grandma's advice of enjoying my own company was solid. It was easier said than done, but if I enjoyed being alone more, I wouldn't be quite so torn up about Delaney's sudden radio silence. When I returned home from their place three days ago, we texted for a solid hour and ended with promises to talk again the next day. The next came and went, with not a single text from her. The ones I sent to her went ignored, much to my annoyance. I'd finally overcome my initial hesitance due to our first encounter, and she ghosted me, just as Beau had. Was my forgiveness just a goal for Delaney to obtain, with no real intent of fostering a friendship? The thought upset me more than I wanted to admit.

Similarly, my texts to Larissa yielded few results. Unlike her cousin, she actually answered. Yet, she danced around the topic of Delaney, not telling me what was going on, just promising me she'd tell her to text. I finally told her don't bother, because I refused to beg someone for their attention, even indirectly. If she wanted to reach out, she'd do so without her cousin's intervention.

Ironically, Beau had begun texting me regularly again. I kept my responses dry, but with Delaney MIA, I couldn't help but think about how fun it had been talking to him, and what a great time we had during our date. Maybe that was why I took him up on his offer to pick me up, allowing him to fulfill his promise to take me on a spin. He'd wanted to hang out, but Mama had taken the car to meet with the lawyer again, leaving me without a ride. Beyond simple greetings, the radio filled most of the silence.

"I love this song," I said as 'State of Shock' by Mick Jagger and The Jacksons began to play. "It's one of my mama's favorites."

It had been one of Grandma's, too, but I didn't want to discuss her. Her intrusions into my dreams took up enough of my sleeping hours, so I tried my best to give her no thought while awake. Today marked a month exactly since her funeral, making it a challenge to fully banish her from my thoughts.

"Your mama has good taste, then," Beau complimented, sidling a glance at me. "You hungry, Mika?"

I nodded, spotting *Jayson's Food Mart* on the horizon. I pointed to it. "We could get something there. They have pre-packed sandwiches, wraps, and salads."

"Where?" he asked, slowing the car down.

I pointed again. "There."

He huffed out a laugh. "You are aware I'm driving, huh? Can't look at you right now, baby."

Baby.

That was new, not that I was complaining. A shudder ran through me, and I cleared my throat, reminding myself that though it was a term of endearment, *'baby'* wasn't necessarily a romantic nickname.

"*Jayson's Food Mart,*" I replied, breathier than I wanted.

As if sensing how much he affected me, he smirked, his grills gleaming in the sunlight. "Whatever you want, *baby.*"

I groaned. "Boy, stop fucking teasing me."

"Who said I'm teasing?" he asked as he pulled into the store's parking lot. "If that's what you wanna be called, I'm happy to oblige."

I didn't want to be called that, per se. I just enjoyed hearing the word roll off his tongue.

"Whatever," I mumbled as he pulled into a parking space.

He exited before me, and by the time I unbuckled my seatbelt, he was opening my car door. My eyebrows lifted in surprise.

"Such a gentleman," I teased as he took my hand, helping me out of the vehicle.

He shrugged, but didn't relinquish his grip as we walked to the entrance. "What can I say? My mama raised me right."

The night of my mother's birthday came to mind. It wouldn't be crazy to say he was a player. A fuckboy with the façade of a gentleman was treacherous. I held my tongue, though, opting to just hum in response. As much as I tried to convince myself otherwise, my need for a distraction was still present, and I wouldn't fuck things up by stirring the pot. As long as I kept in mind that whatever happened with Beau meant nothing, things should be smooth sailing.

"Hey, Jayce," I greeted as Beau and I entered, aiming a smile his way. "Your parents ever give you a break?"

Every time I'd gone into the store, Jayce was manning the cash register.

"Nope. Gotta earn my keep during the summers," he replied, the grin he returned fading when he saw Beau. "Who's this?"

"A customer," Beau barked, the harsh tone taking me aback.

I side-eyed him while Jayce's eyes narrowed. "He just asked a question," I said, feeling the need to come to the boy's defense.

"My name's Beau," he grumbled, the glare he leveled at Jayce wholly unnecessary.

If my memory served me right, he hadn't been rude to our waitress when we'd gone on our date, so I hadn't taken him for the type to be a prick to service workers. Perhaps that was a façade. I saw no other reason he'd be upset at a child's harmless question. Fleur's growth hadn't trickled over to Gaville. As such, Gaville didn't see many newcomers, making Jayce's curiosity natural.

"He's here for work," I volunteered giving Jayce an apologetic smile as Beau fetched a cart.

In my life, I'd only had two traditional job. The first was a local restaurant in Gaville, where Larissa had also worked, enabling us to grow close. The second was the summer after the bullshit with Grandma, I started working as a cashier for a small Miami boutique, a job I held until last year. While my time in the workforce was relatively short, it was enough to let me know that working in customer service wasn't for the weak.

"Oh," Jayce said, looking at Beau as he returned to my side. "What do you do?"

"A little bit of this and that," he answered, looking down at me. "You know what you want?"

I nodded but kept my attention on the teenager I'd known for years. "He's a handyman Jayce."

Beau grabbing my elbow and yanking me away prevented him from responding. I was a respectable 5'6, but Beau had about eight inches on me, meaning he was practically dragging me. When he guided us down an aisle out of view of Jayce, I jerked away. It forced Beau to stop, and when he faced me, I glared up at him, rethinking my decision to spend time with him.

"What hell is wrong with you?" I hissed, rubbing at my sore elbow, flashbacks of my first encounter with Delaney going through my head.

She'd been drunk, but to my knowledge, Beau was sober, so his behavior was inexcusable.

He shrugged. "The kid has a crush on you," he said, as if that explained his bout of assholery.

"So, you nearly yanked my arm out of my socket because you're jealous?" I asked in disbelief.

The first guy I dated had been a rebound from Larissa. I wasn't madly in love with him, but I'd grown to care for him. His eventual infidelity crushed me. As I dealt with my second nasty break-up, Olivia gave me a piece of advice that became a motto of sorts: don't trust peepee owners. She'd said it as a joke to make me laugh, but it was a statement to live by. Men, I'd learned, were raggedy creatures.

Guilt crossed Beau's face, and he rubbed the back of his neck. "You right, that was fucked up. I'm sorry."

Perhaps I was too easy, because his willingness to apologize immediately defused me. Deep down, I knew I needed to dust him, and if I was in Miami, surrounded by friends, I wouldn't have entertained him for so long. But, that wasn't the case. I was a people person, and with a severe lack of people around, I was desperate for human company.

"Apology accepted, but don't do it again," I warned, trying to infuse my previous annoyance into my tone. "First off," I continued, raising my fingers for a countdown. "He's a child, so *ew*. Secondly, I don't date younger, even if they're legal. And third, you and I aren't anything serious. We're barely more than friends, so you can't be jealous."

"The hell I can't," he murmured, raising his hands in surrender when I scowled. He resumed walking, grabbing a jar of spicy pickles off a shelf as we passed it. "Just cuz we aren't anything now—"

"And we won't be anything more than a fling, if that," I interrupted, idly watching as he grabbed pepper flakes. "When our business is sorted, we're both leaving Gaville and returning to our lives."

He chuckled, but even to my ears, it sounded forced. "Damn, girl, so you already planning to cut me off?"

"We *might* remain friends," I offered, though I wouldn't count on it.

Though he was handsome and his company was pleasant, my attraction to him paled in comparison to what I felt for Delaney. If she wasn't ignoring me and Larissa wasn't covering for her, I likely wouldn't have accepted his invitation to hang out. Seeing someone as a second choice isn't a hallmark of a good connection, be it romantic, sexual, or platonic. My relationship with Beau was flirtatious at best, politely cordial at worst. So, I'd enjoy my stint with him, but when it was time for us to part, I'd know that our period together had come to an end.

And oddly, the thought wasn't as upsetting as I assumed it'd be.

Beauden

There was a reason Beau kept away from witches. The natural juju those bitches possessed always made him act a damn fool. It was something he couldn't explain. He'd long chalked it up to the way their blood called to him, whether that was the truth, he couldn't say for sure.

With Kamika, it certainly wasn't.

As delicious as she smelled, and as much as he dreamed of getting another taste of her—in more ways than one—he knew that wasn't the only reason for his attraction, just as his mission wasn't the only reason he wanted to be close to her. The protection spell around her house was weakening. In the meantime, he scoured the libraries of Gaville and Fleur for any records pertaining to Kamika's family, while Cruz claimed to be hunting down people connected to the grandma. It wouldn't be long until Beau and Cruz got what they needed and got the hell out of town.

He pretended the thought didn't disappoint him. Not because he'd grown fond of Gaville, but because Kamika had made it clear their relationship would end when he left.

As mysterious as the effect witches had on him was, the effect Kamika had was even more puzzling. She barely counted as a witch, and he suspected that was the reason she'd been kept in the dark about her heritage. And yet, one whiff of her revealed what species she belonged to, and the sample of her blood he had back at the restaurant let him know the toxins were very much present. That meant she had some type of power. It was likely weak and subtle, but it existed. It had confused him because the last full-blooded witch in her family had been her great-grandmother. At this point, her blood should've been normal. Perhaps a little sweeter, but not as sugary as a witch's.

Then, he dug a little more into her family tree and came to a conclusion.

Her grandfather—her Mama's daddy—had died before she'd been born, and who fathered him wasn't known. Kamika's daddy had died when she was three, and he'd been adopted as a baby. As far as Beau knew, once her old man kicked the bucket, his adopted family lost contact with Kami and her mama. But, he didn't care about that, because the blank slates in her family tree were likely the reason witch's blood continued to flow through her veins.

"Penny for your thoughts?" Kamika asked.

"Worth more than that, girl," he replied, not taking his eyes off the road as he drove to the motel he was staying at in Fleur, finished with the ham and cheese sandwich he'd gotten for her.

In truth, nothing about Kamika beyond her connection to Susanne LeBlanc, LaClair by birth, should've mattered, but that wasn't the case. She'd gotten under his skin, enough for him to act like a jackass because of a little boy's crush. Men equal to Beau's caliber rarely intimidated him, so a scrawny teenager shouldn't have given him such a strong reaction.

Fucking witches. When he was done with this mission, he'd stay far away from them for a long, long time.

"Okay, two pennies," she said.

He smiled at her persistence. "How you normally eat pickles?" he asked, deciding a new subject would be a proper distraction.

Her brows snapped together. "Uh…with my hands? Wait, is that a fucking innuendo, Beau?"

He chuckled at her confusion, fueled by her giggles, the pleasant chime relaxing him more than he wanted to admit.

"Like, what do you put on them?" he clarified.

"Man, you should've just asked that!" she exclaimed.

"My bad, Mika. Now answer the question," he said, shaking his head in confusion as their humor faded away.

"I normally just get spicy pickles and eat them out of the jar. Why?"

"Wanna fix you a snack when we get to the motel," he said, his mouth watering as he thought of his favorite human meal.

Despite many myths saying otherwise, vampires could ingest human food. However, unless it contained blood, it provided no nutrients, and their taste buds didn't pick up mild flavors. To appreciate non-bloody dishes, it had to be overpowering, hence pickles being a favorite. Their saltiness and sourness meant Beau actually tasted something when he ate one, but to truly enjoy it, he spiced it up a bit.

"What does this snack consist of?" she asked.

"Get some spicy pickles, cut them up, and coat them in crushed red pepper, garlic, lemon juice, and lime seasoning."

"Lemon juice and lime seasoning?" she echoed, her nose scrunching up. "I can get behind the garlic and pepper, but I'll pass on the citrus."

"Don't knock it until you try it."

"I'll just steal one of yours and see if I like it."

"Deal," he conceded, pulling into the motel's parking lot.

Just like before, he opened her door and helped her out of the car. He allowed her to gather everything they'd bought, then placed a hand on her lower back as he guided her to his room. She didn't seem to mind, and satisfaction roared through him.

"This place is nicer than I thought," she said when they entered the room he shared with Cruz, who was thankfully absent.

He'd left sometime that morning and hadn't been back since. As they waited for the spell to wear off, they did their own thing. Cruz's new hobby had become terrorizing Fleur's coeds, much to Beau's annoyance. He fed when necessary, to avoid the commotion that Cruz's gluttony had created. Bodies were stacking up, getting the cops' attention, which was never a good thing. Beau would warn him one more time, before he snapped his neck and threw his ass in the bayou while he was out cold.

Hopefully, he'd wake up before the alligators got him. If not, oh well. Beau would be upset, but Cruz would be among one person out of many he'd lost during his centuries of existence.

"You thought I'd be holed up in a dump?" he asked, looking over his shoulder as Kamika set the grocery bags onto the counter above the minifridge.

"Motels don't have a reputation for niceness," she replied, fishing everything out of the bags.

"I'll give you that," Beau said, strolling to the desk and grabbing the remote to hand to her. "Find something to watch while I make our food."

She rolled her eyes, taking the device with a smirk. "Yes, sir," she said sardonically, the playful nickname making heat rush through him.

If he knew where Cruz had gone and how long he'd be away, he would've been bolder, laying it on as thick as he had at the park. It was a goal to get some pussy from her before she dropped out of his life.

"Anything in particular you wanna watch?" she asked from the couch.

"I'm cool with whatever."

"Noted."

He finished preparing the pickles just as *Friday* began playing. He grinned, making his way over to the small sofa and settling next to her.

"This alright with you?" she asked.

He nodded, handing her the small plate he prepared for her that excluded the lime seasoning and lemon. "It's one of my favorites."

"Mine too," she said, popping one of her pickles into her mouth.

He'd made sure to cut back on the garlic and pepper, knowing the amount he enjoyed was too much for a human palate.

She hummed. "Not bad. I really like the spice, but I could've done without the jarlic."

"Jarlic?" he echoed.

"Jarred garlic."

He snickered, then held out his plate. "Try one of mine."

She hesitated before obeying. As she chewed, her face scrunched, her disgust clear. A laugh bubbled up, worsening when she went into a coughing fit. He patted her back, mindful of the amount of strength he used. He didn't want to fling her ass across the room.

"Easy, Mika, just breathe," he soothed through his chuckles, laughing harder when she glared at him.

"Motherfucker, you tried to poison me," she gasped when her hacking died down, swiping at her watery eyes. "What the fuck did you put on that?"

Her abrasiveness only amused him further, his grin growing at how quickly her claws came out.

"Exactly what I told you I would," he answered, getting up for a bottle of water.

She accepted it immediately, twisting the cap off and gulping the entire thing down within seconds.

"Your taste buds are fucking fried if you actually enjoy that."

"It's good," he insisted, eating one of his slices to prove his point, swallowing it without issue. "Delicious."

She gaped at him, then shook her head. "Insanity. Your stomach must hate you."

"Nah, I've built a tolerance."

He ate another pickle to punctuate his point. She huffed out a laugh, then refocused on the television.

"I'll stick to my mild pickles," she declared.

"Whatever floats your boat."

They fell into silence, a quip about the movie here and there the only conversation. Somewhere along the way, his hand navigated to her thigh, and she didn't dislodge his grip on the supple flesh. The quiet camaraderie was nice, until it was interrupted by his friend's return. Beau didn't bother hiding his groan when Cruz strolled in. He stood and positioned himself in front of Kamika when the motherfucker zeroed in on her.

"I wasn't aware we had company," Cruz said with that annoying fucking smirk.

"*We* don't," Beau snapped, wishing they'd gotten their own rooms. "*I* do."

Rooming together had never been an issue before, but neither had such tension existed between them during a job.

"Uh, hi," Kamika said, offering a polite wave, before pausing the movie and standing. "We were just leaving, so…"

"Oh?" Cruz's eyebrows cocked up, likely sensing her lie. "Where to, if you don't mind me asking?"

"Get something to eat," Beau said, going along with her lie. "Then drop her off before it gets too late."

It was a convenient out and would delay the inevitable complaints that would spew from Cruz. What the issue was, Beau didn't know. Cruz was painting the town red, but had an issue with Beau halfway romancing one girl, a girl who was a valuable asset for their mission.

Cruz's eyes roamed to the snacks they purchased at *Jayson's Food Mart*. "Y'all have food here, no?"

"Not a fucking meal," Beau grumbled, grabbing Kamika by the elbow once she collected her things.

"I need to talk to you, Beauden," Cruz said when they were halfway to the door.

Beau paused; Kamika looked at him with a cocked brow.

"Your name is Beauden?" she asked, smiling sweetly when he nodded. "It's a pretty name. French?"

Another nod.

"It means beautiful or handsome," he explained, ignoring Cruz's annoyed sigh.

"Accurate," she said, before clearing her throat. "I'll go wait by the car while y'all talk."

"It can wait," Beau replied, just as Cruz said. "You do that."

Her eyes flickered between the two of them before she escaped Beau's hold and made her way outside. With a huff, he faced Cruz, glaring at his friend.

"What the fuck is it, asshole?"

"Why is she here?" Cruz demanded, crossing his arms and pouting like a child.

"Because I want her to be, motherfucker," he barked, getting in Cruz's face within a second. "You don't get to judge shit that I do, when you're going around fucking up every bitch you see because you're bored."

"So you'd have me starve?"

"I'll have you act like you have some goddamn sense and not cause a mass panic," he snarled, shoving Cruz back, sending him flying into the wall.

A painting fell, and he was thankful the room next to them was vacant. Otherwise, management might get involved and turn a minor incident into a big mess. But, fuck, Beau was getting fed up with Cruz's antics and his judgment. Initially, he was all for Beau getting closer to Kamika, so what had changed?

Cruz recovered in seconds, standing as he rubbed his head. "If you weren't so hung up on her, you would be doing the same thing, so—"

"The hell I would, because I have fucking sense," Beau interrupted, walking to the door and exiting before Cruz annoyed him further.

"Everything okay?" Kamika asked when he came into her line of sight, her brows furrowed in concern. "I heard something crash—"

"Yeah, Mika, it was nothing," he replied, quickly changing the subject. "Where you wanna eat?"

"Do they have a sushi spot here?"

Beau nodded. "Sure do."

Sushi was another favorite of his. Tuna, especially, due to the higher blood content, providing Beau's body with some benefits. But regardless, she could've requested lettuce sandwiches, and he would've taken her to buy one. He wasn't a people pleaser, but he didn't want to leave her disappointed. Most of all, Beau needed to get away from Cruz before he ripped his fucking tongue out. That'd be quite the mess, and put a strain on their already struggling friendship.

When Beau invited Kamika out, he had no expectations of how things would go. Fishing for information hadn't been the goal, because at this point, he realized she didn't know shit. He simply wanted to spend time with her, yet he didn't imagine things would be quite so awkward. Blip after blip kept fucking things up, creating a cloud that refused to dissipate over the date . They'd spent more time listening to music than talking. During their first date, conversation came easily. For their second, neither seemed to know what to say.

As he drove her home, the radio once again echoed in the car. The widening gap between him and Cruz was still on his mind. It was due to Kamika; that much was obvious. Cruz had always been a possessive, sensitive motherfucker, throwing a fit when someone got too close to what he deemed his. Beau, as his best friend, was no exception. Any woman Beau didn't want to share became an object of Cruz's ire, because the asshole had to be the center of attention. It was tiring, especially with Kamika. Their time in Gaville had an expiration date, which meant Beau's time with her had an expiration date. Cruz being a fan wasn't necessary, nor did Beau want the psychotic motherfucker anywhere near her. He just wanted him to get his fucking ass off his shoulders, and act like he had a brain in his head.

That wouldn't happen until they returned to New Orleans and resumed their normal dynamic, but after this job, he'd need to take a break from the prick to decompress.

"Thanks for taking me out," Kamika said as the blue shotgun came into view.

"My pleasure, baby," Beau replied, his tone detached as his thoughts ran rampant.

She noticed. His curtness made her perfect lips tug into a frown. "Uhm, what's your Cash App? I can pay you back. The three nigoris alone were pretty expensive—"

"I'd just send it back to you, Mika," he sighed, scrubbing a hand over his face as he brought the car to a halt. "I'm a gentleman, remember?"

She snorted. "Okay."

Her reaction made him smirk, but that nagging feeling remained. He could blame Kamika's blood, her importance to the mission, or several other factors to explain away how mesmerized he was by her. No matter the reason, he liked her more than he should.

"I know today was a little fucked," he said, giving her his attention. "But I ended up having a good time with you, girl."

She relaxed, granting him a smile. "I did, too. The sushi was really fucking good. Minus the spicy tuna roll, that shit was bloody."

Exactly why he liked it.

"A little blood doesn't hurt anyone, baby," he teased, his mood lightening at the chitchat.

And, fuck, did that piss him off, because it made him feel like a simpering fucking fool.

She shuddered and wrinkled her nose. "I disagree."

Chuckling, he exited the car to open her door, coming alive when she placed her hand in his.

What fucking bullshit.

"You don't have to go through all this trouble," she said, making no moves to pull away as they walked to her porch.

He shrugged. "I want to."

When he first arrived in Gaville, he couldn't approach the property without crippling pain. He didn't know a half-witch could be so powerful, but the bitch was dead, and the spell continued weakening. As they neared her front door, he wasn't struggling to stay standing, so it was an improvement. However, the oppressive feeling settling on his shoulders and the headache forming let him know the hex wasn't completely gone.

Kamika paused on the top step, not seeming to notice Beau's increasing struggles, likely due to the sake she had at the sushi place. "You wanna come in for a minute?"

He waited for a moment to see if her invitation would grant him entry, but he felt just as shitty.

"Actually, baby–" he began, gritting his teeth as he tried to step onto the porch, with no success.

Goddamn witches.

Thankfully, fate intervened.

The opening of the front door interrupted him. Relief slammed into him because it gave him a great excuse to dip. An attractive older woman stepped out, her brows furrowing as she looked between Kamika and Beau. He presumed it was her mother. Amia, if he remembered correctly. Her daughter favored her, and that enticing scent indicative of a witch, though different, was present. While Kamika's aroma was sweet and fruity, Amia's was floral and herbal. Both mouthwatering, but Mika had the edge.

"Who's this, Kami?" she asked with a polite smile.

"Beau, Mama," Kamika answered. She looked between him and her mother. "Beau, my mother, Amia; Mama, Beau."

"Nice to meet you, ma'am," he said, using manners his 'elders' ingrained in him.

In truth, Amia was about one hundred fifty years younger, but he was frozen at 26, and his mama would rise from the grave and whoop his ass if he disrespected someone who presented as older than him.

"The pleasure's all mine," she replied, tension beneath her light tone. "I trusted you treated my daughter right? Used protect—"

"Oh my gosh, Mama!" Kamika exclaimed, the outburst making him laugh. "We only watched a movie and got some food."

He raised his hands, grinning. "I was the perfect gentleman, ma'am." Letting his arms fall back to his sides, he focused on Mika. "I'll text you later, baby."

"Baby?" Amia echoed, raising a brow.

Kamika ignored her mother and gave him a quick hug, "Bye, Beau," she said, before following her mother inside.

He stood outside until the lock clicked, then returned to his car with the knowledge that he and Cruz have to wait just a little longer to complete their mission . Beau missed Snowball, and longed to spend an evening doing nothing but cuddling with his furry baby. He'd jump for joy when the spell had faded, allowing him to finish the job he was hired for. Not only would he return to his feline child, but he'd escape the girl taking up too much of his mental space.

June 24th

Kamila

Today marked one month and two days since Grandma's funeral. It started like any other day: breakfast. Mama had been noticeably gloomier, though we hadn't spoken a word about my grandmother. My falling out with her had resulted in Mama also falling out with her, due to her defense of me. They eventually reconciled, but my mother had spoken often of the strain she felt between them. I'd never known what to say. It made me feel guilty, which made conversation more difficult. Mama always understood and respected that boundary.

Giselle, unfortunately, did not.

"I'll get it," I said, rising from my seat when the doorbell rang.

When I opened the door, I was greeted with the sight of Giselle, carrying a small box, and tears on her face.

"Everything okay?" I asked, taken aback.

"Girl, what's wrong?" Mama inquired when Giselle entered.

She sniffled loudly, and swiped at her puffy eyes, setting the box on the table. "I just...I can't believe she's been gone for a whole month! Lord, it felt like just yesterday she was at my shop, sharing everything with me." A watery laugh escaped her. "No matter how much I tried, that old woman refused to join the Smut Sluts."

"I wonder why," I grumbled under my breath.

I would've paid a lot of money to hear Giselle pester Grandma about joining an erotic book club with such a raunchy name. Despite what my grandmother would have you believe, she wasn't free of sin, but lust wasn't one of them.

Mama gave me a look, but Giselle didn't seem to hear my quip. Far more diplomatic than I, my mother reached a hand out to place on Giselle's, offering her a kind smile. "I know it's hard, Giselle. I still can't believe my mama is gone, and I know how much she valued you. So don't be ashamed—"

"I'm not," she interrupted, sniffling again and reaching for the box. "I came here to bring over some of the things she gave me, the gifts I don't use. Every Christmas and on my birthday, she'd go all out for me. I'd tell that woman I had enough things, but she wouldn't listen."

I clenched my jaw. We were getting her leftovers, and while I could admit the gesture was considerate, I couldn't deny how her words hurt. During her birthdays and on Christmas, Mama would get a card with some money. Grandma had only acknowledge me and Zara at Christmas, sending a generic granddaughter card meant to be shared. The gesture could've been seen as a truce if she'd bothered to return any of my calls. The few times she had picked up, she'd been hostile, so I gave up trying to reestablish a relationship with her.

"That's so kind, Giselle," Mama said, giving no indication she felt a way. "I'll divvy it up between me and the girls."

Giselle nodded, a sad smile spreading across her face. "You know, Miz Susie really took me under her wing during these last couple of years. Said I was the daughter she never had. It was...oh, gosh," she sniffled, swiping at her stupid eyes again. "It was such a blessing to be so close to a great woman during the final years of her life. She was better to me than my own mama, and now she's gone."

Mama stiffened; I glared.

One part of me felt pity for her, as her grief seemed genuine. Yet, I couldn't suppress my annoyance. I didn't know if the subtle jabs were intentional or not, but the shade was present and getting under my skin.

"If it wasn't for me, she would've been all alone," she continued, earning a scowl when she pinned me with a stare. "Y'all were in Miami, and never came to visit—"

"There were some obligations we couldn't get out of, and just because I wasn't present, didn't mean I loved my mother any less," Mama interrupted, shaking her head. "Look, Giselle, I know you mean well, but your comments-"

"Aren't fucking necessary," I snapped, ignoring my sympathy to glare at Giselle. Mama, ever the peacemaker, was being too nice, when that bitch didn't deserve patience. "And don't forget, she fucking barred me from visiting. Don't try to guilt us when there's more to the story, and you know it."

Both Mama's and Giselle's eyes widened.

"Kamika," Mama began, just as Giselle raised her hands in surrender and said, "I'm doing no such thing!"

"The hell you aren't. I'm sorry you lost someone dear to you, but your shade isn't necessary. We lost her too! If you miss her so much, try a fucking séance," I snarled, the collective gasp dulling my anger.

"Oh, Lord!" Giselle exclaimed, making the sign of the cross in my direction. "Fix it, Black Jesus. Guide this child onto the right path…"

I guffawed as she prayed for me under her breath. The hard look Mama fixed me with quelled my humor. I looked down at my feet, clenching my fist, and regretting saying a thing.

"Let me see you out," Mama said, walking next to Giselle. "I'll call you later, girl. We can finish talking then."

I was rooted in the same spot. Giselle didn't spare a goodbye, and I returned the favor. When Mama returned, she smacked the back of my head as she passed me, making me yelp. I finally looked up, rubbing the area of impact.

"What was that for?" I grumbled, my lips pursed into a pout.

"Don't play dumb, girl, you know what the hell that was for," she bit out, the disappointment in her eyes shaming me. "Can't you be the bigger person for once?"

Not to someone who didn't deserve it.

"She waltzed in here, throwing digs and acting like I'm the bad guy!" I retorted, upset she was taking Giselle's side, when she knew the full story. "You know I tried to reach out, and you know Grandma was the one who kept that wall up between us, not me, so I won't be made into the bad guy—"

"*I'm sorry.*"

Just as it had during that day in the park, Grandma's voice sounded in my head. Those two words were so clear that it was as if she stood at my side. But she didn't. Mama gave no indication she heard the apology, otherwise, I would've thought Grandma's spirit spoke. Instead, I recognized it as my brain manufacturing the words I longed for Grandma to say after we fell out.

"She wasn't making either of us into a bad guy, Kami," Mama said, her tone softening as she examined my face and saw how upset I was. "Giselle is just grieving and careless with her words. But, baby, you have to control your temper. When you let people get under your skin, they win."

I swiped at my suddenly watery eyes, feeling like a scolded child. "She was being tactless."

"She was venting," Mama corrected, handing me a napkin. "Her delivery was poor, but that's just Giselle."

"I don't know how you can tolerate her," I grumbled, dabbing away a stray tear with the napkin.

"I've known her since we were children, and she's always been like that. She's a shady heifer, but she's also a clueless one. Believe it or not, she probably don't know what she did wrong."

I wondered if their childhood friendship had softened Mama up to her. I could think of no other reason to willingly subject oneself to Giselle.

"The world is full of Giselles, and by the time you're my age, you learn to co-exist with them," Mama continued, swiping away another tear that slipped from my eye. "Especially when you've known one for a while."

"I don't think I'll ever deal well with people like her."

"Only time will tell, sweetie."

I nodded, though I doubted I'd ever learn to tolerate assholes. Shady hypocrites didn't make for the best company, and if we were back in Miami, I doubted Mama or me would associate with someone like her. But, alas, we weren't in Miami. We were in Gaville, surrounded by people who believed whatever lie Grandma had fed them, a lie that turned me into a villain and her into the innocent victim.

What fucking bullshit.

June 28th

Sarcasm, when understood, can be a great comedic tool. I didn't consider myself a sarcastic person, but I did employ it regularly. Unfortunately, not everyone understands it, and when sarcasm is taken seriously, it leads to a fucked up situation.

Today was a prime example.

Giselle took my sarcastic suggestion, said in a moment of anger, seriously, and I couldn't help but gape at her.

"You want to do...*what*?" Mama stammered, sounding as shocked as I felt.

It was another book club meeting, and once again, I intended to pop in and say hello, then go on my merry way. Perhaps I'd hit up Beau again, or text Delaney to see if she'd returned from hiding, because for better or worse, I wanted to see her. But Giselle's words made those ideas flee from my head.

"Girl, what?" Oletha, whom I'd come to learn was Giselle's best friend, cried. "You wanna fuck with demon shit?"

Ironic, considering she'd punished her daughter for just looking at some 'demonic' books.

"Nothing about Miz Susie was demonic," Giselle countered, sighing dramatically. "Look, the Lord understands my grief, and knows I need to talk to her to overcome it. So, because our Heavenly Father understands my heart, a séance is perfectly acceptable."

"Uhm, okay, y'all have fun with that," I said, deciding that sticking to my original plan was best.

The woman had been tormenting me without provoking her spirit, so inviting her departed soul to enter my life wasn't something I intended to do. There were too many horror movies about the dangers of fucking with the dead for me to partake in Giselle's scheme.

"Text me when you're ready, Mama, and don't get possessed," I called as I walked to the front door.

"Wait!" Giselle cried.

I considered ignoring her and walking out anyway, but Mama's words from days ago about being the bigger person gave me pause. With a sigh, I faced her again.

"Yes?" I asked, peering at Mama to see if she approved of my decision.

Her small smile told me she did, but the wariness on her face hinted that she wasn't wholly on board with Giselle's lunacy.

"The séance will have the most success if something attracts the spirit back to the world of the living," Giselle explained, and I rolled my eyes. "Miz Susie will likely show herself if her kin participate."

"Have you been researching this bullshit?" Oletha asked, outraged.

I scoffed. "So, you want to use me and Mama as bait?"

"I don't believe in séances," Mama declared, drawing all eyes to her. "Once a soul crosses over, nothing can pull them back."

I thought back to the time Zara and her friends bought a Ouija board when she was eleven. I'd been terrified that they would summon a demon, while Mama had reassured me that no such thing was possible, no matter what Hollywood and horror novelists would have you believe. She saw it as a silly game meant to entertain believers and scare wimps, whereas I saw it as an invitation for trouble. When the lights had gone out, I'd taken it as proof, just as Zara and her friends had. Mama, however, insisted it was a coincidence, chalking it up to the bad weather. As much as I'd love to have her fortitude, I was a scary ass bitch, who liked my soul out of the hands of a demon thirsting for blood after being imprisoned for three-hundred years.

"So, then there'll be no harm in staying for the séance if you don't believe in them," Giselle said breezily, giving everyone in the room a triumphant smile.

"Girl, I came here to talk about a book, not plague the dead!" one of the other members called, inspiring murmurs of agreement.

"What she said," Oletha said, pointing to the woman who spoke.

Despite the obvious disagreement, Giselle wasn't giving up. I was half convinced she'd lost her damn mind, her grief driving her mad. No way the hyper-religious, church going woman I knew and hated wanted to contact the dead.

"Do any of y'all honestly think that Miz Susie would bring us harm?" she asked.

Debatable.

"No, Mama wouldn't," my mother said, earning a smile from Giselle.

"That is, if we summon *her*, and not something else," I countered. Everyone tensed at the sound of loud footsteps coming down the stairs.

When Liliana appeared, there was a collective sigh of relief. She looked puzzled and she pursed her lips at the stares we gave her.

"What did I do now?" she asked in exasperation, taking umbrage at the attention.

I didn't blame her. The way those grown ass women talked about her two weeks ago was seared into my mind, and a recipe for a cheap nursing home when Giselle got old and feeble.

"Nothing, girl, we just were worried you were a demon," Oletha huffed, her poor choice of words dawning on no one but me, Mama, and Liliana.

"Ha, very funny," Liliana said, her eyes flashing with hurt and annoyance.

Giselle began to open her mouth, no doubt to scold her daughter. I spoke before she could get a word out, remembering how I felt all those years ago. It crushed me when the town began treating me like an enemy just for dating someone. The reasons for our alienation were different, but I imagined her feelings were much the same. Maybe it was even worse for her. I got to return to Miami, whereas she was stuck in Gaville with her judgmental mama.

"Your mama is talking about a séance, so it has everyone on edge," I explained, sparing Giselle a glance.

"Wait, how come I get my ass beat for reading some books, and you can try to talk to the dead!" Liliana exclaimed, reaching the same conclusion as me and glaring at her mother. "That isn't fair, and you know it."

Giselle stood, stomping to her daughter. "First off, little girl, watch how you talk to me. Secondly, stay out of grown folk business."

"This is why I'm going live with Dad," she retorted.

Panic flashed across Giselle's face. "The hell you are! I didn't give you permission—"

"I don't need permission! You and Dad wanted to arrange custody outside of the courts, so there's no legal reason to stay with you. And if you try to take things to court when I leave, I'll choose him," she yelled, the argument rendering everyone in the room speechless.

I noticed a few dirty looks cast my way, and as bothersome as they were, I couldn't blame them. My attempt to make Liliana feel better had backfired, all because I spoke without thinking.

"Y'all know other people are here, right?" Oletha said, shifting uncomfortably. "This ain't a discussion to be had in front of guests."

"She's right, Giselle," Mama agreed, clearing her throat. "Maybe we can adjourn this meeting—"

"No. We're doing the séance, and that's final," she hissed, glancing around the room before refocusing on Liliana. "Have you spoken to your father about this?"

"He said it's fine, and that he misses me, because unlike you, he actually cares about what I want!"

"Would you stay if your mama suspended your punishment?" I asked, shrugging when Mama shook her head at me.

If they were duking it out in front of everyone, surely, they could understand if others shared their opinions.

Liliana snorted. "As if she would—"

"I don't even see the point of the punishment, because it isn't doing any good," Giselle sniffed, looking at me than back at her daughter. "Answer her question, girl."

"Even if you did, you'd just find another reason to get mad at me. You let Dayton do whatever he wants, even play in that stupid rock band, and I can't even read without getting in trouble!"

"Dayton is almost eighteen, and you two are different children," she snapped, before sighing and shaking her head. "Your daddy lives in Baton Rouge, Liliana. That's a dangerous place, and a hell of a lot different from Gaville."

I was so fucking uncomfortable. While everyone else was watching the argument go down like it was a soap opera, I was inching closer to the door, ready to jet. When Mama noticed, she narrowed her eyes and beckoned me over with her hand. Internally groaning, I returned to her side, wishing we'd go back to talking about séances and ghosts, not witnessing a disagreement that was better discussed in private.

"You say that like it's a bad thing," Liliana said, her arms crossed over her chest.

"I'll allow you to go to the library as much as you want, as long as you go to church," Giselle offered, the pleading in her tone taking me aback.

Even if she was a massive bitch, I suppose she didn't want her daughter to leave her, or to favor her ex-husband.

Liliana dropped her arms, eyeing her mother warily. "And I want to spend weekends with Dad again. It isn't fair that I can't see him because you're angry with me."

"Hold on, you want to get off Scot free—" another book club member began.

"Girl, just shut up," Oletha whispered through her teeth. "They are having a moment."

"Fine, baby," Giselle conceded, sighing heavily. "We'll talk about this later, though."

"...Alright," Liliana muttered, giving everyone one last look before disappearing into the kitchen.

Silence descended over the room, no one knowing how to follow up after what had just happened. When Lilana returned upstairs with a bag of chips, Giselle cleared her throat.

"Uh, well, I think we've wasted enough time," she said with a forced laugh. "Forget the séance idea. We'll do things as normal."

"Thank God," someone whispered, one of the members whose name I didn't know.

I gave Mama a brief hug. "I'm going to go now. Have fun."

"Yeah, baby, I'll call you when I'm ready," she said, no longer stopping my escape.

No one paid attention to me, which was much appreciated. I deeply regretted going back on my vow of attending the meetings. Though I didn't stay for the discussion of the book, just being around the Smut Sluts for more than ten minutes drained me. Drama of some sort seemed to be a given, and Giselle had no issue airing her family's dirty laundry for all to see. That was the last time I'd step foot into that house during book club, and this time, I meant my vow.

June 30th

Kamika

Laney-Lane: Hey

I blinked. A message from Delaney was the last thing I expected to see when my phone received a notification. Like any good phone addict, its buzzing prompted me to check it within seconds. I expected a social media notification, perhaps a message from Olivia or another friend, maybe even a text from Zara or Beau. The Harris girls hadn't crossed my mind.

I considered ignoring her, petty payback for her radio silence. But my fingers began typing out a message, pressing send without input from my mind.

When Beau had ghosted me, ignoring him was so much easier, at least until I needed a pick-me-up. The incident in Burnin' Boots might've played a role, as I didn't appreciate him begging me for attention whilst planning a threesome with his raggedy ass homie. Yet, just thinking about shunning Delaney sent a pang through me, which made no sense. It was pathetic. I'd gone ten days without word from her, in which I'd seethed over her rudeness, wondered what was going on, and felt hurt over my unanswered texts.

All those emotions disappeared at the sight of her text, replaced with relief and elation. I was morphing into a simp, and it shamed me to no end.

Concern slammed into me, the intensity of it shocking me. My condition was more severe than I thought.

> Me: Omg what happened

> Laney-Lane: Allergies morphed into a cold. The medicine had me knocked tf out

> Laney-Lane: I'm good now tho

> Me: That's good

Her texts explained why I hadn't heard from her in nearly two weeks but didn't explain why Larissa wouldn't tell me. Maybe Delaney hadn't wanted me to know? That raised another list of questions, but I'd pretend my theory was the truth and chalk it up to her pride.

> Laney-Lane: Anyway, I'm all better now if you wanna come over 😊

> Me: That emoji 😐

Laney-Lane: What about it?

Certainly, she understood the implications of a winky face accompanying a text inviting me over.

Me: Be so fr

Laney-Lane: Oh

Laney-Lane: Bruh, get your mind out the gutter

It seemed that realization had just dawned on Delaney. I smirked at my phone, enjoying our conversation more than I should. Some might say I had low standards, but they existed and should've allowed me to be petty. Tit-for-tat may not be the hallmark of a healthy relationship or a good person, but I operated on the principle that you get what you give. Even if she had a reason to ignore me, I should've at least left her on read for an hour before responding, but nope.

It was too late now, so I might as well send the message I longed to.

Me: When can I come over?

"Just in time," Larissa said once she opened the door. She guided me to the kitchen, equally as rustic as the rest of the house. "Delaney's mixing the drinks right now."

Delaney waved as we walked in, an array of shit on the island. Whatever she was mixing had her focus. I took a moment to admire the room. The wooden ceiling beams supported black iron cage lights, and the oak cabinetry matched the aesthetic. The black marble countertops, high-end appliances, and expansive kitchen island were a reminder of how luxurious the house was.

At one time, Larissa's home was the kind I aspired to own. Now, I couldn't picture myself living somewhere rustic. I liked bright colors, favored traditionalism, and modern midcentury.

I shook my head. I hadn't gone there to judge the decoration, so I forced myself to give Larissa my undivided attention and acknowledge her words. "Umm, what drinks?"

I didn't turn down alcohol, but it wasn't what I was expecting when she texted me to hang out. The sun was still high in the sky, and at one time, Larissa only indulged in vices at night. But she'd changed so much from the girl who'd stolen my heart, so it was silly of me to expect that rule to remain.

"Prairie Fire."

"What the hell is that?"

"Tequila and Tabasco," Delaney answered, sparing me a smile before focusing on whatever concoction she was creating. Her back to us, she poured shit into a pitcher, allowing me to discreetly admire her. Her leggings highlighted her curves and her ass looked amazing, round and firm. She had fabulously thick, muscular legs. Anticipation filled me at the idea of riding her thigh to discover if those muscles were just for show. "I'm also adding lime."

"You're trying to kill us, mixing hard liquor with fucking hot sauce," Larissa said, pulling me out of my appraisal of her cousin.

Wait...what now?

My perving distracted me from processing the ingredients of the drink, but when I did, I blinked. "Tequila and...and *hot sauce*?"

My stomach churned at the combination, and I thanked Mama for the Caesar salad we had for dinner. It was light, so less vomit to clean.

Larissa laughed. "Yes. We're playing Truth or Drink, and horrible drinks encourage people's honesty."

"How lovely," I said with a frown, shuddering at the thought of downing such a horrid mixture.

Delaney faced us. The moment she looked at me, her tongue swept over her lips, and she gave me a once-over, staring at me with blatant appreciation instead of the covert admiration I had given her moments before.

I stood taller. My blue cropped tank top and orange spandex shorts clung to my figure and left little to the imagination. When her gaze returned to my face, she smiled. By then, I was properly flustered.

She opened her mouth to speak, but the dinging of my phone stole my attention.

"Sorry," I said, fishing it out of my pocket to see who texted me.

Flat Tire: Wassup?

"You know, it's impolite to text when people are talking to you," Delaney lightly chided. However, something about the way she said it made me believe my distraction really pressed her.

"Who are you talking to?" Larissa asked.

"Beau," I said. Deciding to resume the conversation with him another time, I tucked my phone away.

"Beau?" both women echoed.

Delaney sneered, and her cousin's brows furrowed.

"Beauden?" Delaney demanded.

My eyes grew to the size of saucers. "You know him?" I asked, unable to hide my confusion.

"Oh, I know that motherfucker," she snarled, slamming her fist onto the counter. "He's an asshole I met in New Orleans. Stay away from him."

"How do you know it's the same Beauden?" Larissa questioned, pinning her cousin with an intense stare.

I nodded my agreement, watching Delaney closely.

"How many Beaudens have you two met?" she countered, calming down ever so slightly.

"It's a popular name in New Zealand," I offered, shrugging when the two gave me a look. "I Googled it after he told me."

"Are we in fucking New Zealand, Kami?" Delaney demanded, working herself up all over again. "Look, I don't know what he's told you, but I can assure you that you barely know him."

"I met him the same night I met you." I crossed my arms and frowned. I regretted even answering the text. I didn't come over here to be grilled, and if I hadn't answered Beau, I wouldn't have been. "So, by your logic, I barely know you. Should I cut you off, too?"

Sharing the melancholy I felt at the thought would undercut my point, so I'd keep that information to myself.

"Of course not!" she said without missing a beat. "But that's different."

I cocked a brow. "How? What's the difference?"

Delaney opened her mouth, then closed it and glanced at Larissa.

"For one, she's my cousin, Kami," Larissa said briskly. "I wouldn't introduce you to someone who isn't safe."

Valid point, however, how was I going to get to know Beau if he and I didn't speak? Moreover, I'd hung out with him on a handful of occasions, enough for me to get a feel for his character.

"If he wanted to kill me, he could've done so already," I said, unable to recall a time when I felt unsafe around him.

Judging by how both women glowered at me, my words didn't reassure them. Beau vamoosing into thin fucking air had me uneasy, but it was the most unusual thing he'd done thus far. If he was truly a threat, it could've ended with my body floating in the bayou or the Mississippi, and disregarding that incident, he was no more of a threat than your average fuckboy. That compelled me to defend him, even if I was doing a poor job of it.

"What do you mean?" Delaney damn neared snarled, her tone deepening.

I recoiled. Sexy as she sounded, I hadn't known her long enough for me to appreciate such belligerence.

Larissa whispered, "Calm down." Her tone was just loud enough for me to hear. Delaney took in some breaths, then repeated her question, calmer this time.

I was unsure if I should continue. Perhaps, my initial impression of Delaney wasn't too far off. Her show of aggression had my initial wariness returning. Unless she'd taken some sips of the liquor before I'd arrived, her behavior couldn't be chalked up to alcohol.

"The night we met, he was stranded on the side of the road." Another human being was with him, one far worse, so I suppose it didn't wholly count as me being alone with him. "I went out to eat with him at a restaurant. I ran into him at the park—"

"The park people barely go to?" Delaney ground out, interrupting me.

"Some people were there," I said in a vain attempt to soothe her fears. I'd walked out of the situation alive. "Beau didn't murder me and dump my body in the woods or throw me to the gators, so I think I'm safe."

My bad joke earned more scowls. I ignored them and continued speaking. "And last week, when you were *ignoring* me," I said, unable to hide how much that bothered me, "I hung out with him. Even went to his motel room and was alone with him for an hour. The worse thing he did when we were alone was serve me awful fucking pickles."

Delaney's face scrunched. "Lemon, garlic, lime salt, and red peppers?"

My eyebrows shot up, and I nodded. Just how well did she know him? It made me wonder what Beau had done to earn her ire. Maybe her worry had more credibility than I thought.

Larissa took a deep breath, then plastered on a smile. The tick in her jaw made the gesture easy to see through, as did the side-eye aimed at

Delaney. "How about we play Truth or Drink now? Jack is watching the kids in the nursery."

Her casual mention of her family didn't send pain through my heart as it had days ago, a minor victory, in my book. It was cheeky of me to feel that way, and flat-out wrong to lust after a married woman. The fact that I was coming to terms with Larissa moving on relieved me and made it easier to focus on my own romantic prospects.

Namely, Delaney. As gorgeous as Larissa was, her cousin had her beat. And, dammit, looks mattered to me. I was a self-proclaimed vain bitch, which led me to take a seat on an island stool alongside the Harris women so the game could commence. The girl belonged on magazine covers, and even with her oddities, I enjoyed hanging out with her. She was as fun as she was beautiful.

"Okay, the rules are simple," Larissa declared, pouring out the shots. "A question will be asked, and we all drink or answer."

As if we were in a classroom, Delaney raised her hand, and I snickered.

Larissa rolled her eyes. "Girl, you don't have to do that shit. Just ask what you wanna ask."

Another giggle escaped me, and Delaney smirked at me.

"What if I want to ask only one of you a question?"

Larissa shrugged. "One of us would sit a round out. Why? What do you wanna ask Kamika?"

"How do you know she doesn't want to ask you something?" I inquired, curious about her certainty I'd be the target of her cousin's questioning.

"She knows enough about me," Larissa explained.

"So…doesn't that render this game pointless?"

"Enough explanations," Delaney declared. "Let's play. Kamika, what's your ideal woman?"

"You," I blurted before I could stop myself, slapping a hand over my mouth.

Both Larissa and Delaney cackled, their amusement at my expense making me groan. I covered my face with my hands. "Shut up! I'm just being honest."

"Explain what makes me so great," Delaney teased, standing taller, her pretty eyes gleaming with delight.

Awaiting my answer, she stared at me while I contemplated tainting my taste buds with a shot. Delaney was a cool chick, but the primary reason I opted to ignore our first encounter stemmed from my physical attraction to her. Some people were proud of their pretty privilege, while others didn't appreciate the focus on their looks. I didn't know what group Delaney fell into.

I didn't say that, though. Instead, I voiced my second line of thought: the truth. Honesty was the whole point of this game, after all.

"Well, at first it was just because you're fine as hell," I admitted.

She blinked at me. The shock at my blatant admission quickly transformed into smugness, urging me to continue.

"Then, during the times that we've hung out, I enjoyed your company," I admitted, fidgeting with my hands. "You're a talented artist, which is a plus. And even though sickness made you ghost my ass, I enjoy texting you. You aren't dry in any situation, and you're easy to be around, so here I am."

Larissa was beaming, no doubt happy her match-making efforts were paying off.

"You saying I'm the perfect package, huh?" Delaney asked in a sing-song voice, her chest puffed out.

"Girl, fuck off," Larissa said with a snort. "You know she did not say that shit."

"It was close enough," Delaney defended, then reached out to touch my hand. "If it's any consolation, I feel the same way."

"You think you're the perfect woman?" Larissa goaded, snickering when Delaney flipped her off.

"No! I think Kamika is the ideal woman, dumbass," she grumbled, shaking her head, and brushing her hand against mine once again. "You're a catch, babe."

My cheeks burned, a mixture of embarrassment and a surprising warmth spreading through me. Delaney's touch lingered, igniting something unexpected. Heat rushed through me, and I clenched my thighs together.

"Next round," I announced, ready to move on, a light-hearted question already in my head. "If you had a chance to be with a werewolf or a vampire, who would you choose?"

"Werewolf," both women answered without hesitation.

Despite my love for Edward, I nodded in agreement. In most media, werewolves had the privilege of a soulmate. I would kill for that. The dating field was saturated with people who wouldn't make for a suitable fling, let alone the love of my life. If I were with the fictional being, it stood to reason they were meant for me.

Plus, living forever seemed real fucking tiring, and unless those close to you were given immortality as well, loneliness was a guarantee.

Delaney sighed in relief. "Happy we're all on the same page."

"My turn," Larissa stated. "This is for you two because I'm happily married. Describe the perfect first date."

Delaney hummed in consideration, pouring shots of plain tequila as we pondered. We clinked the tiny glasses together, downing the alcohol than sucking on our lime. The liquor flowed through me, warming my body and loosening my inhibitions.

"Okay, answer the question, ladies," Larissa prompted.

"Dinner and dancing," I said without a second thought. "Grabbing a bite to eat to get to know the person, and dancing to work the food off, and because it's fun."

"And a good test of stamina," Delaney chimed, making me and Larissa guffaw.

"Shut your nasty ass up," Larissa said around giggles.

"Oh, so you don't want me to answer?"

"I want you to answer," I said before Larissa could reply, pouring myself another shot. Once it was down, I fluttered my lashes at her dramatically. "Pretty please?"

Hints of red rose to her cheek, and she swallowed. "Uh, in New Orleans, there was this interactive art exhibit that was really fucking cool. Gaville doesn't have one, but an interactive art exhibit followed by dinner would be a good first date."

I nodded in agreement. "They have several interactive museums in Miami, and they're also fun."

"And you can't go wrong with food," Larissa quipped.

"Back to me," Delaney said, tapping on her chin and humming as she thought of a question. When it came to her, she grinned. "Favorite sex position?"

"You are too freaked out," Larissa groaned, shaking her head as I laughed.

"Okay, fine, I'll be good," Delaney conceded with a teasing smile. "Do you two believe in fate?"

"I do," Larissa said without hesitation.

"I'm not sure," I answered after some contemplation. "Some things are just luck of the draw—*fate*. But the choices you make do alter the outcome of your life, so I think it's 50/50."

"Explain," Delaney stated, giving me her undivided attention.

"Well, you can say that a child born to wealthy parents, or a child born with a high IQ are fated to be successful, because they have an advantage over others. But, if that child grows up and makes bad choices, their path changes."

"What about soulmates? Do you believe in that?" Larissa asked.

"I think there are people you're more compatible with than others, but I don't think there's only one person out there for you," I replied, peeking at Delaney.

Sadness wasn't an emotion I expected to see plastered across her face. My heart ached, and I wondered what was going through her head.

"Agreed," she said with a heavy sigh. "Which can be a good thing, because imagine if your soulmate is shitty."

Silence descended upon the room. I cleared my throat, asking the first question that came to mind. "Do y'all have any secret tattoos?"

"Nope," Larissa and Delaney chimed.

"I'm afraid of the pain," Delaney explained, smiling at me, her sadness disappearing as swiftly as it had come. "What about you?"

"Yeah, I have one on my hip," I said, pulling down the left side of my shorts to reveal the black feather that tiny birds flew from. "Got it last year with my best friend. I was supposed to get red, and she was supposed to get blue, but the shop said they couldn't do any color because I'm too dark. It was a spur-of-the-moment thing, so we both got all black."

The alcohol made me too honest, as only Olivia knew why my tattoo was so dull, when I adored vibrancy.

Delaney stopped staring so intensely at my exposed hip, her eyes snapping to my face. Her lips curled. "That's fucking bullshit. One goddamn Google search would reveal it's possible; they just didn't have the skill to do it."

I shrugged. "Yeah, but it's too late now, and I really like the tattoo."

"It's very pretty," Larissa said, before smiling. "Okay, another question for you two, because I'm a married woman," she began, making me and Delaney roll our eyes.

"Bruh, stop cheating by asking questions you won't answer," she ordered, sticking her tongue out when her cousin flipped her off.

"Anyway," Larissa said loudly, looking between us. "Would you hook up with your high school crush today?"

Shit. She was my high school crush. That was a can of worms I was in the process of closing.

As Delaney said, "Nope, she's a bum bitch to me now," I downed a shot of tequila and toad, gagging and grimacing as the abomination slid down my throat.

This might be a long night.

Married life had changed Larissa. No longer could she stay awake until the wee hours of the morning, giggling and gossiping. When the clock struck one, the chick had to run. She was a mother and wife first, a friend second. Even when unwinding, her family wasn't far from her mind.

"Milk came from where?" Delaney asked, gaping at her cousin.

My reaction was similar. Hearing of the trials and tribulations of pregnancy reaffirmed my decision to adopt. Larissa cackled at our faces.

"My armpits. It was fucking awful," Larissa answered with giggles. "Had to wear pads in my shirt to absorb it."

"Oh, hell no," I said, shuddering at the thought.

Footsteps caught everyone's attention. Jack came in, carrying a squirming Shay.

"Babe, are y'all gonna be wrapping up soon? Shay's restless, and the loud talking ain't helping," Jack lamented, a deep frown etched into his face as he bounced his daughter.

Why the fuck his ass looked directly at me when he made the comment, I didn't know. Delaney was just as loud, if not louder. For the sake of harmony, I ignored his shadiness. It was already established that he didn't like me, despite his stupid apology.

"You haven't tried to put her down yet? It's past her bedtime," Larissa said, standing and approaching them.

"I have, but she can't sleep without *you* reading her a bedtime story," he replied, the offense in his voice almost laughable. "She doesn't like how I do it."

"Because it sounds like you're reading a fucking textbook," Delaney inserted, shrugging when the couple glared at her. "What? I've heard how he reads to that child, and no adult should be subjected to that, let alone a baby."

I laughed at her comment. Delaney winked and puffed her chest out, while Jack scowled, and Larissa's eyes narrowed into slits.

"Not too much on my husband now. I don't want to end the night with bullshit."

My humor evaporated. Not only did Larissa love Jack, but she was also sensitive when it came to him.

Bleh.

I sighed and stood; fucking Jack ruining my mood. I wasn't ready for the night to end. Returning to my grandmother's house would weigh me down with grief and worry and curiosity, all emotions I preferred to ignore. And every time I stepped foot in the century-old residence, the past replayed in my mind.

"I'll be going now, so handle your kid, 'Rissa," I said.

"Already?" Delaney whined, her lips pursing into a pout.

Larissa snorted. "Girl, it's late as hell."

Smiling at the exchange, I waved at Delaney before leaving the room. I purposefully ignored Jack as I breezed past him, but I doubted the asshole would've responded if I had bid him goodbye.

As I walked the hallway, my thoughts returned to Larissa. Nowadays, life was different for everyone, and it would never return to how it had been. If I came to Larissa's on the fence about my lingering feelings, I left with full knowledge that the past was gone. It was time to let it go. Perhaps that's why I bowed out gracefully. Or, maybe, confrontation gained me nothing but a reputation for being difficult.

I stepped onto the porch and breathed in deeply. I glanced over my shoulder and stared at the door. Once upon a time, the woman on the other side had been everything to me and I to her. We'd planned a life together before we even got a chance to truly live. But that was a bygone time. She'd found her mate, her happiness; I had to do the same.

Sadness pulling at me, I faced forward again and fanned myself.

Gaville summers were hot and humid, redolent with sweet scents, and alive with the noise of the katydids and other nightcrawlers. The Mississippi snaked along the edge of town, skirting the very forest I'd galloped through earlier.

I wouldn't return to my grandma's on that route. Dark and spooky was one thing, foggy and frightening quite another.

At loose ends, I walked down the porch steps, paused again, and sighed. I contemplated just sitting down and texting my mama to see if she was still awake. Perhaps we could go for a late-night drive. Or watch *Twilight*. Once, she enjoyed the movie as much as me. We'd binged them a thousand times, sharing snacks and laughs as supernatural teenage drama unfolded. It'd been such a long time since we binged the movies, I wasn't sure if her love for them remained.

"Are you okay?"

I jumped at the sound of Delaney's voice. I hadn't heard the door open or her approach, so it shocked me that she suddenly stood next to me.

"Girl!" I placed a hand on my chest, my pulse thumping. "You scared the shit out of me."

She smiled. "Oops. Sorry."

The well-lit property afforded me a good view of her gorgeous face. Laughing, I shook my head. "No, you aren't."

"You're right," she admitted. "I'm not. You were so deep in thought, you didn't notice me standing behind you since you walked out of the house."

I frowned. "It wasn't right after," I protested. "When I walked out and closed the door, I turned and stared at it. You weren't there."

"I was right behind you when you stepped outside," she insisted calmly.

"You're gaslighting me," I snapped. "I know you weren't there!"

She shrugged. "If that's what you want to believe."

"Fuck off. It's what I know."

The moonlight caught her eyes and made them glow. "I didn't come out here to argue with you, Kami," she said softly, my name on her lips warming me from head to toe. "I'm leaving the lovebirds and their whelps to themselves to go for a walk."

"It's late," I said, worried about her walking at night unaccompanied, when I was about to do the same damn thing.

She smiled down at me. "Fresh air always helps me sleep. Let me walk you home."

"Okay," I agreed without issue, falling into step with her.

She reached out, intertwining our fingers. I looked up at her, but she was focused on the path ahead. The corners of my mouth quirked up, and I squeezed her hand. This time, she looked down at me and returned my smile. Our hands fit together perfectly, and her presence was comforting as we walked to my home.

"Tonight was fun," I said idly, my heart fluttering when she gently squeezed my hand, just as I'd done with hers moments before.

"It was," she agreed. "We need to do this again sometimes."

"Definitely."

The rest of the walk home was silent. However, it was the comfortable kind of quiet shared with someone you were close to. Or, in this case, someone you were forging a bond with.

"Good night, Delaney," I said as she walked me up the porch steps and to my front door.

Only when it was unlocked did our hands return to our sides, much to my disappointment. I frowned, immediately wanting to feel her skin against mine again. Fueled by liquid courage, I stood on my tiptoes and planted a kiss on her cheek. I giggled at her shocked reaction and unlocked my door.

"Bye," I cooed in a singsong, disappearing into my house before she could recover.

The sound of a gasp ruined my intention to spy on Delaney through the peephole. Instead, the two figures on the couch came into view, breaking into the haze of alcohol that had descended over my brain. Delaney and tequila had distracted me, blinding me to the presence of Colton's truck. However, seeing him with my Mama, who was sitting on his lap, made him impossible to ignore.

"What the ever loving hell?" I screeched.

Colton smirked at me, but Mama looked like a deer caught in the headlights. She attempted to stand, but he tightened his hold on her and nuzzled her neck.

I staggered forward. "Fucking asshole," I hissed.

Mama stiffened and threw her usual look of warning. "That's enough, Kami," she said, her voice a weird combination of breathy and annoyed. "You won't disrespect my friend."

I looked at her as if she had grown a second head. She must've thought I was born yesterday if I believed they were just friends. My eyes strayed to the empty wine bottle on the coffee table, the papers that'd been strewn across it nowhere to be seen. She'd straightened up just for him, the thought irking me further.

That asshole kissed my mother again, this time on her lips. "We wasn't expecting you back any time soon anyway." He grinned at me. If Mama didn't see his vicious look, I did, and I hated him a little more. "It figures, since you don't have a life of your own and have to stick your nose in your mama's business."

"Colton," Mama hissed, saddling him with a glare.

"What?" he said, feigning innocence.

I waited for Mama to explain what the fuck was wrong with what he said, for her to defend me, but she said nothing. I remembered that was one reason I always preferred my grandmother, until she turned her back on me, too. Mama spoke up for me up to a point, but she generally sided with her men. She did it when she originally dated Colton, and she did it with Zara's father. As a little girl, it crushed me. As a grown woman, it angered me.

"Get out of my house," I ordered, wishing I was big enough to throw his ass out.

"Little girl—"

"Just go, Colton," Mama sighed, stopping whatever bullshit he was about to say.

He looked between us, glared at me, then stomped out, slamming the door behind him. We both jumped at the sound.

"Asshole," I muttered.

"Can't you hold your tongue for once?" Mama said sharply, making me recoil.

"You would've known if I hadn't held my tongue," I replied, crossing my arms. "And Colton? Really? The man who cheated on you? Mama, you're worth more than him!"

"I know that, chile, that's why it isn't anything serious!" she fumed, plopping on the couch and burying her face in her hands. She inhaled deeply, then looked up at me, her narrowed eyes bloodshot. "Let me remind you, child, that I'm still your mama. You don't get to scold me for my choices when I don't scold you for yours."

"The other night with Beau," I began, not forgetting her reaction to him. "You came onto the porch—"

"And asked some questions!" she interrupted. "I didn't insult the boy or antagonize him, like you insist on doing with Colton."

"You could have any man you want, and you chose the one with community dick?" I blurted, tequila making me speak my every thought. "You can do what you want, but that doesn't mean I have to like an asshole who fucked over you."

"Good night, Kami," Mama snapped, standing from the couch and disappearing into the hallway.

I glared at her back. When I heard her bedroom door close, I stormed to my room, slamming the door for emphasis. I hated the hurt rising up in me. Not only had Colton's presence ruined my good feelings, but he reminded me nobody, even my beautiful, kind mother, was perfect. And unfortunately, her form of imperfection made her a wife or a girlfriend first, and a mother second.

My bottom lip wobbled, signaling my impending tears. Another downside of alcohol, it made me so fucking emotional. I grabbed my phone, needing someone to vent to. I tried to call Delaney, but her phone rang to no avail. A text came through.

> Laney-Lane: Talking to Larissa rn, text you later

Sighing, I sent her an 'Okay'. How she got home that quickly was a mystery, but my head hurt too much for me to dwell on it. Instead, I scrolled to my second choice, the one person who could understand what I was feeling perfectly.

Zara.

> Me: Guess who Mama is dating now?

At first, I doubted that she'd answered. It was late, after all. But, within a minute, my phone chimed.

> Zara: Who?

> Me: Colton.

> Zara: WHAT?!

I snickered, though my amusement at Zara's reaction didn't lessen my upset. I explained what I walked in on, her texts mirroring how I felt. Her relationship with our mother was more strained, but our hatred of Colton was mutual. If only Mama felt the same way and barred that slimy toad from her life for good.

July 2nd

Kamika

With Mama's secret out of the bag, she had no issue flaunting her relationship with Colton. I understood well the appeal of using a fling as a distraction; I just wish she'd chosen somebody different. Despite her declaration that it wasn't anything serious, I worried that her heart and her mind would have different ideas. She'd always been a lover, not a luster. And if her relationship with Colton rekindled completely, I'd have no choice but to kill him.

Okay, well, that was a little extreme. I felt guilty taking the lives of bugs, barring roaches and mosquitoes, so I knew killing a human was out of the question, even someone as lowdown as Colton. However, though I might not employ violence, I would use everything in my arsenal to steer him away from my mother should they become an official item, and not a situationship.

What fucking bullshit. My 45-year-old mother was in a *situationship* with her ex. I thought her maturity would protect her from such a bad decision, but I was wrong.

I huffed, groaning into the cushion. I'd been lying on the couch since she left for her date with him, unable to muster the energy to do anything but fret. The trashy reality TV show barely held my attention. Mama had made it clear she didn't want me sticking my nose in her business, and while her reasoning was understandable, agreeing with her bad choices without question was impossible.

I swear, raising a parent could be so damn difficult.

Unable to focus on the messy antics of the women on screen, I searched for another program. Unfortunately, nothing caught my eye. I switched to streaming, but even the movies and shows on my watchlist seemed uninteresting. Today, I had nothing to distract myself.

My calendar was clear for the rest of the week…the month…my summer in Gaville. Unless I returned to Miami. I gazed around the room. For all the progress Mama had made going through Grandma's things, so much remained. If I had the energy, I might straighten up a bit. Alas, I didn't. Besides, Mama had a certain way of organizing things. She hadn't shared her method for this mess with me, so I wouldn't know what went where. Maybe I'd text Delaney and see if she wanted to grab a bite to eat. Our conversations were brief, but we'd been texting daily for the past three days.

I turned off the TV, gazing at the dark screen and cringing at my exhausted reflection. Yesterday, I was hungover and upset. Today, I was just upset, too down to do a goddamn thing. Perhaps, instead of being social or productive, I'd just sleep. Eventually, I opted to stare at the ceiling. The longer I lay, the heavier my eyes grew. Wanting to rest my mind, I allowed my lids to shut.

Barely cognizant, I turned to my side to get more comfortable. Instead, I tumbled off the couch and landed on the wooden floor.

"Shit!" Miraculously, my head avoided the edge of the coffee table. My foot, however, wasn't spared. "Goddammit."

Pain radiated upwards, snatching my dawning relaxation. Annoyance swamping me, I sat up. I'd been in a bad mood since Mama left for her date, and this proved to be a breaking point. In a fit of irrational rage, I shoved a pile of old magazines off the table, then cussed myself out. Now, I had to clean that shit up.

"Stupid bitch," I muttered, crawling to the mess and gathering the magazines.

The violent swipe off the coffee table opened many of them and revealed their contents. Instead of gossip articles from decades ago and 1980s beauty tips, I found aged papers taped to the pages.

What the hell?

My mess was momentarily forgotten. I flipped through the magazines, curiosity overwhelming me. As I skimmed the first page, my eyes widened. The topic of coven ownership confused and shocked me. More perplexing was the repeated mention of my great-grandmother's name, Marine LeClair. Per the date, she would've been carrying my grandmother at the time. Reading the next page sent me into a tailspin. My great-grandmother and her two eldest children lived on land owned by the Harris *pack*, headed by Martin Harris.

I reread it over and over again to connect the dots. I was missing something. The papers seemed to focus on the supernatural. *Covens* suggested witches and *packs* recalled wolves. Or, in this case, *werewolves*.

Ludicrous.

Such creatures didn't exist outside of fiction and fairy tales. But, if so, why were there so many papers—hidden ones, at that— mentioning such things? Two possibilities came to mind. The first, my great-grandma had been penning a self-insert supernatural novel. The second, she was a fucking nutjob.

"Try again."

How ironic. I was calling my great-grandmother a nutjob, when I was hearing the voice of a dead woman on the regular now. Either I'd gone insane, or she was haunting my ass. Even in death, she couldn't let me rest.

Sleep had lost its appeal. I cleaned up the mess I'd created, then got to my feet. Sulking would do no good, and whatever I'd just read had given me a headache. It would be so easy to dismiss it as nonsense, but something told me there was more to the story. That could've just been a sign of my dwindling sanity.

My phone dinged. Opening it up, I saw a message from Delaney. Instantly, my mood lifted, warmth spreading through me as I thought about the peck I'd given her a couple of days ago. It was an innocent kiss on the cheek, but I couldn't stop thinking about it. I'd accepted my status as a simp and knew nothing could be done about it. Next time, I'd be even bolder and kiss her on the lips.

Laney-Lane: I'm bored and hungry. Meet me at La Mer?

Food and company were exactly what I needed, a perfect distraction to the fuckery I'd uncovered.

Delaney

Two things had been on Delaney's mind since the night of Truth or Drink, both having to do with Kamika. The tattoo on her hip and the kiss she'd gifted her with. The peek of skin had mesmerized Delaney, and the tattoo adorning Kamika's flesh had made the glimpse all the more tantalizing.

And, fuck, but the bit of red lace she'd seen had almost sent her into heat again.

She shook her head as she walked into the restaurant, forcing her mind to remain out of the gutter. The memory of Kamika's soft lips on her cheek made the endeavor difficult. Nothing had been raunchy about the kiss, but the fact that her mate had initiated such intimate contact short-circuited her. The tequila had slowed her reaction time, and if she hadn't been shocked out of her goddamn mind, that kiss could've turned into something much steamier. As it was, she'd needed to rub one out before she slept. The instant Larissa had finished chewing her goddamn head off, she'd fled to her room to take care of her issue.

Turned out, her cousin hadn't forgotten her reaction to Beau and had grilled Delaney until she confessed to dabbling in bounty hunting in New Orleans. Thankfully, Aunt Galena was pulling an all-nighter at the hospital, and Jack had been sworn to secrecy. That was the best outcome she could've hoped for.

Well, other than tracking Beau down and beheading him before anyone found out, but she hadn't a clue where he was staying, and that ship had sailed.

"Table for one?" the hostess asked as Delaney entered La Mer.

She shook her head. "No, I'm waiting for someone."

The girl nodded, then gestured to the benches against the wall. "You can have a seat, and I'll get you two a table as soon as the other party arrives."

"Thank you," Delaney said, settling on the bench closest to the hostess stand.

She played *Fruit Ninja* on her phone to pass the time. The game might've been old, but it was a classic that Delaney continued to enjoy.

"Hey," Kamika greeted, drawing her attention.

Delaney's pupils dilated when she laid eyes on her, unable to focus on anything but her mate. Her white halter top made her dark skin glow. The blue midi skirt she wore was decorated with white flowers, and had a high slit on her left side, revealing glimpses of her tattoo. Her floral sandals and flower earrings matched the skirt, and made Kamika look nice and summery.

"Hey," Delaney breathed, standing and pulling her into a hug.

As subtly as possible, she inhaled Kamika's scent. Warmth enveloped her body, her cheeks burning as she remembered how that strawberry and caramel body spray had comforted her doing her heat, and enhanced her sessions with *David*.

"You look nice," she complimented when they separated.

Kamika smiled at her. "Thank you." She swept her gaze over Delaney, her tongue swiping over her glossed lips when she homed in on her pierced belly button. "You do, too. We're kind of matching."

That was debatable. They both wore blue bottoms and a white top, but Delaney's pinstripe jeans and off-the-shoulder sweater were decidedly more casual. Sure, she wore a chain and hoop earrings, and her sneakers were pristine white, but Kamika still outdressed her.

"Nah, babe, you outshine me," Delaney said, giving her another once-over. "And we're dressed for different seasons."

"You're dressed for inside a cold-ass restaurant," Kamika corrected. "I'm dressed for Louisiana's heat."

"That works, too," she replied with a small smile, then nodded her head at the hostess stand. "C'mon, let's get a table."

The two people ahead of them were seated quickly, and they didn't have to wait long before they were escorted to a table.

"Your waiter will be with you shortly," the hostess stated with a polite smile, before returning to her station.

"I didn't know you had any piercings," Kamika said when they were alone. Her eyes flickered to her earrings. "Well, besides your ears, but you know what I mean."

Delaney nodded. "They're less scary than a tattoo."

Kamika cocked her head to the side. "How? A needle is a needle. Pain is present for both."

"Yeah, but piercings are quicker, and the needles are different."

Delaney always wanted a tattoo, but the method used for humans wouldn't cut it for a werewolf. By the time the artist got to the last part of the tattoo, the first part would've been absorbed into the skin. The needle needed to be silver for a tattoo to stick for a shifter, and wolfsbane needed to be present in the ink. It would trick the body into thinking the tattoo was a scar, leaving it unabsorbed. Yet, that method hurt like a motherfucker. She'd tested it as a teenager, giving her arm a fake beauty mark. That tiny prick had been excruciating, and she knew that a large, noticeable piece would have her passing out.

The waiter appeared, a man who appeared to be in his 30s. "Hello, I'm Alex, and I'll be taking care of y'all tonight," he greeted with a smile, examining both Delaney and Kamika. "Can I get you two started with a drink?"

"I'll have a grapefruit beer," Delaney announced, the item her go-to whenever she ate at La Mer. "And some fried gator bites."

"Excellent choice," the waiter said, winking at her before looking at Kamika. "And for you, ma'am?"

"Mango iced tea, please, and the seafood spinach cheese dip."

"Great. I'll send those out shortly."

When he disappeared to put their orders in, Delaney tsked dramatically. "You're expensive."

Kamika's eyebrows shot up. "How?"

"The dip is the priciest appetizer on the menu."

"Well, it has crab in it, and I'm paying for my food, so—"

"No, you're not," Delaney interrupted, snickering at Kami's shock. "I invited you, so I'm paying."

Her expression became sheepish, a realization seeming to dawn on her. "Oh."

Delaney cocked a brow, noting how Kamika fidgeted with her menu. "Whatchu thinking about, babe?"

"I just realized that this is sorta date," she confessed, gnawing on her bottom lip. Delaney couldn't help but laugh, earning a scowl from her mate. "Girl, that shit isn't even funny."

"No, but it's adorable," Delaney countered. "And take the 'sorta' out of it. This *is* a date. If you want it to be," she quickly added.

She was still terrified of scaring Kamika off, and didn't want one misstep to undo everything. It'd be crushing if she refuted her, but she'd respect her decision for the time being. However, if she didn't protest the declaration, Delaney could say their relationship had officially been taken to the next level.

"I do," Kamika said quietly, her posture relaxing as she set her hands on the table. "You probably guessed from the other night, but I really like you. More than I thought I would when we met."

Delaney cringed at the memory. She'd acted like a jackass, but she hadn't expected to encounter another potential mate, so soon after breaking things off with Toria. Another witch, at that. It seemed like fate was mocking her, but after getting to know Kamika, she understood that the two women couldn't be more different.

"Yeah, that wasn't my proudest moment," Delaney replied after a heartbeat of silence. "And I'm happy you're giving me a real chance."

Kamika's sweet smile was comforting. Delaney opened her mouth to speak, but a grating voice interrupted her.

"Here you are," Alex chirped. As he set their order on the table, Delaney frowned at his awful timing. "Have you ladies decided what you want, or do y'all need more time?"

"More time, thank you," Kamika said, making the man nod and scamper off.

The moment ruined, they fell quiet, munching on the food and sipping their drinks. Jazz and blues played throughout the restaurant, preventing awkwardness from descending on the table. But Delaney still longed to get back to the previous discussion. Unfortunately, she didn't know what to say, especially because Kamika didn't seem inclined to rekindle their conversation.

"I have a question," she began, her nerves returning as she gave Delaney her attention.

"I assume I have the answer," Delaney replied with a smile, though her mate's reaction made her anxious.

Kamika gave a courtesy giggle, then nodded. "You do, because it has to do with your family."

Delaney froze. Kamika's eyes darted all over her face, and Delaney forced her expression to stay neutral. She wouldn't give anything away until she heard the question, even as *her* mind ran wild with what the question would be. It could be anything from asking about her relationship with her parents before they passed, to an inquiry about Harris family history, or God forbid, an assertion of the truth.

"I'm all ears, babe," Delaney said, forcing her smile to stay plastered on her face.

"Can you tell me a little about Martin Harris?"

On the surface, the question was harmless enough, but the reason behind it was unknown, making relaxing a challenge.

"He was the grandson of the town's founder," Delaney stated. "And Larissa's great-grandfather, through her Daddy's side."

When slavery ended, humans began settling around their village, prompting Martin Harris' grandfather to push for Gaville to become an incorporated town to have greater local control and autonomy.

"You two are related via y'all's mothers?"

She nodded. "Yeah. Why the sudden interest in our family tree?"

Delaney tried to keep her tone light, but her words sounded sharp even to her ears.

"His name was mentioned in one of my grandmother's old documents, and I got curious," Kamika explained, her lips downturned. "Turned out, he knew her mama."

Well, shit.

Kamika's eyes were sharp and assessing, hinting that there was more to the story. Delaney couldn't say if she knew the truth, but she definitely knew more than she was letting on.

"Gaville was even smaller back then, so it isn't shocking," Delaney said evenly, her guard up high.

Her plan to tell Kamika the truth excluded prematurely revealing family details or dropping a bomb on her mid-meal at a restaurant. Delaney wouldn't say anything incriminating unless Kamika directly asked, and even then, she'd avoid answering directly until they were somewhere private.

"The Harrises have been here since before Gaville was founded, right?"

Delaney nodded. "Since the early 19th century."

"Can you tell me a bit more about y'all's family?" Kamika pushed, prodding for an answer she found satisfactory.

Delaney reasoned that she couldn't possibly know the truth, as no one from the pack would've told her. Beau might've, but shielding Kamika from the supernatural world would keep her guard down, making whatever raggedy reason he had for growing closer to her easier. That left the possibility of her finding out independently, likely through whatever document that mentioned Martin Hariss' name.

"Why the sudden probing, Kami?" Delaney asked.

She shrugged. "I don't know. I just find it interesting that our families have known each other for so long."

Nothing about Kamika's demeanor indicated the words were a lie, and Delaney relaxed ever so slightly.

"So...can you?" Kamika requested, leaning back against her seat. "Please?"

"Nope," Delaney said with faux cheer, pretending the way Kami's face dropped didn't bother her. "I've been sworn to secrecy."

Her eyes widened, then narrowed as she clicked her tongue. "Haha, how hilarious. I'm fucking rolling."

Delaney grinned. "I know, I'm a comedy genius."

"Yep," Kamika agreed, her face softening as her tiny smile returned. "Up there with Eddie Murphy and Bernie Mac."

"The glazing is appreciated, babe, but there's no need to lie," she joked, praying she dropped the discussion.

"Now, be for real. This is serious. I've been sworn to secrecy is Hollywood-level corny."

Delaney winced. Kami wasn't lying. She could've come up with a better line, but the investigation caught her unawares. Looking at the stubborn tilt of her mate's head, she knew the subject wouldn't be dropped, so she scrambled for an acceptable version. In truth, she did struggle to remember the exact story of her pack's origin. It had taken so many twists and turns over the years, the truth was lost well before she was born. Out of all the legend and lore, she'd been told only two held any validity.

"Well, from what I understand, an ancestor of Martin Harris, an upper crust Creole, fucked over his fiancé, a Creole from an even higher stock. This woman had a very powerful family and a French daddy, and they didn't take kindly to this. The mistress ended up pregnant and went to the dude's future father-in-law." Delaney warmed to the story and rolled her shoulders. "He fled New Orleans to escape the wrath of the Demontlizants and came to the place that eventually became Gaville." She ended the story with a wide smile. "That's as much as I know."

"Why would he have to flee? Wasn't it commonplace for wealthy men in Antebellum New Orleans to take lovers?"

"Clearly, her family didn't believe in that."

"Actually, it was common everywhere," Kami said, ignoring Delaney's comment. "Wealthy men had wives and mistresses, so why would Martin's ancestor have to flee?"

Because there was no wife. It was a witch who dabbled in Voodoo, and she cursed her unfaithful lover, his kin, and all future generations to become werewolves, then revealed his secret to all of New Orleans. He'd come to the area to avoid being hunted down and killed.

"The girl was half-French," Delaney reminded her. "Martin's ancestor, though powerful, would've been considered a downgrade, because he was a regular Creole."

Aka, *colored*, making his infidelity an offense that couldn't go ignored. Being *Passé Blanc* likely saved his life, but if the woman he wronged knew the truth, she had the potential to get him killed.

"Besides, it's just a story, Kami," she continued, considering offering the other accepted story of Harris family history.

In the second version, a collection of Creoles and Free People of Color—*les gens libre de couleur*—who suffered the affliction of lycanthropy, banded together and created a village where they wouldn't have to hide. Likely, the truth lay somewhere in the middle. But in both versions, others of their kind joined the pack and adopted the surname 'Harris' to honor the family who created their safe space, and to create a cover story that they were all related.

"Ready to order?" the waiter interrupted.

"Not yet—"

Delaney snatched her menu. "I am. I'm starving."

"I haven't looked at the menu yet," Kami said. "And neither have you."

"How about I give you five more minutes?"

Before Delaney could stall further, the man walked off.

"Do you know what I find interesting?" Kami snatched the menu and snapped it open. "The papers mention *covens* and *packs*."

Fuuuuuuuucccccccckkkkkkkkk.

No, fuck. Make that fuckity, fuck, fuck, fuck.

"That's supernatural shit," Delaney said with a breezy laugh. "Right?" she asked, snatching her water glass and gulping.

"Yep. Know anything about that?"

Oh yeah. Delaney set the glass down and licked her lips. "Nope."

"Mama isn't a believer either," Kami revealed, searching Delaney's face. "So, I understand if this is weird. I thought it was weird, too."

"Maybe your grandma was writing a novel."

Kami smiled. "That's what I said. And it would've been my great-grandmother. Remember?"

That small detail was lost in fear and fuckery. "Not really, babe. I'm sorry."

"And here I thought you'd hang onto my every word."

"Never doubt that," Delaney returned, wondering if she'd really get off so easily or if Kami was arming herself with another round of questions to throw at her.

She'd probably need to tell Aunt Galena. The covens and packs were notoriously unfriendly to each other. She wasn't sure what would happen once Amia, or even Kami, discovered their true bloodlines. Susanne's presence had been tolerated because of whatever agreement had been made with her mother, but that agreement didn't extend to grandchildren or great-grandchildren, leaving Kamika and her mama out to hang.

Sometimes, Delaney really fucking hated how convoluted the supernatural world was.

They fell into another stretch of silence, this one filled with a different type of unease than before. The weight of the lies she'd told Kami kept Delaney quiet. Judging from Kami's looks, Delaney *hadn't* gotten off so easily. She was suspicious but had stopped asking questions.

Delaney wasn't sure which was worse.

Forewarned is forearmed. Now that she knew Kami was on a seek-and-find mission, she was better prepared, so she pushed her empty plate away and broached the topic again.

"Maybe, you can finish this book, babe. Pick up where your great-granny left off."

"It was weird. The documents were hidden, taped to magazine pages. It seemed less like a novel and more like a history. Or the rantings of a lunatic."

"Def. I'd go for that one." Clearly, Kami couldn't bring herself to accept the truth, which was why she kept searching for other explanations. "Sorry, babe, but your great-granny was stark, raving mad. I suppose she went out and howled at the moon, hoping to draw the werewolves out."

Kami laughed and shook her head. "That would be a no. My family belonged to the coven. Yours to the pack."

Clocked it.

"Fuck, babe, we're going to spend the evening discussing supernatural shit or what?" Diversion was the best underhanded tactic in her arsenal. Besides the blatant lies she'd been handing out.

Delaney knew that would breed mistrust and resentment once Kami found out the truth. Delaney's untruths had the potential to ruin them. The only way to stop the train wreck in the making was to find another topic.

"You're right," Kami said reluctantly. "Tell me about New Orleans. I've always wanted to visit. Do you know French?"

"A few words here and there. Nothing deep. I know more Louisiana Creole, but it's useless, because who the fuck do I have to converse with? It's a dying language."

"Isn't it a dialect of French? My grandma always called it bayou French."

Delaney's lips quirked up. "Not entirely inaccurate, but it's a distinct language, drawn from French vocabulary but influenced by indigenous, West African, Spanish, and English languages. The same as Haitian Creole. A Creole language, but different from Louisiana Creole. Both have their own linguistic structures and features. In Haiti, it's the official language. In Louisiana, it's a dying language."

"That's so sad. It's an important part of the state's history. It should be preserved."

Delaney nodded. "I agree. My daddy's side of the family spoke it fluently, but he didn't teach me much before he died."

She couldn't keep the sadness out of her words. He'd been far from a perfect man, but he was still her father, and she still mourned the absence of her parents.

Kamika reached out, grabbing Delaney's hand and squeezing gently, just as she had the other night. It drew Delaney back to the present and destroyed the unease that had settled in her gut. It seemed that her mate was touchy when she was comfortable.

"I didn't mean to bring up any bad memories, asking about your family history—" Kamika began, but Delaney interrupted her.

"Nah, babe, the motherfuckers you were talking about are long dead, and probably aren't even related to me," she said, returning the favor and squeezing Kami's hand. "I never understood why they couldn't keep their own surnames. That's why so many people think we're an inbred cult."

Kamika's laugh lifted her spirits and brightened the atmosphere. "Let the record show that I've never thought that."

Delaney chuckled. "Duly noted. And I have a question of my own for you."

It was decidedly less intense. Kamika's remark about bayou French sparked curiosity, leading to Delaney wanting to know more.

"I have an answer," Kamika said, mimicking Delaney's earlier words.

"You know any Louisiana Creole? Or 'bayou French' according to your granny."

"A little, but Grandma didn't teach me much," she confessed, her shoulders slumping and expression falling. "No matter how much I asked her to, she never did. I just stopped asking after a while."

Yet another strike against Susanne. Delaney's daddy hadn't taught her everything he knew, nor did he share any of his knowledge with her mother. She'd suspected it was because he wanted to talk shit with no consequences, and bet Susanne's reason had been the same.

"But, I know some basics," Kamika continued. "*Bonjou*, of course, is hello. *Koman sa va* is 'how are you.' *Mo bon* is 'I'm okay.' *Adyeu* is goodbye. *Mo pele* is 'my name is.' *Tanpri* is please, and *mersi* is thank you. *Mo linm twa* is 'I love you,' and *mo linm twa tou* is 'I love you too.' And that's the extent of my knowledge."

Delaney gave her a round of applause, her pronunciation impressing her. "You ate that, babe."

Kamika rolled her eyes. "You're just gassing me up."

"I am, but it's deserved," Delaney agreed, grinning when her mate perked up again.

"Thank you. Also, did I tell you about the fuckery I walked in on the other day?" Kamika questioned, tugging her hand away to take a sip of her drink, and filling Delaney with a pathetic sense of loss.

"You did not," she replied, taking a sip of her own beer, relishing the coolness of the fruity liquid.

"My mama is back together with her ex, and I found out because..."

Kamika launched into the full story, explaining in great detail what unfolded once she arrived back at her place after Truth and Drink. Delaney felt a surge of anger hearing what Colton said to her, but most of all, she felt relief that the topic of Martin Harris and his family had been dropped. A nagging feeling in the back of her mind told her that this wasn't the true end of discussing her pack's history, but she'd cross that bridge when she got there.

The only thing she could do was be better prepared, and if Kamika was going to become her true mate, she needed to know what she was getting herself into.

July 4th

Kamika

Once the awkwardness of my sudden interrogation of Delaney faded, our date got back on track. I still had many more questions, but it was clear she didn't want to answer them, and I didn't want to ruin things. If it was important, she'd tell me when she was ready. However, I knew that most likely, it wasn't. Everyone involved was dead, and I was 98.8% sure that the papers weren't speaking in the literal sense. The believer in me didn't want to completely dismiss it as nonsense, and

Delaney's reaction hadn't helped matters. Yet, I wasn't the lunatic my great-grandmother might've been, so the chances of the documents holding any truth were slim.

That didn't stop me from constantly thinking about them.

The papers also reinforced my belief that the house was haunted. Ghosts, in my opinion, were far more likely than witches, werewolves, and vampires. Grandma's house dated back to the 1910s, and the land it was built on had been inhabited far longer. A soul or two sticking around wasn't out of the realm of possibility, and my grandmother's presence in my thoughts and dreams made me believe she was one of them. Every bump and creak freaked me out 10x more than before, and I was absolutely terrified of seeing an apparition.

Should that happen, I was getting the fuck out of there, my promise to Mama be damned.

Though my promise was proving futile. She didn't want my help going through her mother's things and had yet to tell me what she and the lawyer discussed, claiming she'd reveal everything to me when the business was settled. It made me all the more curious about the papers I saw. It felt like she was trying to hide something, making it hard to dismiss the talk of the occult as strict nonsense.

Worse than that, she was insisting on getting closer to Colton, even opting to go to the crawfish boil the Samsons were hosting, instead of accepting my invitation to the Harris's Fourth of July festivities. She claimed the former celebration was more age appropriate, but I called bullshit. The time she spent with him only made my presence feel unnecessary. She didn't want my help, and now, she didn't even want my company. If it wasn't for Delaney, I might've hopped a flight back to Miami and called Mama daily to check on her.

"Shouldn't you start getting ready?" Mama asked as she breezed into the living room, her braids tied back in a ponytail, and her ears adorned with golden star earrings.

She looked so pretty, and her cobalt blue sundress was gorgeous and flattering. The haltered top's deep V-neck and the skirt's leg split revealed plenty of skin. Knowing she dolled herself up for Colton annoyed me, but it was an argument I wouldn't get into.

"I'm just wearing a swimsuit and shorts, and it doesn't start for another two hours," I replied, glancing at my phone's clock to confirm I had some time to lounge around.

The Samsons' boil had started at 2:30 PM, half an hour ago. Why they wanted to languish when the sun was bright and mighty, I had no idea. But I wasn't going, so I wouldn't say shit about it.

Disapproval flickered across Mama's face, a look I'd gotten used to seeing since we arrived in Gaville. Something in the town's air just made people more judgmental.

"You're not bringing anything to cover up with?"

"It's a pool party, so why does it matter?" I countered, peering at her over my phone.

I was, indeed, bringing a mesh top with bright sequin details to wear over my swimsuit, as well as a cardigan in case I got chilly when the sun dropped, and a pair of panties hidden in my purse when I got tired of swimming. Yet, I'd explain none of it to my mother. She claimed not to be one to meddle, making an explanation unnecessary.

"Don't drink too much if you're gonna be swimming," Mama warned, swapping her house slippers for the sandals she kept by the door. "In fact, you probably shouldn't drink at all."

"I won't have much," I assured, trying to stamp down my exasperation.

Before seeing her with Colton on the very couch I lay on, which I made sure to wipe down the next day, I would've appreciated her concern. Now, it just pissed me off. It was a solid piece of advice meant to avoid drowning, but her defense of Colton—her very relationship with him—made me more critical of everything she said. It was ingrained pettiness I couldn't shake, and I hoped she was telling the truth when she said she was keeping things casual. However, it seemed as if that was just a lie to shut me up.

"You shouldn't have any," she repeated, grabbing her keys from the hook by the door.

I shrugged. "We'll see."

She examined me for a moment, not hiding her frown. "Something the matter?"

Besides her relationship with an old school fuckboy? Nope. Not a thing.

"I'm fine, Mama. Have fun," I answered, giving my phone my full attention.

The huff of air she released indicated her annoyance, but she only said, "Yeah, you too," before leaving the house and slamming the door behind her. I couldn't help but roll my eyes and wondered if the underlying tension wafting from her was due to anger at me or knowledge that getting closer to Colton was a stupid thing to do. But, hey, as she reminded me, it wasn't my damn business. And when it inevitably blew up in her face, I'd comfort her as any good daughter would and hate the motherfucker she was fucking with a little more. However, I was a bad enough person that I'd feel some satisfaction, taking solace in the fact that I was indeed right.

I'd done my part and voiced my opposition. Now, all that remained was to await the results of her choices.

Chased by annoyance and images of that slimy bastard chatting up my mother, I left an hour after Mama. A leisurely walk to Magnolia Mist hopefully calmed me down. It took twenty minutes to walk there at a reasonable pace, longer with a detour. Since there was still an hour to go before the party officially started, and several before shit started getting lit, I saw no harm strolling through the park. I didn't want to stay in that house, full of unwanted memories, new and old. I'd hoped that being surrounded by nature would calm me, but that didn't happen. It left me even more irritated because it gave me time to think about Mama's pissy attitude toward me since I caught her with that man.

Yes, she was my mother, and I was supposed to listen to her advice and whatever shit she handed me. However, I was a grown ass woman with common damn sense. It should've worked both ways, especially since she'd already been burned once by the same man. Well, that was on her if she touched that stupid stove again.

I got to Magnolia Mist just as the clock struck five. Some guests were already in attendance, milling about the property. I forced myself to respond to the few greetings thrown my way. They'd gone all out for the party with red, white, and blue banners, and American flags dotting the place. It shocked me to see three dogs lounging under the tree. I'd never seen any pets on the property, let alone giant motherfucking dogs. Big, wolfy creatures that looked scary, especially when they homed in on me each step of the way.

Perhaps, I should've arrived later, as the dogs might've been put away as more people showed up.

The hairs on the back of my neck stood as the canines, with eyes too intelligent, examined me and a handful of other guests. My paranoia was more blame to lay at the feet of the women in my family. If Great-Grandma hadn't written that stupid shit and Grandma hadn't died, then Mama wouldn't have been sorting papers that I had the misfortune to read.

The early hour meant it wasn't as crowded as it would be later. Since the extended family was so large, a mix of generations always packed the place. The scent of barbecue and spice tantalized the air. Music drifted from the veranda, where huge speakers stood. Long tables filled with covered dishes sat in strategic locations. Hopefully, by the time the buffet was ready, I would have an appetite.

Halfway across the lawn, I finally spotted Jack and Larissa, sitting under a big oak tree, not far from that pack of fucking spy dogs, and I redirected my steps toward them. Larissa saw me first and smiled, waving at me. Jack glanced in my direction and nodded. I returned the gesture, no longer feeling such ire for him.

Delaney helped to ease my acceptance of him, but why look a gift horse in the mouth?

"Hey, girl," Larissa greeted, fanning herself. "You're here early."

Jack swung his gaze toward me and lifted a brow. "Guess she's excited to see y'all," he drawled, the sarcasm I detected worsening my mood.

Okay, motherfucker, don't make me regret easing up on you.

"What's up with you?" Larissa said, ignoring her husband.

"Nothing much." I scowled, holding back the slew of words I wanted to say.

"Larissa!" Miss Galena called from the porch. She waved at me. "Come and help with the potato salad."

"Mama," Larissa groaned, then jumped to her feet. She kissed Jack and paused to address me. "Delaney is near the barbecue pits," she said and hurried off.

Her departure left me standing awkwardly with only *Jack* for company.

"I thought your mother was coming," he said in a neutral voice.

Distaste sat heavy in my gut, and I frowned. Not at him for a change, but of course, that's the way he took it. This day couldn't get any shittier.

"Delaney is probably waiting for you," Jack said coldly, any friendliness disappearing.

I didn't have it in me to explain myself, so I turned and marched across the grounds, which estates tended to have. A mere yard was way too pedestrian. Before I reached Delaney, her laughter floated to me, and it instantly lifted my mood. A goofy grin spread across my face, and I picked up my pace. I was happy that I didn't have to walk all the way around the side to the barbecue pits. She was leaning against a tree, her back to me.

She flipped her locs, adjusted her position, threw back her head, and laughed again. I was closer now, able to hear more. The high-pitched giggles joining her rich laughter shocked me and…and…hurt me, too. But I halted, knowing the stress of the day had me overreacting. Delaney wasn't that type of woman. She wouldn't pretend to be so into me and chat up another chick, aware I planned to attend the celebration.

I plastered a smile on my face and started forward, modifying my stride when I realized I was damn near running.

Delaney turned as I approached. I saw no sign of guilt. The way her face lit up when she saw me burned away my jealous panic. She straightened and pulled me into her arms. I hugged her tightly, holding her just a little longer than necessary, the toll of the day getting to me. It felt good being in the company of someone who wanted me around.

"Hey, babe, you okay?" Delaney released me and studied my face. "What happened?"

"Colton—" I started on a huff.

"Delaney," the other girl inserted.

Delaney's irritation pleased me, but she stepped aside so I could see the intruder. She was extremely pretty with an unusual yellow brown eye color made all the more outstanding by her reddish-brown skin and dark hair. The little dress she wore barely concealed her curves.

"Do you still want to help me with my meat?" she purred.

I narrowed my eyes and cocked my head to the side, reminding myself to act mature and reasonable, and not jump to conclusions. As difficult as it was, ignoring the innuendo would be best for everyone.

Delaney shook her head. "Kami is dressed for swimming, not standing over a hot ass barbecue pit, Malika."

"You said it was just going to be you and me."

"I thought Kami was coming later."

That wasn't what I wanted to hear.

"By the way, Kamika, this is a relative of mine, Malika Harris." Delaney nudged me, an arm draping around my waist. "I call her Queen. Malika, this is Kamika LeBlanc."

Relief swamped me. Delaney's little history lesson let me know that the name 'Harris' didn't mean that blood was shared, but the way she referred to Malika was reassuring. Unless they were on some Alabama, blue people shit, nothing was going on between them.

I extended my hand to her, pasting my smile back on. "Our names are pretty similar," I noted, an attempt to break the ice.

"So they are," she sniffed, ignoring my outstretched hand to focus on Delaney. "Is this...her?"

What the fuck did that mean?

I stiffened, wondering if I should leave before my temper got the best of me, and the gloves fully came off. Sensing my growing anger, Delaney's grip on me tightened, and her curt nod offered no insight. Releasing my waist, she interlaced our fingers together, throwing Malika a dirty look.

"Come on, babe. I want to show you something," she said, her gentle smile a contrast to the glare she'd just thrown seconds before.

"Can I come?" Malika asked.

"See to your fucking meat," I snapped, too through with her.

Did this bitch just growl? Malike narrowed her unusual eyes, and I swore they glowed. Or, maybe, it was a trick of the early evening sun.

Delaney yanked me forward. "I've been waiting for the barbequed smoke sausage, Mal," she threw over her shoulder, an underlying warning in her tone. "Get to it."

Across the way, the dogs were standing, pacing, and pawing the ground in between staring at me. Jack glared at me too, jumped to his feet, and stormed to that pack of mutts. Whatever he said calmed them down instantly.

Props to him.

Perhaps he was a dog trainer. It wasn't out of the realm of possibility, as I knew jackshit about him outside of his connection to Larissa.

I wasn't about to show my unease when I realized we would pass by the dogs, but I sidled closer to Delaney. As we passed, Jack planted himself in front of the hellhounds, met Delaney's gaze, and nodded. To ease myself, I peeped at her through my lashes in time to see her return the gesture and glare at the beasts.

Even when they were a good distance behind us, I felt watched, and a shiver went through me. Delaney tucked me closer to her body. Finally, we reached the dirt path that led to the clearing where the kickbacks were held. She lessened her hold on me.

"Green never looked as good on anyone as it did you, babe."

I didn't pretend ignorance. "I was not jealous!" I said with mock indignation. "I was just...uh...*protective*."

"You're so full of shit," Delaney said, laughing. "But it's cool, Kami. I kind of liked it, anyway."

"Well, in that case..." I allowed my voice to trail off. We halted and turned to each other. "You're right. I was green with it."

Delaney hummed in her throat, settled her hands on my hips, and pulled me closer. She brushed her lips over mine, and I melted, all the day's awfulness dissolving. Her tongue slipped past my lips. She tasted sweet and a little minty, and the combination went straight to my head. But it was her scent, an earthy combination of sandalwood, bergamot, and honey, that invaded my brain, leaving desire pooling in my core.

With joy, I realized this was our first proper kiss.

It made all the bullshit of the day worth it and left me pitifully horny. If she'd wanted us to fuck right there, out in the open, I wouldn't have cared. Something about her, a strange thing that I couldn't put my finger on, loosened my boundaries. When we were near each other, I was consumed solely by her presence, everything else be damned.

All too soon, she pulled away, breathing as heavily as me. She rubbed my arms and leaned in for another kiss. This one was far too quick. I wanted more.

"Come on," she said huskily, her tender gaze searching my face and looking at me in wonder. "I really do have something to show you."

"We're all alone," I breathed, my mind immediately going to the gutter. "You can show it to me here."

That earned me another, longer kiss. "Can't," she said when we came up for air.

"Why not?" I whined.

"Because it's my cabin. I want to show you how close it is to being finished."

"You need some ideas for décor?" I joked, trying to get hold of myself.

The prospect of a private tour of her new home excited me.

She chuckled and shrugged. "If you'd like. Or we can chill until more people arrive, or hide there all night long. Whatever you want, babe."

"How long have they been building it?" I asked, a pep in my step as I followed her to her future home.

"They started about a week before I arrived," she answered, looking down at me with a smile. "And by the way, you look very nice."

"Right back at you," I replied.

My breath hitched when she reached out and traced the orange starfish made of sequins that decorated the mesh top, located right above my breast.

"I like this, especially," she continued, her teasing not making her falter.

The same couldn't be said for me. I nearly tripped, her touch leaving me lightheaded.

Her arms were quick to encircle my waist when I stumbled. She paused to steady me, her proximity sending electricity through me. I longed for her to kiss me again. Whatever we had going on had no label, and I didn't know how long it would last. But for the time being, I wanted to savor our time together, and that would include locking lips many, many more times.

"Careful," she said, not relinquishing her hold on me even when I regained my ability to stand. "I know I'm amazing, but you don't have to fall for me."

A bark of laughter escaped me. "Girl, that joke was lame as hell."

"It isn't a joke if it's the truth," she countered, words fading away as she brushed her lips over mine.

It was sweet and brief, and I couldn't help but pout when she pulled away.

"You're teasing me," I accused, my hand again finding hers as we resumed walking.

"Nope, savoring you," she corrected with a smirk. "I've been wanting to kiss you since...well, since I first met you, so I'm making up for lost time."

"You don't have much time to make up for, since we haven't known each other long," I reminded her, a fact that boggled my own mind.

The night we met, she hadn't acted like she wanted to kiss me. But that was in the past, and now, all I wanted was for her to kiss me more. Never had I gotten hooked on someone so quickly. Two months ago, I had no clue she existed. Now, my heart ached knowing that my return to Miami would end whatever we had going on.

"By the way, did Larissa ever mention me to you?" I blurted, the question escaping before I could stop it. "Because she never mentioned you. Neither did Miss Galena."

"Well, I left for school two years before y'all started dating, and before that, I was a bit of a troublemaker, so I wasn't the most popular person," she said with a laugh, shaking her head. "Nah, scratch that. I was a raging bitch. I'm shocked Aunt Galena didn't beat my ass out the door."

Giggles escaped me, before they abruptly stopped when her words processed. "You know me and Larissa dated?"

"Yeah, she told me a few weeks ago. It doesn't change anything between us, so I didn't see the point in bringing it up."

Wow.

That was a mindset I could only aspire to.

"That's...very mature of you," I said, my admiration clear. "And you didn't answer my question."

She shrugged. "Not by name, but she did talk about a girl she was seeing a few years back, right before she met Jack. I assume that was you."

"Probably."

I wondered if I'd known about Delaney, if things would've turned out any differently. Maybe, I would've harbored a crush on her, preventing me from getting with Larissa. The age difference between me and Delaney was no big deal now, but as teenagers, four years is a lot. Being hung up on her might've prevented my relationship with Larissa, thereby avoiding my falling out with my grandmother. Or maybe, it would've delayed it. Regardless, I would've been in Grandma's life longer, and Delaney would've been in my life earlier.

That notion alone made me long for that to have been the reality I existed in, instead of the one where my grandmother died hating me, and Delaney and I hadn't known each other for a full season.

"We're here," she announced as the elaborate log cabin came into view.

"Wow," I breathed, admiring the craftsmanship of the structure. "It's bigger than expected."

"My cabin has three bedrooms and two baths," she said, leading me up the covered porch. "Once they finish up some things, I'll be free to move in."

"Cabin is a little misleading," I admitted, craning my neck to look everywhere. "This is more like a house."

She fished a key out of the pocket of her jeans. "I'm a simple woman. I prefer cabin," she said, unlocking the door and stepping aside so I could enter.

"Okay, simple woman," I teased, brushing past her.

She flipped on an overhead light and closed the door. It wasn't furnished, and there were still signs of construction with ladders and toolboxes next to lengths of wood and several saws. White cloths hung from the windows, and as she took me from room to room, I saw drop cloths on the floors.

"That'll be cozy," I remarked when I laid eyes on the stone fireplace in the den. "Pointless, because it stays hot, but still cozy."

"Girl, you know as well as I do that it gets cold down here," she said, shaking her head.

I ignored her correct assertion. "I could see a little cat curled up in a basket by the fireplace. That'd make for a good postcard during the holidays."

"I thought you preferred birds?" she asked, a small smile on her lips.

"I said I wanted a hyacinth macaw, not that I can't admire the cuteness of other animals," I reminded her. "Besides, I won't be here often, because it won't be my home. It'll be yours."

"You'll be visiting, and I aim to be a good host," she said, pulling me to her chest and resting her chin on my head.

I adored how well we fit together, but even it wasn't enough to ignore my sadness as I realized I wouldn't get to enjoy her home for long. "Yeah, we can chill here until I return to Miami."

Her entire demeanor shifted at my remark. She pulled away as if burned, and the loss of her body against mine saddened me further.

"Yeah," she murmured, sighing heavily. "That's right. I'm, uh, going to check something real quick."

With that enigmatic comment, she retreated down the hallway. I wasn't wildly patriotic, but I normally enjoyed Fourth of July celebrations. This year, however, was proving to be a bust, filled with one disappointment after another.

Delaney

There were times when emotions overcame Delaney, and she'd feel her wolf right below the surface, restless and eager to come out. Kamika's little reminder upset her beyond words and agitated her wolf. Her looming departure had been tormenting Delaney and wooing her felt all the more urgent. She'd hoped that by the time August rolled around, she'd consider staying. Or, if nothing else, be open to a long-distance relationship with frequent trips to Gaville, financed by Delaney. Both would require a serious discussion, but she wasn't sure their relationship was at that point. After all, stolen kisses didn't equate to dating.

She waited until she felt normal again before exiting her incomplete bathroom and returning to the living room. Kamika stood right where she'd left her, by the fireplace. It crushed Delaney to see how sad she looked.

"Sorry about that, babe," she said, pasting on a smile, guilt swamping her. "Just...wanted to check my toilet."

"I call bullshit, but whatever," Kami grumbled, her arms crossed over her chest.

Delaney's smile turned genuine. Kamika's bluntness was something she adored.

"It's inevitable that I leave," she continued, immediately wiping Delaney's grin away. "It shouldn't be a big deal. You've known that since the beginning, and it doesn't erase that we're cool for the summer."

"It still fucking sucks," she grumbled, looking down at her painted toenails.

She usually just trimmed them, forgoing color. But her sandals would expose her toes, and she wanted to look as cute as possible for Kamika. She'd enlisted Larissa's help for the endeavor, and the sparkly white polish was an upgrade from her typically bare nails.

"I'll be going back home, Laney, not to fucking Mars. We could still text, and call, and do video chats, and all that shit," Kamika said, stepping closer. She placed her slender fingers under Delaney's chin, tilting her head up. "Going back to Miami doesn't mean we have to lose contact, and it doesn't warrant you lying about toilets, of all the goddamn things."

Delaney chuckled. "I went to the bathroom, so it wasn't a complete lie."

She grabbed Kamika's hands and kissed her knuckles. Her lips would become well acquainted with her mate's flesh now that kissing was on the table.

"I didn't want to bring down the mood," Delaney confessed, not releasing Kamika's hands.

She snorted. "Girl, my mood was already fucked up."

"I noticed. What were you saying about Colton when you arrived?"

Kamika groaned, retracting her hands to cover her face. "Don't get me started on that motherfucker. He cheated on my mama back in the day, now she's back with him, and deciding to spend all her free time with that asshole. He's a whack ass cheater with no game, and insufferable to be around."

Delaney had never met the man, but just from Kamika's description, she despised him on principle.

"I'm sorry to hear that, babe," she soothed, pulling her back into her arms when she started to pace. "If he makes you that upset, I can beat his ass for you."

Delaney was deadly serious, but Kami took it as a joke, throwing her head back and laughing. "I'll keep that offer in mind."

She smiled, brushing a stray loc from Kamika's face. "Do that. In the meantime, why don't we go get a drink and some barbecue?"

"Do we have to walk past those big ass dogs again?"

"They should be put away by now," Delaney reassured, keeping her tone even.

Those dogs were, in fact, wolves. 13-year-old shifters who had the misfortune of experiencing their first change on America's birthday. A quirk of werewolf twins, triplets, and so on was that they tended to all transition for the first time together. Often, something triggered the first shift. Their mother had shared with the females of the pack that the youngest triplet had been introduced to Aunt Flow, and the fluctuations of hormone levels induced the change.

"Whose dogs are they, anyway?" Kamika asked as they exited the cabin.

"A friend of Aunt Galena's," Delaney replied, smirking at her. "But don't worry. I'll protect you from the big bad wolves, babe."

Kamika rolled her eyes, but her giggles betrayed her amusement. "I'll hold you to it."

Kamika

    Hours after the sun set, I could barely stand on my two feet. Liquor had flowed freely, though the pool was off limits to anyone who'd had more than two drinks. Delaney and I had gone for a dip after our first cocktail. Even surrounded by people, it felt like it was only the two of us. We were in our little bubble, laughing and cuddling without a care in the world. Colton, Mama, Grandma, Malika, and everyone who'd dragged the day down was forgotten. During our second drink, Larissa and Jack joined us, their kids supervised by older children somewhere out of sight. They'd shared a few old folks also chilled with the youngins, just to keep them under control and tend to the babies amongst the group, such as Cyrus.

Whatever was in the mixed drinks was strong, so by the third drink, everything was becoming fuzzy. I wasn't sure what I'd drunk; I stopped counting after my fifth. Delaney, sweetheart that she was, offered to walk me home. She'd had a couple more drinks than me, but the alcohol showed no signs of affecting her. The same couldn't be said for me, and as she led me to my house, I required her assistance to keep me up.

"You're so pretty," I cooed, playing with the ends of one of her locs. Our closeness allowed me to inhale her scent in all of its citrusy, earthy glory. "And you smell sooo good."

She snickered, holding me a little more snugly. "You're fucking wasted, babe."

"Nuh-uh," I protested, her laughter triggering mine. "Just a lil' tipsy."

She snorted. "You ain't fooling anyone, Kami. You had eleven damn drinks, which is why you can barely stand up. A regular person would be knocked out in the grass right now, and likely need their fucking stomach pumped."

"M'regular!" I protested, pouting up at her. "I'm just an ordinary girl with a high alcohol tolerance."

"Whatever helps you sleep at night, sweetheart," she drawled, the nickname sending shivers through me.

"Sweetheart," I repeated, my eyelids growing droopy. "I like that. Sounds right coming from you. Makes your accent pop."

The bright blue siding of Grandma's house came into view. Relief ran through me. All I wanted to do was sleep, and I was unsure if I would've been able to make it much further.

"I do not have an accent," she complained, which, ironically, made her Southern drawl even thicker. Despite what she thought, it was very much present.

"Everyone has an accent," I replied, my voice slurred to my own ears. "*I* have an accent. Probably sounds Southern to people not from the South, but not as Southern as yours, because you're from the Deep South, and I'm from the...uh, whatever Miami is."

By the time I finished my drunken ramblings, Delaney's shoulders were shaking with laughter. "Kamika, baby, you're going to have a killer fucking headache tomorrow."

"I like your voice a lot," I stated around a yawn as she helped me up the porch steps.

The car was still absent, and the porch light wasn't on, so I knew Mama wasn't home yet.

"Yeah?" she said, fishing into my small purse and retrieving my keys.

She unlocked the front door, guiding me to the couch. My initial reservations about someone dying on the sofa had faded weeks ago, and when I was on the verge of passing out, all I cared about was that it was a comfy, soft surface.

"Mmhmm. It's deep and raspy and fucking sexy. No wonder that bitch was all over you."

"Malika?" she questioned, amusement lacing her tone.

"You see...you know she's a bitch. Thirsty heifer," I mumbled, gripping her hand when she tried to pull away. "Nooo, stay with me."

Even in my drunken stupor, I could see the conflict on her face. She was taller than me, and based on how toned she was, it was likely she was stronger, too. If she wanted to escape my grasp, I didn't doubt that it would be a breeze for her.

"Sweetheart, I have to get home," she protested weakly, though she didn't resist when I tugged her next to me. "And you need to get to bed."

"Stay with me until Mama gets home." I wrinkled my nose. "I can't believe she's spent all day with fucking Colton. I hope they're using protection. I don't want him to be my stepdad because he got her pregnant."

"Kamika, fucking ew," Delaney groaned. "Instead of thinking about your mom getting creampied, let me help you to your room."

"Eww!" I shrieked, shuddering at her words and swallowing back a gag. "That's so gross!"

"How else does pregnancy happen, babe?"

"You didn't have to say it like that," I complained, yawning loudly. "M'so tired…need to sleep." Keeping my eyes opened suddenly became a Herculean task. I plopped my head on Delaney's lap, my cheek against her bare thigh. "Mmm, you're so soft."

"Girl, tell me where your room is so you can take your ass to bed," she ordered, pulling me into her arms and standing up.

I mumbled some words, but my head was too foggy for me to process what they were. I hoped they were directions to my bedroom. However, it didn't matter much, as Delaney's arms were comfortable enough for me to fall asleep in. As I slipped into oblivion, I snuggled closer to her, wishing she'd be there when I woke up.

Delaney

After tucking Kamika into bed, Delaney knew she should leave. Perhaps wait on the couch until Amia got home from fucking Colton, since Delaney didn't have a key to lock the door. Yet, instead of waiting in the living room, she stood over the bed, hovering above Kamika's form.

Was it creepy? Yes.

Did it make her stop? No.

She wished she had her drawing tablet to capture how angelic and peaceful Kami's beautiful face looked in the moment. Her long lashes swept across her high cheekbones, soft snores escaping her parted lips. Snoring normally annoyed the shit out of Delaney. Even with Toria, she found the sound grating. With Kamika, she found it adorable.

It was said that every shifter had dozens of potential mates, people they were so compatible with that it transcended normal attraction. It was an instinctual pull, and in the modern era, it remained mystical. Some argued that because werewolves had many potential mates, it was a sign they were naturally a polyamorous species. Harems were permitted in some packs, though only for the highest-ranking members. Delaney had always disagreed with that theory and had been raised on the idea that the one you chose to solidify the mate bond with was the one you were meant to be with. As she gazed at Kamika,

Delaney wholly believed that Kamika was the 'one'.

The third time was the charm, after all.

The first time Delaney felt that all-too-familiar pull, it was with a girl from a visiting pack, the only other shifter she'd ever felt drawn to. Delaney had never formally come out; it was just always a fact that she liked girls. The same couldn't be said for the visitor she'd been so infatuated with. She was still in the closet and cornered Delaney to swear her to secrecy that one of her potential mates was another woman. Disappointed as she was, she'd respected her choice. After Delaney moved to New Orleans, she fucked around with some girls, but entertained nothing serious.

Enter Toria.

Even the strings of fate hadn't been enough to make her relationship with the witch healthy. They'd been toxic, and there were many times she doubted that Toria felt anything for her. Sex was frequent, but Toria resisted completing the solidification process. Year after year, she claimed it was too soon. Delaney figured once college was a thing of the past, Toria would be ready to dedicate herself.

What a fucking joke.

Toria's graduation present to Delaney had been infidelity, forcing her to come to terms with the fact that the witch truly didn't care for her. When Kamika came into the picture, she captured Delaney's wounded heart, and left her mesmerized.

Toria could hold a grudge forever, whereas Kamika was forgiving, almost to a fault. She had no problem stating what was on her mind, whilst Toria loved to keep shit hidden, then throw a fit that people couldn't read her mind to fix a problem they didn't know about. Kamika was funny, and knew how to have a good time, whereas Toria could be a giant fucking stick in the mud. How Delaney had tolerated that bitch for so long was a mystery, but Kamika's presence had cleansed her of the pain Toria left.

Delaney had heard before that out of the many potential mates a shifter could have, the pull would be stronger for some than it would be for others, leading to a belief that amongst your pool of potential mates, you were only truly meant to be with only a handful. In a little over a month, Kamika had consumed Delaney's being. She was constantly on Delaney's mind, and never did she feel more alive than when her mate was in her presence. The electricity that sparked between them when their lips touched reinforced that Kami was the one, and Delaney could only imagine what she'd feel when they finally made love.

Lord, just the thought drove her wild.

The slamming of a car door interrupted her admiration of Kamika. It seemed Amia was home from her date, signaling it was time to go. When she heard the keys being inserted into the front door, Delaney bent down and pressed her lips to Kamika's forehead.

"Sweet dreams, baby," she whispered to her, smiling at her sleeping form.

With one last quick kiss, she left the bedroom, taking care to softly close the door behind her. As she was exiting the hallway, Amia was entering it. When the older woman saw Delaney, she froze.

"What are you doing here?" Amia questioned, folding her arms over her chest, the scent of alcohol, cigarette smoke, and sweat clinging to her skin.

"Just dropping Kamika home, ma'am," Delaney answered, the hostility taking her aback. "I'll, uh, be going now."

She'd long known of Amia, but this was the first time Delaney was meeting her face-to-face. There was nothing she could've done to offend her, and she wasn't sure that she even knew who Delaney was.

"Wait," Amia called, halting Delaney's retreat. "You're Delaney, huh?"

Well, turned out she did know her.

Nodding, she faced Amia again, pasting on a smile. "Yes, ma'am." She stuck out her hand.

"It's nice to meet you. I've heard a lot about you."

"All good things, I hope?" Amia replied, taking her hand for a brief handshake.

"Of course," Delaney said, lying through her teeth.

The way she handled her raggedy ex certainly wasn't a good thing, but ultimately, it wasn't her business. Nor would she cause bullshit by exposing what Kamika had told her.

"Well, I can't say the same," Amia stated, her eyes narrowing.

Delaney bristled. "Excuse me?"

There were a few possibilities that could explain Amia's words. The first was that her mother had talked trash about her prior to her death. Susanne hadn't been a fan of the Harrises, Delaney included. The second was that Amia heard rumors from the townsfolk, a holdover from Delaney's days as a wild child. The final, and most painful option, was that Kamika had said something about her. Her heart ached at the thought.

"You see, my mama left behind some journals," Amia continued, the relief that flooded Delaney stopping her from immediately processing the words. When they did, she tensed back up. "Your family comes up a lot, Delaney, and let me say, everything in there ain't too favorable. She wasn't a fan of y'all."

"Well, from my understanding, your mother wasn't a fan of most people," Delaney replied, searching Amia's face, wondering just how much she knew.

"My mama was hard to impress, and harder to please, but what she said about y'all...how much is true?"

Shit.

"I don't know what she said, but I guarantee you—"

"You have a hunch of what she said," Amia interrupted, shaking her head. "I didn't believe it at first, and I still don't believe everything. But my mama wasn't stone-cold mad, and if even a portion of it was true, you and your family are a threat to my daughter."

Fury surged through Delaney, the very suggestion that she'd do anything to harm Kamika pissing her off to no end.

"No, we aren't," she snapped, her nails digging into the palm of her hand. "Your mother had delusions, delusions that you best forget about."

Amia stepped back, unease flickering across her face. "Is that a threat, little girl?"

"It's a piece of advice, because if your mama really knew what she was talking about, she'd know that me and my family don't mean no harm to anyone, especially someone like Kamika."

Harming a pack member's mate was a grave offense that warranted extreme punishment. The fact that Delaney was courting her made her off limits.

"You don't have to like me, Amia," Delaney continued. "But you sure as hell don't get to make vague accusations because a bigoted woman wrote some bullshit down."

"Watch it—"

"I won't tell Kamika about this." Not yet, anyway. "I hope you'll do the same."

"You don't dictate what I say to my daughter. She doesn't belong to you."

That one statement enlightened Delaney, giving her an idea of the contents of whatever Amia read. Some other supernaturals had a false perception of the concept of mates, believing there was no choice in the process, when the opposite was true. Susanne had been an old woman with an outdated mindset and stuck in her ways. The likelihood that she painted mate bonds as oppressive was high.

"I'd best get going, ma'am," Delaney said, deciding to end the conversation there.

She wouldn't tell Amia anything that she hadn't told Kamika. Seeing as Delaney had told her jackshit, Amia would stay in the dark as well. It was a risky gamble, as unlike Kamika, Amia had a negative view of the Harrises.

"I believe that's for the best," she grumbled, trailing behind Delaney as she made her way to the front door.

The moment she stepped onto the porch, the door slammed behind her, rattling the frame. The confrontation left a bad taste in Delaney's mouth, and she knew that the time to tell Kamika the truth was fast approaching. As she walked home, she thought of a dozen different ways to drop the bomb. Shifting in front of Kamika was likely the easiest way to get her to believe, but it'd also come as the biggest shock. On the other hand, words alone might not be enough for her to accept the facts.

God, why couldn't it be easier to tell the girl you cared about you were a werewolf?

By the time she got home, her head was hurting, the slight buzz she'd acquired wearing off. All the humans were gone, but her family was still milling about. Some were cleaning up, others were playing spades or racing, and many were indulging in the leftovers. Jack and Larissa were in possession of their children again, sitting by the bonfire. Larissa held a sleeping Shay while Jack rocked Cyrus.

"Hey, cuz," Larissa called, waving her over.

She stalked to them and plopped down, putting her head in her hands and groaning, her ponytail veiling her face.

"Uh, you good?" Jack asked, prompting Delaney to look up.

"I need a fucking drink," she grumbled, massaging her temples. "I think Amia knows the truth, and Kamika is catching on, too."

Her confession made both freeze. Jack recovered before Larissa did.

"Isn't that a good thing? That means you could court her properly," he said, his tone uncharacteristically gentle.

Delaney accepted the cocktail Larissa handed her, the cup full. "I didn't want to tell her yet, and Amia thinks the mate bond is brutish ownership."

She didn't even question if her cousin had taken a sip, instead, she gulped down the fruity concoction, emptying the cup within seconds.

"We'll help you tell her," Larissa reassured. "And she'd need a few days to recover from the shock, but as long as you give her time and answer her questions, things should work out."

Delaney nodded, going quiet. She hoped like hell her cousin spoke the truth, because at this point, losing Kamika wasn't an option she'd entertain.

CHAPTER TWENTY-NINE

July 7th

Beauden

Despite the space Kamika was taking up in his thoughts, Beau admission to the fascination he'd developed with her flipflopped. He'd had many women in his lifetime, several of whom made Kamika pale in comparison. Even before Alosia claimed him and stole away his mortality, he'd never struggled with getting the attention of beautiful women. Becoming a vampire only enhanced his appeal to the opposite sex.

He could have any woman he wanted, and yet, one who barely seemed interested in him had become a permanent occupant of his mind.

How fucking pathetic.

He'd become so pathetic in fact that he'd begun selecting women who resembled Kamika to fuck. All had left with their lives, much to Cruz's dismay. However, most of the time, Beau didn't drink to kill, especially on a job where laying low was needed. Of course, there were exceptions to that rule, but he wasn't reigning terror on a sleepy corner of Louisiana like Cruz was.

Their relationship was strained almost to the breaking point; their longtime banter and camaraderie had devolved into awkward silences and petty spats. It wasn't the first time they'd been on the outs, but women rarely damaged their relationship, and never to this extent. It made Beau's fascination with Kamika even more annoying.

Beau didn't allow himself to get close to many people, women especially. To him, they were food and fucktoys. Yet, for the sake of his mission, he'd gotten close to Kamika, and learned how witty, funny, and entertaining she was to be around. He found himself having fun with her, and felt care free in her presence. It didn't hurt that she was beautiful, and that her blood called to him. But as much as he wanted to chalk it up to only her blood, he knew that wasn't the only reason for 'his little crush', as Cruz put it.

A growl of frustration left him. He quickened his thrusts, driving into the woman beneath him with more gusto. Crystal, he believed her name was. Or at least, it was her stage moniker. Muffled moans and whimpers flowed from her lips, her large, possibly fake breasts jiggling. Facially, she could be Kamika's sister, but her body was obviously artificial. It hadn't stopped him from taking her back to the motel room, nor had Cruz voiced any complaints. Sharing Crystal was a peace offering of sorts to recapture how they'd been before they arrived in Gaville.

"That's it," Cruz crooned, holding her turned head in place as he thrust into her mouth. He looked at Beau with a smile, his eyes glimmering. "How is she, Beauden?"

"Tight," he grunted, slipping a hand between their sweaty bodies to rub circles over her clit.

The walls of her pussy fluttered around his pistoning shaft, her pleasured squeal muted by Cruz's cock. Idly, Beau wondered what sounds Kamika would make as he fucked into her, a shudder running through him as he imagined how tight her cunt would be. Tension built in his core, his muscles growing taut as he neared his peak. His balls tightened, and with a roar of completion, his orgasm swept over him. Cum shot from his throbbing dick, ecstasy racing through him as he emptied himself inside the stripper. All the while, his thumb never faltered, continuing to circle her clit until she too came.

"Beautiful," Cruz breathed.

When Beau opened his eyes, he found Cruz's gaze glued to his face.

Cruz pulled out of Crystal's mouth, his seed dribbling down her chin. Beau withdrew from her pussy, admiring the mess he made of her. He'd only just stepped away from the bed when Cruz dove between her thighs, burying his face in her pussy and making her squeal.

"Oh, shit!" she mewled, threading her hands through his hair and throwing a leg over his shoulder. "You nasty motherfucker, keep going..."

Beau rolled his eyes, cursing at the lewd scene as wet slurps filled the room. She wasn't wrong about the motherfucker being nasty. It seemed to be a kink of Cruz's, eating out a woman after she'd been creampied.

As much as he wanted to turn away, he couldn't. Each time she moaned or trembled or rolled her hips, Beau saw Kamika in her place. He wanted to see Kami's face in the throes of ecstasy. He didn't care about Crystal, but she was all he had at the moment. He wrapped his fingers around his aching cock and began to stroke. The louder she groaned, the faster he pulled his dick.

"I'm coming," she cried.

Closing his eyes, Beau threw back his head, his nuts tingling and—

An agonized scream cut off the pleasure coursing down his spine, and he looked at Cruz and Crystal. Cruz rose up, his fangs extended, blood dripping down his chin. Shock interfered with Beau's responses, so he didn't stop Cruz from leaning in and sinking his teeth into Crystal's neck.

"Stop!" Beau roared before Cruz tore her throat out or drained her completely of blood.

Glaring at Beau, Cruz hissed and bit her breast, her arm, her belly, ignoring her twitches. She was going into shock from her rapid blood loss. He aimed at her thigh and Beau flew to Cruz, not wanting the stupid motherfucker to sever her femoral artery.

"What the fuck are you doing?" Beau demanded, shoving Cruz away. "We didn't bring her here as a meal."

"Do you think I don't know why you've been picking broads resembling that witch bitch?" He pushed Beau away and turned to Crystal again. "Fuck you. She dies. Just as Kamika will."

Beau snatched Cruz by the shoulders and tossed him away. "I swear to all that's fucking holy if you don't back the fuck off, I'm fucking done with you. Do you hear me? I'm fucking done!"

Cruz froze, and his eyes widened. Seeing Beau's seriousness, he raised his hands, his bloodlust disappearing as quickly and as unexpectedly as it came.

"Get the juniper, motherfucker," Beau ordered, watching as Cruz scurried to do his bidding.

He always made sure to carry dried juniper berries and leaves. It was an effective antidote against their venom and could be dangerous to young vampires. Those unfortunate fuckers could burn from the inside if they ingested too much. Both he and Cruz were old enough that the only thing juniper did to them was raise their body temperatures, allowing them to masquerade as human with ease.

"Here," Cruz grumbled, sticking his lip out to pout as Beau retrieved a Styrofoam cup.

He spat in the cup thrice, then threw the juniper in. Mixed with his saliva, the plant should heal Crystal's wounds, and a little compulsion should have her forgetting about this entire incident.

His cellphone rang but he ignored it, too caught up in saving Crystal. Maybe, it was because of her resemblance to Kamika. Or, maybe, it was because he didn't have the need to kill as Cruz did. No matter the reason, he picked her up and brought her to the shower to wash away the blood. She was limp—probably dead. The bleeding had all but stopped. Once she was cleaned of blood and semen, he wrapped her in a towel and laid her on the bed again, annoyed when his phone rang yet again.

"It's Lavina," Cruz announced, back to his smugness. He didn't stay subdued for long, but Beau knew his threat to walk away would keep him in line. "It's Lavina, Beau."

Beau groaned. Lavina Blackwood was the head of the coven that hired him. Chances were, she was calling for an update, with little changing from when she last checked in.

"I'll call her back," he growled, applying some of the antidote to Crystal's bites before sitting her up and forcing what little was left between her lips. She only needed to swallow a drop. Hopefully, she did.

His chest rising and falling as if he had air in his lungs, he lay her back down and waited. Five minutes later, she sat up, groggy and swaying, but alive.

"Wh-what happened?" she squeaked, hoarse.

"Time to go, Crystal," Beau announced, tossing her clothes to her.

It cheered him to see her attempt to catch them. They floated into her lap, but at least she'd made the effort. She blinked, studying him, and blinked again. "Y'all ain't letting me stay the night?" she asked with a frown.

So she remembered their original agreement. Good, but bad, too.

He walked to her and tipped her chin up, staring into her eyes, forcing her to focus on him. An insane part of him wanted her to remember their fucking, but that was too dangerous.

His phone rang again, and he gritted his teeth. That fucking witch needed to back off.

Beau brushed his lips over Crystal's, trailing to her neck and sucking ever so slightly, infusing her with just a tad more of his venom.

He pulled her to her feet. She stumbled.

Lifting her hands, she braced herself against his chest. "You're such a fine motherfucker."

At the moment, he was even more of whatever he wanted her to see.

"Get dressed," he ordered, backing away.

She bore no visible injuries. Internally, it would take her a couple of days to recover.

"Did we fuck?" she asked, pulling on her clothes with jerky movements.

"No, now get out," he said, looking at Cruz as the phone started ringing again. "Our boss calling, man."

Crystal squinted at the clock and stiffened. "It's almost 4 AM, you lying asshole. What the fuck kind of job you have—"

"None of your goddamn business," Beau barked, annoyed by her audacity and the entire situation.

A half-dead stripper was the last person who should be judging the hours of someone's job.

"Just go, sweetheart," Cruz interjected as if he hadn't tried to fucking drain her. "I'll be seeing you again soon."

No that motherfucker wouldn't.

She smiled, not detecting the underlying threat. "I'll be counting on it."

Beau stormed to the door and held it open. "Out."

She staggered past him. To any passersby, she'd appear wasted. If everything wasn't going to shit, he'd bring her home to ensure her safety.

"Bye, Beau," she said thickly.

"Eat some liver," he ordered, and slammed the door behind her, scowling at Cruz's snicker.

By now, they'd missed two more calls from Lavina. Instead of fucking up Cruz, he dialed Lavina's number, and she picked up on the second ring. Beau put the phone on speaker and tugged on some pants, while Cruz made no effort to clothe himself.

"Now why the fuck didn't you two nocturnal motherfuckers answer me at first?" she demanded.

Cruz cackled at her crudeness. "Hello to you, too," he called, lounging back on the mattress, naked as the day he was born. "'Tis always a pleasure to speak to such an eloquent lady."

Beau snorted at the sarcasm. Lavina was classless, confrontational, and had the mouth of a sailor. Her sheer power was the only reason she'd been given the chance to represent her coven. In his mind, she was a poor choice, better suited to be an enforcer of their laws than the leader. But he wasn't getting paid to pass his opinion about the coven's governance, and he wasn't going to interfere with his payday by pissing Lavina off.

"We were busy," Beau explained, not going into more detail.

He doubted she'd wanted to hear about their three-way with a stripper they picked up from a club.

"Please tell me what the fuck you two were doing, because I've made it clear that I expect my calls to be answered immediately," she replied, her tone pissing him the hell off.

Beau had always hated employers who were too hands-on. They were a hindrance to their mission and often hard to reason with. Lavina was a prime example of that. She didn't seem to understand they didn't have the power to make the mission go by any quicker. Only a formidable witch could create a protection spell like the one around Susanne's house. The fact that a half-breed could maintain an enchantment so strong was a testament to Marine's power. It was weakening by the day, but not to a point where they could enter the house and retrieve the requested documents.

"Actually, I know what you two have been doing," Lavina continued, sounding more annoyed by the second. "Wreaking fucking havoc. Tell me, why the hell are y'all trying to slaughter half the damn town? What part of 'lie low' is hard for you two ignorant motherfuckers to comprehend?"

"Did you call to insult us, or did you want something?" Beau snapped.

He'd admonished Cruz over his behavior multiple times, but he wouldn't have Lavina calling them so late just to be an insulting heifer.

"Forgive me, Lavina, but I get hungry," Cruz said, his casual tone only irritating Beau further. "A man must eat, no?"

Getting Cruz to take shit seriously was a challenge, and this was no different.

"Then go on a diet, because you're too goddamn greedy," Lavina retorted. "Your crimes are receiving statewide attention, and whatever fuckery you're up to is delaying you two doing your goddamn jobs."

"The protection spell hasn't worn off." Beau sighed, scrubbing a hand over his face. "I've checked several times. That shit is strong."

"What goddamn protection spell?" Lavina demanded. "This is the first I'm hearing of this? How could Susanna LeBlanc, a half-breed—" she spat that insult— "place a protection spell?"

"I was thinking the same thing," Beau confessed. "It must've been her mother. Susanne was Marine's only child, so it made sense she'd want to protect her."

Lavina cackled, then abruptly stopped. "*Not*, you dimwitted bloodsucker. She had two other kids, and that woman's been dead for decades. *Her* protection spell would've worn off ages ago. No, it must've been Susanne. Somehow," she sneered. "Fucking bitch. Marine always thought that bitch was better than us."

"Is it possible Susanna's father had warlock blood?" Cruz asked, deciding to contribute to the conversation instead of trying to stare a hole into Beau's head. "There has to be some explanation for how she hexed her place."

"Did I ask you?" Lavina snapped. "I've known Mr. Valois for a good while, and that carnage that's going on in Gaville isn't his style. That's on you, so shut the fuck up. If I want your input, I'll ask you. But don't hold your breath." She laughed again. "Oops, sorry. You don't have any."

Cruz growled, but Beau held up a hand to calm him. Lavina was such a shady bitch.

"Keep your corny insults to your goddamn self," Beau ordered, Lavina's grating laughter raising his hackles further.

He might be sick of Cruz's shit, but he wouldn't allow a fucking witch to down his friend with lame ass jabs.

"You know, Beau," she said, switching gears. "You and your pardner are said to be some of the best around, yet this shit looks real amateurish. I would've thought y'all had charms at your disposal to counter fucking troublesome spells, or a goddamn contact to dismantle it completely."

"Getting another person involved is more trouble than it's worth." And often came with a cost. "Moreover, we weren't properly prepared, because you didn't give us all the fucking facts. You said Susanne was clever, but weak. A weak witch couldn't do that spell."

He bit back a flurry of insults. He'd known Lavina since the 1980s, when the bitch was in college and less of a headache. Her annoying tendencies could've been chalked up to youth, but as a woman nearing senior citizen status, that excuse had long since faded.

"I didn't know, asshole," she huffed. "And that's no excuse for zero progress. Her house ain't the only place she could've kept shit."

"Well, it's the only place that's fucking hexed," Cruz called, disregarding her previous words.

"Didn't I tell you to shut up?" she snapped. Both men exchanged a look, their spat with each other forgotten as Lavina worked on both of their nerves. "Go to Susanna's lawyer, Beau. Get me goddamn answers or your services will no longer be needed. I'll also expect my money back since you haven't produced any fucking results. You have a week."

She disconnected.

July 9th

Kamika

"All right, Mama, I'm about to go," I said, gathering my keys from the coffee table. She was sprawled out on the couch, reading glasses equipped as she scanned through another document. "I'll text you when I'm on the way back."

The sun was dipping below the horizon, and the cicadas were starting to sing as the moon rose in the sky. Earlier, Delaney had invited me to grab a drink this evening, and I accepted without a second thought. Because alcohol would be the equation, I decided against taking the car.

Mama lowered the document, examining the layered mustard romper I wore. "You going to the Harris's again?"

I shifted at her scrutiny, and frowned at her tone. "Yeah, I'm just gonna hang with Delaney for a few hours."

"You've been spending a lot of time around them," she said with a frown of her own, disapproval in her voice. "Around *her*. Don't you have other friends you could see?"

Back in the day, *before,* she never had a problem with the Harris family. Yet, her relationship with Colton was bringing out the worst in her. More and more, she was starting to remind me of Grandma. Instead of enjoying my mother's company, I was starting to dread it.

"I lost contact with my other friends, Mama," I said with remarkable patience. I hated it when we argued, so I'd do my best to keep my cool. "Larissa and I reconnected by pure coincidence, and Delaney is the only other friend I have in town."

We were more than friends at this point, but I didn't think Mama would like that piece of information.

"Just be careful."

I nodded, and she returned to her document. Slipping into the low platform sandals I kept by the door, I double checked I had my phone and my wallet, then prepared to leave.

"Oh, wait, baby, you know another girl went missing?"

I paused. Since we arrived, eight women had disappeared from Fleur. One was visiting her family, five had been college students, and two had been a tourist passing through town. Now, a ninth had been added to that list.

"A local or a tourist?"

"Local, but it doesn't matter. See if one of the Harris girls can bring you home."

I nearly snorted but managed to refrain. "If a serial killer is on the loose, what could they do?"

"Safety in numbers."

"Then they'd have to walk home alone and put themselves at risk."

She huffed out a breath, indicating her growing agitation. "They can handle themselves. Just trust me, girl. It's for your own good."

I nodded. And with nothing else to say, I offered a wave before going on my way. I kept an extra-tight grip on my keychain, thankful for the attached stun gun. It was little but mighty. If worse came to worse, I'd tase a motherfucker, and then run like hell.

Burnin' Boots was one of the oldest surviving juke joints in the country, having been around for about a century. It'd survived by modernizing when needed, but still maintained an old-timey feel that kept people coming back for decades. In a dying breed, Burnin' Boots was living history. My grandmother had many stories about the place. Years prior to seeing Acrylic Bayou, I'd snuck in once or twice as a teenager, resulting in an ass whooping from Grandma. She'd loved to remind me I wasn't too old to get beat for disobedience, a threat she backed up whenever I challenged her.

"You look good tonight," Delaney whispered to me, her hand on my lower back as we weaved through the crowd milling outside. "Then again, you always do, baby."

Located over the tracks on the other side of town, the juke joint was bumping tonight. Old people and young stood around, smoking and laughing. A stone fire pit lit up the night, and people sat on the rocky stools, sipping beers and conversing.

I laughed, but the noise around us drowned out the sound. "Flattery does you good."

If honkytonks were for country music fans, the juke joint was all blues. Nowadays, Burnin' Boots allowed an array of musical acts to perform on their stage, but the soulful sound of the blues was still often heard. Like tonight. The worried notes of a flattened fifth scale cried through the open door.

"Got to keep favor with my girl," she whispered in my ear, her raspy voice sending a shiver down my spine.

Her girl.

A smile spread across my face, not slipping even as Delaney steered me to the bar. The building was a small, wooden structure with a faded sign hanging from the center of a roof beam. Though I received a few nods, Delaney was offered warm greetings. It wasn't as crowded inside as it was out, yet it was so much noisier. Album covers, street signs, and folk art hung on the walls. Colorful lights hung from the ceiling, casting the place in a kaleidoscope of shades.

I glanced at the stage, occupied by older gentlemen performing fast-beat blues songs. It wasn't as packed as it was the night that Acrylic Bayou had performed, allowing more room for dancing.

Delaney guided me to the bar. "Hey, Boots," she called over the noise of the guitar and the singer. "Give me two growlers." She dug in her back pocket and came up with a twenty-dollar bill, throwing it on the bar.

As the music ended, Boots swiped the money and turned to the old-fashioned register.

The aging man was the great-grandson of the founder, and his daddy had been good friends with my grandma. He and his father had been some of the people Grandma made me talk to after church services ended, but years had passed since we'd spoken, he only offered me a nod of acknowledgment. Once he completed the transaction, he bent and came up with two capped, amber-colored jugs, then slid one to me and held the other out to Delaney.

"Still stingy with the tips," he said, shaking his head, topped with knotty grey hair. His teeth flashed white against his dark skin, smooth despite his age. "You your daddy's girl."

"And you your father's son, cuz," Delaney replied with fondness.

"And damn proud of it."

As he should be. It was the efforts of his father that'd revitalized the dying juke, affording me something to do before crawling back home to Miami.

Delaney turned to me, her hand still lingering on my back. Her touch was comforting, in a strange way.

"I'd like you to meet—"

"Kamika," a deep voice interrupted, that whisper of a rich drawl winding around me.

My toes curled, and I stood straighter. "Beau?" I said, too breathless for my own damn good.

Delaney stiffened, and I swore she growled. Fucking *growled* like a dog.

"Haven't seen the likes of you around here in a minute," Boots sneered.

I blinked. "You've visited Gaville before? You said you were just passing through."

That was already established to be a lie, so it shouldn't have been shocked that he's been to Gaville before. It would explain the familiarity of which he navigated the town, though I hadn't a clue why he wanted to keep it a secret.

Beau shrugged his wide shoulders, his expression never changing. A liar caught in his own games would at least break a sweat. "I am. Doesn't mean I haven't been here before." He glared at Boots, then nodded to Delaney. "Laney," he murmured, smooth as hell. "It's a pleasure to see you."

"Wish I could say the same," Delaney retorted.

Their undercurrents alarmed me. I didn't wish to be thrust into the middle of...whatever was going on. Delaney never told me just how they knew each other. I snatched the growler. "Thank you for the moonshine," I said with as much dignity as possible. "I'm going to enjoy it at home."

"Don't let him run you away, Kamika," Delaney said sharply.

Beau glared at her, his beautiful, dark eyes growing colder. "Excuse you. She's trying to escape *you*, Laney."

"I'm trying to escape you both," I clarified and scowled at Beau. His behavior made sense now. "I won't be used to make anyone jealous. No wonder you've been following me."

"I haven't followed you!"

Another growl escaped Delaney; I turned and frowned at her, almost impressed by her dog sounds. She should try out voice acting.

"And I especially am not trying to make Delaney jealous." His nostrils flared, and I shrank back at the hateful look he gave her. "She's not my type."

Unafraid, she smirked at him. "Correction, you aren't mine, though I know you wish you were, motherfucker." She grabbed her jug of moonshine, placed a hand on my shoulder, and steered me toward the exit. "Fuck him, girl. No-good, filthy ass-sucker," she finished with a snarl as we stepped outside.

"What happened between you two?" I asked as the hot night air swirled around us.

She shrugged, uncapped the jug, and drank deeply. "It's complicated, but trust me," she said, recapping the moonshine and licking her lips. "You don't need him. He doesn't have good intentions."

"That's an assumption."

"That's a fact."

"Based on?"

"Does it matter? You haven't been here in years. I should know the folks around here."

"Ain't that the pot calling the kettle black, because you haven't been around lately, either," I said, glaring up at her.

"I visited over the years," she sniffed, changing topic before I could call her out again. "And hasn't Beau already lied to you by saying he was just passing through?"

"Yeah, but—"

"No buts." She took my hand in hers and tugged me forward. "I'll walk you home, Kami."

Disappointment swarmed me; we didn't even finish our drinks in the juke joint while enjoying the music. Beyond that, I was relishing Delaney's company. Going home meant being without her presence, explaining to Mama what had happened, and struggling to fall asleep.

I frowned. "You really gonna let an asshole ruin our night?"

"He's a special kind of asshole, so yes." She sighed, scrubbing a hand over her face. "Trust me, it's for your own good."

"No, Delaney," I snapped, crossing my arms over my chest. "Tell me what the fuck is going on, and then take me back inside so we can dance."

I expected pushback on my order. Instead, her lips twitched into a smile. "It's cute when you're bossy."

"Compliments won't get you out of this."

Her lips thinned into a line. She was silent for several seconds, contemplating. Finally, she huffed out a breath and nodded. "Promise you won't judge, but...Beauden and I worked...uh...a less-than-savory job together."

My eyebrows shot up to my hairline. Was I about to hear a criminal confession? Would keeping her secret make me an accomplice?

"What, y'all sold drugs or some shit?" I joked, attempting to lighten the mood. I laughed at my own weak jest; she didn't. My eyes went wide. "Wait, y'all really sold drugs?"

Well, I'd be damned. I'd cast aside my second theory about Beau's career as nonsense, but it turned out that I was right on the money.

"Keep your voice down," she hissed, looking around and stepping closer. "And like I said, it's complicated, but I needed money for college."

"Was it hard drugs?" I asked.

"Does it matter?"

I thought for a moment, then nodded. "Selling weed is different than selling crystal meth or black tar heroin."

She shook her head, snickering. "I never sold anything that hard, but I can't say what that motherfucker did. He'd sell his own mama for a paycheck."

His lying about being a contractor wasn't shocking, as he wouldn't confess the truth. Yet, it begged the question of why he was bouncing between Gaville and Fleur. Wouldn't New Orleans have a healthy enough drug market?

"Just tell me what he did, Delaney," I said, searching her face to see if she was playing a joke on me.

I found zero signs of her words being a prank or a lie. I swallowed as I realized she was serious, and a part of me questioned my morality, because my attraction to her wasn't hindered by this information. Then again, why would it? I'd indulged in weed a handful of times, and even hung around some small-time dealers in Miami. Looking at her differently would make me a hypocrite.

"We used to be cool," she began, her voice low. "We ran in the same circles and would hang out at the same places. We worked together a few times. Shit was straight, but then a deal went left, and he left me out to hang. He promised to keep me safe, Kamika, then left me to fucking die."

My heart ached at the emotion in her voice. Beau doing something so fucked up sickened me. It finally made sense why he never spoke much about his job. Not only was he a criminal, but he also lacked the honor to look out for those he worked with.

"I'm sorry, Laney," I said quietly, placing my hand on her cheek. "That's so fucked up."

"Tell me about it," she huffed, leaning into my touch. "So now you know."

"Now I know," I confirmed with a nod. "And it changes nothing between us. You're still you."

Her face softened, the anguish that'd settled over her features melting away. Wrapping an arm around my waist, she pressed her mouth to mine. I parted my lips, granting her access. Our tongues brushed, the kiss growing hot and heavy very quickly. Only the sounds of hoots and hollers broke us apart. My cheeks heated as Delaney scowled at the drunk patrons egging us on.

"Look away, motherfuckers," she barked, glaring at the people—mostly men—staring at us.

"Keep the show going, baby!" one called, earning chuckles.

I wrinkled my nose; Delaney snarled. She shoved her drink into my hand and began to descend the steps. I followed her, stepping in front of her path.

"They're just drunk assholes, Laney." Who'd likely overpower her, even with alcohol in their systems. They were a group of men; she was one woman. "Let's go inside and dance. Have another drink and forget about all the dicks we've ran into tonight."

With one last glare over my shoulder, she nodded, taking her drink from my outstretched hand. "Yeah, babe, you're right. C'mon."

We returned to the bar, snagging two empty barstools. Beau was nowhere to be found, thankfully. Knowing how much of a motherfucker he was made my blood boil, and the first thing I'd do when I got home was delete his fucking number. It was one thing to be a drug dealer, it was another to not look out for your comrades and go back on promises.

"It was pretty fucking hot that you wanted to defend my honor," I said, just to end the awkward silence that'd settled between us. "But you could've gotten hurt, so please don't do that shit again."

She laughed, flexing her biceps, her tank top revealing just how muscular she was. "You underestimate me, babe."

I swallowed, her strong arms sending heat through my core. "Well, you aren't superwoman," I murmured, my voice huskier.

I quickly took a swig of my moonshine, my mouth suddenly dry. Grinning, she did the same. We finished our jugs quickly, a buzz settling over me by the time I drank the last drop. Hopping off my seat, I held a hand out to her.

"Let's dance," I said, wiggling my fingers when she didn't immediately take my hand. "Please, Laney?"

Her smile still stretched big, she placed her hand in mine, allowing me to guide her to the dance floor. Somewhere amid the drama, more people migrated to dance. We found a place on the edge, where the stage was barely visible. Watching the performers wasn't our priority, though, so neither of us made a fuss about it. The music pulsed through our bodies, driving our movements and melting away our stress. Her hand found mine as we moved to the beat, the harshness of the earlier confrontation replaced by a quiet intimacy and plain fun.

"Oh, shit, I fucking love this song," Delaney exclaimed as the band began covering 'I Walk on Gilded Splinters' by Dr. John.

"It's hard to dance to, though," I replied, the people retreating from the dance floor seeming to agree with me.

"Girl, you can dance to anything if you got the skill," she teased, leading me closer to the stage. "Just follow my lead."

With that, she started to sway to the beat, her hips moving in a decidedly seductive manner, her waist whining with skill I simply didn't possess. Still, I tried to mimic her, even though I felt a tad silly. Her hands found my hips, guiding my movements when I began to falter, my self-consciousness getting the better of me.

"Just like that, baby," she cooed as we synced up, her encouragement making me swallow coarsely.

Based on the glint in her eyes, she knew exactly how her words could be interpreted. At that moment, I could only focus on Delaney and admire the way her eyes sparkled with a mischievous light, how her small smile was so breathtaking. The world outside of this sweaty, vibrant shack ceased to exist. Only the music of the band, Delaney's touch, and the intoxicating feeling washing over me registered in my mind.

The next song covered was 'I Want You (She's So Heavy)' by the Beatles. My grandma adored the group and often spoke about how disappointed she was that she couldn't attend their only performance in New Orleans. I wasn't as big a fan, but 'She's So Heavy' was a favorite of mine.

"See, you're getting the hang of it," Delaney encouraged as I relaxed, my love of the song melting away any lingering tension.

"Only thanks to you," I replied, shuddering when her grip on my hips tightened a fraction.

We stayed close for the song, any shame we had going out the window as we practically grinded against one another, putting on a show for anyone who looked our way. Thankfully, there were no drunken creeps to catcall us and ruin the moment.

"What the fuck kind of lineup do they have?" I questioned as the Beatles cover faded into 'Iko Iko' by The Dixie Cups. "And isn't Mardi Gras over?"

"You can enjoy a good song year round, babe," Delaney said, releasing her grip on me, much to my disappointment. "C'mon. Let's go get another drink."

I nodded, following her to the bar. As we sat down, she didn't relinquish her grip on my hand. Boots was in the middle of helping another customer, one who appeared to be hogging his time. When he gave the guy his beer, and he continued to yap, Delaney grew impatient.

"Hey, cuz, we're thirsty," she called, interrupting the continuous conversation.

"Girl, couldn't you see I was busy?" Boots griped, no real venom behind his words. "Always been impatient, chile."

"The guy got his drink, and I can't let my girl dehydrate," she fired back, looking at me. "Another growler good with you?"

"Yeah," I said, eyeing Boots nervously.

As much as I loved hearing her refer to me as her girl, Gaville was still Gaville, and Boots's daddy had been close with my Grandma.

"Your girl, huh?" Boots repeated, his tone teasing rather than judgy. "You mean it how I think you mean it?"

"Sure do," she announced with pride, holding up our joined hands.

I waited for the look of disgust, for a biting comment, but none came. Instead, he laughed, looking at me and shaking his head. "Good luck to you, Kamika. You gonna need it with this one."

"Oh, c'mon, that's blatant slander," Delaney complained, handing him another twenty when he slid our drinks over. "Show your lil' cuz some respect."

His answer was another bout of laughter. Some other customer beckoned his attention before he could properly respond. His easygoing reaction was a relief and left me feeling lighter.

"Are you two really related?" I asked.

She nodded. "Boots' is my daddy's third cousin once removed through his mama."

I stared at her blankly. Cousin once removed was always a conundrum.

"Okay," I said simply, deciding to pretend I knew what the hell she just said.

She cackled, sensing how lost I was. "Kami, sweetheart, third cousins share the same great-great-grandparent, and once removed means they're of a different generation.

"I know what a third cousin is," I argued, feeling the need to defend myself.

"Boots is a boomer, born back in 1963," she continued, her only reaction to my words a smirk. "My Daddy was born in 1973. Gen X."

"Like my mama," I said after a swig of moonshine. "Or she's an elder millennial. I don't know the age ranges."

"Yeah, cusp years always confuse this shit out of me," she agreed.

"Alright, that'll be all from us, folks," the leader of the band said, capturing our attention.

The bar didn't provide the clearest view of the stage, but we saw the singer's slight bow at the round of applause. The songs the group performed may have lacked cohesion, but their talent couldn't be denied.

"Wonder who's playing next," I said when the stage was vacated.

Boots grabbed a remote from a counter behind the bar. He pressed a few buttons, and old blues songs started to ring out once again.

"Probably another cover band," Delaney replied.

She was proven right ten minutes later. Their introduction took at least five minutes, but just as we finished our growlers, the new band began playing 'Tennessee Whiskey' by Chris Stapleton, one of the few country songs I tolerated. Their cover was decidedly more bluesy, but they still maintained the original essence of the song.

"Huh, country in a juke joint," Delaney muttered, just as I squealed, "Dance floor, now."

"Always so demanding," she teased, taking my hand and leading me back onto the dance floor.

The song was the slowest of the night, allowing us to dance closer than before. Delaney's hands were perched on my waist, and my arms were thrown over her shoulder, locking us in a slow dance. Her scent enveloped me, the warmth of her body leaving me unable to focus on anything but her. An awkward giggle left me, the intimacy of the moment overwhelming me.

"Hi," I whispered when she cocked a brow.

She chuckled, a smile spreading across her lips. "Hi, baby."

We stayed close even as the song ended, unable to look away from one another. The air between us felt electric, and never had I felt more drawn to her. There was a pull between us, one that couldn't be denied, and one that I know she felt, too. I could've stayed like that for an eternity, in her arms with music pulsing around us.

Unfortunately, the moment was interrupted by the last person I wanted to see.

"Can I get a turn?" Beau asked, appearing out of nowhere.

"No," Delaney and I echoed, glaring at him.

Knowing what he'd done to her was a wake-up call. The few times we'd hung out didn't mean I knew him, and I wasn't going to get involved with a criminal who'd leave his associates to die.

He ignored Delaney entirely, focusing on me. Despite his smirk and relaxed demeanor, the intensity in his eyes left me anxious. He stepped closer, infringing on my space. I huddled closer to Delaney, relaxing as soon as her arms wrapped around me.

"Fuck off," she barked, lifting me up and setting me behind her, her taller body shielding me from view.

The ease in which she manhandled me was so fucking sexy, but Beau's presence prevented me from dwelling on it for too long.

"Crawl back into the wretched hole you came from, and leave Kamika the hell alone," she ordered, frowning at me when I peered around her to look at him.

Beau put his hands up and stepped back, that annoying smirk remaining. "No need to growl at me like a dog, Laney. After how much fun Kamika and I had at the motel, I just thought she'd be eager to spend more quality time with me."

I bristled, and another dog-like growl escaped Delaney.

"Motherfucker, you know nothing happened—"

My own shocked gasp cut off my words, prompted by Delaney punching the fuck out of Beau. I truly underestimated her strength, because the blow sent him flying. He landed on an empty table, and everything screeched to a halt at the crash. All eyes turned to us.

"You fucking overgrown mutt," he snarled, rebounding with surprising speed. "I'll kill you for that."

My blood ran cold, dread settling in my stomach at the venom in his tone. I grabbed her hand to tug us to the exit, but she shrugged me off.

"Bring it, you lowdown asshole—"

Suddenly, water splashed onto Beau, a spicy fragrance of orange blossoms seeping into the air. He hissed, scratching furiously at his own skin. Much of his flesh was covered, but on his neck, I swore a blister or two appeared. I realized what was thrown on him wasn't regular water, and was causing an allergic reaction. Before I could suggest an ambulance, Boots' angry voice rang out.

"What the hell is going on over here?" he yelled, tossing the empty aluminum bowl onto the floor. Delaney opened her mouth to speak, but he held up a hand. "Actually, I don't give a damn." He zeroed in on Beau, his lip lifting into a sneer. "You, motherfucker, leave. And if you know what's good for you, you won't come back."

He ceased his scratching, but his body trembled with rage. He looked at Delaney, an ugly scowl on his face. "This ain't over, bitch."

"Just go," I snapped, the night thoroughly ruined.

He spared me a glance, then stormed out of the building. Other patrons parted like the Red Sea, allowing me to keep an eye on him until he exited the building. When Beau was gone, Boots turned his attention to us.

"You two, out," he ordered, a tad less aggressive than he'd been with Beau. "I'll see y'all to the door."

"C'mon, Boots, he started it—"

"I don't care if the ghost of Michael Jackson started it, y'all ain't coming up in here and disrupting my business," he hollered, grabbing Delaney's wrist. "Now come on. We're having a long talk later, girl."

I hurried behind them, too flabbergasted to say a thing. After what I witnessed, I knew Delaney was allowing herself to be pulled by him, so I didn't make a fuss about it. Moreover, I didn't want to be on Boots' shitlist, as I enjoyed Burnin' Boots. Only when we were outside did he release her, and he walked with us until we reached the edge of the property. Digging into his pocket, he pulled out four vials. He handed two to both of us.

"Take that, ladies, and be safe," he said, looking at me. "Let Delaney bring you home, and if that motherfucker bother you again, pour it in his eyes, nose, or mouth."

My brows furrowed. The contents of the vial looked like murky water, and Boots' words had my mind drifting back to what I read. If supernaturals existed, it stood to reason that they had weaknesses. As insane as the notion was, I couldn't dismiss the thought, nor would that sinking feeling in my stomach go away.

"Boots," Delaney hissed.

He shrugged. "Better safe than sorry, Laney. I'll be seeing y'all around."

He glanced between us, then retreated into the shack. Little was said on the walk to my home. My mind was going a mile a minute. Our night had started rocky and ended terribly. I wished I'd declined her invitation, even with the fun we had in between. I was unable to rid my lips of the pout marring them. Out of the corner of my eye, I saw Delaney frequently glance at me, which I ignored. Her strength, too, made me think of the documents and the claim that the Harrises were a bunch of wolves. Pure lunacy that wouldn't leave my mind, and only left me more shaken up.

"All right, bye," I sniffed as we reached my grandmother's house, breezing past Delaney. "Be safe, and all that shit."

My words were callous and childish, but I was thoroughly disappointed. Beau was worse than I could've imagined. His history with Delaney was incredibly sordid, and both possessed a violent and criminal streak. Yet, I wasn't as angry with her as I should be. I was overwhelmed, and that made my demeanor chilly.

A sound close to a whine made me pause, and a firm grip on my wrist stopped me from getting far. Had she made that noise?

Turning, I came face-to-face with a sulking Delaney, her lip nearly dragging the ground. "Kamika, please don't be upset. I'll take you back to Boots another time."

I opened my mouth to blast her for causing such a scene, for provoking someone who she knew was lowdown and underhanded and putting us both at risk. Yet, all my complaints died on my tongue when I gazed into her wide, pleading eyes. Eyes didn't lie, and hers told me that she regretted her actions. She looked so distraught, and a pang went through my chest at the thought of making her feel even worse.

I flung an unruly loc behind her shoulder and allowed my hand to linger. "Imma hold you to that, 'Laney."

At my use of her nickname, she smiled, and the tension left her body. "I'll make it up to you, I swear."

She made no effort to remove my hand. Likewise, I allowed hers to stay wrapped around my wrist. We stared at each other, neither of us speaking. She licked her lips and leaned closer. I didn't back away.

Quite the opposite. I inched toward her and my hand wandered to her cheek.

"Can I?" she murmured, her gaze glued to my mouth.

In answer, I brushed my lips over hers. With a growl, she wrapped her arms around my waist and responded with fervor. She slanted a knee between my thighs and drove it upward, the thin fabric of my romper allowing my core to be stimulated. Her gentle nips at my lips made me gasp. She seized the opportunity to invade my mouth with her tongue, gently stroking the pink appendage against mine. The movement of her leg didn't falter. She deepened our kiss and slid her hands to my ass.

She smiled against my lips as I ground against her knee. I feared I'd soak through my panties and reveal my arousal to the world. Even so, it was a minute worry. I was on the verge of orgasm, easily wound up because of my dry spell. Right now, my release was the primary focus.

Or, it was, until the front door swung open. In record time, Delaney and I flew apart. We were both panting, our lips no doubt swollen from the steamy make-out session.

Clutching her robe, my mother stepped outside, glowering at us. I made it a point to look everywhere but at her, embarrassment filling me.

"Uh, hey, Ma," I murmured, my gaze glued to the porch.

She didn't answer, and it seemed as if the night sounds increased in volume. Trooper that she was, Delaney took it upon herself to break the awkward silence.

"Ms. LeBlanc...hi," she said.

From the edges of my vision, I saw her extend a hand to my mother. She didn't accept the peace offering. After a few seconds, Delaney dropped her arm back to her side.

"Another Harris girl, huh, Kami?" Mama asked.

I snapped my head up.

A snarl escaped Delaney. She slapped a hand over her mouth.

Mama released a humorless laugh. "And this one can make dog noises. How shocking."

"Mama!" I exclaimed, taken aback by her rudeness. I glared at her. "What's wrong with you?"

Gone was the sweet mother I knew and loved. She'd always been her mother's twin looks-wise, and right now, it seemed she'd adopted her prejudice, too. The idea hurt my soul. I'd been rejected once for who I was by someone I loved dearly. I couldn't go through that pain again. Especially by my own mother, the one person who always had my back.

"Imma go now, Kamika," Delaney breathed, her tone utterly dejected. "I'll text you."

"I think that'd be best," Mama said, quickly ushering me inside as Delaney disappeared into the night. Her exit didn't comfort my mama, though. "I told you to let one of them walk you home, not stick their tongue down your throat."

"What does it matter?" I snapped. I rarely lost my temper with my mother, but the way she treated Delaney was out of pocket. "I'm grown, remember? What happened to staying out of *my* business? Isn't that the excuse you used when I walked in on you and Colton?"

"That's different, Kamika, because I knew what the hell I was getting myself into! You don't!" she yelled, her temper still burning hot. "I told you to be careful around them, and what do you do? Jump from one cousin to another."

I bristled at her words. "Oh, so I'm just a whore who jumps from cousin to cousin, is that it?"

"Stop twisting my words—"

"I'm not twisting anything, when you're standing up here shaming me for seeing Delaney! Would you have preferred Beau, Mama? Is that the issue?"

"I would prefer neither one of them," she spat, angrier than I'd seen her in a while. "What's wrong with dating someone else, someone normal? Or just being single for a while?"

The sheer hypocrisy of her statement stopped me from dissecting what she meant by 'normal'. An indignant snort left me. "That's rich, when you went back to your cheating ex because you were lonely."

"Trust me when I say as lowdown as Colton is, he's a better choice than either of them."

My jaw dropped, the insanity of her statement robbing me of words. My eyes darted around her face, looking for any evidence that she doubted her statement. I found none. Exhaustion slammed me, and my shoulders slumped, the fight gradually leaving my body. I'd dealt with enough drama tonight, and I knew this was a fight I wasn't going to win.

"Whatever," I muttered, beelining for my room and slamming the door closed before she responded.

Kamika

When you start getting comfortable, you become reckless. Larissa and I had taken precautions to hide our relationship, especially from my grandma. I suspected her family knew, but her mother hadn't said a thing to me, nor had Larissa told me they'd found out about us. Thus, it remained a hunch, one I tried to ignore whenever I went over to her place. She claimed her family wasn't bigots, but I could imagine no other reason for her to want to keep our relationship on the down low. That was the primary reason I hadn't told my grandma about us. Even my mother didn't know. Not because I thought she'd be unsupportive, but because I didn't want her to accidentally expose me during their nightly phone calls.

I knew my grandmother loved me. However, I also knew she was from an older generation, one that had certain ideas they couldn't shake. One such idea was the unnaturalness of same-sex relationships. Never did she say she hated queer people, but the comments she'd made over the years made it clear that people who dared to be attracted to the same gender disgusted her.

Knowing that she'd see me as repulsive if she discovered my relationship with Larissa Harris terrified me.

"What's on your mind, Kami?" Larissa murmured into my hair.

"My grandmother," I answered, my face in her neck.

We were intertwined on my bed, half-naked and sated for the time being, listening to my playlist of shuffle. Currently, 'Meant to Be' by Bebe Rexha played. It made me smile. I couldn't imagine being meant for anyone else but Larissa, so the song felt fitting.

And yet, even that thought didn't take away the sense of foreboding I felt, one that worsened the closer it came to Grandma returning home. She had a church function to go to, and those lasted well into the night. At least, we had another hour together before Larissa and I had to become decent and navigate to the living room.

Larissa tsked. "Stop worrying. It doesn't end until 9 PM, baby. It's only 8 o'clock."

"What if it ends early?"

She snorted. "When have you ever known that pastor to end services early? If anything, your granny won't be coming home until 10 AM tomorrow."

I giggled, my worry trickling away. "You're so stupid."

"I can't be stupid if I'm telling the truth, dummy," she retorted, her laughter joining mine.

When we fell silent again, she tilted my head up. Leaning down, her lips found mine. The kiss quickly grew heated, and when we pulled apart, we were both panting.

"Round two?" I asked, placing my hand on her upper thigh.

She nodded, parting her legs and granting me access.

Looking back, I wasn't sure if I was comfortable, or plain cocky. The night Grandma caught me with Larissa, we decided to take another nap after fooling around, instead of getting up and heading to the couch as we normally did. That had been our downfall. She

was right about services lasting longer than intended, but it didn't matter, because we only woke up when my bedroom door flew open.

"Kamika!" Grandma yelled, jolting me awake.

Once again, I was an observer to my memory, unable to do anything but watch chaos unfold as my grandmother discovered my secret in the worst way possible.

"What the hell is going on here?" she screeched as we hurried to cover ourselves.

"There's no need to yell, ma'am," Larissa said, glaring at Grandma.

Back then, she was bolder, and her sense of shame was nearly nonexistent.

"The fuck their isn't," Grandma hissed, walking over to the bed and yanking me out, forcing me away from Larissa. "Not when I just caught my granddaughter in bed with a goddamn filthy mutt."

At this point, I was expecting my other Grandmother—the dead one—to appear and offer her input. So, when she spoke, it didn't come as a surprise.

"You never did figure out what I mean, huh, girl?" she asked, materializing by my side. "Just thought I was hurling a slur at her."

"Well, you called me a dyke right afterwards, so excuse me for being confused."

Maybe I was imagining things, but I swore regret crossed her face. With a sigh, she snapped her fingers. My dreamland transformed her into a genie, so that simple gesture allowed the scene to fade away into the limbo version of her living room.

"I didn't handle things correctly, but you have to understand, I was shocked, and it wasn't natural," she said in earnest. "For more reasons than one."

There was no bite to her words, but it didn't stop me from laughing in her fucking face as I put distance between us.

"If that's your attempt at an apology, it's ass," I snapped, pacing the length of the room. "Not only did you insult me and Larissa, but you humiliated me, dragged my name through the mud. Why, Grandma? What had I ever done to you to deserve that?"

My voice cracked, and at that moment, I felt like that hurt sixteen-year-old who's world had just been shattered by a woman she held in such high regard.

"Nothing, Kami. That was wrong of me, and for that, I'm sorry," she stated plainly. "But after catching you with her, I knew it was best if you stayed away from town, and my words served their purpose."

"Oh, how righteous of you, shaming a teenager to...to...to what? What reason did you have to drive me away?"

"I should've told you before I died. I knew I was dying, but I didn't know how to reconcile. Never did I think your choice was Godly, but I understand now it wasn't my place to pass such harsh judgment. I should've set you up with a good boy, guide you to the right path—"

I decided to ignore her proposed solution, the first part of her rambling catching my attention. "Told me what, Grandma? You keep speaking so cryptically, and expect me to understand!"

"Back then, would you have believed me if I told you Larissa was literally a dog?" she questioned.

My lips parted in surprise, and for several seconds, I could only stare at her. When I caught my bearings, I scoffed. "Hell, no, because my eyes clearly told me she is a human female."

"What if I told you she could turn into one? That her entire family could, that—" She stopped abruptly, wincing as if in pain. She swallowed and shook her head. "Back in April, when the doctors told me there was nothing they could do—"

"You were sick?" I asked, my heart shattering.

Her official cause of death had been a heart attack. Never had she told us she had a terminal disease.

"Did Mama know?"

"No one did," she confessed, a sad smile spreading across her face. "Once word got out, I

knew what would happen. My mama had enemies, and when she died, I inherited them."

"Those documents…were they…how much of it was the truth?"

"Whatever your instincts are telling you, believe them," she replied, composing herself quickly.

My instincts were telling me those documents weren't the ramblings of a lunatic or the musings of someone with an overly active imagination. Yet, just thinking that those wild words held some truth made me feel like a fool, no matter what my gut feeling was telling me.

"You know, the year we fell out, I was going to invite you, your Mama, and Zara down for Christmas, and tell y'all the truth. Fate had different plans, I suppose."

"You still could've," I whispered, imagining how different life would've been if she'd followed through with those plans. "You didn't have to shun me, no matter the reason."

"I need you to listen to me closely, Kamika. When you wake up, go to my journals."

"Which ones? You have dozens."

"Look for the journals with these dates," she ordered, beginning to list the dates before I could reply. "February 15th, 1960."

A week after Grandma's 13th birthday.

"June 16th, 1993."

Five days after Mama's 13th birthday.

"August 6th, 2009."

The day Mama found out she was pregnant with Zara.

"June 4th, 2018."

The day I arrived in Gaville that year.

"August 15th, 2021."

The day I left Gaville, just three days after Grandma discovered me with Larissa.

"And finally, April 4th, 2025. That day, I found out I would be dead by the end of the year. And lo and behold, they were right."

"Those are a lot of fucking days," I grumbled, trying to ignore the overwhelming grief that slammed into me at her words.

Because, despite the heartache she'd caused me, I hadn't wanted her to die. She'd been dead to me because I'd been dead to her. All I had really wanted was an apology and reconciliation.

"The last one is the most important, baby, but reading all of them will give you the full picture," she said gently. "You have nearly two months to read them, so don't feel the need to rush."

Duly noted.

"And, after I read these journals, what am I supposed to do, Grandma?"

"Talk to your Mama and Zara and share what you read. Do what I should've done years ago."

Passing her burden onto the grandchild she shunned, how sweet of her. What a lovely posthumous present.

"Although," she continued. "They probably know. Zara definitely does."

"Please stop being so cryptic," I begged, uncaring of how whiny I sounded.

Death was never easy, and I knew emotional turmoil would be a staple of this summer. But everyone speaking in riddles wasn't something I anticipated. Everyone around me shared a giant secret, it seemed. Yet, they withheld it from me, leaving me to wonder what the hell was going on. It was maddening.

"Please, just speak plainly," I continued, hoping my plea gave me the results I craved.

If I was awake, I'd wager I'd have a massive headache.

"I swear I will, Kami, after you discover the truth," she promised.

I groaned in frustration, but before I could get a word out, the limbo I was becoming so familiar with was fading away. And with it, my grandmother, once again leaving me with more questions than answers.

July 11th

Kamika

The first thing I did when I woke up was write down the dates Grandma had mentioned. They were still fresh in my head, and I didn't want to forget them. However, I didn't immediately follow through with the instructions plaguing me. Each time I intended to, more bullshit was flung my way. When I left Gaville humiliated, betrayed by my grandmother, and forced away from Larissa, I thought nothing would ever compare to my heartache and pain. Then Grandma died, and I swore I *didn't* feel heartache and pain. But after the scene between Mama and me, I'd become a non-entity to my mother. She wouldn't talk to me or even smile at me, and she made sure to take her meals without me, leaving dirty dishes as evidence.

I'd never felt such devastation. No matter our disagreements and different outlooks, I always believed in my mother and put her on a pedestal. Just like I did Grandma. And just like Grandma, Mama deserted me.

It left me numb, unable to muster the energy to find the diaries or call my sister and ask what *she* knew. I especially couldn't bring myself to tell Mama. She already looked at me with disdain, if she bothered to glance in my direction. I couldn't have her studying me like a specimen in a lab if I told her a dead woman was giving me instructions and also informed me she'd died of a terminal illness.

Hadn't she been autopsied? Wouldn't they have discovered her exact cause of death? Dealing with my grief, for my mother, for my grandmother, even for Beau made me long to escape and go back to Miami.

If it wasn't for Delaney, I would have. I hadn't seen her since the disaster of Burnin' Boots. She still texted me but something about her seemed off, too. Was I looking at her through a different lens? One in which my grandmother told me to trust my instinct, and both she and Mama referred to Larissa and Delaney as *mutts*?

Come to think of it, hadn't Beau referred to Jack in a similar way?

In what alternate reality did I fucking exist?

Mama walked into the living room, dressed in denim shorts, a sleeveless red top, and hoop earrings. She sat her oversized purse on the chair and grabbed her sandals. "I don't know what time I'm returning tonight, Kamika," she said briskly, deeming to speak to me for the first time in days. "Or if I'm returning." She nodded to her bag. "I may spend the night at Colton's."

How did she expect me to respond? I could've reminded her I'd stayed in Gaville *for her*, but it wouldn't have done any good. I'd disappointed her and lost her love and support.

That crushed me. Blinking, I drew in a deep breath, swallowing the sob rising up.

"What are your plans?"

"Does it matter what I do, Mama?" My voice sounded hoarse. Distraught. Defeated.

"Of course it does, Kamika," she said, sounding exasperated, as if I was the problem. "I love you, and more importantly, it matters what you *don't* do."

"Why don't you bring this same energy to all the people who deserve it?" I demanded, glaring at her, near my breaking point. "Like Giselle and your raggedy man. Zara's daddy. Like all those women at the book club and most of the people who came to Grandma's funeral?"

Her nostrils flaring, she stormed to her bag and snatched it up. "Look, little girl, you don't get to tell me what to do. I refuse to lower my dignity to their levels. Something I tried to impart to you. They go low? We go high."

"Not in my book," I snapped. "They go low? I go lower, because going high don't get you nowhere but the company of assholes."

"Then you'll be cavorting with serpents and demons if you aren't careful."

"Exactly what Colton Sampson is, a damn yellow-bellied snake and a demon."

"That's enough…" She lifted her hands as if she needed to stop *me*. "You know what? No matter what you think, I know how to handle Colton, more than I can say about you concerning Delaney. One day, you're going to wish you'd listened to me about that girl."

"If you said something worth hearing, I'd listen to you."

A honking horn interrupted whatever she would've said. Without another word, she left, slamming the door behind her to underscore her anger and disapproval.

I jumped to my feet, too through. Fuck them all. I'd done nothing wrong. Loving Larissa…loving Delaney…no, I didn't love her, but I did care about her, and I wanted a relationship with her. I thought Mama would've been happy that I'd finally found someone I might be able to call my own.

Admittedly, I could've handled some situations better. Did I have a bad temper and a smart mouth? I did have Grandma's DNA. Although I could've been more respectful at times, I didn't have the patience for the dumb shit. I said what I had to say and moved on.

Maybe, I *should* leave. Find the journals with the dates Grandma gave to me and then fly home. But last-minute plane tickets were expensive as hell and my bank account was broker than my heart.

Needing a distraction, I headed to Grandma's room, now the place where my mother slept, brave woman that she was. Not that it mattered. I would think my grandmother would've missed her room and visited Mama. Instead, she plagued my dreams and took us to the living room to hang out.

I halted, and my eyes widened. Did that mean she resided there, floating in some invisible world that she stepped out of when the mood hit her? It was where she died.

A chill swept over me. Spooked, I returned to the living room and looked around, my gaze touching every corner. As I did so, I made the sign of the cross.

"You're being foolish, girl."

Nope, nope, nope. I sure wasn't.

"Find the damn journals, Kamika."

I'd lost my mind.

"You're very much sane. You're made of sterner stuff. Get to work."

I jumped at the yelled directive, turned and ran to the bedroom. I thought about closing and locking the door, but shit, what good would that do? Couldn't ghosts float through walls? I wasn't sure where to start and Grandma decided to clam up instead of telling me where these journals might be. They had been on the coffee table. Mama had moved them. Grandma's room was as neat as always, smelling of myrrh and frankincense, her favorite incense fragrance.

I ignored the meaning behind those religious connotations and tipped forward, as if I feared waking the dead when it seemed like one particular dead person never slept. As I passed by the dresser, an old photo in a faded black frame caught my attention. The picture, from my sixteenth birthday, when Granda surprised me with a visit to Miami, showed me standing next to her just after she'd arrived. I saw the tears on my cheeks.

I'd been an emotional child.

The picture had been right here when I'd arrived that next summer. I'd avoided the room brimming with evidence of Grandma's life, and hadn't stepped foot into it since Mama had cleaned it up. I figured once she put me out, she would've thrown any memories of me away. That she didn't...

It meant more to me than anything else. It meant, somewhere inside her, I'd still mattered. Snatching the picture, I hugged it to me, unable to stop the wave of grief swamping me, admitting how much I missed her and wanted her back here with me. She always knew how to make everything better. Until she didn't.

Stumbling to the bed, I sobbed for what could never be. What should've been but never was. Bitter tears escaped me. Tears that were forged in pain but honed by mourning. Not just for my grandmother's life, but the happy girl I'd been, believing love cured everything.

The sound of a text message alert broke through my weeping and I picked up my phone, laying the picture next to me.

Laney-Lane: You busy?

Sniffling, I swiped at my cheeks.

Me: No. Why?

Laney Lane: I'd like us to watch a movie here at the house. Just us.

Just hearing from Delaney calmed me down, and the prospect of being alone with her was enticing. Maybe, it'd help me feel better, and allow me to ignore the feeling that everything I'd known was crumbling all around me.

Me: What time?

Laney Lane: In an hour.

Me: See you then.

Laney Lane: Bet.

Like Mama, I needed a break too, and Delaney happened to be one of my favorite people in the entire world. Chilling with her always cheered me up and her perspective usually helped me.

Standing, I returned the picture to the dresser. I wasn't sure how long I'd be out tonight, so I decided to take a quick peek in the closet, where I hit the jackpot. All the journals that had been on the coffee table, were stacked on the floor, amongst Grandma's shoes and handbags. The dates Grandma wanted me to find spanned 65 years, so that would be in several different journals. Her advice had been ringing through my head since I woke up, allowing me to remember most of the days.

Chewing on my lip, I decided to look for the most recent one first. Luckily, it was near the top just as I suspected. It took me ten minutes to find the journal from 2021 and and the one from 2009.

Wasn't there a date in between? I searched my mind for important dates. Yes, that's right! It was 2018. June 4th.

Unfortunately, I wanted to change into something cuter before I left, so I had to abandon my exploration. For now, I'd content myself with the three journals. Grandma said not to rush. I had two months before I left Gaville, although I'd amended my intentions to never return. I'd *have* to return to see Delaney.

My mood brightening for the first time in days, I shoved the journals in my sock drawer, burying the notebooks in a sea of colors, before I hopped to my feet and headed to my closet.

I felt unreasonably happy as I rang Larissa's doorbell and waited for Delaney to open it. My mind ran wild as I imagined how we'd greet each other. Would we pick up with the kiss that had been so rudely interrupted? Maybe we'd just hug, watch the movie, and then talk about everything.

I *did* have questions, but I'd been so miserable I'd pushed my curiosity aside.

Or should I demand answers *first* and get the tough shit out of the way? Confirming that my almost-girlfriend was a fucking *wolf* might ruin the relaxing evening I needed. However, how did one live as a human in a world populated by supernaturals?

I was just about to ring the bell again when the door swung open. I scowled at Jack, insulted at how anger darkened his face the moment he saw me.

"Delaney invited me."

"She's not here."

"Ha, ha, very funny, but I don't believe you."

Scowling, he stepped aside. "See for yourself, Kami."

I stomped past him, ignoring how he slammed the door, and dogged my steps all the way to the kitchen, where Larissa and Miss Galena sat at the counter, less than pleased. I lost some of my steam.

"Uh, Delaney...Delaney invited me over," I squeaked, shifting my weight. "For a movie."

"She left with Queen," Miss Galena said, sitting straighter and drumming her fingers on the countertop.

Queen? "I, uh, I...who's that?"

"Malika," Larissa said, her lips turning down unhappily.

Right. Delaney had said that was her nickname. That heifer had been all over Delaney, unable to catch on that she wasn't interested. Certainly, she wouldn't have blown me off for her.

Unless, she was interested and just hid it well.

Wait, no.

That'd be incest, so they couldn't possibly have anything going on.

Right?

My head was spinning. For the sake of my sanity, I chose to believe it was a joke. A cruel, stupid joke, but one I still laughed at. No one joined in. Even Jack looked distinctly uncomfortable.

"She's a Harris, isn't she?" I asked, refusing to read more into this situation. "Where'd they go? Delaney told me to get here in an hour. She must be on her way back."

"She's a Harris by association, not blood," Miss Galena spat, disgust coating each word. "We don't know when they'll be back."

I glanced from her to Larissa. I even looked at Jack, but he could no longer meet my eyes.

Snatching my phone from my pocket, I fired off a quick text to Delaney.

> Me: I expected you to greet me with open arms and a big kiss, not be out with Malika.

> Delaney: I can't talk right now. We're busy. Sorry.

A noise escaped me. A sob or a squeak. Maybe, a cross between the two.

The words on the screen blurred.

"It's best that you leave, Kamika," Miss Galena ordered.

Backing away, I turned and ran, my heart shattering. Or the part not already in pieces from all that had happened over the past few days.

"Kamika!"

Ignoring Jack's call, I ran blindly. I couldn't bear his gloating or his sympathy. I'm not sure which would've been worse.

Before I could open the gate and make it out onto the road, those three fucking dogs from the 4th of July leapt in front of me, growling and pawing the dirt. The smallest of those overgrown monsters positioned itself to jump. Suddenly, a wolf with a winter white coat soared through the air and landed in the space between me and baby Cerberus. All three of them immediately cowered, even though they were bigger.

The moment they moved, I opened the gate and rushed through it, alarmed when the white canine followed me out.

"Get back in there," I ordered through my tears. I pointed. "Go!"

The dog ignored me.

"Kami," Larissa called.

I couldn't deal with her right now. Before she reached me, I ran off, aware of the beast hot on my heels. Halfway home, I paused. "Go away, you mangy mutt!"

The dog was actually beautiful, and it seemed to know that, judging by the growl I received.

Huffing, I continued toward Grandma's house. I'd text Larissa and let her know her damn dog decided to follow me. Her dog?

I paused, and the dog did, too. Carefully, I studied it, taking in its beautiful coat and blue eyes. Its proud stance and fierce look.

"You're a dog, not just a wolf, aren't you?" I questioned, deciding it was likely a wolfdog.

As if it understood, it cocked its head to the side.

Hysterical laughter escaped me, and I tipped my head back, blinking at the dark sky, dotted with stars, and a slivered moon. The night was warm and sultry, the air smelling of night-blooming jasmine.

"Werewolves only come out during full moons," I muttered.

I swore the dog frowned. It reminded me of Olivia's chihuahua. Though multiple times bigger, this dog was just as expressive as that barky little menace.

A honking horn scared the shit out of me. I realized I'd stopped in the middle of a road, and a car was fast approaching.

"Come on, girl," I said frantically, refusing to leave the dumb dog behind.

We moved out of the way just in time.

"Asshole!" I yelled, kicking at the air. "You're all assholes! All of you," I bawled, plopping down on the sidewalk.

Had my emotions been more stable, my dramatics might leave me ashamed. Instead, it felt like I was on the verge of a breakdown, leaving me feeling justified for falling apart so publicly.

The dog nuzzled me, my only fucking friend in the world, and I wrapped my arms around its neck and sobbed. Being so comfortable around an unfamiliar animal wasn't my wisest decision, but lately, I was full of bad ideas. Thankfully, it stood still as if it knew I had nothing else to comfort me. Finally, I got to my feet and made my way home.

Once I unlocked the door, I beckoned the dog. "Come inside until someone gets you," I instructed as if it understood me. It sat on the porch and began to pant. "You're thirsty? I'll get you some water. It's cool inside and—"

"Who the hell are you talking to?" Mama demanded.

Groaning, I opened the door since I had only cracked it and found my mother sitting on the sofa.

"The dog," I said hoarsely, and pointed.

Her gaze fell on the animal, and she narrowed her eyes. "Get the fuck out of here," she yelled, flying toward it, but unable to injure it because it turned and sprinted away.

I started to run after it. Mama yanked me back and dragged me into the house, slamming the door shut.

"What's wrong with you, Mama?" I cried, bewildered by her actions. She was an animal lover through and through. "Have you gone insane?"

That could be the cause of her recent behavior, explaining why my sweet mama had been acting so out of character.

She pointed a trembling finger at me. "No, but you have. Where were you?"

"What does it matter?" I clapped back. I knew it wouldn't. "As a matter of fact, why are you here? What happened to your all-nighter?"

"Colton happened, and unlike you, I know when to walk away from a bad situation." She swept me with a look. "Why the hell would you bring a goddamn wolf into this house, girl? Asking me if I've gone insane, when you should be asking yourself that!"

"That was a dog," I growled. "Are you blind?"

Mama straightened. "I'm not but obviously you are," she said darkly. "You know what? It might not be such a bad idea if you went back to Miami, Kami. You're better off there than here."

Her voice cracked on the last word, her face falling and her bottom lip wobbling. Her statement seemed to hurt her as much as it crushed me, but I refused to show any emotion. Just like her mama, she was throwing me away, too. "Finally, something we agree on, Mama," I said, and stalked away.

With that, I retreated to my room. The sob that floated to my ears sent a pang through me. I hated it when my mother cried. I wanted to return to the living room and tell her not to cry because it'll be alright, words she said to me often during my childhood. However, my pride prevented me from venturing outside my room, even as I hoped she'd be the bigger person she typically was and rescind her words. If her remark was said in a moment of anger, and she didn't mean it, she was free to come to my room to talk things out.

She didn't.

The next day, Mama was gone by the time I woke up. I didn't know where she'd disappeared to, and I didn't care. I felt numb, and all I could think about was leaving town. The trip had gone to hell, doing more damage than anticipated.

After I fixed myself some coffee, I navigated to Olivia's number and texted her, explaining the situation. I threw out my dignity and begged her to lend me the money for an expensive plane ticket. Angel that she was, she sent the money via Cash App minutes after reading my text. Before doubts could set in, I purchased the ticket. My departure was slated for the next day, so I started packing.

"I'm leaving tomorrow," I told Mama when she finally returned.

Her face crumpled, but she nodded. "Okay."

That simple reply was all she said to me before retreating to her room. She left early the next morning again, again neglecting to tell me where she was going. Despite our argument, I hoped she would return before I left at noon. By 10 AM, I realized she wouldn't, so, in a fit of pettiness, I found the other three journals and packed all six away. Whatever secrets the notebooks contained would only be revealed if I wanted to share. The act was a small

consolation and allowed me to pretend my
world hadn't just crashed around me.

July 19th

Kamika

The moment I touched down in Miami, I regretted my decision. Mama, Larissa, and Delaney had all reached out to me, but I was too proud and too emotional to answer their texts or calls. Delaney blowing me off to be with Malika was crushing, just as Mama continuously choosing Colton over me. The meek woman I knew and loved had disappeared, turning into a hellcat quick to defend her raggedy man. Her claws remained extended to criticize my choices and insult the woman I'd grown to care about. Ultimately, her warnings about Delaney weren't wrong, but Mama's condescension was my breaking point.

Well, that, and her outright telling me to leave.

If our relationship hadn't become so strained, I might've dismissed her words as a meaningless remark said in an argument. That wasn't the case, and she didn't make the effort to rescind the comment. It reminded me why I had grown to resent Gaville. It was a toxic little town that infected everyone within its boundaries with low-motherfucker syndrome.

Yet, that didn't stop me from missing it, and a week after I left, I was already considering returning. Reading the journals didn't help, and it left me even more torn. Apparently, I *did* live in a world where werewolves, witches, and *vampires* existed. The latter was such a problem, that Grandma and her mama had to cast a spell over the town to prevent them from entering. At times, I accepted that possibility as if it was okay and that we weren't fucking insane. Grandma for writing it, and I for entertaining it. I couldn't tell Olivia because she *would* call me crazy. Maybe, she'd even turn away from me, or worse, encourage me to seek therapy. They, in turn, might believe I needed to be committed.

I just didn't know anything anymore, including who to trust or how to feel.

The journals and not being able to talk to anyone about them were part of the reason I missed Mama and Delaney so much. I could've discussed it with one, if not both. Even Grandma—her ghost—had deserted me. It almost made me try one of the spells contained in the notebook to summon her and investigate the realness of all the claims on my own.

Three things stopped me.

For one, I didn't want to summon a demon and cause my primary place of residence to become haunted beyond belief.

Two, it felt fucking silly, like one of the those spells you did when you were in elementary school because the internet told you it would transform you into a mermaid.

And finally, I didn't know if I was capable of doing it, of mustering the energy to try something so outlandish, while feeling so alone and dejected.

The modest Miami townhome I shared with my mother felt empty without her, and spending time with Delaney had grown to be a regular part of my routine. The absence of them both left me empty. Perhaps I'd been too rash in my decision. Maybe I should've gotten a room at Gaville's tiny, decrepit inn, or packed an overnight bag and taken an Uber to Fleur, renting a decent motel room until I cooled off.

Alas, I hadn't, and now I had to live with the results of my temper. Because, surprise, surprise, children, actions had consequences.

"Girl, cheer up," Olivia grouched, nudging me with her elbow. "Just text them if it's bothering you so much."

"I'm fine," I snipped, my obvious lie earning me the side-eye.

She huffed out a laugh. "Could've fooled me."

Sighing, I plopped back on the beach towel, staring at the blue sky. Olivia thought a beach day would cheer me up, and any other time, it would've. The beaches were one of the things I loved about Miami, but the warmth of the sun and the salty sea breeze did little to help my mood.

"Hey," Olivia coaxed, nudging my side until I looked at her. The air was making her curls sway, and the beams of sunlight brought out the natural red highlights in her dark brown hair. Her hazel eyes were soft as she looked at me. "Kami, girly, if you don't want to do it, I'll send the text for you. But it's obvious that you're upset about what happened. Replying to them might make you feel better."

Or lead to more bullshit. As much as I wish I hadn't left, I feared that forgiveness would lure me back to Gaville, just for the drama to continue.

"I'll text them soon," I said, sitting back up and grabbing the flask I'd packed in my beach bag. "Let's talk about something else. How are things with Benson?"

"Chile, don't get me started on that motherfucker," she huffed, grabbing the flask from my hand once I took a swig, and taking a big gulp. "You know he was texting Nicki on the low? When he knows how I feel about that bitch."

"That asshole!" I exclaimed, infusing indignation that I didn't feel into my voice. "He's green for that."

Yes, Nicki was a lowdown heifer and intolerable to be around, but I couldn't muster up the energy to feel genuine outrage. Numbness had been my constant companion since I'd left Gaville, and during the moments that it gave me some reprieve, I only felt hurt and regret.

"Right? I should've let Bones chew his ass up," she declared, making me snicker.

Her little white chihuahua had earned his namesake, being a vicious creature despite not even weighing ten pounds.

"And like, you know I'm not the jealous type—shut up," she said when I snorted. Olivia was very jealous when it came to relationships, no matter how much she denied it. "But Nicki is unbearable, and I don't know what she has against me, but I swear that hoe always chases the guys I go for."

Olivia's bad history with Nicki dated back to high school, when they went from friends to enemies. I didn't know the details of what happened, and today, I was too down to ask for the info I didn't know. So, I just nodded along, showing the anger she wanted to see from me whenever required. She needed to vent, and I wouldn't spread my misery by being a shitty friend.

If only Mama and Delaney had been so protective of my feelings.

"Oh, by the way," I said when Olivia paused to take another swig of liquor. "Megan is letting me take pictures for her baby shower and do her maternity shoot."

Olivia cocked a brow. "For free?"

"Girl, no. I'm doing it lower than the market value, but not for free." I waved a hand dismissively. "Anyway, it should be enough to pay you back.

She studied me for a moment, then shook her head. "Nah, girl, it's okay. My parents actually gave me the money to give you, and they weren't expecting it back. You're going through enough right now."

Gratitude slammed into me. Olivia's family was well-off, and as the baby, she was wildly spoiled. What she wanted, she got, and as her best friend, the same courtesy extended to me. However, I didn't realize it would extend to something so expensive, especially when it had nothing to do with their daughter.

"Are y'all sure?" I asked, eyes wide. "The ticket was expensive, and—"

"And nothing. I told them how badly I wanted you to come back, and that was enough for them," she said with a shrug.

Speechless, all I could do was lean over and hug her, infinitely grateful that at least one person was in my corner.

Hours after I returned from the beach, I sat in the living room, watching TV, stuffing my face with junk food, and sipping on a bottle of wine I swiped from the fridge. Evidence of my seaside lounging had been washed down the drain, and despite a couple of invites to go out and turn up, I didn't have the energy. Olivia's revelation had lifted a weight from my chest, as owing money was never a good feeling. But in the solitude of the townhome, the sadness that'd been weighing on me made a grand return. I wanted to sulk and bask in my misery for a couple of days longer, hiding away like a hermit and appearing outside just enough to avoid accusations of depression.

"Oop," I mumbled around a mouthful of chips, watching as a fight broke out on the reality TV that held my attention.

Just as I finished the bag of fried potatoes, an emergency weather broadcast interrupted the TV show. I groaned as the news anchor droned about the incoming thunderstorms and the flood risk, the needless information ruining my distraction. I finished off the bottle of wine, placing the empty container on the table as I impatiently waited for the report to go away.

"Booo!" I shouted when ten minutes passed, the broadcast still going strong.

Frustrated, I grabbed the remote and shut the television off, the ensuing silence deafening. I hated how quiet the house was. It made me miss Mama even more and think about when Zara lived with us, before the argument that sent her running to her father last year. For months, I'd judged her decision and couldn't understand how one fight could make someone do something so monumental. Now, I understood perfectly.

For several moments, I just sat on the couch, staring at the black screen. It felt like a Herculean effort to stand, but after some minutes ticked by, I forced myself to undertake the challenge. I dusted the crumbs from my pajamas, then made my way to my room.

Unlike my bedroom in Grandma's house, my room in the townhome had a queen-sized bed, giving me ample space to stretch out and stare at the ceiling. Typically, I'd be scrolling on my phone, but I was avoiding the device so I wouldn't have to see any notifications from Mama or the Harris girls, especially Delaney.

I'd lost my mind. Missing them, but committed to avoiding them. What a fucking conundrum.

Sighing, I stood and made my way to my desk, where my laptop was stationed and the journals were stacked. I ignored the device and grabbed the sixth and final journal. With nothing else to do, I'd burned through the other five journals over the week, going in the order they were written. They captured my attention almost immediately. The claims written on their pages kept me flipping through the notebook, seeking answers. Instead, I was only left with more questions and an array of theories, my mind not allowing me to easily believe what was written.

However, what reason would Grandma have to write such outrageous things in her private entries?

The only journal not meant for her, I realized, was the most recent one, written back in April. It began by addressing us—me, Mama, and Zara—causing me to lock in immediately.

~~Dear family~~
~~Dear Girls~~
~~To Amia, Kamika, and Zara~~
Clearly, I don't know how to start this shit. Nothing sounds right. I've made a lot of mistakes during my day, and this fucked up beginning would just be another added to the list.

Ignore that. Let me try again.

Laughter bubbled up at her words, but my chest still felt heavy as I continued. For all her flaws, Grandma could be so unintentionally funny, and it was something I missed about her.

My beloved girls,

There's so much I should've said to y'all over the years. This, in truth, should be said face-to-face, but I've burned my bridge, preventing that from happening. Today, I heard words I never wanted to hear: I'm dying. You start to die from the moment you're born, but when you're young and healthy, it feels like you have forever before you have to face your mortality. I, however, am neither young nor healthy. I'm an old woman with a terminal disease. Turns out, decades of smoking have consequences.

The ink was smudged, the page slightly transparent. It was evident she'd been crying as she was writing this, and that knowledge worsened the melancholy that'd become my companion.

Firstly, I want to apologize. To you, Amia, for making you feel as if you have to tiptoe around everyone and putting so much on your young shoulders. When your daddy died, I should've been there to comfort you. Instead, I fell apart, leaving you to deal with things no child should have to handle, and giving you hostility when you needed love.

To you, Zara, for never making the effort to be close to you. My resentment for your daddy clouded my judgment, but you were my daughter's child, and that should've been enough for me to forge a bond with you. I want you to know that despite the gap that was forever present between us, I love you. You're my blood, my descendant, and I want nothing but the best for you.

Lastly, I owe the biggest apology to you, Kamika. My first grandbaby, and for the longest time, my pride and joy. I allowed fear and disgust to destroy our closeness. I won't pretend I agree with your choices, but I will admit I handled that situation poorly. A bad decision doesn't erase all the good in you, and what happened should've stayed a private matter between us and the Harrises. Instead, I opened my mouth to Giselle to vent, knowing that girl couldn't keep a damn secret to save her life.

So, Giselle had been the one to spread the news around town. Fucking figures.

However, she was my late best friend's daughter, and I swore to her mama I'd treat her like one of my own. I thought that meant sharing sensitive information with her, even when it wasn't the smartest decision. However, you truly are my own, my flesh and blood, kind, smart, and witty. Even with your temper and smart mouth, you're the best granddaughter I could've asked for. So many times over the years, I wanted to reach out, but didn't know what to say. It's easy to hurt people when you're upset, but it's hard to ask for their forgiveness. If I wasn't faced with my own mortality, I doubt the words would be coming to me. And even now, I'm too much of a coward to mail this to you. Pride is a bitch. There's a reason it's a sin, and I'd argue it's the worst of them all. But whenever you're reading this, Kamika, be it I somehow mustered the courage to send it to you—

Tears pricked my eyes, because that hadn't happened. If she had sent me a letter, I would've flown down to Gaville in an instant, even if it meant delaying my graduation. Somehow, I continued reading, even as my heart felt heavier.

—or if you're reading this when I'm gone. If that's the case, I'm doubly sorry for being a coward and hope you can find it in your heart to forgive me.

Despite my many wrongs, I love all y'all, and just know that I'm watching over y'all from above. Or below, because only the Lord himself can dictate which direction I go in.

A sound escaped me, half giggle, half sob. She'd kept her promise, even if at times, it scared the shit out of me.

"Oh, grandma," I sniffled, swiping at my eyes.

The diary was a bittersweet balm to my soul. Her ignorance hadn't been erased by the time she died, but the words I longed for her to say were present. It reaffirmed that even in the end, after years of radio silence, she still loved me. I thought back to the picture she'd kept on her dresser, tangible evidence that she continued to care for me.

My tear drops joined the ones already present on the page. I set the book aside, grabbing sheets of tissue from my nightstand and dabbing away my tears. Fanning my face, I gave myself a couple of minutes to calm down before I continued reading. Inhaling deeply, I picked up the journal again and flipped to the next page.

Believe it or not, that was the easy part. Please, girls, read the next part with an open mind.

The bombshell she was about to drop was one I already knew, but though I anticipated what I was about to read, tension still coiled within me.

Although, Zara, I'd wager your raggedy daddy already told you most of this.

Holy shit. Roman knew of the supernatural world. Was he a paranormal being, as Grandma claimed we were? Was that why Zara had deserted us, because her father convinced her of the truth?

If not, here it goes. Those fairy tales about things that go bump in the night? Most of them are true. Some humans truly do shift into animals; some people truly can cast spells and possess special powers; blood-craving undead are more common than you'd believe; mermaids inhabit the waters—

Wait, what?

I'd become used to all the mentions of vampires, werewolves, and witches, but another supernatural being thrown into the mix took me aback. Likewise, the mentions of faeries and demons made the hair on the back of my neck stand. The chill that ran through me was so bad that the familiar mentions of ghosts were comforting. Because my life had gone so off the rails, invisible dead people were no longer quite terrifying.

Now, you're probably thinking I'm a crazy old bitch who's gone senile. I wouldn't blame you, but I ask you to finish reading before you dismiss me.

First, the Harrises can back up my claims because they're giant dogs. Werewolves, as most would say. If you're in town, give them a visit and ask them. If they deny it, they're fucking idiots. Luckily for you, girls, an incantation could call them out on their bullshit. Latin is a dead language, but spoken by the right tongue, it continues to be a powerful one.

Ostende mihi veritatem.

Oh-sten-day/me/very-tot-ta-meh

That means 'Show me the truth.' Say it right, now, as otherwise, it won't do shit. I'm not an expert on Latin, so I can't say how accurate the pronunciation is. However, that's how I say it, and it never fails to work.

Fuck me. If I were in Gaville, I could settle this matter with one trip to Magnolia Mist. Then again, it might be a good thing I was in Miami. If it didn't work, I'd look like an insane jackass. If it did and they turned into wolves as Grandma said they would, then I could end up being a meal, assuming that werewolves ate people as they did in fairytales.

Then again, wolves had been sighted over the years in Gaville. A rarity, but not unheard of, though an attack was never recorded…

Hold up.

My eyes grew to the size of saucers, and I slapped a hand over my mouth. The 'dogs' under the tree on the Fourth of July, the white 'dog' that followed me home last week. They all were so very wolf-like, and all came from Harris' property.

Holy fucking shit.

I couldn't believe it took me so long to put two and two together.

Feeling like a dumbass, the only thing I could do was continue to read. I needed to know more, needed to know how many glaring signs I'd missed.

Now, the Harrises might help you confirm the truth, but they can't teach you what I'm about to. Your Aunt Melanie and your Uncle Norman in New Orleans might shed some light, assuming they aren't dead by the time you read this.

No news of their deaths had come to me, so I imagined they were still alive. Then again, I'd never been close to them, and during my life, I'd only met them a grand total of three times.

Those fuckers are uppity with a superiority complex, so deal with them as a last resort. However, if you opt to make yourself suffer, here are their numbers. 504...

I reached for my phone. Ignoring the many messages, I opened my notes app and copied the phone numbers down, just in case I needed them.

If you have access to this journal, you have access to the other ones, so you'll learn the history of our family soon enough. But, unless my old ass brain is failing to remember shit, I've never jotted down spells, rituals, and incantations for y'all.

She had indeed written down a handful of spells and the like. However, the journals containing those were written decades before this one, so it'd reason that she didn't remember the few spells she'd documented.

All of y'all should be able to do these. Amia and Kamika, I don't know much about your daddies' origins, but both of those men weren't fully human. More common than you think.

The words should've come as a massive shock to me, but at this point, they were just water under the bridge.

Zara, your daddy definitely isn't human. I'd say he's a demon who crawled out of hell, but I want to stay respectful and don't want to confuse you.

A huff of laughter left me. She was on point with that comparison, because Roman was a motherfucking bastard. As I flipped onto the next page, I noted it was also stained, though not with tears. The amber tint hinted that whatever hard liquor she'd been drinking had sloshed onto the paper.

I'm sorry for never telling y'all. It's my biggest regret after losing contact with y'all. I fancied myself protecting you three. Even though I sensed the power flowing through y'all, I didn't want to confront the truth. The supernatural world is a dangerous, wretched thing, and I wanted to keep that sordid mess away from y'all. My daddy, bless his soul, was a human man, for that I am sure. My mama, though, she was a witch not to be crossed. But even with someone like her as a mother, I was mocked and looked down on, made into a target because they thought I was weak. My domain, after all, was dreams. Awake, I wasn't defenseless, but I was nowhere as strong.

That explained why she held so much power over my mind when I slept but could only occasionally whisper to me when I was awake. Dreamland was her domain.

Barring Roman, your fathers didn't know about their heritage, either. Their blood was nearly human, but off enough for me to know something was up with them. However, they never brought it up, so neither did I. I carried the same attitude with my precious girls.

I smiled at the way she described us, my index finger stroking the words. As much as a shock that this would've been to receive months ago, I wish she had sent this as a letter before she passed. I would've stayed by her side during her final days and eagerly learned whatever she wanted to teach me.

I thought that if you three didn't know, it wouldn't hurt y'all. Then, Roman waltzed on into your life, Amia, and I realized the fruitlessness of my efforts. If anything, I see that it put y'all more in harm's way, but by the time I figured that out, telling y'all seemed impossible. Even now, as I'm a goddamn emotional mess and half-drunk, it's no easy feat.

Time for the spells. I don't feel like writing the pronunciation for all of them, so y'all just gotta figure that shit out. I have enough shit to write.

Wow, how considerate.

In this circumstance, I don't believe in saving the best for last. So, here's the most important one. Nullae me tenebrae tangent, nullae me laedent mala. That means 'No darkness will touch me, no evil will hurt me.' It's an incantation that protects the user. If you want it to apply to multiple people, you say 'Nullae nos tenebrae tangent, nullae nobis mala nocebit.' For it to work, you'd need to be touching them. To protect a defined area, you say, 'Hanc aream nullae tenebrae intrabunt, nullae hoc loco mala calcabunt.' You need to mix salt and cayenne pepper and encase the perimeter of the area in it. Next, determine the center of the area. The bigger it is, the more of a hassle the motherfucker is to find, but I have faith y'all would manage. Bring a bundle of dried herbs, consisting of sage, lavender, St. John's Wort, and rosemary. For protection of people, make a tea from those herbs. That flower shop on Main Street should have them all, if y'all are in Gaville. If not, good luck.

I made a note to go out and purchase all the listed herbs. During our senior year, Olivia was big into herbology, so I knew all the plants mentioned were said to repel evil. At the time, I thought it was bullshit. Ironically, now that Olivia thought it was mumbo-jumbo, I was giving it credence. However, even if she no longer believed in the power of plants, I knew she'd tell me where to find them if I asked.

Some raggedy motherfuckers would argue that there are more important spells, but to me, nothing is more important than protection. God's Grace will ensure nothing happens to you before your time, but ain't nothing wrong with taking precautions.

Ever the good Christian woman. It was an oxymoron, almost, a hyper-religious witch.

Here's another quick ritual. Ghosts are easy to summon in your sleep. Be warned that not everyone can contact the dead, and if you don't know what you're doing, you can have unintended consequences. But our line is powerful, so it should present no issue. If you ever wanna talk to me, take some mugwort before you fall asleep, and say 'Excita ánimam meam et adfer mihi.' It means 'Awaken the soul and bring it to me.' You'll say my name, and then 'Ego voco te. Veni.' I am calling you. Come.

In theory, this could work with any departed person, but you need some connection to them. If you don't have one, you can summon the wrong person or being, and that could lead to a whole world of trouble. I recommend casting the protection spell before summoning anyone. Otherwise, the rituals to get rid of a ghost or demon are long, so if that happens, my advice is to welcome the entity to its new home and get the hell out of the newly haunted house. You may be homeless, but at least you'll have your soul.

What a lovely thing to read when you're all alone, a dead woman warning you of the dangers of undead entities. I shivered in spite of myself. First thing tomorrow, I was locating those herbs, because I would be damned if I'd get haunted or possessed.

After that little warning, Grandma ran down many more hexes. The incantations, ingredients, and rituals needed for each other took several pages, and I didn't foresee myself using most. The spells to inspire love and lust felt dubious, and those meant to harm others felt like bad juju, only to be used as a last resort. The niche spells felt almost unnecessary, as the situations were too outlandish to imagine myself in. Some spells were simple, meant to be used in little everyday chores, but they seemed to be more trouble than just doing the damn task yourself. My attention lulled at times, and it wasn't until I was nearing the end of the small journal that I locked back in.

Now, girls, if you've made it to the end, I take that to mean y'all are putting some stock into what I'm saying.

Ding, ding, ding.

But, even if that's the case, doubt may linger. So, I've compiled spells suited for each of y'all, based on what I suspect your powers are. Amia, you've always been so emotionally intelligent—

I snorted. As a whole, the assessment wasn't inaccurate, but the last few weeks contradicted that statement. Of course, grief and fear could reduce the smartest person to a bumbling idiot, doubly true when they were overwhelmed.

Mama's spells were geared toward emotions. Zara's, too, as well as clairvoyance. I thought back to the times she'd texted me when I was in Gaville, each after a dream had left me shaken. Had she somehow sensed that I needed someone at that moment? If so, why hadn't she reached out since I returned to Miami?

I made a mental note to call Zara tomorrow, then continued onto the spells meant for me. Unlike my mama and sister, they had nothing to do with emotions.

Kamika, you're a testament to my mama's power. Heat never bothered you, like the opposite of that one princess Zara used to love.

I chuckled at the memory. As a child, *Frozen* was her obsession.

Mama was an elemental, you see. Fire was her element. They say those who can control the elements are descended from the fae. My mother was an ethereal woman, so I believe it. You look just like her, Kami, albeit a darker version with more nappy hair.

I rolled my eyes, my lips pursing. Shady to the end, Grandma was. I suppose it was too ingrained in her for her to change the habit, but her prejudices were easily her greatest flaw.

It makes sense you'd have a version of her power. Emotions, clairvoyance, and dreams are all connected to each other, so I'm sorry that I don't have as many spells for you, Kamika. Fire isn't my realm of expertise, so Mama didn't teach me many spells for her powers. But I know a handful. Here's the first. Get a candle—

I paused, considering if I wanted to test the spell written, or be a passive reader. It was a choice a struggled with longer than I should've, and it wasn't until a crack of thunder sounded that I made my decision. I was buzzed, lonely, and bored, with nothing to lose by doing Grandma's spell. If nothing happened, I could just blame the alcohol for my silliness, and laugh it off.

My mind made up, I set the journal aside, scurrying off the bed to collect the candle on my dresser. I'd gotten it right before I learned Grandma died and never had a chance to use it. As luck would have it, it was a rosemary and lavender candle, two of the herbs mentioned before. It was meant to inspire better sleep hygiene, but utilizing it for a ritual was a far more exciting use. Just to be safe, I grabbed my lighter, then returned to the bed.

—Likely, you'll need to use a lighter. Just to be safe, go outside.

…Goddammit.

The prospect of having to travel such a far distance—my backyard—was daunting. However, reading the journal gave me a feeling of tranquility I didn't want to lose, and made me feel connected to my grandmother. So, I dragged my ass out of my room, the candle in one hand, the lighter in the other, and the diary under my arm. Rain was starting to fall, but the covered portion of the patio kept me dry. I plopped down on the concrete, keeping a safe distance from anything flammable. Setting the candle and lighter in front of me, I resumed my reading.

If you don't follow my instructions, I'm not responsible for the house burning down, girl, so don't go cussing my ass. Now, get some salt—

Fuck me sideways.

Huffing in annoyance, I scanned over the spell to see what the hell else I'd need. A knife, scarily, was one of the requirements. However, both were in the kitchen, so after making another trip, I was finally ready to go. I followed the instructions as I read them, my palms growing sweaty, my heart racing in anticipation.

—and pour it around the candle. Make sure it's a solid circle. Light the candle. Now, here's the scary part. Take the knife, or whatever sharp tool you have, and slice your finger. Let it drip on the flame. Your blood will act as an accelerant. Other options don't require you to injure yourself, but unless you're dead, you're guaranteed to have some blood on hand. If the flame grows larger, it's a good sign. Remember, blood is mostly water, so normal, liquid blood will not be combustible.

I might've truly gone mad, because instead of stopping there, I picked up the knife and pressed the tip to my thumb finger. I hissed as it sliced through my skin and quickly let the drops of blood drip onto the candle. The small flame nearly doubled in size, licking at the sides of the container. My lips parted in surprise. Putting my wounded finger in my mouth, I sucked the blood away as I read, the sweet, metallic taste not bothering me.

Now, for the moment of truth, Kami. Put your index fingers and thumbs together. Point your index fingers at the fire, and your thumbs at yourself, then say the following:

Ignem appello, ferum, divinum.

Flamma, surge!
Ardeat extra circulum ductum

I reread the words several times. She didn't provide a translation. Either she didn't know what it meant, or she was tired of writing them. I imagined penning this took her multiple hours, so both were in the realm of possibilities. Perhaps a little of both. Sounding them out in my head, I mustered the courage to speak them aloud. I stumbled over the words several times, but after about five attempts, I became more confident. Nodding, I decided it was good enough.

Praying the neighbors weren't outside, I started to chant the words. "*Ignem appello, ferum, divinum. Flamma, surge! Ardeat extra circulum ductum.*"

The third time around, a barely perceptible light formed in the circle. If it wasn't for the sun dipping below the horizon, I might not have noticed it. I held my breath, unsure of what to expect next. I got my answer when another drop of blood escaped my thumb, trickling down my hand and falling onto the flame. The glow strengthened, and within seconds, the ceramic container broke, courtesy of the enlarged flame.

A horrified screech left me. I jumped back, staring at the roaring fire with a gaping jaw. The wax and broken glass seemed to fuel it, and soon, the entire circle was burning. It didn't cross the boundary of the salt. Still, the flames lapped at the edges, heightening my anxiety. Taking a deep breath, I grabbed the galvanized bucket by the patio door, the metal rusty from lack of care.

Thinking on my feet, I poured half of the box of salt onto the fire. It sizzled as it hit the inferno, and I couldn't help but flinch. When I covered the fire with the bucket, hoping to smother the flame, plumes of acrid salt billowed from under the bucket's edge. The sharp scent of burnt wax and the tangy odor of blood filled my lungs. My nose scrunched up, and my eyes watered. My heart hammered against my ribs, even when the smoke blew into the night and the noise from under the bucket quieted. Slowly, I cautiously lifted the bucket, relief washing over me when I found the flames extinguished.

A disbelieving laugh escaped me as what had just happened processed. I'd successfully done a fire ritual. Against all the odds, despite how ridiculous I felt, I'd fucking done it. Grandma's words weren't insane lies; I'd seen firsthand that they held some truth. The claims that I'd struggled to accept had just been proven to have weight. My mind ran wild with the implications.

Mama, Zara, and I were witches.

Larissa and Delaney were werewolves.

A host of other supernatural creatures walked the Earth.

I stumbled onto one of the outdoor chaise lounges, my head whirling. Reading wild claims, no matter what your gut was telling you, was different from finding out they were true. In truth, I didn't know how to feel. That teenage girl who was obsessed with paranormal romance novels rejoiced. The Christian values that had been hammered into my head by my grandmother resulted in panic. Everything I'd known had been turned on its head, fueling the panic. And even still, the logical side of my mind scrambled for another explanation. Yet, the excuses I came up with seemed even more impractical, dismissing what I'd seen with my own two eyes. Thus, I was left with two options.

I was stone-cold, raving mad, to the point that fiction and reality had fused together, presenting itself as fact to my twisted mind.

Or, my sanity was very much intact, and all the fairy tales I'd grown up hearing were in fact true.

I much preferred the second option, but no matter which was true, the implications were life-changing. One thing was for certain, however. Several times, Grandma said that Zara, thanks to Roman, would be aware of the truth. No longer did I doubt her words. Calling Zara was paramount. I couldn't wait until the morning.

Instead of cleaning up my mess, I returned to my room, the franticness I felt almost comical. On the grand scale of things, this changed nothing. Yet, on a personal level, my entire world was rocked.

Grabbing my phone, I dialed her number. The first call went to voicemail. Growling in frustration, I called again.

"Answer, goddamnit," I hissed to myself, wondering if I'd have to drive to Roman's house.

Thankfully, she answered the second time around, preventing me from being in her father's miserable presence.

"Kami—"

"Is it true?" I interrupted, the words coming out in a rush. I detected how frenzied I sounded, so I took a breath. "I...I read Grandma's journals. The stuff they talk about...it's outlandish, but I have reason to believe it, and she says you know. That your father knows. Is it true?"

I heard her sharp intake of breath and the coarse swallow that followed. Then, silence. Seconds turned into a minute.

"Hello?" I urged, needing an answer, needing to know I wasn't insane, that what just happened was real.

"What truth are you talking about, Kami?" she finally said, her voice low.

I breathed deeply, mustering up courage for my question. "If I said….if I said my blood fueled a fire, would you call me insane?"

"…No."

Her tentative reply gave me the confidence to continue. "And if I told you…an incantation made it grow larger, that the circle of salt was glowing…would you believe me?"

The silence stretched longer this time, fraying my nerves.

"Say something, Zara," I demanded.

"This isn't a conversation to be having over the phone, Kami," she said quietly, sounding so much older than her fifteen years. "I'll come over tomorrow, and we'll talk."

That was good. Grandma's words were addressed to her, too, so tomorrow would give her the chance to see them.

"Would your father allow that?" I questioned, knowing that Roman was doing everything in his power to isolate Zara.

"Daddy said being with him would be best for everyone and protect y'all," she confessed, her voice small. "If you know…there's no reason I shouldn't be able to come over."

There it was. An indirect confirmation.

"And yes, I would believe you, about the glowing circle and shit," she continued. A door opened in the background, and I heard Roman calling her name. "I…uh…love you, bye."

That put an end to the call. Maybe I was mistaken, but I swore I heard fear in her voice. It made me hate Roman more.

I stood still for several moments, rooted in place. When the urgency of the situation faded, I returned to the patio. I'd clean the mess tomorrow, but I wouldn't leave the journal outside, vulnerable to the elements. It held answers to questions I'd long wondered, and for questions I hadn't thought to ask. It was an insight into my grandmother's mind during her final weeks, and a reaffirmation of her care. The words I read were cathartic, healing scars left by their author. The past would never be forgotten, but it could be forgiven. My world had shifted in a major way, and yet, I felt lighter, all thanks to the diary. As of today, it had become my most important possession, one I wouldn't let anyone take from me.

Thank you for reading part one of Kami's story. I hope you enjoyed reading it as much as I enjoyed writing it. The Latin at the end is Google Translate, so please excuse any errors. I had no other way to access the language. If you, per chance, speak Latin and see any glaring flaws, feel free to reach out. Please consider leaving a review of <u>Mesmerized</u> at the point of purchase, (please keep it constructive and respectful), and if you want to contact me, shoot me an email at <u>nev.ryn.writer@gmail.com</u>. You can also message me on one of my socials, linked below.

Thank you again for reading and have a lovely rest of your day.

THE PLAYLIST

TOO CLOSE TO THE MIRROR BY EDDIE RUTH BRADFORD
SHE WOLF BY SHAKIRA
OFF THE WALL BY MICHAEL JACKSON
SUCKER FOR PAIN FROM THE SUICIDE SQUAD
SWING BY SAVAGE
MANNISH BOY BY MUDDY WATERS
I'LL BE AROUND BY CEELO GREEN FT. TIMBALAND
I'VE GOT A WOMAN BY RAY CHARLES
CLOSER BY NINE INCH NAILS
STATE OF SHOCK BY THE JACKSONS AND MICK JAGGER
SIMP BY FULL TAC FT. LIL MARIKO AND RICO NASTY
HOUSE OF MEMORIES BY PANIC! AT THE DISCO
KISS ME MORE BY DOJA CAT FT. SZA
COOL FOR THE SUMMER BY DEMI LOVATO
RAIN BY SLEEP TOKEN
MY GIRL BY THE TEMPTATIONS
I WALK ON GUILDED SPLINTERS BY DR. JOHN
I WANT YOU (SHE'S SO HEAVY) BY THE BEATLES
IKO IKO BY THE DIXIE CUPS
TENNESSEE WHISKEY BY CHRIS STAPLETON
EYE DON'T LIE BY ISABEL LAROSA
MEANT TO BE BY BEBE REXHA AND FLORIDA GEORGIA LINE
BAD IDEA BY CORDAE FT. CHANCE THE RAPPER

Scan to listen on Spotify

Instagram:
https://sqr.co/Neveah-Ryn-Instagram/

Threads:
https://www.threads.net/@nev.ryn

Facebook:
https://sqr.co/NevaehRynFacebook/

Goodreads:
https://sqr.co/Goodreads-Neveah-Ryn/

TikTok:
https://www.tiktok.com/@neveahryn

Website:
https://nevaeh-ryn.square.site/

Since she was young, twenty-one-year-old Nevaeh Ryn has had a passion for storytelling. Writing is Nevaeh's escape and platform for underrepresented literary voices. Nevaeh's storytelling shapes her, and she hopes to have a positive impact. When she isn't lost in her own world, Nevaeh is pursuing a BFA in Creative Writing at Full Sail University to hone her craft. Between classes, Nevaeh spends her free time gaming on her PC, cooking up new recipes, and of course, reading and writing. She's an avid Sims player and expresses herself through an ever-growing collection of tattoos.